# About Shirley Jump

*New York Times* bestselling author Shirley Jump didn't have the will-power to diet, nor the talent to master under-eye concealer, so she bowed out of a career in television and opted instead for a career where she could be paid to eat at her desk—writing. At first, seeking revenge on her children for their grocery store tantrums, she sold embarrassing essays about them to anthologies. However, it wasn't enough to feed her growing addiction to writing funny. So she turned to the world of romance novels, where messes are (usually) cleaned up before The End. In the worlds Shirley gets to create and control, the children listen to their parents, the husbands always remember holidays, and the housework is magically done by elves. Though she's thrilled to see her books in stores around the world, Shirley mostly writes because it gives her an excuse to avoid cleaning the toilets and helps feed her shoe habit.

To learn more, visit her website at **www.shirleyjump.com**

# Return of the
# Last McKenna

Shirley Jump

First published in Great Britain 2012
by Mills & Boon, an imprint of Harlequin (UK) Limited.
Harlequin (UK) Limited, Eton House, 18-24 Paradise Road,
Richmond, Surrey TW9 1SR

© Shirley Kawa-Jump, LLC 2012

ISBN: 978 0 263 22798 7

Printed and bound in Great Britain
by CPI Antony Rowe, Chippenham, Wiltshire

TM

To the most heroic military man I know—my husband,
who served his country, and has made me proud
to be his wife in a thousand different ways.
Not to mention, he's the kind of guy
who brings home cupcakes just because I had a hard day.
He knows me well!

# CHAPTER ONE

Brody McKenna checked his third sore throat of the morning, prescribed the same prescription as he had twice before—rest, fluids, acetaminophen—and tried to count his blessings. He had a dependable job as a family physician, a growing practice, and a close knit family living nearby. He'd returned from his time overseas none the worse for wear, and should have been excited to get back to his job.

He wasn't.

The six-year-old patient headed out the door, with a sugar-free lollipop and a less harried mother. As they left, Helen Maguire, the nurse who had been with him since day one, and with Doc Watkins for fifteen years before that, poked her head in the door. "That's the last patient of the morning," she said. A matronly figure in pink scrubs decorated with zoo animals, Mrs. Maguire had short gray hair and a smile for every patient, young or old. "We have an hour until it's time to start immunizations. And then later in the afternoon, we'll be doing sports physicals."

Brody's mind drifted away from his next appointment and the flurry of activity in his busy Newton office. His gaze swept the room, the jars of supplies, so easy to order and stock here in America, always on hand and ready for any emergency. Every bandage, every tongue depressor, every stethoscope, reminded him. Launched him back to a hot country and a dusty dirt floor hut short on supplies and even shorter on miracles.

"Doc? Did you hear me?" Mrs. Maguire asked.

"Oh, oh. Yes. Sorry." Brody washed his hands, then dried them and handed the chart to Helen. Focus on work, he told himself, not on a moment in the past that couldn't be changed. Or on a country on the other side of the world, to those people he couldn't save.

Especially not on that.

"Lots of colds going around," he said.

"It's that time of year."

"I think it's always that time of year."

Helen shrugged. "I think that's what I like about family practice. You can set your watch by the colds and flus and shots. It has a certain rhythm to it, don't you think?"

"I do." For a long time, Brody had thought he had the perfect life. A family practice for a family man.

Or at least, that had been the plan. Then the family had dissolved before it had a chance to form. By that time, Brody had already stepped into Doc Watkins's shoes. Walking away from a thriving practice would be insane, so he'd stayed. For a long time, he'd been happy. He liked the patients. Liked working with kids, liked seeing the families grow and change.

It was good work, and he took satisfaction in that, and had augmented it with volunteer time with different places over the years—a clinic in Alabama, a homeless shelter in Maine. When the opportunity to volunteer assisting the remaining military overseas arose, Brody had jumped at it.

For a month, he'd changed lives in Afghanistan, working side by side with other docs in a roving medical unit that visited villagers too poor to get to a doctor or hospital, with the American military along for protection.

Brody had thought he'd make a difference there, too. He had—just not in the way he wanted. And now he couldn't find peace, no matter where he turned.

"You okay, doc?" Mrs. Maguire asked.

"Fine." His gaze landed on the jars of supplies again. "Just distracted. I think I'll head out for lunch instead of eating at my desk."

And being around all these reminders.

"No problem. It'll do you good to take some time to enjoy the day." Mrs. Maguire smiled. "I find a little fresh air can make everything seem brighter."

Brody doubted the air would work any miracles for him, but maybe some space and distance would. Unfortunately, he had little of either. "I'll be back by one."

He stepped outside his office and into a warm, almost summer day. The temperatures still lingered in the high seventies, even though the calendar date read deep into September. Brody headed down the street, waving to the neighbors who flanked his Newton practice—Mr. Simon with his shoe repair shop, Mrs. Tipp with her art gallery and Milo, who had opened three different types of shops in the same location, like an entrepreneur with ADD.

Brody took the same path as he took most days when he walked during his lunch hour. He rarely ate, just walked from his office to the same destination and back. He'd done it so many times in the last few weeks, he half expected to see a worn river of footsteps down the center of the sidewalk.

Brody reached in his pocket as he rounded the corner. The paper was crinkled and worn, the edges beginning to fray, but the inked message had stayed clear.

*Hey, Superman, take care of yourself and come home safe. People over here love and miss you. Especially me. Things just aren't the same without your goofy face around. Love you, Kate.*

Brody had held onto that card for a month now. He ran his hands over the letters now, and debated the same thing he'd had in his head for weeks. To fulfill Andrew's last wishes, or let it go?

He paused. His feet had taken him to the same destination as always. He stood under the bright red and white awning of Nora's Sweet Shop and debated again, the card firm in his grip.

*Promise me, Doc. Promise me you'll go see her. Make sure she's okay. Make sure she's happy. But please, don't tell her what happened. She'll blame herself and Kate has suffered enough already.*

The promise had been easy to make a month ago. Harder to keep.

Brody fingered the card again. *Promise me.*

How many times had he made this journey and turned back instead of taking, literally, the next step?

If he returned to the thermometers and stethoscopes and bandages, though, would he ever find peace?

He knew that answer. No. He needed to do this. Step forward instead of back.

Brody took a deep breath, then opened the door and stepped inside the shop. The sweet scents of chocolate and vanilla drifted over him, while soft jazz music filled his ears. A glass case of cupcakes and chocolates sat at one end of the store while a bright rainbow of gift baskets lined the sides. A cake made out of cupcakes and decorated in bridal colors sat on a glass stand in a bay window. Along the top of the walls ran a border of dark pink writing trimmed with chocolate brown and a hand lettered script reading Nora's Sweet Shop. On the wall behind the counter, hung a framed spatula with the name of the shop carved in the handle.

"Just a minute!" a woman called from the back.

"No problem," Brody said, stuffing the card back into his pocket. "I'm just…"

Just what? Not browsing. Not looking for candy or cupcakes. And he sure as hell couldn't say the truth—

He'd come to this little shop in downtown Newton for forgiveness.

So instead he grabbed the first assembled basket of treats he saw and marched over to the counter. He was just pulling out his wallet when a slim brunette woman emerged from the back room.

"Hi, I'm Kate." She dried her hands on the front of her apron before proffering one for him to shake. "How can I help you?"

Kate Spencer. The owner of the shop, and the woman he'd thought of a hundred times in the past weeks. A woman he'd never met but heard enough about to write at least a couple chapters of her biography.

He took her hand, a steady, firm grip—and tried not to stare. All these weeks he'd held onto that card, he'd expected someone, well, someone like a young version of Mrs. Maguire. A motherly type with her hair in a bun, and an apron around her waist, and a hug ready for anyone she met. That was how Andrew had made his older sister sound. Loving, warm, dependable. Like a down comforter.

Not the thin, fit, dynamo who had hurried out of the back room, with a friendly smile on her face and her coffee colored hair in a sassy ponytail skewed a bit too far to the right. She had deep green eyes, full crimson lips and delicate, pretty features. Yet he saw shadows dusting the undersides of her eyes and a tension in her shoulders.

Brody opened his mouth to introduce himself, to fulfill his purpose for being here, but the words wouldn't get past his throat. "I...I...uh," he glanced down at the counter, at the cellophane package in his hands, "I wanted to get this."

"No problem. Is it for a special person?"

Brody's mind raced for an answer. "My, uh, grandmother. She loves chocolate."

"Your grandma?" Kate laughed, then spun the basket to face him. "You want me to, ah, change out this bow? To something a little more feminine? Unless your grandma is a big fan?"

He glanced down and noticed he'd chosen a basket with a Red Sox ribbon. The dark blue basket with red trim, filled with white foil wrapped chocolates shaped like baseballs and bats, couldn't be further from the type of thing his staid grandmother liked. He chuckled. "No, that'd be me. I've even got season tickets. When she does watch baseball, my grandma is strictly a Yankees fan, though you can't say that too loud in Boston."

Kate laughed, a light lyrical, happy sound. Again, Brody realized how far off his imaginings of her had been. "Well, Mr. Red Sox, let me make this more grandma friendly. Okay? And meanwhile, if you want to put a card with this, there are some on the counter over there."

"Thanks." He wandered over to the counter she'd indicated, and tugged out a card, then scribbled his name across it. That kept him from watching her and gave his brain a few minutes to adjust to the reality of Kate Spencer.

She was, in a word, beautiful. The kind of woman, on any other day, he might have asked out on a date. Friendly, sweet natured, with a ready smile and a teasing lilt to her words. Her smile had roused something in him the minute he saw her, and that surprised him. He hadn't expected to be attracted to her, not one bit.

He tried to find a way around to say what he had come to say. *Promise me.*

He'd practiced the words he needed to say in his head a hundred times, but now that the moment had arrived, they wouldn't come. It wasn't the kind of subject one could just dump in the middle of a business transaction, nor had he quite figured out how to fulfill Andrew's wishes without giving away why. He needed to lead up to it, somehow. Yeah, easier to climb Mt. Everest.

"So…how's business?" he asked.

"Pretty good. We've been growing every year since

we opened in 1953. Mondays are our only slow day of the week. Almost like a mini vacation, except at the beginning of the week."

"You make all the cupcakes and candy things yourself?"

She shook her head and laughed. "I couldn't. It's a lot of work. Nora's Sweet Shop has been a family business for many years, but…" she trailed off, seemed to look elsewhere for a second, then came back, "anyway, now I have a helper who's invaluable in the kitchen. Why, you applying?"

"Me? I'm all thumbs in the kitchen."

"That can be dangerous if there are knives involved." She grinned. "But seriously, baking is something you can learn. I never had formal training. Learned it all at my grandmother's knee. And if a hopeless case like me can grow up to be a baker, anyone can."

"Sounds like you love working here."

"I do. It's…therapeutic." The humor dimmed in her features, and her gaze again went to somewhere he couldn't see. He didn't have to be psychic to know why sadness had washed over her face. Because of choices Brody had made on the other side of the world.

Damn.

Brody cleared his throat. "Work can be good for the soul."

Or at least, that's what he told himself every time he walked into his practice. Ever since he'd returned from Afghanistan, though, he hadn't found that same satisfaction in his job as before. Maybe he just needed more time. That's what Mrs. Maguire said. Give it time, and it'll all get better.

"And what work do you do, that feeds your soul?"

She colored. "Sorry. That's a little personal. You don't have to answer. I was just curious."

"I'm a doctor," he said.

She leaned against the counter, one elbow on the glass, her body turned toward his. "That's a rewarding job. So much more so than baking. And not to mention, a lot more complicated than measuring out cupcake batter."

"Oh, I don't know about that," he said. "Your job looks pretty rewarding to me. I mean, you make people happy."

"It takes a lot of sugar to do that." She laughed. "But thank you. I try my best. Three generations of Spencers have been trying to do that here."

Brody's gaze drifted over the articles on the wall. Several contained accolades and positive reviews for the sweet shop, a third generation business that had enjoyed decades of raves, as evidenced by some of the framed, yellowed clippings. Brody paused when he got to the last article on the right. The page was creased on one side, as if someone had kept the paper in a book for a while before posting it on the wall. A picture of a handsome young man in uniform smiled out from the corner of the article.

Shop Owner's Brother Dies in Afghanistan

Brody didn't have to read another word to write the ending. In an instant, he was back there, in that hot, dusty hut, praying and cursing, and praying and cursing some more, while he tried to pump life back into Andrew Spencer.

And failed.

Brody could still feel the young man's chest beneath his palms. A hard balloon, going up, going down, forced into moving by Brody's hands, but no breath escaping his lips. Andrew's eyes open, sightless, empty. His life ebbing away one second at a time, while Brody watched, helpless and frustrated. Powerless.

Damn. Damn.

No amount of time would heal that wound for Kate and her family. No amount of time would make that better. What had he been thinking? How could buying a basket ever ease the pain he'd caused Kate Spencer? What had Andrew been thinking, sending Brody here?

Brody's hand went to the card in his pocket again, but this time, the cardboard corners formed sharp barbs.

"Sir? Your basket is ready."

Brody whirled around. "My basket?"

Kate laughed and held it up. The arrangement sported a new pink and white bow and the sports-themed chocolates had been changed for ones shaped like flowers. "For grandma?"

"Oh, yeah, sure, thanks." He gestured toward the article on the wall. He knew he should let it go, but he'd made a promise, and somehow, he had to find a way to keep it. Maybe then he'd be able to sleep, to find peace, and to give some to Kate Spencer, too. "You had a brother in the war?"

A shadow dropped over her features. She fiddled with the pen on the counter. "Yeah. My little brother, Andrew. He died over there last month. We all thought he was safe because the big conflict was over, but there were still dangers around every corner."

"I'm sorry." So much sorrier than he could say. He wanted to step forward, but instead Brody lingered by the counter. All the words he'd practiced in his head seemed empty, inadequate. "That must have been tough."

"It has been. In a lot of ways. But I work, and I talk to him sometimes, and I get through it." She blushed. "That sounds crazy, I know."

"No, it doesn't. Not at all."

She smoothed a hand over the counter. "He used to work here. And I miss seeing him every day. He was the organized one in the family, and he'd be appalled at the condition of my office." She laughed, then nodded toward the basket. "Anyway, do you want to put your card with that?"

"Oh, yeah, sure." He handed Kate the message he'd scribbled to his grandmother and watched as she tucked the small paper inside the cellophane wrapper. Again, he tried to find the words he needed to say, and again, he failed. "I've, uh, never been to this place before. Lived in this neighborhood for a while and I've seen it often, but never stopped by."

"Well, thank you for coming and shopping at Nora's Sweet Shop." She gave the basket a friendly pat. "I hope your grandmother enjoys her treats."

"I'm sure she will." For the hundredth time he told himself to leave. And for the hundredth time, he didn't. "So if you're Kate, who's Nora?" He asked the question, even though he knew the answer. Andrew had talked about Nora's Sweet Shop often, and told Brody the entire story about its origins.

"Nora is my grandmother." A soft smile stole over Kate's face. "She opened this place right after my grandfather came home from the Korean War. He worked side by side with her here for sixty years before they both retired and gave the shop to my brother and me. She's the Nora in Nora's Sweet Shop and if you ask my grandfather, she's the sweet in his life."

"She's still alive?" Ever since Brody had met the jovial, brave soldier, he'd wondered what kind of people had raised a man like that. What kind of family surrounded him, supported him as he went off to defend the country.

"My grandparents are retired now," Kate said, "but they come by the shop all the time and still do some deliveries. My brother and I grew up around here, and we spent more time behind this counter than anywhere else. I think partly to help my grandparents, and partly to keep us out of trouble while my parents were working. We were mischievous when we were young," she said with a laugh, "and my brother Andrew served as my partner in crime. Back then…and also for years afterwards when we took over the shop from my grandma. He had the craziest ideas." She shook her head again. "Anyway, that's how a Kate ended up running Nora's."

Brody had heard the same story from Andrew. Both Spencer children had loved the little shop, and the indulgent grandparents who ran it. Andrew hadn't talked much about his parents, except to say they were divorced, but he had raved about his grandparents and his older sister.

It had been one of several things Brody had in common with the young soldier, and created a bond between the two of them almost from the first day they met. He'd understood that devotion to grandparents, and to siblings.

"My grandmother runs a family business, too. A marketing agency started by my grandfather years ago.

My brothers and I all went in different directions, so I think she's pinned her hopes on my cousin Alec for taking it over when she retires."

She cocked her head to one side and studied him, her gaze roaming over his suit, tie, the shiny dress shoes. A teasing smile played on her lips, danced in her eyes. Already he'd started to like Kate Spencer. Her sassy attitude, her friendly smile.

"And you, Mr. Red Sox ribbon, you are far from the business type, being a doctor?"

He chuckled. "Definitely."

"Well, should I ever feel faint," she pressed a hand to her chest and the smile widened, and something in Brody flipped inside out, "I know who to call."

For a second, he forgot his reason for being there. His gaze lingered on the hand on her chest, then drifted to the curve of her lips. "I'm right around the corner. Almost shouting distance."

"That's good to know." The smile again. "Really good."

The tension between them coiled tighter. The room warmed, and the traffic outside became a low, muted hum. Brody wished he was an ordinary customer, here on an ordinary reason. That he wasn't going to have to make that smile dim by telling her the truth.

Kate broke eye contact first. She jerked her attention to the register, her fingers hovering over the keys. "Goodness. I got so distracted by talking, I forgot to charge you."

"And I forgot to pay." Brody handed over a credit card. As he did, he noticed her hands. Long, delicate fingers tipped with no-nonsense nails. Pretty hands.

The kind that seemed like they'd have an easy, gentle touch.

She took the credit card, slid it through the register, pushed a few buttons, then waited for a receipt to print. She glanced down at his name as she handed him back the card. "Mr. McKenna, is it?"

He braced himself. Did she recognize the last name? But her smile remained friendly.

*Yes, I'm Brody McKenna. The doctor who let your brother die.*

Not the answer he wanted to give. Call him selfish, call him a coward, but for right now, he wanted only to see her smile again. He told himself it was because that was what Andrew had wanted, but really, Brody liked Kate's smile. A lot.

"Yes. But I prefer Brody." He scrawled his name across the receipt and slid it back to her.

"Well, thank you, Brody." His name slid off her tongue with an easy, sweet lilt. "I hope you return if you're in the neighborhood again."

"Thank you, Kate." He picked up his basket and headed for the door. As he pushed on the exit, he paused, turned back. He had come here for a reason, and had yet to fulfill even a tenth of that purpose. "Maybe someday I can return the favor."

"I didn't do anything special, just my job. If you want to return the favor, then tell all your friends to shop here and to call on us to help them celebrate special moments." And then, like a gift, she smiled at him again. "That'll be more than enough."

"No, it won't," he said, his voice low and quiet, then headed out the door.

## CHAPTER TWO

WHAT had he been thinking?

He'd gone into that little shop planning…what?

To tell Kate the truth? That her little brother had charged him with making sure his sister was okay. That Brody was supposed to make sure she wasn't letting her grief overwhelm her, and that she was staying on track with her life, despite losing Andrew. Instead Brody had bought a basket of chocolates, and chickened out at the last minute. Damn.

"Tell me you're quiet because you're distracted by that pretty hostess over there," Riley said to Brody. The dim interior provided the perfect backdrop for the microbrewery/restaurant that had become their newest favorite stop for lunch. Brody had called Riley yesterday after his visit to Nora's Sweet Shop, and made plans for lunch today. That, he figured, would keep him from making another visit. And leaving without saying or doing what he'd gone there to do.

"Why are you mentioning the hostess?" Brody asked. "Aren't you getting married soon?"

"I am indeed. But that doesn't mean I can't keep my eye out for a pretty girl…" Riley leaned across the table and grinned, "for *you*. You're the last of the

McKenna boys who isn't married. Better pony up to the bar, brother, and join the club."

"No way. I've tried that—"

"You got engaged. Not married. Doesn't count. You came to the edge of the cliff and didn't jump."

"For good reason." Melissa had been more interested in the glamour of being a doctor's wife than in being *Brody's* wife. Once she'd realized he had opted for a small family practice instead of a lucrative practice like plastic surgery or cardiac care, she'd called off the engagement. She didn't want a man who spent his life "sacrificing," she'd said. No matter what Brody said or did, he couldn't fix their relationship and couldn't get it back on track. Brody's family dream had evaporated like a puddle on a summer day.

Brody picked up the menu and scanned the offerings. "How's work going?"

That drew more laughter from Riley. "Don't think I'm falling for that. You're changing the subject."

"You got me." Brody put up his hands. "I don't want to talk about the hostess or my love life or why I didn't get married. I want to visit with my little brother before he attaches the ball and chain to his ankle."

"No need for that. I'm head over heels in love with my wife to be." A goofy grin spread across Riley's face. "We're working out the final details for the wedding. Got the place—"

"The diner." A busy, quaint place in the heart of Boston where the former playboy Riley had worked for a few weeks when their grandmother had cut him off from the family pocketbook and told him to get a job and grow up. Now, a couple of months later, Riley had turned into a different man. Stace had brought out the best in Brody's little brother.

"Gran had a fit about us having the wedding at the Morning Glory, because she wanted us to get married at the Park Plaza, but Stace and I love that old diner, so it seemed only fitting we seal the deal there. Stace has her dress, though I am forbidden from seeing it until the wedding day. And you guys all have your suits—"

"Thank you again for not making me put on a tux."

Riley grinned. "You know me, Brody. I'd rather wear a horsehair shirt than a tux. Finn's the only formal one out of the three of us. He actually *wanted* a tux. Says I'm killing a tradition with the suit idea." Riley waved a hand in dismissal. "I'm sure Ellie will talk some sense into him. That wife of his has been the best thing ever for ol' stick in the mud Finn."

Brody shook his head. "I can't believe you're talking about wedding plans. You've changed, little brother."

"For the better, believe me. Meeting Stace made me change everything about myself, my life. And I'm glad it did." The waitress came by their table to take their orders. Riley opted to try the new Autumn Lager, while Brody stuck to water.

Riley raised a hand when a few of their mutual friends came in. Then he turned back to Brody. "Want me to invite them over to join us?"

Brody thought of the small talk they'd exchange, idle chatter about women, work and sports. "I don't feel much like company. Maybe another time."

"You okay?"

"I'm fine." Brody pushed his menu to the side of the table and avoided his brother's gaze.

"Sure you are. Brody, you're still struggling. You should talk about it."

The waitress dropped off their drinks. Brody thanked her, then took a long sip of the icy water. Talking about it hadn't done any good. He'd lost patients before, back when he was an intern, and in the last few years, seen a few patients die of heart disease and cancer, but this one had been different. Maybe because he'd lacked the tools so easy to obtain here.

Either way, Brody didn't want to discuss the loss of Andrew. Of the three McKennas, Brody kept the most inside. Maybe it came from being the middle brother, sandwiched between practical Finn and boisterous Riley. Or maybe it stemmed from his job—the good doctor trying to keep emotion out of the equation and relying on logic to make decisions. Or maybe it stemmed from something deeper.

Admitting he had failed. Doctors were the ones people relied on to fix it, make it better, and Brody hadn't done either.

"By the way," Brody said, "if you guys don't have a cake picked out yet for the wedding, there's this bakery down the street from my office that does cupcake wedding cakes. They had a display in the window. I thought it looked kind of cool. I know you and Stace are doing the unconventional thing, so maybe this would be a good fit."

"Changing the subject again?"

Brody grinned. "Doing my best."

"Okay. I get the hint. No, we don't have a cake decided on yet. We planned this whole thing pretty fast, because all I want to do is wake up next to Stace every day of my life." Riley grinned, then narrowed his eyes.

"Hey, since when do you bring dessert to a get-together? Or heck, offer anything other than a reminder to get my flu shot?"

Brody scowled. "I thought it'd be nice for you and Stace."

Riley leaned forward, studying his older brother's face. "Wait…did you say bakery? Is it the one owned by that guy's sister?"

"Yeah." Brody shrugged, concentrated on drinking his water. "It is. But that's not—"

"Oh." Riley paused a second. "Okay. I get it. Good idea."

"I'm just offering to help defray the costs of your wedding."

"Whatever spin you want to put on it is fine with me." Riley chuckled. "Stace talked about baking the cake herself, but she's so busy with the diner, and then planning this thing. Let me talk to Stace and see if that works for her. I'll do that right now, in fact."

"You don't have to—"

"I don't mind, Brody. Not one bit." Riley's face filled with sympathy. Riley knew very little about Brody's time in Afghanistan. A few facts, but no real details, and only because Riley had brought over a six-pack of beer to welcome Brody home, and by the third one, Brody had started talking. He'd told Riley one of the military guys who had died had been local, that he'd struck up a friendship with the man before he died. But that was all. Brody had hoped broaching the subject would be cathartic. Instead, in the morning he had a hangover and ten times more regrets.

Riley flipped out his cell phone and dialed. "How's the prettiest bride in Boston today?"

Brody heard Stace laugh on the other end. He turned away, watched the hum of activity in the restaurant. Waitstaff bustling back and forth, the bartender joking with a few regulars, the tables filling and emptying like tidal pools.

"Stace loves the idea," Riley said, closing the phone and tucking it back into his pocket. "She said to tell you our colors are—"

"Your colors?" Brody chuckled. "You have a color scheme there, Riley?"

A flush filled his younger brother's cheeks. "Hey, if it makes Stace happy, it makes me happy. Anyway, go for bright pink and purple. Morning glories, you know?"

Brody nodded. His brother had told him about the meaning behind the diner Stace owned. The one started years before by her father, and decorated with the flowers that he had said reminded him of his daughter. A sentimental gift to a daughter he'd loved very much. "That'll be nice."

"Yeah," Riley said, as a quiet smile stole across his face, "it will."

How Brody envied his brother that smile. The peace in his features. The happiness he wore like a comfortable shirt.

It was the same thing Brody had been searching for, and not finding. He'd thought maybe if he stopped by and talked to Kate, made a step toward the promise he'd made, it would help. If anything, it had stirred a need in him to do more, to do…something.

Hence, the cupcakes. Now that he'd opened his big mouth, he'd need to go back there and place the order.

Damn.

"So how is work going?" Brody said before Riley turned the conversation around again. His brother had started an after school program at the arts centered high school he'd once attended. For creative, energetic Riley, the job fit well.

"Awesome. The kids at the Wilmont Academy are loving the program. So much, we opened it up to other kids in the area. We're already talking about expanding it in size and number of schools."

"That's great." The waitress brought their food and laid a steaming platter of mini burgers and fries in front of Riley, a Waldorf salad in front of Brody.

"Why do you eat that crap?" Brody said. "You know what it's doing to your arteries. With our family history—"

Riley put up a hand. "I love you, Brody, I really do, but if you say anything about my fries, I'm going to have to hurt you."

"I just worry about you."

"And I appreciate it. I'll do an extra mile on the treadmill tonight if that makes you feel better."

"It does. Did you get your flu—"

Riley tick-tocked a finger. "Don't go all doctor on me. I'm out to lunch with my brother, and we're talking about my job. Okay?"

Brody grinned. "Okay."

As if to add an exclamation point to the conversation, Riley popped a fry into his mouth. "Things at Wilmont, like I said, are going great. We've got classes in woodworking, dance, film, you name it. They're filling up fast."

"That's great."

"Oh, yeah, before I forget. We're having a career day

next month and we're looking for people to speak to the kids about their jobs. Answer questions about education requirements, things like that." Riley fiddled with a fry. "Maybe you could come in and do a little presentation on going into medicine. You know, a day in the life of a doctor, that kind of thing."

Brody pushed his salad to the side, his appetite gone. "I don't think I'm the best person to talk about that."

Riley's blue eyes met his brother's. Old school rock music flowed from the sound system with a deep bass and steady beat. "You're the perfect one. You've got a variety of experiences and—"

"Just drop it. Okay?" He let out a curse and shook his head. Why had he called his brother? Why had he thought it would make things better? Hell, it had done the opposite. "I just want to get you some damned cupcakes. How many do you need?"

Riley sighed. He looked like he wanted to say something more but didn't. "There should be fifty guests. So whatever it takes to feed that many. We're keeping it small. I figure I've lived enough of my life in the limelight. I want this to be special. Just me and Stace, or as close as we can get to that."

Brody nodded. Tried not to let his envy for Riley's happiness show. First Finn, now Riley, settled down and making families. For a long time, Brody had traveled along that path, too. He'd dated Melissa for a couple years, and he'd thought they'd get married. Then just before he took over Doc Watkin's practice, he'd spent two weeks working for free in a clinic in Alabama, tending to people who fell into the gap between insurance and state aid. He'd been in the middle of stitching up a kid with a gaping leg wound when Melissa had called to tell him she was done, and moving on.

"Thanks," Brody said, getting to his feet and tossing some money onto the table. He turned away, shrugged into his jacket. "I'll let the baker know about the cupcakes."

"Brod?"

Brody turned back. "Yeah?"

"How are you? Really?"

Brody thought of the physicals and sore throats and aches and pains waiting for him back in his office. The patients expecting him to fix them, make them better. For a month, in Afghanistan, he'd thought he was doing just that, making a difference, until—

Until he'd watched the light die in Andrew Spencer's eyes.

"I thought I was fine," Brody said. "But I was wrong."

# CHAPTER THREE

KATE stared at the pile of orders on her desk, the paper-work waiting to be done, but found her mind wandering to the handsome customer who had come in a couple days ago. The doctor with the Red Sox basket, who had been both friendly and...troubled. Yes, that was the word for it. She'd joked with him about spreading the word about the shop, told him it would be enough to repay her work on the basket, and he'd said—

*No it won't.*

Such an odd comment to leave her with. What on earth could he have meant? She hadn't done anything more for him than she'd do for any other customer. Changed a bow, added some feminine touches. It wasn't like she'd handed over a kidney or anything. Maybe she'd misheard him.

Kate gave up on the work and got to her feet, crossing to the window. She looked out over the alley that ran between her shop and the one next door, then down toward the street, busy with cars passing in a blur as people headed home after work. The sound system played music Kate didn't hear and the computer flashed messages of emails Kate didn't read.

Her mind strayed to Dr. Brody McKenna again. She

didn't know much about him, except that he was a Red Sox fan who'd been too distracted to notice the basket he'd picked out was more suited to a male than a female. Maybe he was one of those scattered professor types. Brilliant with medicine but clueless about real life.

She sighed, then turned away from the window. She had a hundred other priorities that didn't include daydreaming about a handsome doctor. She'd met two kinds of men in her life—lazy loafers who expected her to be their support system and driven career A-types who invested more in their jobs than their relationships.

Few heroes like Andrew, few men who lived every day with heart and passion. Until she met one like that, dating would run a distant second to a warm cup of coffee and a fresh from the oven cookie.

The shop door rang. Kate headed out front, working a smile to her face. It became a real smile when she saw her grandmother standing behind the counter, sneaking a red devil cupcake from under the glass dome. Kate put out her arms. "Grandma, what a nice surprise."

Nora laughed as she hugged her granddaughter. "It can't be that much of a surprise. I'm here almost every day for my sugar fix."

Kate released Grandma from the hug. "And I'm thrilled that you are."

Growing up, Kate had spent hours here after school, helping out in the shop and sneaking treats from under the very same glass dome. The sweet tooth came with the family dimples, she thought as she watched her grandmother peel the paper off the cupcake.

"Don't tell your grandfather I'm sneaking another cupcake," Nora warned, wagging a finger. "You know he thinks I'm already sweet enough."

"That's because he loves you."

Nora smiled at the mention of her husband. They had the kind of happy marriage so elusive to other people, and so valuable to those blessed with that gift. Unlike Kate's parents, who had turned fighting into a daily habit, Nora doted on her husband, always had, she said, and always would.

Nora popped a bite of cupcake in her mouth then looked around the shop. "How are things going here?"

"Busy."

"How's the hunt for a second location?"

Kate shrugged. "I haven't done much toward that yet."

"You had plans—"

"That was before, Grandma. Before..." She shook her head.

Nora laid a hand on Kate's shoulder. "I understand."

When Andrew had been alive, buying and opening new locations had been part of their business plan. But ever since he'd died, she'd had to work at keeping to that plan. Months ago, she'd found a spot for a second location in Weymouth, but had yet to visit it or run the numbers, all signs that she wasn't as enthused as she used to be.

Her grandmother smiled. "I like the idea of another Nora's Sweet Shop, but I worry about you, honey. If you want to take some time off, I'd be glad to step in and help. Your grandpa, too."

Kate looked at her eighty-three-year-old grandmother. She knew Nora would step in any time Kate asked her, but she wouldn't expect or ask that of Nora. "I know you would, and I appreciate that but I'm okay. You guys do enough for me making the daytime deliveries."

Nora waved that off. "It keeps us busy and gets us out of the house. You know we like tooling around town, stopping in to see the regular customers."

"You two deserve to enjoy your golden years, not spend them working over a hot oven. Besides, I'm doing fine, Grandma."

Nora brushed a strand of hair off Kate's face. "No you're not."

Kate nodded, then shook her head, and cursed the tears that rushed to her eyes. "I just…miss him."

She didn't add that she regretted, to the depth of her being, ever encouraging her brother to join the military. Maybe if she'd pushed him in another direction, or dismissed the idea of the military, he'd be here today.

Tears shimmered in Nora's eyes, too. She had doted on her grandson, and though she'd been proud of his military service, she had worried every minute of his deployment. "We all do. But he wouldn't want you to be sitting around, missing him. If there was one thing your brother did well, it was live his life. Remember the time he went parachuting off that mountain?"

Despite the tears, Kate smiled. Her brother had been a wild child, from the second he was born. He approached life head on—and never looked back. "And the time he skydived for the first time. Oh, and that crazy swim with the sharks trip he took." Kate shook her head. "He lived on the edge."

"While the rest of us stayed close to terra firma." Nora smiled. "But in the end, he always came back home."

"His heart was here."

"It was indeed," Nora said. "And he would want you to be happy, to celebrate your life, not bury it in work."

Before he left for Afghanistan, Andrew had tried to talk to her about the future. When he'd started on the what-ifs, she'd refused to listen, afraid of what might happen. Now, she regretted that choice. Maybe if she'd heard him out, she might have the secret to his risk taking. Something to urge her down the path they had planned for so long.

Andrew had soared the skies for the rest of them while the other Spencers offered caution, wisdom. She missed that about him, but knew she should also learn from him. Remember that life was short and to live every moment with gusto. Even if doing so seemed impossible some days. Kate swiped away the tears. "I'll try to remember that."

"Good." Nora patted her granddaughter on the shoulder. Then her gaze shifted to the picture window at the front of the shop. She nodded toward the door. "Ooh. Handsome man alert. Did you put on your lipstick?"

Kate laughed. Leave it to Nora to be sure her granddaughter was primped and ready should Mr. Right stride on by. Her grandmother lived in perpetual hope for great grandchildren that she could spoil ten times more than she'd spoiled her grandchildren. "Grandma, I'm not interested in dating right now."

"I think this guy will change your mind about that. Take a look."

The door opened and Brody McKenna strode inside. Kate's heart tripped a little. The doctor's piercing blue eyes zeroed in on hers, and the world dropped away.

She cleared her throat. "Back for another basket, Doctor?"

*Way to go, Kate, establish it as a business only relationship.* In the end, the best choice. Hadn't she watched her parents' marriage, started on a whim, with major differences in goals and values, disintegrate? She wanted a steady, dependable base, not a man who made her heart race and erased her common sense, regardless of the way Brody's lopsided smile and ocean blue eyes flipped a switch inside her.

"I just came by to thank you," he said. "The basket was a big hit. My grandmother sends her regards and her gratitude for the cherry chocolates. Especially those. In fact, I'm under strict orders to buy some more."

"Those are my favorites, too," Nora said. She leaned over the counter and put out a hand. "I'm Nora Spencer."

He smiled. "Ah, the famous Nora in Nora's Sweet Shop." He shook hands with her, and Kate swore she saw her eighty-three-year-old grandma blush. "Brody McKenna."

Nora arched a brow. "You're a *doctor,* you said?"

Kate wanted to elbow her grandmother but Nora had already stepped out of reach. Under the counter, she waved her hand, but Grandma ignored the hint.

"Yes, ma'am," Brody said. "I own a family practice right down the street from here. I took over for Doc Watkins."

"Oh, I remember him," Nora said. "Nice guy. Except for when he was losing at golf. Then he was grumpy. Every Wednesday, he played, so I learned never to make an appointment for first thing Thursday morning."

Brody chuckled. "Yep, you have him down to a tee."

Kate and her grandmother laughed at the pun. Then Nora tapped her chin, and studied Brody. "Wait... McKenna. Aren't you that doctor that volunteers all the time? Or something like that? I read about a charity your family heads up. Doctors and Borders or something like that."

"Medicine Across Borders." He shifted from foot to foot. "Yes, I'm involved in that. We travel the country and the world, providing volunteer medical help to people in need."

The name of the organization sounded familiar to Kate, but she figured maybe because she'd seen something in the news about it. Brody McKenna, however, seemed unnerved by talking about the group. His gaze darted to the right, and his posture tensed. Maybe he was one of those men who didn't like his charity work to be a big deal. A behind the scenes kind of guy.

Nora leaned in closer to him. "So tell me, Doctor McKenna, is there a Mrs. Doctor?"

"Grandma," Kate hissed. "Stop that." Still, Kate checked his left hand. No ring. The doctor was a single man. And she didn't care. At all.

Uh-huh.

"No, ma'am, there isn't a Mrs. Doctor," Brody said. "But I am here about a wedding that's in the near future."

Disappointment filled Kate. She told herself to quit those thoughts. She'd seen the man once for a few minutes and she didn't care if he married her next door neighbor or the Queen of England. For goodness sake, she'd turned into an emotional wreck today. And it was only Tuesday.

"I'd be glad to help you with that," she said, pulling out an order pad and a pen. "What do you need?"

"It's not for me. It's for my brother."

"Wonderful," Nora said. "In that case, we're even more glad to help you."

"Grandma, stop," Kate hissed again.

"It is nice to find such helpful and beautiful service in this city," Brody said with a smile.

Nora elbowed Kate. A little thrill ran through her at his words. Why did she care?

Darn those eyes of his.

"Oh, don't worry," Brody said. "I'm as far from getting married as a man can be. This is for my little brother, Riley. He's getting married next Saturday and it's a small, private affair, but I thought it would be nice to provide the dessert so his new bride doesn't have to cook it. She owns a diner in the city. Maybe you've heard of it. The Morning Glory."

"I've seen it before when I've been in the city," Kate said, stepping in with a change of subject before her grandmother found a way to turn a diner, a brother's wedding and a cupcake order into an opportunity for matchmaking. After all, hadn't Brody just said he had no interest in marriage? That screamed stay away, commitment-phobic bachelor. "Didn't the diner host an animal shelter thing a month ago?"

"It did. Went well. The diner's main chef is on a trip to Europe and they've got a new one filling in, but I think doing the dessert *and* the food might be a bit over-whelming for him. Plus it's a nice way for me to show my support for my brother and his new wife. As well as give some business to a local shop."

It all sounded plausible, but still, something about the story Brody told gave Kate pause. She couldn't put her finger on it. Why come here? To this shop? There were a hundred bakeries in the area, several dedicated to weddings. Why her shop?

She decided to stop looking a gift horse in the mouth.

She needed the income, and she'd be crazy to turn down the opportunity to get Nora's Sweet Shop name out there. Especially if she sthe tuck to the plan about expanding, every public event was an opportunity to spread the word, ease into new markets.

"You've come to the right place," Nora said, as if reading Kate's mind. "We've done lots of weddings."

"Yeah, I saw that cupcake thing you had in the window. My brother and his fiancé thought it'd be a great idea because they're having their wedding and reception at the diner. It's going to be more low-key than your traditional big cake and band kind of thing. They aren't your typical couple, either, and loved the idea of an atypical cake."

Kate thought a second while she tapped her pen on the order pad. "We could do a whole morning glory theme. Put faux flowers on top of the cupcakes and arrange them like a bouquet."

Brody nodded. "I like that. Great idea. And I know Stace—that's the bride—will love it, too. The diner is important to her."

The praise washed over Kate. She'd had dozens of customers rave about the shop's unique sweets. Why did this one man's—a stranger's—words affect her so? "How many people are we serving?"

"Uh, about fifty. I think that's what my brother said."

"Sounds great." She jotted some notes on the order pad, adding the details about the cupcakes, his name and the date of the event. Considering the number of orders already stacked up in her kitchen, adding his one into the mix would take some doing. Thank God she had her assistant Joanne to help. Joanne had the experience of ten bakers and had been with the shop for so many years, neither Kate or Nora could remember when she'd started.

"And what about a phone number?" Nora piped in. Kate shot her grandmother a glare, but Nora just smiled. "In case we need to get a hold of you."

Brody rattled off a number. "That's my office, which is where I usually am most days. Do you want my cell, too?"

"No," Kate said.

"Yes," Nora said. Louder.

Brody gave them the second number, then paused a second, like he wanted to say something else. He glanced across the room, at what, Kate wasn't sure. The cupcake display? The awards and accolades posted on the wall? "So, uh, thanks," he said, his attention swiveling back to her.

"You're welcome. And thank you for the order."

"You said spread the word." He shrugged and gave her a lopsided grin. "I did. I'm sorry it wasn't more."

She chuckled. "I appreciate all business that comes my way."

Again, he seemed to hesitate, but in the end, he just nodded toward her, said he'd call her if he thought of anything else, then headed out the door. Kate watched him go, even more intrigued than before. Why did this doctor keep her mind whirring?

"Why did you keep trying to fix us up?" Kate asked Nora when the door had shut behind Brody.

"Because he is a very handsome man and you are a very interested woman."

"I'm not at all."

"Coulda fooled me with those googly eyes."

Kate grabbed the order pad off the counter and

tucked the pen in her pocket. "My eyes are on one thing and one thing only. Keeping this shop running and sticking to the plan for expansion." Her gaze went to the article on the wall, the only one that truly mattered. To the plans she'd had, plans that seemed stalled on the ground, no matter how hard she tried to move them forward. "Because I promised I would."

Brody tried. He really did. He put in the hours, he smiled and joked, he filled out the charts, dispensed the prescriptions. But he still couldn't fit back into the shoes he'd left when he'd gone to Afghanistan. After all his other medical mission trips, he'd come back refreshed, ready to tackle his job with renewed enthusiasm. But not this time. And he knew why.

Because of Andrew Spencer.

Every day, Brody pulled the card out of his wallet, and kicked himself for not doing what he'd promised to do. Somehow, he had to find a way to start helping Kate Spencer. He'd seen the grief in her eyes, heard it in her voice. Andrew had asked Brody to make sure his sister moved on, followed her heart, and didn't let the loss of him weigh her down, and do it without telling her the truth. That he had been the one tending Andrew when he'd died.

*She doesn't handle loss real well, Doc. She'll blame herself for encouraging me to go over here, and that'll just make her hurt more. Take care of her—*

*But don't tell her why you're doing it. I don't want her blaming herself or dwelling on the past. I want her eyes on the future. Encourage her to take a risk, to pursue her dreams. Don't let her spend one more second grieving or regretting.*

When Brody had agreed, the promise had seemed easy. Check in on Kate Spencer, make sure she was okay, and maybe down the road, tell her about the incredible man her brother had been, and how Brody had known him. But now...

He couldn't seem to do any of the above.

Maybe if he wrote it down first, it would make the telling easier. He could take his time, find the words he needed.

The last patient of the day had left, as had Mrs. Maguire, and Brody sat in his office. His charts were done, which meant he could leave at any time. Head to his grandmother's for the weekly family dinner, or home to his empty apartment. Instead, he pulled out a sheet of blank paper, grabbed a pen, then propped the card up on his desk.

*I never expected to bond with Andrew Spencer. To me, he was my guardian—and at times, a hindrance to the work I wanted to do, because he'd make me and the other doctors wait while he and his fellow troops cleared an area, double checked security, in short, protected our lives.*

*All I heard was a ticking clock of sick and dying people, but he was smarter than me, and reminded me time and again that if the doctors died, then the people surely would, too. That was Andrew Spencer—putting the good of all far ahead of the good of himself. He risked his life for us many times. But the last time—*

Brody's cell rang, dancing across the oak surface of his desk. He considered letting it go to voicemail, but in the end answering the phone was easier than writing the letter. "Hello?"

"Dr. McKenna, this is Kate down at Nora's Sweet

Shop." Even over the phone, Kate's voice had the same sweet tone as in person. Brody liked the sound of her voice. Very much. Maybe too much. "I'm calling because there's a problem with your cupcake order. I…I can't fill it. My assistant had to go out of town today because her first grandchild came a little early, and that leaves me short-handed with a whole lot of orders, not to mention a huge one due tonight. Anyway, I took the liberty of calling another bakery in town and they said they'll be happy to take care of that for you. No extra charge, and I assure you their work is as good as mine."

Kate Spencer was in a bind. He could hear the stress in her voice, the tension stringing her words together. He thought of that card in his pocket, and of the promise he'd made to Andrew to help Kate. Now, it turned out that Brody's order had only added to her stress level.

"Anyway, let me give you the name and number of the other bakery," she said. "They're expecting your call, and have all my order notes."

Brody took down the number, jotting it on a Post-it beside the letter he'd been working on. His gaze skimmed the words he'd been writing again. *That was Andrew Spencer—putting the good of all far ahead of the good of himself.*

It was as if Andrew was nudging Brody from beyond the grave. Do something, you fool. You said you would. "Is there any way I can help?" Brody asked.

She laughed. "Unless you can come up with an experienced baker in thirty minutes who is free for the next few days, then no. But don't worry, we'll be fine. I do feel bad about the last minute notice on changing suppliers, but I assure you the other bakery will do a great job. Thanks again for the business, and please consider us in the future."

"In case I ever have another wedding to buy a cake for?"

"Well, you *are* a doctor," she said with a little laugh. "You know, most desirable kind of bachelor there is. God, I can't believe I said that. Something about being on the phone loosens my tongue to say stupid things." She exhaled. "I'm sorry."

"No, no, I'm flattered. Really. Most people who come to see me are complaining about something or other. It's nice to get a compliment once in a while."

She laughed again, a light lyrical sound that lit his heart. For the first time in days, it felt like sunshine had filled the room. "Well, good. I'm glad to brighten your day. Anyway, thanks again."

"Anytime." She was going to hang up, and his business with Kate Spencer would be through, unless he found a reason to buy a lot of chocolate filled baskets. He glanced again at the words on the page, but no brilliant way to keep her on the line came to mind.

"Thank you for understanding, Dr. McKenna." She said goodbye, then the connection ended. He stared at the phone and the number he'd written down for a long, long time. He read over his attempt at the letter, as half hearted as his attempts to keep his promise, then crumpled it into a ball and tossed it in the trash. Then he got his coat and headed out the door, walking fast.

Thirty minutes wasn't a lot of time to change a future, but Brody was sure going to try.

# CHAPTER FOUR

WIND battered the small building and rain pattered against the windows of Nora's Sweet Shop. A fall storm, asserting its strength and warning of winter's imminent arrival. Kate sat at her desk, flipping through the thick stack of yellow order sheets.

She had two corporate orders. Three banquets. And now, the McKenna wedding—well, no, that one was safely in another bakery's hands. A lot of work for one bakery, never mind one person. On any other day, she'd be grateful for the influx of work. But today, it all just felt…overwhelming. She glanced over at the folder on her desk, filled with notes about expansions and new locations, then glanced away. That would have to be put on hold. For a long time.

Always before, baking had been her solace, the place where she could lose herself and find a sweet contentment that came from making something that would make people smile. But ever since Andrew's death, that passion for her job had wavered, disappearing from time to time like sunshine on a cloudy day.

Now, without her assistant on board, she knew getting the job done would take a Herculean effort. Best to just roll up her sleeves and get it done.

She glanced at the dark, angry sky. "I can't do this without you," she whispered to the storm above. Thunder rumbled disagreement. "We were supposed to expand this business together, take Nora's Sweet Shop to the masses. Remember? That's what you always said, Andrew. Now you're gone and I'm alone and trying like hell to stick to the plan. But…" she released a long, heavy sigh, "it's hard. So hard. I'm not the risk taker. I'm not the adventurer. You were. And now, the shop is in trouble and I…I need…help."

The bell over the door jingled. Kate jerked to her feet. For a second, she thought she'd round the corner and see Andrew, with his teasing grin and quick wit. Instead, she found the last answer she'd expect.

Brody McKenna.

He stomped off the rain on his shoes, swiped the worst of the wet from his hair, and offered her a sheepish smile, looking lost and sexy all at the same time. A part of her wanted to give him a good meal, a warm blanket, and a hug. She stopped that thought before it embedded itself in her mind. Dr. McKenna embodied dark, brooding, mysterious. A risk for a woman's heart if she'd ever seen one.

"Dr. McKenna, nice to see you again." She came out from behind the counter, cursing herself for smoothing at her hair and shirt as she did. "Did you have a problem with the other bakery?"

"No, no. I haven't even called them yet." He shifted his weight from foot to foot. The rain had darkened his lashes, and made his blue eyes seem even bluer. More like a tempestuous sea, rolling with secrets in its depths. "I, ah, stopped by to see if you had eaten."

She blinked. "If I had eaten?"

"I live near here and every night when I walk home, I see the light on." He took two steps closer. "Every morning when I leave for work, I see the light on in here." He took another two steps, then a few more, until he stood inches away from her, that deep blue ocean drawing her in, captivating her. "And it makes me wonder whether you ever go home or ever have time to have a decent meal."

"I…" She couldn't find a word to say. No one outside her immediate family had ever said anything like that to her. Worried that she'd eaten, worried that she worked too hard. Why did this man care? Was it just the doctor in him? Or something more? "I won't starve, believe me. I have a frozen meal in the back. I'll wolf it down between baking."

"That's not healthy."

She shrugged. "It's part of being a business owner. Take the bad with the good. And right now, the good is…well, a little harder to find." She didn't add that she planned on keeping herself busy in the kitchen because it kept her from thinking. From dwelling. From talking to people who were no longer here.

Brody leaned against the counter, his height giving him at least a foot's advantage over her. For a second, she wondered what it would be like to lean into that height, to put her head against his broad chest, to tell him her troubles and share her burdens.

Then she got a grip and shook her head. He was asking her about her eating habits, chiding her about working too much. Not offering to be her confidante. Or anything more.

"Listen, I eat alone way too often," he said. "Like

you, I work a lot more hours than I probably should and end up trading healthy food for fast food."

She laughed. "Doctor, heal thyself?"

"Yeah, something like that. So why don't we eat together, and then you can get back to baking or whatever it is you're doing here. It's a blustery night, the kind when you need a warm meal and some good company. Not something packaged and processed."

Damn, that sounded good. Tempting. Comforting. Perfect.

Despite her reservations, a smile stole across Kate's face. "And are you the good company?"

"That you'll have to decide for yourself." He grinned. "My head nurse thinks I'm a pain in the neck, but my grandmother sings my praises."

She laughed. "Isn't that what grandmothers are supposed to do?"

"I do believe that's Chapter One in the Good Grandma Handbook."

Kate laughed again. Her stomach let out a rumble at the thought of a real meal. Twice a week she went to Nora's for dinner, but the rest of her meals were consumed on the run. Quick bites between filling baking pans and spreading icing. Brody had a point about her diet being far from healthy. "Well, I am hungry."

"Me, too. And I don't know about you, but I…I don't want to eat alone tonight."

She thought of the gray sky, the stormy rumbles from the clouds and the conversations she'd had with her dead brother. "Me, either," Kate said softly.

Brody thumbed to the east. "There's a great little place down the street. The Cast Iron Skillet. Have you been there?"

The rumble in her stomach became a full-out roar. "I ate there a couple times after they first opened. They have an amazing cast iron chicken. Drizzled with garlic butter and served with mashed sweet potatoes. Okay, now I'm salivating."

"Then drool with me and let's get a table."

Drool with him? She was already drooling over him. Temptation coiled inside her. Damn those blue eyes of his.

She hesitated for a fraction of a second, then decided the work had waited this long, it could wait a little longer. She wasn't being much use in the kitchen right now anyway, and couldn't seem to get on track. Not to mention, she couldn't remember the last time she'd had a meal that hadn't come from the microwave. She grabbed her jacket and purse from under the counter, then her umbrella from the stand by the door. "Here," she said, handing it to him, "let's be smart before we go out in the rain."

But as Kate left the shop and turned the lock in the door, she had to wonder if letting the handsome doctor talk her into a dinner that sounded a lot like a date was smart. At all.

The food met its promise, but Brody didn't notice. He'd been captivated by Kate Spencer from the day he met her, and the more time he spent with her, the more intrigued he became. What had started as a way to get to know the person whom Andrew had raved about, the one who had written that card to her brother and sent Andrew so many care packages he'd joked he could have opened a store, had become something more. Something bigger.

Something Brody danced around in his mind but knew would lead to trouble. He was here to fulfill a promise, not fall for Andrew's sister.

Kate took a deep drink of her ice water then stretched her shoulders. She'd already devoured half her dinner, which told Brody he'd made the right decision in inviting her out. Like him, he suspected she spent more time worrying about others than about herself.

For the tenth time he wondered what had spurred him to invite her to dinner, when he'd gone over to the shop tonight to just check in on her, ask her how business was going, and somehow direct the conversation to expansions. Drop a few words in her ear about what a good idea that would be then be on his way, mission accomplished. Once again, his intentions and actions had gone in different directions. Maybe because he was having trouble seeing how to make those intentions work.

"I forgot…what kind of medicine do you practice?" she asked, as she forked up a bite of chicken. The restaurant's casual ambience, created by earth tone décor and cozy booths, had drawn dozens of couples and several families. The murmur of conversation rose and fell like a wave.

"Family practice," Brody said. "I see kids with runny noses. Parents with back aches. I've administered more flu shots than I can count, and taped up more sprained ankles than the folks at Ace bandage."

She laughed. "That must be rewarding."

"It is. I've gotten to know a lot of people over the years, their families, too, and it's nice to be a part of helping them live their lives to the fullest. When they take my advice, of course." He grinned.

"Stubborn patients who keep on eating fast food and surfing the sofa?"

He nodded. "All things in moderation, I tell them. Honestly, most of my job is just about...listening."

"How so?"

"Patients, by and large, know the right things to do. Sometimes, they just want someone to hear them say they're worried about the chances of having a heart attack, or scared about a cancer diagnosis. They want someone to—"

"Care."

"Exactly. And my job is to do that then try to fix whatever ails them." Which he'd done here, many times, but when it had counted—

He hadn't fixed Andrew, not at all. He'd done his best, and he'd failed.

"Where did you start out? I mean, residency." Kate's question drew Brody back to the present.

"Mass General's ER. That's a crazy job, especially in Boston. You never know what's going to come through the door. It was exciting and vibrant and...insane. At the end of the day, I could have slept for a week." He chuckled. "The total opposite of a family practice in a lot of ways. Not to say I don't have my share of emergencies, but it's less hectic. I have more time with my patients in family practice, which is nice."

"I have a cousin in Detroit who works in the ER. I don't think he's been off for a single holiday."

"That's life in the ER, that's for sure." Brody got a taste of that ER life every time he went on a medical mission trips and again in Afghanistan. "That's one of the perks Doc Watkins told me about when I took over the practice. There are days when all those runny noses can get a bit predictable, but by and large, I really enjoy my work."

"Same with cupcakes. Decorated one, decorated a thousand." She laughed. "Though I do like to experiment with different flavors and toppings. And the chocolates—those leave lots of room for creativity."

"Do you ever want to step out of the box, and do something totally different?"

"I have plans to." She fiddled with her fork. "My brother and I always wanted to expand Nora's Sweet Shop, to take it national, maybe even start franchising. Andrew was the one with the big, risky ideas. I'm a little more cautious, but when he talked, I signed on for the ride. He was so enthusiastic, that he got me excited about the idea, too."

"And have you expanded yet?" Brody crossed his hands in front of him, his dinner forgotten. Here was what he had come here to discuss, though he got the feeling it wasn't a subject Kate really liked visiting.

She shook her head. "I've thought about it. Even found a property in Weymouth that I saw online, but..." Kate sighed, "ever since Andrew died, it's been hard to get enthusiastic about the idea again. I know he'd want me to push forward but...it's hard."

Guilt weighed heavy on Brody's shoulders. Maybe if he'd been a better doctor, if he'd found a way to save Andrew, her brother would be here now, and Kate wouldn't be debating about opening another location. She'd be celebrating with Andrew.

*Promise me.*

Andrew had asked him to watch out for his little sister, to make sure she was moving on, living her life. Taking her to dinner was part of that, Brody supposed, but he knew Andrew had meant more than a platter of chicken Alfredo and some breadsticks.

"You should expand anyway. Your brother would want you to," Brody said, wondering if she knew how true that was. "And if it's a matter of financing, I can help if you want."

She laughed. "You? What do you know about franchising or opening new locations?"

"Uh...nothing. But I think it sounds like a great idea and if you need financial backing—" Was that what he was going to do? Throw money at the problem and send it away? "—then I am more than happy to provide that."

"You hardly know me. Why would you give me money, just like that? And how can you afford it?"

"I'm a McKenna, and part of being a McKenna means having money. I inherited quite a lot when my parents died, and my grandparents were good investors. Even after paying for medical school and my own practice, I've been left with more than I know what to do with." He leaned forward, wishing he had the magic words he needed. "I've tasted your cupcakes and chocolates. That's a business worth backing."

"Well, I appreciate the offer, but..."

"But what?"

"I'm not ready for expanding or any kind of a big change yet." She toyed with the fork some more. "Maybe down the road." She raised her gaze to his. Green eyes wide, looking to him for answers, support. "I think part of it is fear of the unknown, you know? Andrew was good at that, just leaping and looking afterwards. I'm one of those people who has to peek behind the curtains a few times before I do anything." She twirled some noodles onto her fork. "I'm the one in the back of the scenes, not out there leading the charge."

He watched her take a bite, swallow, then reach for her water. Every time he saw her, he saw the memory of her brother. They had similar coloring—dark brown hair, deep green eyes, high cheekbones. Andrew had been taller than Kate, tanned from his time in the desert. But Brody could still see so much of the brave young man in his younger sister.

A part of Brody wanted to leave, to head away from those reminders. To bury those days in Afghanistan and his regrets deep, so deep he would never remember them, never have them pop up and send him off-kilter again.

Except that would be the coward's way out, and Brody refused to take that path.

"I used to be that way, too," he said. "Afraid of the unknown. Then I went on my first medical mission trip, and it cured the scare in me."

"How?"

"You get dropped into a new place, with new people and new equipment, and you have to sink or swim. If you sink, then other people get hurt. So I had no choice but to buck up and get over my worries that I wouldn't be a good enough doctor."

But had he been a good enough doctor? Sure he'd helped people in Alabama, Alaska, Costa Rica, even here in Newton, MA, but when it came down to a moment that mattered, a moment when death waited outside the door, he hadn't been good enough after all. He had tried his best and he had failed.

Medical school had taught him over and over again that sometimes, people just die. Maybe that was true, or maybe it was just that the wrong doctor had been in charge that day. He had rethought every action of that day a hundred times, questioned every decision, and retraced his steps. But in the end, it didn't matter because no matter how much he did the day over in his head, it wouldn't bring Andrew back.

"I think just taking care of people like you do, and giving back on those trips you take, is brave enough," she said.

"I don't know about that. It's my job and I just try to do the best I can." Would he ever be brave enough to take on another mission? Or spend the rest of his life afraid of regretting his mistakes?

"My whole family has always been the kind that believes in giving to others," Kate said. "From bringing food to the shelters to donating to good causes, to giving people who need a second chance a job. That's easy, if you ask me. But doing what you do, going to a strange city or country and caring for people…that takes guts."

"There are others who do far gutsier jobs than I," he said. "They're the ones to admire, not me."

"I don't know. You've worked the ER at Mass General." She laughed. "That takes some courage, too."

He had no desire to sit here and discuss courage and himself in the same sentence. He'd come here to keep a promise, and knew he couldn't leave until he did. "Courage is also about going after your dreams, which is what I think you should do. Open that new location." He placed his hand on the table, so close he could have touched her with a breath of movement. "My offer to back you stands, so just know whenever you need me, I'll be there."

"You barely know me," she said again.

"What I know looks like a very good investment."

Her cheeks filled with pink, and she glanced away. "Well, thank you. I'll let you know if I move forward."

Damn. She didn't sound any more enthused about the idea now than she had before.

The other diners chatted and ate, filling the small restaurant with the music of clanking forks and clinking glasses. Waiters bustled to and fro, silent black clad shadows.

"I forgot to get more of those chocolates my grandmother wanted when I was at the shop the other day. She wanted me to also tell you that she liked those chocolate leaves you had in the basket," he said, keeping the topic neutral. Away from the hard stuff. "She said they were so realistic, she almost didn't want to eat them."

The pink in her cheeks deepened to red. "Thank you."

"Don't be embarrassed, Kate. It's clear you enjoy your work by how good the finished product turns out."

"I'm just not used to being the one in the spotlight. For years, I was the one in the back, baking. My grandmother was the face of Nora's for a long time, then Andrew and now…"

"You."

She smiled. "Me."

"You make a good face for the company. Sweet, like the baked treats." The words were out before he could stop them. Damn.

"Keep saying things like that, Dr. McKenna, and I'll never stop blushing." She grinned, then grabbed another breadstick from the basket.

"I wouldn't complain." What the hell was he doing? Flirting with her? He cleared his throat and got back to the reason for being here—a reason that eluded him more and more every minute. "It sounds like you enjoy your job a great deal."

"I do. Except when there's a huge stack of orders and I'm short on help. And…" She glanced at her watch. "Oh, darn, I almost forgot I have a delivery to make tonight." She pushed her plate to the side and got to her feet. "Thanks for dinner, but I have to go."

He rose and tossed some money onto the bill. "Let me walk you back."

She smiled. "It's only a couple blocks to the shop. I'm fine by myself."

"A gentleman never lets a lady walk home alone. My grandfather drilled that into me."

"A gentleman, huh?" The smile widened and her gaze assessed him. "Well, I wouldn't want you to disappoint your grandfather."

They headed out the door, back into the rain. Brody unfurled the umbrella over them, and matched his pace to Kate's fast walk. He noted the shadows under her eyes. From working hard, maybe too hard. She was doing exactly what Andrew had predicted—spending her days baking and wearing herself into the ground. Not taking care of herself. Hence the microwave dinners and shadows under her eyes. "Do you make many deliveries yourself?"

She shook her head. "My grandparents make the daytime deliveries—they enjoy getting out and seeing folks in the neighborhood, but they don't like to drive at night, so I handle those. I don't mind, but when I've been working all day…well, it can make for some long days."

"You need not one assistant, but a whole army of them."

She laughed. "I agree. And as soon as Joanne gets back and I have some time to run an ad and do some interviews, I'll be hiring, so I don't end up in this boat again."

They had reached the shop. Brody waited while she unlocked the door and let them inside. He set the wet umbrella by the door. Kate turned toward him. "Thanks for walking me back."

"No problem."

"And, I'm really sorry about having to send you to another bakery for the cupcake order. If there was a way to fit that in my schedule, believe me I would. I just had too many existing orders and not enough time." She grinned and put her hands up. "There's only one me."

"You could get a temp," he said. "I've hired them when my nurse is on vacation. And during busy seasons."

She waved that suggestion off. "Trying to find someone trained in cooking and willing to work just those few days…it's almost more work to do that than it is to just handle it myself. And right now, my time is so limited, I can't imagine adding to my To Do list."

She reminded Brody of himself when he had been an intern in medical school, burning the candle at both ends, and sometimes from the middle, too. "How are you going to get all the orders done? And make deliveries and do paperwork and all the stuff that goes with owning your own business?"

"Working hard. Working long hours. I do most of the baking after the shop closes, which means for very long nights sometimes." She shrugged. "I've done it before. I can do it again."

He saw the tension in her face, the shadows under her eyes, the weight of so much responsibility on her shoulders. Andrew had told him, in that long, long conversation that had lingered long into the night while Brody prayed and medicine failed, that his sister had poured her whole life into the shop, giving up dates, parties with friends, everything, to keep it running when the economy was down, and get it strong enough to take on the next challenge of expansion. Baking made her happy, especially during the tumultuous years of their childhood and after their parents' divorce, Andrew had said, and seeing his older sister happy had become Andrew's top mission. The business had meant as much to Andrew as it did to Kate. Andrew would never let it falter, even for a few days.

Nor would he want Brody to just keep throwing words at the problem. He had tasked Brody with making sure Kate moved forward, found that happiness again. That meant doing what Brody did best—digging in with both hands.

"What if I helped you?" Brody said.

"You?" She laughed as she crossed the room and flipped on a light. "Didn't you tell me you're all thumbs in the kitchen?"

"Well, yeah, but I can measure out doses." The urge to help her, to do something other than buy a damned basket of chocolates, washed over him in a wave. She wouldn't let him back her next location, and he didn't know enough to just go out there and buy one for her, but he could take up some of the slack for her. He followed her into the back room. "I'm sure I can measure flour and sugar and…whatever. And if I can take the temperature of a patient, I can add stuff to an oven. I may not have the best handwriting in the world—"

At that, she laughed.

"But I can handle putting some flowers on some cupcakes."

"I appreciate the offer, but I'm sure you're busy with your practice, and this would be a heck of a job to just jump into. I'll be fine." She had pulled a paper off the wall and read it over. The order that needed to be delivered, he surmised. At night, maybe to a less than desirable neighborhood, alone.

A thick stack of orders were tacked to the wall, waiting to be filled after she did this one. Piles of bakery supplies lined the far counter. Sacks of flour and sugar, tubs of something labeled fondant. A huge work load for anyone. Not to mention someone still reeling from a big personal loss.

Once again the urge to walk away, to distance himself from this reminder of his greatest mistake, roared inside him. If he did this, he'd be around Kate for hours at a time. At some point, the subject of her brother would come up. How long did he think he could go before the truth about why he was here came out?

*Promise me.*

Damned if he'd let her struggle here on her own. Andrew wouldn't want that.

Once she was stronger, ready for the rest, he would tell her how he had come to be in her shop that day. Andrew had warned Brody that his sister looked tough, a cover for a fragile heart, and cautioned him against telling Kate the truth. Brody suspected Andrew did on his deathbed what he'd done all his life—protected the sister he loved so much.

And now he'd given Brody that job. He'd deal with the rest when he had to, but for now, there was Kate and Kate needed help. He took a step closer. "Let me help you, at least with the delivery, and if we work well together, then maybe I can help you in here, too."

"I don't know. I—"

"It'll only be for a few days, you said so yourself. And I'll work for free. We can get that cupcake order done for my brother and I can be the hero of the wedding." He grinned. "Just let me help. I'll feel better if I do."

She leaned closer, her green eyes capturing his. "Why?"

"Because you need the help. And I...I need something to occupy my nights."

"Why?"

He could have thrown off some flippant answer. Something about being single and bored, or a workaholic who needed more to do, but instead, his gaze went to the far corner of the room, where a sister had pinned up an article about a brother who'd given his all, and the words came from deep in Brody's heart. Not the whole truth, but something far closer than he'd said up until now. "I'm working through some stuff. And I just need something to...take my mind off it, until I find the best way to handle it."

She worried her bottom lip, assessing him. "Okay, we'll start with the delivery. It's a simple one, just getting those cupcakes," she pointed to a stack of boxes on the counter, "over to a local place for a party they're having tonight."

"Okay." He hefted the boxes into his arms, careful to keep them level, then followed Kate out the back door and over to a van she had parked in the alley between her shop and the one next door. The words Nora's Sweet Shop reflected off the white panels in a bright pink script. Kate slid open the side door, and he loaded the boxes on racks inside the van.

She climbed into the driver's seat and waited for him to get in on the passenger's side. "Before we go, I better warn you, that this place can be a little…rowdy."

"Rowdy? In Newton?"

"Sort of. You'll see." She put the vehicle in gear, a bemused smile on her face. He liked her profile, the way the streetlights illuminated her delicate features.

They headed down the street, bumping over a few potholes. Kate drove with caution, keeping one eye on the road and one on the cargo in the back. He kept quiet, allowing her to concentrate on the still congested city roads. A few turns, and then they pulled into the parking lot of the Golden Ages Rest Home.

"A rowdy rest home?" He arched a brow.

She just grinned, then parked the van, got out and slid open the side door. "I hope you wore your dancing shoes."

"My what? Why?"

But Kate didn't explain. He grabbed several of the boxes and followed her into the building. Strains of perky jazz music filled the foyer. No Grandma's basement decorations here. The rest home sported cream and cranberry colored furnishings offset by a light oak wood floor and a chandelier that cast sparkling light over the space. A petite gray haired lady rushed forward when Kate entered. "I'm so glad you're here. The natives were getting restless." She placed a hand on Kate's arm. "Thank you so much for helping us out again. You are an angel."

Kate hefted the boxes. "An angel with dessert to the rescue! I'm always more than happy to help you all out, Mrs. White."

The older lady waved the last words off. "You know that calling me Mrs. White makes me feel as old as my grandmother. Call me Tabitha, Kate, and you'll keep me young at heart."

Kate laughed. "Of course, Tabitha. How could I forget that?"

"Maybe you're getting a little old, too, my dear," Tabitha said, with a grin. She beckoned them to follow. They headed down the hall and into a room decked out for a party.

A pulsing disco ball hung from the ceiling, casting the darkened room in a rainbow of lights. Couches had been pushed against the walls, but few people sat on them. Jazz music pulsed from the sound system, while couples and groups of seniors danced to the tunes, some on their own, some using walkers and canes as partners. On the far wall, sat a table laden with food and drinks, and a wide open space waiting for dessert.

A tall elderly man with a full head of thick white hair and twinkling blue eyes, came up to Kate as soon as she entered the room. "Miss Kate, are you here to give me that promised dance?"

"Of course, Mr. Roberts." She rose to her toes and bussed a kiss onto his cheek. "Let me get dessert set up and I'll be ready to tango."

"Glad to hear it. Oh, and I see you brought a partner for Mrs. Williams." The man nodded toward Brody. "I didn't know you had another brother."

"Oh, he's not my brother."

"A beau?" Mr. Roberts grinned and shot a wink at Brody. "That's wonderful, Miss Kate. You deserve a man who will treat you right." He eyed Brody. "You *are* going to treat her right, aren't you?"

Brody sputtered for an answer, but Kate saved him by putting a hand between the men. "Oh, no, Brody's not a beau. Just a…friend."

Friend. The kiss of death between a man and a woman, Brody thought. But really, did he want anything more? Brody wanted to help Kate, not be her boyfriend.

Yet the thought of them having nothing more than a cordial relationship left him with a sense of disappointment. A war between what he wanted and what he should have brewed in his chest. He opted for the should have. Help her through this bump in her business, make sure she got back on track, that she was happy and secure again, then go back to his life. No more. No less.

"What, are you nuts, boy? This woman is a catch and a half. If I was thirty, okay," Mr. Roberts winked, "fifty years younger, I'd marry her myself."

"Mr. Roberts, you are an incorrigible flirt."

"Keeps me young." He grinned. "And keeps the ladies around here on their toes."

"Speaking of people on their toes," Kate said, "I better get dessert on the table before dinner is served."

She and Brody headed across the room, and started loading the cupcakes onto the waiting trays. A flock of eager and hungry partygoers lingered to the side, waiting for them to finish. Several people greeted Kate by name, and raved about her cupcakes. When she and

Brody were done, they stowed the empty boxes under the table, and stepped to the side.

"Tabitha wasn't kidding." Brody glanced around the room. "People are dying for those cupcakes. I think if we waited any longer, you'd have had a riot on your hands."

Kate laughed. "It's that way every month. I donate dessert for the Senior Shindig, and people are always already lined up to get one, sometimes before I even get here."

"That's because everyone here loves your desserts, and you," Brody said.

She brushed the bangs off her forehead and watched the residents shimmy to a fifties be-bop tune. "This place has always had a tender spot in my heart. Bringing the dessert for their events has sort of become a family tradition. When Andrew and I were kids, my grandparents used to bake for them. My great grandparents, Nora's parents, lived here, and from the beginning, the shop donated treats. On the weekends, Andrew and I would help deliver the cupcakes. The residents got to know us and we got to know them. We've cried when people have passed away, celebrated when they hit milestones, and helped them weather storms whenever we could."

"Weather storms?"

She leaned against the wall, while her gaze scanned the room. "This place was started by a husband and wife team who wanted to provide a low-cost but really nice option for retirees who needed a caring place to live. Because of that, it's faced some financial challenges, so my brother and I followed in my grandparent's footsteps, and over the years, we donated our time and talents to help them out. As a result, a lot of these residents are…well, friends. Sort of an extended family."

All in keeping with the jovial, caring hero that Brody had met in Afghanistan. A young man who would put his life in front of another's without thinking twice. Kate possessed those same admirable traits. Brody's esteem for her rose several notches, and so, too, did his connection with her. He could see some of the same spirit that had driven him into medicine, shining in her eyes as she took in the room. Kate was what Brody's grandmother would call a "good soul," the kind of woman who put others ahead of herself. "So you're not just the baker, but the dance partner as well?"

She laughed. "I like coming here. The residents remind me of what's important and what I get to look forward to."

"You're looking forward to the days of walkers and canes and wheelchairs?"

"In a way, yes. I mean, look at them." She waved toward the people around them. "These truly are their golden years. These are people who are happy and content with who they are. They've achieved their goals, realized their dreams, for the most part, and now they want to enjoy their lives. If a red devil cupcake can help in that a little bit, I'm more than happy to bake a few dozen."

"But doesn't that put you behind on your other work?"

"Some work," Kate said, her voice soft while she watched the crowd of people move about the room, "pays so much more than money. That's what Andrew always said, and it's true."

"I agree." Brody watched the happy faces of the residents as they greeted Kate, complimented the cupcakes. "That's how I feel about working in medicine. It's not about the money—and the medical mission work is all volunteer, so there's no money there at all, it's about the return on my time. The satisfaction at the end of the day is—"

"Priceless." She turned to him and smiled. "Then that's something we have in common."

He could feel the thread extending in the space between them, interlocking him more and more every minute with Kate Spencer. "It is indeed."

They were bonding, he realized, doing the very thing he had told himself not to do. But a part of Brody couldn't resist this intriguing woman who blushed at compliments and gave of her heart to so many around her.

Mr. Roberts stepped up to Kate and put out his arm. Just as she put her hand on the older man's arm, the perky elderly woman who had greeted them at the door sidled up to Brody. "Care to dance, young man? I hope you know the foxtrot."

"Be careful." Kate laid a hand on Brody's. "Tabitha can cut a rug better than Ginger Rogers."

"Now don't say that, Kate," the other lady said. "You'll scare off my dancing partner."

"I'm not much of a dancer." Brody offered up a sheepish grin. "That's my brother Riley's department."

"You're young and you have your original hips," Tabitha said. "That's good enough for me. Come on, honey, let's show those young kids we can outdance them." She took his hand and led him to the floor, followed by Kate and Mr. Roberts. The music shifted to a slow paced waltz, and Brody put out a hand and an arm to Tabitha. The older lady slipped into the space with a very young giggle, and they were off, stepping around the room with ease.

He tried to keep his attention on the chatty woman in his arms, but Brody's gaze kept straying to Kate. She laughed at something Mr. Roberts said, her head thrown back, that wild mane of rich dark brown hair cascading down her shoulders, swinging across his back, begging to be touched. Her lithe body swung from step to step, a sure sign she'd danced dozens of times before. As she danced a circle with Mr. Roberts, the people in the room said hello, thanked her for the cupcakes, and each one received a kind word or a friendly smile in return.

Too often, Brody had seen business people who cared about dollars and cents, not about people. Kate had that unique combination of heart and grace, coupled with killer baking skills. He admired that about her. He admired a lot about her, in fact.

Mr. Roberts swung Kate over to the space beside Brody, then sent a wink Tabitha's way. "Hey, Tabby, isn't it partner *change* time?"

"Partner change time?" The other woman gave him a blank look, paused, then a slow, knowing nod. "Oh, yes, of course. Partner change time. Thanks for the dance, kiddo." She stepped out of Brody's arms and into Mr. Roberts's, leaving Kate standing on the floor.

She laughed and watched the older couple spin away. "Not exactly subtle, are they?"

"About as subtle as a bull horn." Until that moment, Brody hadn't realized how much he had been waiting for an opportunity to dance with Kate. To feel her in his arms, instead of watching her in another's. This woman had intrigued him, captivated him, and even as he told

himself this was a *bad idea* on a hundred levels, he put
out his arms. "Shall we, partner?"

"I think we shall." She stepped into the circle created
by his embrace, and they began to move together to the
music. The big band sounds swirled in the air around
them, as other couples whooshed back and forth in a
flurry of colors and low conversations.

As they danced, the other people in the room disappeared, the lights narrowed their focus, and every ounce
of Kate's attention honed in on Brody. She could have
been dancing on the moon and wouldn't have noticed
a thirty-foot crater underfoot. Her heart beat in rhythm
with the steps, and her body tuned to his hand pressed
to the small of her back, the warmth of his palm against
hers, the way his dark woodsy cologne wrapped around
them in a tempting cloud. She could see the slight five
o'clock shadow on his chin, watch the movement of his
lips with each breath, and she wondered how it would
feel if he kissed her.

*Working through some stuff.*

That was what he had given as his reason for wanting to help her. Kate wanted to ask, to probe, to find
out what had caused the shadows in his eyes. What he
wasn't telling her—and what had been in all those odd
comments that he'd never explained. But Kate Simpson
didn't want anyone asking about the shadows in her own
eyes, so she sure as heck wasn't going to ask about his.

And that meant not letting one dance distract her, or
wrap her in a spell. She'd stick to business only. Period.

"Thank you again for dinner and for helping me with
the delivery tonight," she said.

"I wasn't a bad cupcake transporter?" he asked as
he turned her to the right, exerting a slight bit of pres-

sure to help her move. How she wanted to lean into that touch, but she didn't.

She knew better than to try to step up and solve another man's problems. To be the shoulder he cried on, the heart he leaned on, only to leave her alone in the end when he returned to his busy life. How many times had she seen her mother crying, alone? How many times had she heard their fights, watched the destruction of their marriage a little at a time? She'd come close herself to repeating that mistake with her last boyfriend, and had no intentions of doing that again.

"Not bad at all," she said.

"Thanks." He chuckled. "It's always nice to have a back up career, should there ever be a sudden need for cupcake transportation throughout the greater Massachusetts area."

She laughed. The song had come to an end, and they broke apart, and made their way to where the parquet met carpet, carving out a corner of the room for themselves, apart from the others. Despite her reservations, and her determination to keep things platonic, she liked Brody. Liked spending time with him. He had a wit that could coax a laugh out of her on her worst day, a smile that made her forget her stress, and eyes that inspired all kind of other thoughts that had nothing to do with work.

It might not be so bad to have him around, particularly when the days got long and her thoughts drifted toward Andrew, and she found herself ready to cry. Her brother, she knew, wouldn't want her to do that, but getting past the loss was far from easy.

Easier, though, when Brody was around, she'd found. Maybe it wouldn't be so bad to have him in her kitchen for a time. "If you want to learn the baking business,

I'd be a fool to turn down free help. Especially sort of experienced free help."

Brody nodded toward Mr. Roberts and Tabitha, who were watching from the sidelines. Tabitha sent up a little wave. "I do come with the recommendations of Tabitha. Wait, that was just for my dancing skills. Is there a lot of call for dancing in your bakery?"

"Not so much, but I'm sure we can figure something out." She put out her hand. "Just remember—in the cupcake operating room, I'm the one in charge."

"Yes, ma'am." He grinned, then took her hand and when they shook, the warm connection sent a tremor through Kate's veins.

She dropped his hand and vowed that no matter what, the only thing she'd be cooking up in her kitchen over the next few days was dessert. Not a relationship with a handsome doctor. She could see in his eyes, in those shadows and in his soft words, that he needed someone.

And the one thing Kate vowed never to be again was the kind of person who filled that gap. To be a temporary pillow before the man returned to his driven life and discarded her like a forgotten towel on the floor. Because her heart was already scarred and one more blow would surely damage it forever.

# CHAPTER FIVE

THE logistics of Brody's plan required more finesse than negotiating a peace treaty. A busy family practice doctor couldn't just up and walk out of the office to bake cupcakes. He'd told Mrs. Maguire he needed a bit of breathing room. "Just to get back into the swing of things," he'd said. "It's been a big change coming back from being overseas."

She'd put a hand on his shoulder, her brown eyes filled with kindness. "I understand. You take care of you and I'll take care of the schedule."

In a matter of hours, she'd managed to free half his days for the coming week. Brody made a mental note to send Mrs. Maguire a big box of chocolates and a gift certificate to her favorite restaurant. Maybe two gift certificates.

The day brightened as the sun began its journey to the other side of the sky. Odd how the same sun that warmed Boston's streets created an oven in Afghanistan. And how the same sun that shone over a quiet neighborhood street could shine over a war zone peppered with the wounded and the dead.

The dead—like Andrew Spencer. Cut down before he'd lived a fraction of his life.

Guilt washed over Brody, teemed in his chest. He'd done all he could, but still, it never seemed he'd done enough. Had he missed something? Forgotten something? Taken too few risks—

Or too many?

The what ifs had plagued Brody ever since Andrew's last stuttering breath. They'd been a heavy blanket on his shoulders as he'd boarded a plane to return to his family, knowing another plane had brought Andrew home to his family, stowed in a wooden casket in the cargo hold.

He could still see Andrew's wide green eyes, trusting Brody, hoping that Brody would pull off an eleventh hour miracle. Then trust had given way to fear, as the reality hit home. All the while, Brody battled death, tending to Andrew, then to the other wounded soldiers, assessing wounds based on survivability, and making his priorities off that grim reality.

Those who would die no matter what were put to the end of the list. While those who had a chance were helped first. Brody and the other doctor with him had worked on the others, knowing Andrew's chances...

Brody cursed as he drew up short outside the cupcake shop. Why had he agreed to do this? And why would Andrew pick him, the doctor who had tended him until his last breath, to watch over Kate? The task loomed like a mountain, impossible.

Inside the building, Kate crossed into his line of vision. She saw him outside and shot him a wave. Today, she had her hair up in a clip that poufed the back in a riot of curls. The style accented her delicate features, drew attention to her emerald eyes.

Maybe not impossible, just tough as hell. As he

watched Kate, he decided no matter what mountain faced him, it would be worth the climb.

Brody opened the door and stepped inside. Sweet scents of vanilla, chocolate, berry, wrapped around him like a calorie laden blanket. "Damn, it smells good in here."

"Thanks." Kate smiled. "If you ask me, it smells like temptation on a stick. Working here makes staying on any kind of diet impossible."

His gaze traveled over her lithe frame. She had on a V-necked black T-shirt emblazoned with the shop's logo and a pair of body hugging jeans. Tempting was exactly the word he'd use, too. "I'd say you're doing just fine in that department."

Had he just flirted with her? What the hell was he thinking?

A pale pink flush filled her cheeks, and the smile widened. "Well, thank you again." Her eyes lit with a tease. She wagged a finger at him. "But don't think you're getting out of dishes just because you complimented me."

"Damn," Brody said, then grinned. "And here I thought you'd go easy on me."

"And why would I do that?"

"Because of my charming good looks and great bedside manner, of course."

She laughed. "That might work with the nurses, but I'll have you know, I am a tough taskmaster."

He closed the gap between them, and his gaze dropped to her lips. Desire warred with his common sense. "How tough?"

"Very." She took a breath, and her chest rose, fell. "Very tough."

The urge to kiss her roared inside him. If there was one woman on this planet Brody shouldn't date, it was her. Already, he'd gotten too close, gotten too involved, when he had promised to help her, not fall for her.

Damn. Holding back the truth only made it worse. Everything in Brody, all the practical, logical, deal with the facts sides of him, wanted to tell Kate who he was. But Andrew had been firm—

*Don't tell her. I don't want her to dwell on what happened to me or to blame herself for suggesting I enlist. I want her to move forward.*

Telling her, Andrew had said, would leave Kate hurting, in pain again. That was the last thing Brody wanted to bring to Kate Spencer's life—more hurt and pain. He was here to make her laugh, not cry.

"Here." Kate thrust a bright pink apron between them. "Sorry I don't have any in more manly colors."

"This'll be fine." He slipped it over his head. "Reminds me of med school when one of my roommates did the laundry one week and washed the lab coats with a red sweatshirt. We were all pink for a while."

Kate laughed. "My brother said the pink made him look approachable to the ladies."

"I'll keep that in mind."

"Though, I have to say, Andrew was one of the most manly men I've ever known. When the war started, he told me he wanted to make a difference. So I said he should…" She shook her head and her eyes misted. "He joined the National Guard, and really took to the job. Everything Andrew did, he gave a hundred and ten percent."

Brody swallowed hard. "I'm sorry for your loss."

Such inadequate words. He'd said them many times

over the years of being a doctor, but never had they run more hollow than right now. Maybe because he knew Andrew, and knew that loss didn't even begin to describe the hole now left in the world.

"It's okay. I've always wondered and wished..." She shook her head again and bit her lip. "Anyway, he died doing what he loved. And although I miss him every single day, I'm proud of him." She swiped at her eyes, and let out a long breath. "Now let's to get to work so he can be proud of me, too."

Brody followed her into the kitchen in the back. Stainless steel countertops and machines gleamed under the bright lights. Here, the sweet scents were stronger, a tempting perfume filling the space. "So, where do we start? With Riley and Stace's cupcakes?"

"Not yet. We'll be making those closer to the date of the wedding, so they'll be fresh. Right now, we have another cupcake order to complete." She pointed to a huge sack on the floor. "You offered to be the muscle, so let's see how much muscle you have. I need five pounds in that mixer there."

He lifted the heavy bag, then gave her a blank look. "Do I just dump the whole thing in?"

She laughed. "No. Weigh it in that container on the scale, then when I tell you, you're going to add it, a little at a time." She dropped sticks of butter into the mixing bowl, then added sugar and turned on the beaters. "Have you ever cooked anything before?"

"Does making grilled cheese with an iron count?" He grinned. "Old college trick. Some wax paper from a cereal box, a loaf of bread, a package of cheese and an iron, and dinner is done."

"All I can say is thank God you went into medicine

instead of the restaurant industry." She added eggs, one at a time, keeping the beaters whirring until the mixture blended into a pale yellow ribbon. She crossed to Brody and added the rest of the dry ingredients to the flour. "Now remember, add a little at a time, otherwise the flour will go everywhere and we'll get covered. I'm baking cupcakes, not you and me."

Heat flushed her face. What was that? You and me? *Focus, Kate, focus.*

So she did, concentrating on the recipe instead of on Brody McKenna. And the reasons why he was here. Why he had cut his schedule in half to help her. And why work with her, of all the people in the city of Boston?

A few minutes later, the two of them scooped the batter into cupcake liners, then popped the trays into the oven. Kate started melting some chocolate, then laying out molds for the candy orders. "We'll pour these, then make the pink flowers that go with them. By then the cupcakes should be cooled and ready to frost. If you want to start the buttercream frosting, I'll get the ingredients out for you. Frosting is pretty simple. Dump and mix."

"That I can handle." He shot her a lopsided grin, then he paused and stepped forward. The streetlights glimmered outside, casting a golden glow over the counter under the window. The city's busy hum had dropped to a whisper. The storm had broken, and from time to time, a night bird called out.

Kate's gaze met Brody's. He had the bluest eyes she'd ever seen. A color as rich and true as the ocean. Eyes that studied her and analyzed her, and made her heart trip.

What the heck was she doing here?

Because right now it didn't feel like baking cupcakes. At all.

"You're good at this," he said.

"Thanks."

"I can make a huge mess just heating up restaurant takeout. But you…" he gestured toward the kitchen counters, "you manage to keep this place clean from start to finish."

The flush returned to her cheeks. "Oh, I'm not that neat. You should see my bookshelves and my closets." Had she just invited him to her apartment? If she danced any closer to the edge, she'd fall over—and fall for Mr. Wrong. She wanted steady, dependable, quiet, not a man who turned her insides into Jell-o and sent a riot of desire roaring through her whenever he smiled.

"I didn't say you were that neat," he said, and the grin played again on his lips, "because you, uh, have some flour…"

He reached out a finger, slid it down her cheek. A warm, slight touch. Sexy in its innocence. She drew in a breath, held it. "Right there," he finished.

"Thank you." The words were a whisper. Her heart hammered in her chest.

"Anytime." His voice dropped, low, husky, tempting.

His hand lingered against her cheek for a long, dark second. Was he going to kiss her? Did she want him to?

Then the oven timer beeped and broke the spell. She stepped back. "We…we should get back to work."

"Yeah." Those blue eyes locked on hers. "We wouldn't want anything to get burned."

"No. We wouldn't." She grabbed a pair of potholders and turned toward the oven before she could question whether he was talking about cupcakes—or them. She opened the oven, took out the trays and laid them on the counter to cool for a minute before she could remove the cupcakes and set them on racks.

Brody stood to the side, watching her. "You go a million miles a minute here. No wonder you never have time to eat."

"There are days when it's slow." Then she looked at the list of orders clipped to the board against the wall and laughed. "Though I have to admit, there aren't too many of those. Thank goodness."

"Admit it. You're just as Type A as I am."

She bristled. "I'm as far from Type A as you get."

"You run your own business, work too many hours, dig in and get the work done regardless of the obstacles in your way." He flicked out fingers to emphasize his list. "That defines Type A to me."

"You've got me all wrong." She turned away, and started taking the cupcakes out of the pans. Just as she'd thought. He'd admitted he was the exact kind of career focused man she tried to avoid. The kind who swept a woman off her feet, then left her in the dust when his job called. "My father was type A-plus. He worked every second he could. Took on extra shifts because he was convinced no other surgeon could do as good a job as he could."

"Your father was a doctor, too?"

"Yes. So that means I know the type. Come home at the end of the day, dump an emotional load on the family dinner table, then leave again when it's time for play practice or violin lessons. That is *not* me." How could he see her in that same light? She had a life, a world outside this bakery. Her gaze dropped to the cupcakes before her. Didn't she? "At all."

"Not all doctors are the same. And even so, being driven isn't always a bad thing, you know," he said. "That's the kind of trait that encourages you to do things like expand the business, open new locations."

"You're here to help, Dr. McKenna, not analyze me or my life choices." Suddenly he seemed much closer than when he'd been touching her a moment ago. She didn't need anyone to hold a magnifying glass to her life, or her choices. Because when they did that, all she could see was mistakes. "I'd appreciate it if you stuck to mixing dough and left the personal issues to the side. You stay out of my personal life and I'll stay out of yours. I'm sure you don't want me analyzing why you're working here instead of taking care of patients."

He stared at her for a long moment. His jaw worked, then he let out a long breath. "Yeah, I agree. Keeping this impersonal is best for both of us."

"Agreed." She should have been relieved that he agreed. Then why did a stone of disappointment weigh on her chest? She stowed the baked cupcakes in the refrigerator then removed her apron and laid it over a chair. "We're done here tonight."

"Yeah," he said quietly. "We are."

That couldn't have gone worse if he'd lit a flame to the night and set it ablaze. Regret filled Brody the next morning, heavy and thick. He sat in a booth at the Morning Glory, thinking for a man intending to do the right thing, he kept going in the wrong direction.

"Hey, Brody, how you doing?" Stace plopped a coffee cup before him and filled it to the brim with steaming java.

"Great, now that I have some coffee." He grinned. "How about you? Getting nervous about the wedding?"

She cast a glance toward Riley across the room, talking to one of the other customers. Riley caught his fiancé looking at him and gave her a wide smile. "How can I be nervous when I'm marrying the man of my dreams?"

Jealousy flickered in Brody. Finn had Ellie, and wore the same goofy smile as Riley every day. His two brothers had found that elusive gift of true love. To Brody, a man who measured everything in doses and scientific facts, it seemed an anomaly worthy of Haley's Comet.

The door to the diner opened, and instead of his older brother striding in, as Brody had expected, his grandmother entered. Stace went over and greeted her, followed by Riley. Mary said hello, then headed straight for Brody's table.

Mary McKenna wasn't the kind of woman to make social calls. Even as she eased out of her position at the helm of McKenna Media and groomed her grandnephew Alec to take the top spot, she spent her days with purpose. There were lists and appointments, tasks and goals. So when she slid into the seat opposite him, he knew she hadn't come by to chit-chat.

"Gran, nice to see you." He rose, and pressed a kiss to her cheek.

"Brody. I missed you at dinner the other night." It was an admonishment more than anything else. His seventy-eight-year-old grandmother, Brody knew, worried about him, and that meant she liked to see him regularly so she could be sure he wasn't wallowing away in a dark corner.

"Working late. Sorry."

"Working late…baking?"

"How'd you know that's where I was?"

"Your brothers are worse than magpies, the way they talk." A smile crossed her face. "Riley said you missed your regular lunch with him and when he asked Mrs. Maguire where you were, she said you were making cupcakes. He told Finn, and Finn told me."

His brothers. He should have known. Finn and Riley had found their happily ever afters and seemed to be on a two-man mission to make sure Brody did the same. They'd done everything short of bring him on a blind date shotgun wedding. Brody rolled his eyes. "I wish my brothers would stay out of my life."

"They only interfere because they love you." She pressed a hand to his cheek. "And so do I."

His grandmother had been a second mother to him for so long, there were days it seemed like it had always been just his grandparents and the McKenna boys. They'd been a rock in a turbulent childhood for all three boys, and stayed that way long after the McKennas graduated college, moved out on their own and became adults. After her husband's death three years ago, Mary had taken over the full time running of McKenna Media, but still doted on her grandsons with a firm but loving touch.

Brody's gaze softened, and he covered his grandmother's hand with his own. "I love you, too, Gran."

"And thank you for following up with my doctor this morning. You know you don't have to do that."

"I just worry about you, Gran. Wanted to make sure he covered all the bases."

"You do enough worrying for five doctors." She gave

his hand a squeeze. "I'm fine. Just suffering from a little old age."

He chuckled. "Glad to hear it."

Stace brought over a cup. "Some coffee, Mrs. M?"

"Goodness, no, dear. I'll slosh out of here if I drink any more." She pressed a hand to the belly of her pale gray suit. "But thank you."

"No problem. Let me know if you want to order anything." Stace headed off to another table.

"I like that girl," Mary said. "Sassy, strong, smart, and most of all, perfect for Riley." She returned her attention to Brody. "I just suffered through a long, excruciating meeting with the head of Medicine Across Borders. That's why I came by today. Finn is meeting me here in a second, so we can chat about the group."

His eldest brother had become more involved with the McKenna Foundation's overseas mission work after he'd married Ellie and adopted Jiao, an orphan from China. He'd been instrumental in organizing fundraisers and getting the word out.

"Was Larry at the meeting?" Brody asked. The assistant director had gone on his own mission a few weeks prior. Brody had always liked the older man, who had dedicated his life to the charity. Both Brody and Larry had a special place in their hearts for Medicine Across Borders because it took what he and other doctors did in the United States and multiplied it around the world.

"No, he's still in Haiti. It's been rough, he said." Gran sighed. "He lost a few patients last week. One of them a child, and it hit him hard. He said he wished that you were there because you're the best doctor he knows."

Brody shook his head. "Larry doesn't need me."

"I don't know about that," Gran said. "Larry talked to

me about that time you worked that clinic in Alabama. He said you changed those people's lives. They raised enough money to hire a second doctor after you left, and the mortality rate there has dropped significantly, in part because of those diabetes and heart disease awareness programs you started."

"I just did my job."

"You don't give yourself enough credit," Gran said. "You always were the one who worried too much and made it your personal mission to fix everything. Ah, Brody, you don't have to take so much on your shoulders."

"I'm not doing that, Gran."

"You do it and you don't even realize it. You protect the family, you protect your patients, and I suspect you're even protecting that pretty bakery owner. Sometimes, people have to face their worst fears and face the worst possible outcome in order to learn and grow. Protecting them can do them a disservice." She read his face, and let out a sigh. "You disagree, but maybe you'll think about it. Anyway, Larry said to say hello to you. He should be home in about a month. He says there's still a lot of need for basic medical care in Haiti, but he's making a dent, one patient at a time."

Brody listened to his grandmother's news about the charity, but his mind kept drifting to Kate Spencer. He had dodged her question, and dodged an opportunity to tell her the truth. Why?

He knew why. Because he was starting to like her. As much as he'd told himself he had no right to get involved with her, and no room in his life for a relationship right now, he had started to fall for her. She was sweet and funny and despite everything, upbeat and cheery. She was like a daisy in the middle of a lawn that had filled with weeds.

And if he told her—

It would devastate her. She'd relive her brother's death, hold herself responsible for him being there.

Maybe his grandmother had a point. Maybe in protecting her, he was hurting her more.

"Brody? Did you hear me?" his grandmother asked.

"Huh? Uh...sorry. My mind drifted for a second. What'd you say, Gran?"

"I asked if you would deliver the speech for the fundraiser next week. I realize it's short notice, but Dr. Granville broke his leg skiing in Switzerland and won't even be stateside again in time."

"Gran, you know I hate speeches. And hate tuxes even more."

Finn slid into the booth beside his brother. "You and Riley, couple of tux-phobics. What is wrong with the two of you?"

"We're not as uptight as you, hence our more casual formal wear," Brody quipped.

"Nah, you're not as debonair as me." Finn jiggled his tie. "My wife says I make this look sexy."

Brody laughed. "She's biased."

"She is indeed." The same smile that had been on Stace and Riley's faces winged its way across Finn's. Gran sat across from the boys, pleasure lighting her eyes. The whole family was in some kind of happiness time warp. Brody rolled his eyes.

Riley plopped onto the seat beside Gran. "What'd I miss?"

"The hard work." Finn shot him a grin.

"Hey, I've matured. Become a taxpayer, a fiancé *and* a responsible adult, all at the same time."

Brody arched a brow. "You have two of the three. Bummer on the third."

Mary let out an exasperated sigh. "You boys still act like children. My goodness. Celebrate with each other, not tease each other."

Riley pressed a kiss to his grandmother's cheek. "If we did that, we'd have no fun at all, Gran. Besides, Finn and Brody are big boys. They can take whatever I can dish out."

"And deliver it back to you with a second helping," Finn said.

Mary just shook her head, and smiled. "Well as much as I would love to sit here and chat all day with you boys, I do need to get back to the office. So, Brody, will you do the keynote? I think it will do the attendees good to hear about the experiences of someone who actually went overseas and helped people."

Brody swallowed hard. "No one wants to hear what I went through."

His grandmother leaned forward and covered his hand with her own. "You need to talk about it. Maybe if you did—"

"It wouldn't change anything." He shook his head and bit back a curse. "I can't."

His brothers cast him sympathetic looks. "If it helps, we'll sit in the audience and heckle you," Riley joked. "Or just give you a thumbs-up."

Brody shook his head.

"Think about it." Gran got to her feet. Her eyes were kind as she looked down at Brody. "Promise me you'll think about it."

"I will." He intended to do no such thing. But he'd never say that to Gran. He could see the worry in her features, and refused to add to her burdens. He'd find another reason to back out, and line up another speaker for her. That way, she wouldn't be in a bind and he wouldn't be stuck delivering a speech. Maybe Finn would do it for him. "I'll be fine, Gran. And I'll be at the next family dinner."

"Good. And since Riley will be on his honeymoon—"

"Basking on the beach with my beautiful new wife," Riley put in.

"—and we'll have room at the table, I want you to make sure you bring that bakery owner. No excuses."

"Gran, I don't think that's a good idea."

"I want to thank her in person for those chocolates. So don't forget. Sunday afternoon at two. Oh, and when she comes to dinner, tell her to bring more of those chocolates. An old lady needs to have at least one vice, and I've decided mine will be those chocolates." Gran winked, then headed out of the Morning Glory.

Brody tossed some singles on the table for his coffee and started to get to his feet. Finn put a hand on his arm. "I gotta get back to the office."

"You have a minute. I haven't seen you in a while, Brody. And you know, you look like crap."

"Hey!"

"I mean it in the nicest way possible," Finn said.

"He does," Riley added. "Or as nice as Finn can be."

Finn scowled at Riley, then went on. "If you ask me, you've been stewing too much and talking too little. You're a proactive guy, Brody. One who gets in there and makes it right. If you want my advice—"

"I don't." He brushed off Finn's touch. "Thanks for the concern, but I'm doing fine on my own."

"Are you?" Finn asked.

Brody didn't answer. Instead he headed out of the diner. As he did, he realized Finn had a point. Buying a basket of chocolates, bringing cupcakes to a retirement home and adding flour to a mix were not proactive events. None of them were, in fact, in keeping with the kind of thing he normally did. Brody McKenna was a hands-on guy, in a hands-on industry. And until he found something that let him do that, he knew he wouldn't be able to fulfill Andrew's last wishes, or get Kate Spencer moving forward.

And in the process, find a little peace for himself.

# CHAPTER SIX

*Two days later*

HE'D last seen Kate two days ago. And yet, she hadn't been out of his mind once in all that time. He'd come so close to kissing her that night in her shop—too close. He'd called her on Friday, making up an excuse about not being able to help that night, then spent the evening with a bottle of Merlot and a lot of junk TV.

Hadn't changed anything. He still thought about her too much, still worried about her, and still didn't see a way out of the web he'd woven. Finn had been right— he needed a proactive approach to the problem. One that did not involve kissing her.

Brody slipped on a pair of shorts, an old T, and his running shoes, then grabbed his iPod and headed out into the fall sunshine. Most mornings, he had just enough time to run the three mile circuit around his own neighborhood, but on Saturdays, his appointments started later in the morning, which left him extra time to extend his run to the picturesque Chestnut Hill Reservoir.

Dozens of runners, walkers and dog owners strolled the park, greeting the regulars with friendly waves and quick conversations. Late summer flowers peeked through the still green foliage, while the water glistened under the rising sun, twinkling back at him as Brody made the 1.6-mile loop. The sandy packed path was soft under his feet, and soon he slipped into the rhythm of running, oblivious to anyone around him.

He rounded a bend, turning into a gentle breeze skipping over the surface of the water. Ahead of him, Brody spotted a familiar figure.

Kate.

She'd pulled her dark brown hair into a ponytail, and she'd traded her usual jeans and T-shirt for silky navy shorts and a Red Cross T-shirt. Her legs were long and lean, the muscles flexing with each step. She had good form, a steady pace, all signs she ran often. Working off those cupcakes, he presumed. He smiled to himself.

Damn she looked good. Enticing. For the thousandth time, he wished he had kissed her back in the bakery. The magnet of attraction drew him to her again and again. Hunger—yes, that was the word for it—hunger to know her better, to see her more, brewed inside him.

Brody increased his pace until he drew up alongside Kate. "I owe you an apology."

She tugged an earphone out of her ear and glanced over at him. Her skin glistened in the sun. "Brody. I didn't even see you, sorry. I get into a zone when I'm running and don't notice anything around me."

"Me, too." But he had noticed her. He had a feeling no matter what he was doing, he'd be distracted by Kate Spencer. "I wanted to apologize for the other night. You're right. I have no business telling you how to run your life."

She slowed her pace a bit and exhaled. "You might

have been a teensy bit right. I do tend to put in more time at work than I should. And yes, sometimes use work to avoid the hard stuff."

"I can relate to that. Though, sometimes work can be therapeutic."

"True. Or it can be an avoidance technique. Whichever it is, I've got plenty of it to keep me busy." She chuckled. "I appreciate the apology."

He shot her a grin. "You sure you don't want to say anything more? Bash me a bit? Because this is a prime opportunity to get me back by telling me everything I'm doing wrong."

"Oh, I would, but I'm trying to save my breath for running."

He laughed at that. They settled into a comfortable mutual rhythm of running, their steps matching one another as they rounded the sparkling waters of the reservoir. Geese honked as they flew overhead, their bodies forming a perfect V. Brody and Kate neared an empty bench, and slowed their pace.

"I've never seen you running here before," Kate said when they stopped, her words peppered with gasps as she drew in several deep breaths. She propped a leg on one end of the bench and bent forward to stretch.

He did the same on the other end, trying not to watch her. And failing. "During the week, I don't have enough time to make it over here. Most days, I do a quick jog through my neighborhood and then get to work. I run here on the weekends."

"And weekends are my busy time for deliveries, so I get most of my longer runs in during the week." She bent over to stretch her hamstrings, and Brody reminded himself again to be a gentleman and not stare at the creamy length of her legs.

Instead he propped his foot against a nearby post and stretched his calves. Still his gaze stole over to Kate several times, watching as she bent this way and that, working out the lactic acid in her legs.

Beautiful. Absolutely beautiful woman.

And absolutely off limits.

Kate got to her feet, and opened her mouth to say something, then stopped. Her eyes misted, and she turned away. Her body tensed and the good humor left her. Brody's gaze followed where hers had gone.

A dark-haired man in an ARMY T-shirt ran past them, pounding the pavement at a fast clip. He had the crew cut and honed build that spoke of current military service. The close resemblance to Andrew caused a stutter in Brody's chest. Kate paled, and exhaled a long breath.

"Hey," he laid a hand on her shoulder, "you okay?"

"Yeah. That guy over there just looked so much like my brother that for a second I thought..." She shook her head and tried a smile, but it fell flat. "Andrew's gone. Sometimes I forget that. And when I remember..."

"It hurts like hell."

"Yeah." She sighed. "It does."

"Here, sit down for a minute." Brody waved toward the bench, and waited for her to take a seat. In these unguarded moments, Brody got a peek beneath the layers of Kate's grief.

*Take care of my sister,* Andrew had said. *Don't let her wallow in grief. Make sure she's happy. Living her life.*

"Thank you," she said.

"I'm sorry," Brody said. "I know that's so inade-quate when you're hurting, but I am sorry." The words sat miles away from the true depth of his regret. He watched emotions flicker across her face, and wres-tled with what more to say. A thousand times, he'd had to counsel patients, offer advice. And now, when it counted, he froze.

He knew why. Because he'd started to care about her, had allowed his heart to get tangled.

"Have you ever lost someone you were close to?" Kate asked.

Brody picked a leaf off a low-lying branch near the bench and shredded it as he spoke. "My parents."

"Your parents died? Both of them?"

He nodded. "When I was eight. Car accident. The whole thing was sudden and unexpected." And tough as hell. He hadn't talked about that loss in so long, but there were times, like now, when it hit him all over again.

"You were only eight? Oh, God, that's awful."

"I had my brothers, which made a difference, but yeah, it was still tough." He let out a long breath, and suddenly, he was there again, sandwiched on that overstuffed ugly floral couch in the living room be-tween Finn and Riley while his grandfather delivered the news. Finn, the stoic one, seeming to grow up in an instant, while Riley fidgeted, too young to know better. Brody had stared straight ahead, trying to fit the words into some kind of logical sense, and failing. "I remember when my grandfather told me. It was like my whole world caved in, one wall at a time. Everything I knew was gone, like that." He snapped his fingers. "My grandparents took me and my brothers in. They did their best, but it's never the same as having your mom and dad around, you know?"

"Yeah." She watched the geese settle on the grass across from them, and waddle fat bodies toward the water. "I spent most of my childhood with my grandparents. My parents fought all the time, and Andrew and I hung out in the bakery. To escape, I guess. Then, finally, they got divorced when I was in high school. My dad moved to Florida and my mom moved to Maine, and Andrew and I stayed here with our grandparents. That's part of why Andrew and I were so close. And my grandparents, too. We formed our own little family here."

Andrew had told him that Kate had taken the divorce hard. That she'd been heartbroken at the breakup of the family, as fractured as it was. Andrew had taken it on his shoulders to cheer up his sister, to keep her from dwelling on the major changes in her life. He could see in Kate's face that it still affected her, even after all these years. A childhood interrupted, just like his. "I'm glad you had each other," he said. "Like my brothers and I had each other."

"Yeah. But I don't have him anymore now, do I?" She cursed, let out a long breath, then turned to Brody. "It was my fault, you know." Her eyes filled with tears, and everything in Brody wanted to head off what was coming. "I was the one that encouraged him to sign up. He kept talking about wanting to make a difference, wanting to change lives, and he was such an adventurer, you know? It just seemed perfect. I thought the war was over, how dangerous could it be?" She shook her head and bit her lip. "I shouldn't have said anything. I should have—"

She cursed. Brody ached to tell her the truth, but how could he do that without adding to her pain? Recount the story of Andrew's death, and his part in that moment, and see her go through that loss all over again. He bit his tongue and listened instead.

"A part of me feels like..." at this her eyes misted again, and Brody wanted to both hold her and run for the hills, "if I hadn't encouraged him, if I had told him to become a hiking instructor or skydiver or something instead, he'd be here today."

He put a hand on her shoulder. "Kate. It's not your fault. Your brother loved—"

"My brother died because of me, don't you see that?" Tears streamed down her cheeks, and she swiped them away with a quick, hard movement. "I'm the one that encouraged him, pushed him. If I never said a word, he'd be here today and I'd..."

He reached for her hand. "You'd what?"

She exhaled, a long, slow breath. "I'd forgive myself."

Brody's heart ached for her. How he knew that pain. That guilt. "You can't blame yourself, Kate. People do what they want to do. Andrew was an adult. If he didn't want to join, he would have told you. You said yourself he loved his job."

She shook her head. "Every day, I live with that regret. Every day, I wish I could take the words back. I go to work and I stand there, and I wish I could do it over. It's like I'm standing in cement, and no matter how hard I try, I can't pick my feet up again." Pain etched Kate's features. Brody saw now why Andrew had been so adamant about protecting his sister. She did blame herself, and the worst thing Brody could do was add to that burden.

*I don't want her blaming herself or dwelling on the past. I want her eyes on the future. Encourage her to take a risk, to pursue her dreams. Don't let her spend one more second grieving or regretting.*

Andrew's words came back to him. Somehow, Brody needed to find a way to redirect Kate's emotional rudder.

She sat for a moment, then shifted in her seat to face him. "Before the soldiers even knocked on my door, I knew. I fell apart right then, a sobbing messy puddle on the floor. That pain," she exhaled a long, shaky breath, "that pain was excruciating. As if someone had ripped out my heart right in front of me." She drew her knees up to her chest, and hugged her arms around her shins. "What if I'd said 'be careful' one more time, or told him I loved him again? Would it have ended differently?"

"I think you did everything you could. Sometimes… these things just happen." Every instinct in him wanted to make this better for her, to ease her pain. And somehow do it without violating the promise he had made. "When I was in med school, I lost a patient. I'd seen him a couple times before, and had gotten to know him during the time I was working there."

It was a story Brody had never fully told before. The words halted in his throat, but he pushed them forward. He had promised to help Kate, and maybe, just maybe, knowing she wasn't alone would do that. "He loved to walk the city," Brody went on. "But he was legally blind, and in a city that busy…"

"Accidents happened."

Brody nodded. "Construction projects springing up

out of nowhere create obstacles that he couldn't see or anticipate. He had a cane, and was thinking about getting a guide dog, when he was hit by a car."

"Oh, Brody. That's awful."

"He was just crossing the street. One of those senseless deaths that shouldn't happen." Brody sighed and shook his head. "I tried so hard to keep that man alive. So damned hard. I kept pushing on his chest, up, down, up, down, yelling at him to hold, to keep trying, don't die on me—"

At some point he'd stopped talking about the patient in Boston. His mind had gone back to that dusty hut in Afghanistan, to a moment that could have been a carbon copy of the one at Mass General. Young man, cut down in the prime of his life, and Brody, powerless to prevent his death.

"It was too late," Brody went on, his voice low, hoarse. In that instant, he didn't see the pedestrian hit by a car, he saw Andrew's eyes again. So like Kate's. Wide, trusting, believing the doctor tending to his wounds would know what to do. So sure that Brody could save his life. "It's in your hands, doc," Andrew had said. He'd given Brody his life—

And Brody had let him down.

Brody heard the choppers in his head, the pounding of the rotors, the shouting of the other soldiers. Heard himself calling out to the other doctors, asking for supplies they didn't have. Too many wounded at one time, too few resources, and too few miracles available. Brody flexed his palms, but he could still feel Andrew's chest beneath his hands. The furious pumping to try to bring him back, and the silent, still response.

"They had to stop me from doing CPR," Brody said.

The other doctor, pulling him off, telling him it was too late. There was no hope. "I just...I wanted him to live so bad, but it wasn't enough. Not enough at all."

Now her hand covered his, sympathetic, understanding. "Oh, Brody, I'm so sorry."

On the other side of the reservoir, Brody saw the gray flash of the soldier's T-shirt moving down the path. Guilt and regret settled hard and bitter in Brody's stomach. Did he want to see Kate living with that the rest of her life?

He wasn't here to assuage his own pain. He was here to help her with hers.

"How did you..." she took a breath, let it out again, "how did you get past that loss?"

"For a long time, I blamed myself," Brody said, his mind drifting back to those difficult days in med school. "For a while, I thought I should do something else, something outside of medicine. I felt so damned guilty, like you do."

She nodded, mute.

"He was always joking, that patient of mine. It got so that I even kidded him about walking the streets of Boston, told him to keep an eye out. He thought that was the funniest damned thing he ever heard. It became a running joke between us. He'd thank me for stitching him up and joke that he'd be back for another appointment next week. I did the same thing you did, Kate, I blamed myself. What if I didn't joke with him? What if I'd lectured him about being careful?" He tossed the remains of the leaf onto the ground and turned to her. "For weeks, I was stuck, like you. Then I realized I wasn't doing myself, or his memory, any good." His gaze swept over Kate's delicate features. He thought of all she had told him in the last few days, and of what Finn had said. Do something proactive. That was what Brody had done all those years ago, and what Kate needed to do now. "I ended up going down to city hall and petitioning them for an audio crosswalk at the intersection where my patient was hit. The kind that beeps, warns people with vision problems. It might have been too late for him, but it wasn't for the next person. Doing that helped me a lot. It made me move forward."

"That's what I need to do." She sighed. "Someday."

Then he knew how he could help her. How he could get her out of that self-imposed cement. Something bigger, better than baking cupcakes and delivering desserts. "How do you feel about taking a trip to Weymouth this afternoon?"

"Weymouth? Why?"

"Let's go look at that location you were considering. See if it's good enough for another Nora's Sweet Shop."

"Oh, Brody, I can't—"

"Can't? Or won't? I'll be done with patients at three, and last I checked, the sign on the door said you close at three. I'd say that's a sign we should go. Do something proactive, Kate, and maybe..." his hand covered hers, "maybe then you can move forward again."

She studied him for a second then a smile curved across her face. "You're not going to let me say no, are you?"

"Not on your life."

"Okay. Meet me at the shop at three. I'll give the realtor a call this morning."

He got to his feet, put out a hand and hauled her to her feet, too. Now she stood close, so close, a strong breeze would have brought them together. His thoughts swirled around the sweet temptation of Kate Spencer. Her emerald eyes, her beautiful smile, her slender frame. And then to her lips, parted slightly, as if begging him to kiss them. How he wanted to, and oh how he shouldn't. "Then it's a date."

A date.

Kate pondered those words all day while she worked. Joanne had called and said she'd be tied up for a few more days with her daughter. "She's finding out a new baby is a lot more exhausting than she thought," Joanne said, "and my son-in-law couldn't take any more time off from work to help her. Are you sure you're going to be okay without me?"

"I have temporary help," Kate said. "You just enjoy that new grandbaby." She and Joanne chatted a bit more about the new baby, then Kate hung up. She glanced at the clock, saw the hands slowly marking time until Brody arrived.

Nerves fluttered in her stomach. Crazy. He might have used the word *date,* but that didn't mean he meant it. They were going to look at a piece of real estate, for goodness' sake, not go dancing.

That word conjured up the memory of dancing with Brody, of being in his strong, capable arms, pressed to his broad, muscled chest. He'd had a sure step, a confident swing, and when she'd been in his arms, she'd felt—

Safe. Treasured.

*Nope, nope, nope.* Her goal today involved real estate, not potential husbands.

Still, a part of her really liked Brody. He'd told her not all doctors were the same, and the more she got to know him, the more she wondered if he was that one rare animal in the room. Could this man who volunteered in needy areas, who'd taken the time to help a stressed out baker, could he be the one for her? Or too good to be true?

The last thing she wanted to do was repeat her mother's mistakes and rush into a relationship that was doomed from the start, then spend the rest of her life fighting to make it into something it could never be. Better to be cautious, to find a quiet, gentle man. Not one who sent her heart into overdrive.

Easier said than done.

Kate fussed with her hair. Checked her lipstick twice. Rethought her choice of a skirt instead of jeans at least a dozen times. Ever since she'd met Brody, her mind had been working against her resolve to business only. First peppering her dreams with images of him, then flashing to his smile, his eyes, at the oddest times. She was hooked, and hooked but good.

A little after one, the bell over the door rang, and Kate had to force herself not to break out in a huge smile when Brody walked into the shop. "You're here early. I thought you said you wouldn't be over until three."

"My one o'clock appointment canceled, and I had an hour until the next one, so I thought I'd stop by and see how you were doing."

Thoughtful. Sweet. Because he liked her? "It's been a busy day."

"Too busy for lunch?" He held up a bag from a local sub shop.

She snatched it out of his hands. "Bless you. I was about to eat the fixtures." She glanced up at him, trying to read the intent behind his blue eyes. "You're always taking care of me."

"I'm trying to, Kate." His gaze met hers and held.

"Well, thank you." The intensity in his eyes rocked her, and she turned on her heel, heading for the kitchen, rather than deal with the simmering tension between them.

He followed her out back and sat across from her while she ate.

She finished up the sandwich. "Thank you again. I don't think I've ever eaten that fast in my life. And one more healthy meal from Doctor McKenna. This is becoming a habit."

"All part of the service, ma'am." He grinned. "Besides, it'll be on my bill."

She laughed. "Well maybe I should charge you for cupcakes consumed."

"Who me?" He snatched one of the miniature ones she'd just frosted, and popped it in his mouth. "I don't know what you're talking about. Show me the evidence."

"I'll do better than that." She wagged a finger at him. "I'll make you work harder next time we're in this kitchen."

He glanced around the room, at the stacks of orders on the counter, the tubs of supplies waiting by the mixer. "If you want, we can tackle whatever is on your To Do list after we see that property today."

"That would make for a really long day. Wouldn't that interfere with your plans?"

"Plans?"

A flush filled her cheeks. She got to her feet, and tossed her trash into the bin. "Well, it's Saturday and

I didn't want to assume you didn't have…" *Push the words out, Kate, you'll never know unless you ask,* "a date or anything."

"I don't have a date." He came over to her, lowered the apron to the counter. "Not tonight."

"What about tomorrow night?" Who was this forward woman? Hadn't she vowed a thousand times not to get involved with a man like him? To be cautious, look for someone who didn't inspire her to run off to the nearest bedroom? But a part of her wondered if Brody was different, if the risk in falling for him would end in the kind of love story her grandparents had enjoyed. And that part wanted to get that answer. Very, very badly.

"Not tomorrow night, either. I'm not dating anyone right now." He reached up a hand and captured the end of her ponytail, letting it slide through his fingers. She inhaled the dark woodsy scent of his cologne. "In fact, I don't even have a date for my own brother's wedding."

"That's too bad. Especially if there's dancing." A smile curved across her face. "I bet Tabitha is free."

"I'd much rather take someone closer to my own age. Someone who could use a night off." He twirled the end of her hair around his finger, his blue eyes locked on hers. "Someone like you."

Her heart hammered in her chest. Her pulse tripped. She reminded herself—twice—to breathe. "Are you asking me on a real date, Brody McKenna?"

"I am indeed."

Now the smile she'd been trying to hold back did wing its way across her face. Her heart sputtered, then soared. "Then I accept."

"Good." His hands took hers, and he pulled her to

him. "You know, I haven't been able to stop thinking about you all day. I would be talking to a patient, and end up thinking about you. Or I'd be trying to write up my notes, and think about you. I even called poor Mrs. Maguire Kate today instead of Helen."

"Because of my cupcakes?"

He traced a finger along her face, down her jaw, over her lips. She breathed, and when her lips parted, his finger lingered on her lower lip. Tempting. "Because of your smile. Because of your eyes. Because of the way you make me hope and dream of things I…well, I hadn't wanted before. You…you're not what I expected."

Another odd comment. Brody McKenna seemed full of them. The man had more dimensions than a layer cake. "What you expected?" She laughed. "It seems my reputation has preceded me, if you had expectations." She lifted her jaw to his, sassy, teasing. "Have other people been talking about me and saying I'm this boring old fuddy duddy who does nothing but work?"

"That's not it."

"Then what expectations did you have? Because you seem to have a heck of a bead on everything about me. As if you knew me before you met me."

The humor dropped from his face, and he took a step back, releasing her hands. He turned away, facing the wall where she had hung the plaques and reviews of the shop. "I'm not…not who you think I am, Kate."

"Not a doctor?" She grinned. "Don't tell me you're actually a nurse."

"No, no, it's not that. It's—"

A ding sounded from the oven. "Oh, the cupcakes are done. I have to get them out of the oven or they'll burn." Kate pivoted to take the trays of baked cupcakes out of the oven and set them on the racks to cool. "God, what a busy day. Good thing you're taking me to Weymouth this afternoon, or I'd be liable to work until I passed out. In case you haven't noticed, I'm still working on the prioritizing thing. Like learning to add a little fun into my day and keep my eye on the bigger goal."

"Which is?"

She placed her hands on the counter and glanced out the window at the clear blue sky. "Continue the legacy my grandparents started, while learning not to waste a second of my life on grief. Someone gave me some advice about that today, and I'm still trying to take it in." She gave Brody a watery smile. "I'm working on it anyway."

"Good." Brody handed her another batch ready to go, then helped her load liners and batter into the next set of cupcake pans.

"So, what'd you want to tell me?" she asked. "What did you mean when you said you're not who I think you are?"

He gave her that grin she was beginning to know as well as her own. "Well, first, that I'm not a baker, not by any stretch."

"That I noticed." She sensed shadows lurking behind Brody's words, like secret passages that led to parts of himself he'd closed off. She wanted to quiz him, wanted to press him, but the cupcakes were waiting to be frosted, and the orders were piled up, and time was of the essence if she hoped to get out of here on time. So Kate let it drop for now, intending to come back to serious topics when they had more time.

Kate added a pink fondant flower to the top of one of the baked treats. "I used to send care packages to

Andrew's unit overseas, and one time, I sent him a whole batch of cookies with pink flowers on top, as a joke. He said they were the best damned thing he and the guys ever ate, and asked me to send more. So I did. Pink and blue and purple flowers. He said it was like a garden exploded when he opened the box." She laughed, then shook her head, as the laugh turned to tears. "Oh, damn. See what I mean? I'm trying, but I'm not doing so good at the last one. I miss him. God, do I miss him."

Brody turned to her at the same time she turned to him. He gathered her to his chest, and she let the tears fall. She'd promised herself she'd never again rely on a man, never fall fast and hard, but Brody seemed different. Like the kind of man she could trust. Lean into. Depend upon.

Then like a wave, the loss of her brother hit her all over again. He was gone, and she'd never again see his smile or hear him tease her, or look for treasures in the yard. He was gone…and she was here, without him.

"Andrew was the strong one, you know? When our parents got divorced, he was the one who told me it'd all be okay. He was the one who dragged me down to the bakery day after day. He saved me." She shook her head, tears smearing into the cotton of his shirt. "I don't know what I would have done without him. And I don't know what I'll do without him now."

"You'll go on, and put one foot in front of the other. Because he would want that."

She raised her gaze to Brody's. Damn. This man read her like a book. "He would."

"He'd want you to keep running this shop and keep your family's legacy going. He'd want you to go look at that location this afternoon, and move toward the future. He wouldn't want you to stand around and cry for him."

"You talk like you know him." She swiped at her face. "That's exactly what Andrew would say. Actually, he'd say it far more direct and with far more colorful language." She laughed, and the sorrow that had gripped her began to ease a bit. "I wish you had met him. He was an amazing man."

"I feel like I have met him," Brody said quietly. "He's in every part of this shop and everything you do and... it's like he's here with us."

"It is." She bit her lip and nodded. "Thank you for lunch, for being here, for cheering me up."

"Kate—" The clock on the wall chimed quarter to the hour, at the same time Brody's cell phone began to vibrate. "Damn. My time's up. I have to get back to the office for the last couple of appointments." He pressed a kiss to her lips, then cupped her jaw. "I'll be back. And we'll talk then, okay?"

"I can't wait." And as she watched Brody McKenna leave, Kate thought there was nothing closer to the truth than that.

She was beginning to fall for the doctor, and fall hard.

# CHAPTER SEVEN

ONE hour later, true to his word, Brody returned to the shop. The sight of him caused a hitch in Kate's breath. "You're on time," she said. "Quite impressive for a doctor."

He chuckled. "That's a pet peeve of mine. I hate to be late, for anything, and I work hard to make sure my practice runs on time. Makes for happier patients—"

"And a happier doctor."

"That, too." He swung his car keys around his finger. "You ready? I thought I'd drive, so you could concentrate on the building and neighborhood."

Thoughtful. Nice. Again. Did the man like her, or just see a pity case?

And why did she keep wondering about that?

"I won't turn that offer down." She tucked her apron behind the counter then headed out of the shop behind him, locking the door as she left. At the curb, Brody opened the passenger side door of an older Jeep, its dark green paint a little worse for wear. "What, no Mercedes?"

"I told you. I'm not the typical doctor. This is the car that got me through my college years, and I've had it so long, it's part of the family." He shrugged. "Whether

I can afford a Mercedes or not isn't the point. I don't need a sixty thousand dollar piece of metal to prove I'm successful. I'd rather let my patients speak to that."

"You are different," she said. "In a good way." She got into the Jeep, and waited while Brody came around to the driver's side. Every time Kate thought she had him pigeonholed, he added another dimension to his character. Maybe she'd misjudged him. Seen him through jaded eyes. Every minute she spent with him, Brody McKenna came closer to the kind of man she thought didn't exist.

Still, she suspected Brody McKenna kept a part of himself back. She wasn't sure what it was, or why he was keeping himself distanced from her, but she knew better than to try to force a bridge when there was only a rope across the river between them. If he was interested, he'd open up, and if he didn't...

She didn't need to fall for a mystery. Her mother had made that mistake, and she refused to do the same.

"So, tell me about this property." Brody put the Jeep in gear—a stick shift, which impressed Kate a little more—and pulled away from the curb.

"It's a thousand square feet, which is pretty much the same size I have now, and it's on a corner lot, beside a coffee shop and a florist. Busy location, with a lot of foot traffic."

"Sounds perfect. And like the kind of location that would let you do some partnering and cross-marketing with your neighbors." He flashed her a grin. "Sometimes I listened when my grandparents talked about work."

Kate laughed. "We'll see. I've looked at it online, and talked to the realtor a few weeks back, but this is my first in-person visit. Sometimes what you get in person isn't as good as the advertisement."

"Sort of like online dating, huh?"

"Speaking from personal experience, Doctor?" Curiosity about Brody's dating past sparked inside her. What had kept such an eligible, smart, handsome man from marrying? Was he really that gun-shy or had he been burned before, like her?

"Nope, can't say I've ever tried that," he said. "I'm old-fashioned. I like to meet people, see if there's a connection, and then take the next step."

"You said you came close to settling down before. What happened to that connection?"

Brody sighed. "Melissa and I got engaged right out of college, then I went on my first medical mission trip, and she broke up with me while I was gone."

"She did? Why?"

"She expected that being a doctor's wife meant shopping on Fifth Avenue and vacationing in Italy, not visiting third world countries to treat malaria and set broken bones. And, I was distant, and didn't put in the time I should have with the relationship." He sighed. "I tried to fix things, but I was too late."

"And that burned you forever on the idea of love?"

"That and…a few other things. I guess at a certain point, I gave up on finding someone who shared my goals."

She chuckled. "Now you sound like me. Two jaded souls. Destined for…"

"What?" he asked.

"I don't know. You tell me."

He raised and lowered a shoulder, a grin playing on

his lips. "Last I checked, psychic abilities weren't on my résumé."

She laughed. "No fair. You can't go all mysterious on me."

"Me? Mysterious? I'm as easy to read as a prescription."

That made her laugh even harder. "Written in a doctor's handwriting? That makes it illegible."

"I never said figuring me out would be easy." He grinned.

"Oh, I agree. You are far from easy to decipher. You're a Sphinx with a stethoscope." Kate sat back against the seat, wondering about this other side of her that being around Brody encouraged. She didn't trade flirty repartee with men. She worked hard, kept her nose to the grindstone, and yes came up for air once in a while to go on a date. But never had she met a man who made her exchange...

Banter.

Or met a man who made her blush like a schoolgirl. A man who made butterflies flutter in her stomach. A man who made her begin to dream again of things she'd given up on long ago. Not like this, she hadn't. A part of her threw up a huge Caution side while another part craved more.

The whole ride to Weymouth went like that, the two of them exchanging barbs, always with a hint of flirting on the side. The sun shone bright, and Brody had the windows down, letting in a nice fresh breeze. When they turned off on the Route 18 exit, disappointment filled Kate as they neared their destination.

A few minutes later—and after getting turned around once—they pulled in front of the location, a cute little storefront smack dab in a part of Weymouth dubbed Columbian Square. From the historic homes bordering the square to the old style storefronts, Kate could see vestiges of Weymouth's historic roots. Across the street from the shop sat the Cameo Theater, an old-style movie house that harkened back to the days of Model T cars. "Quaint, isn't it?"

"It looks perfect for a second Nora's." Brody came around and opened her door then the two of them headed for the storefront. People walked along the sidewalk, popping in and out of shops, chatting and enjoying the warm fall day. Traffic slowed at the stop signs, drivers casting quick glances at the shop wares before continuing on their way.

A wiry dark-haired man came hustling down the street, a packet of papers under one arm, a briefcase in the opposite hand. He extended his free hand as he came upon Kate and Brody. "Hello, hello. You must be Miss…Spencer? Here about the building?"

"Kate Spencer." She shook with the other man. "Owner of Nora's Sweet Shop in Newton. Thank you for meeting me today."

"No problem." He turned to Brody and shook. "I'm Bill Taylor." He turned and unlocked the door, then led them inside. "Nora's Sweet Shop, you said? Sounds like just the thing for our little community. We have lots of shops here that can compliment a bakery. And with the hospital around the corner, there's always a demand for gift baskets and the like."

As Bill talked about square footage and lighting, Kate took the time to look around, to imagine a counter here, a display there. The shop had housed a deli before, and the kitchen would need minimal changes to meet Kate's needs. All in all, the shop had the space and equipment to house another Nora's, not to mention a prime location.

"Looks perfect," Brody said to Kate. "Not that I'm an expert in these kinds of things, but it sure seems ideal to me."

"It is perfect. Right town, right space, right location."

"And right for you now?" Bill asked, already reaching into his stash of papers for an offer sheet.

Kate looked around. Nerves threatened to choke her. Brody had told her to be proactive, but now that the moment to take that step forward had arrived, she stalled. "I, um, I don't know. I need some time to think about it." She thanked Bill for his time, promised to call the realtor with any other questions, then headed out to the car. Brody opened her door, then climbed in the driver's seat.

"Why didn't you make an offer?" he asked. "I thought you said that place was perfect."

"I just don't think now is the right time to be adding locations." She watched the storefront grow smaller as the Jeep headed down the street. A mixture of disappointment and relief washed over her. Disappointment that she'd let the location go. Relief that she didn't have to tackle a major task like a second location. Maybe next month. Or the month after. Maybe she'd wait till spring when the weather improved, and people spent more time strolling the streets. Valid reasons? Or stall tactics?

"Do you want to talk about it?" Brody asked.

No, she didn't, but Brody had driven her here and deserved an answer. Maybe if she got her reservations out on the table, the worries would ease.

"It's scary to take that next step, you know?" she

said. "And I'm just not sure that I'm ready for it. I mean, adding a second location splits me in two, and I have my hands full with the Newton location as it is."

"Your assistant will be back soon, and you talked about hiring others, so that will free up your time," he pointed out. "I agree that the next step is scary as hell. You could fail, or you could succeed. But you won't know either unless you try."

She watched the streets of Weymouth pass by outside the window. Neat houses in neat rows, flanked by businesses on either side. A bustling, growing community, one that seemed much like Newton. One that could support a Nora's Sweet Shop, if she dared to make the attempt.

Fail...or succeed. Either prospect sent a shiver of worry down her spine. She turned to Brody. "How did you do it?"

Brody flipped on the directional, then merged onto the interstate. His gaze remained on the road, his hand shifting the gear as they accelerated and entered the fray of automobiles. "Do what?"

"Take those risks, fly to other cities, other countries, and step into a strange environment? How did you know it would work out?"

"I didn't. I had to trust in my skills as a doctor. And sometimes, I succeeded. And sometimes," he let out a long, low breath, "I failed."

"That's what I'm most afraid of, I guess. Andrew was the risk taker, the one who would go all in on everything from poker to tic-tac-toe." She fiddled with the strap on her purse. Andrew had traveled the world, leapt out of airplanes, climbed mountains. While all her life, Kate had stayed in the same town, worked in the same business, seen the same people, baked the same things. "I know he'd want me to do it, but…"

"You're afraid of letting him down."

"Yeah." She sighed. "And myself. And my grandmother. And all those people who love Nora's Sweet Shop."

"I can relate to that. When someone gives you a huge responsibility, it can be scary. You worry about whether you are up to the task. Whether you'll fulfill their wishes, the way they wanted. Whether…you're doing the right thing at all." Little traffic filled the highway, few people traveling in or out of the city on a fall Saturday afternoon. "Maybe you should wait then. Give it a little time."

"Maybe." Or maybe she should throw caution to the wind, as Andrew had done, and just go for it. Leap off the edge and trust the winds to carry her.

As the miles clicked by and the city drew closer, Kate realized she didn't want the day to end. Brody had been good company, and joking with him on the way out here had brightened her day, eased the tension in her shoulders. Whenever she spent time with him, he had the same effect. He made her forget, made her think about the day ahead, rather than the past.

She liked him, as a friend, and as something more, something she wanted to explore, taste. She wondered about the things he kept to himself, wondered how it fit with the man she'd gotten to know. "I'm not sure what your plan is for today, but if you're free, I'd like to invite you over for dinner. Nothing too fancy, because I'm not exactly cook of the year, but it'll be edible, I promise."

"I've tasted your cupcakes. You can definitely cook."

"Bake, not cook. They're two different sciences. I'm

great with things that are exact and precise, but with cooking, a lot of it is a pinch of this, a dash of that, and it gets me all flustered." She shook her head. "Don't even ask me about the Thanksgiving turkey debacle."

He laughed. "Now that I'd like to see. You flustered."

"You'll see that, and the parts of my life that aren't so organized." Inviting him over meant opening a door to herself. She hadn't done that in a long, long time. She thought of her brother, and how he approached his days with a what's-the-worst-that-could-happen attitude, and decided she'd take a cue from Andrew, and dance a little closer to the edge of danger.

"You'll be shattering my image of you as the perfect woman, you know," Brody said.

She pivoted in her seat. "You think I'm the perfect woman?"

He turned toward her, but his eyes remained unreadable behind dark sunglasses. "I think you're pretty damned amazing."

Her face heated, and a smile winged across her face. Her heart skipped, as if she'd been rocketed back to middle school and the cute boy in math class had dropped a note on her desk. "Amazing, huh? You're not so bad yourself, Doctor."

"Well, there's a rousing endorsement." He laughed. "I'll have to add that to my online dating profile."

She gave him a coy smile. "I can't be throwing out compliments left and right at you. You could get a swelled head."

"I doubt that's going to happen. I have my brothers to remind me that I can still be a dork sometimes."

"You? A dork? I don't think so." She took in the sharp line of his jaw, his tousled dark hair, his defined, strong hands. The last word she'd use to describe Brody was *dork*. Sexy, mysterious, intriguing, tempting…

A hundred other words came to mind when she looked at Brody McKenna.

"Hey, don't underestimate me. I read medical journals in my spare time. And watch operation shows on TV. I've never been in the cool kids clique." He grinned.

She waved that off. "That's overrated if you ask me."

He grinned. "Oh, were you in the cool kids group?"

"I was a cheerleader." She shrugged. "Membership came with the pom-poms."

"You were a cheerleader?" A grin quirked up on one side of his face. "You do know that when you tell a man that, it gives him ideas?"

"Does it help to know I was terrible at it?"

He thought a second. "Ummm…nope."

"Well, just don't ask me to rah-rah and we'll get along just fine."

"Even if I say please?"

"Even if you say please." She laughed, but still a simmering sexual tension filled the car, rife with the innuendos and unspoken desires hanging between them. Maybe later, she'd explore a little of that with Brody McKenna. Take a chance for once, and let the man not just into her house, but into her heart.

They neared her exit, and she gave Brody directions. In a few minutes, he had reached the driveway of her townhome. "Home sweet home," he said, and shut off the engine. The Jeep clicked a few times, then fell silent.

Nerves bubbled inside her. She'd invited men into her home before, but this time seemed different. Because she'd started to like Brody—a lot? Because being around an enticing man like Brody embodied taking a risk?

Either way, the few steps it took to get from the driveway to the front door seemed to last forever. She unlocked the door, then flicked on the hall light and stepped inside, with Brody following. "Can I get you something to drink?"

"Sure."

"Um, beer, water, soda?"

He opted for water. She filled two glasses, then led him to the small sunroom at the back of her townhouse. Screened in the summer, shuttered in the winter, the room offered large windows and a fabulous peek of the outdoors. "This is my favorite room. It's not very big, but it has a fabulous view." She waved toward the picture windows, and the thick copse of woods that ran along the back of the property. She'd hung birdfeeders on several of the trees when she first moved in, which provided a constant flurry of winged activity.

Brody sat on an overstuffed floral patterned love-seat, a tall man on a feminine couch. Somehow, Brody made it work. "I can see why you love it," he said. "It's hard to get something like this so close to the city, with woods and everything. Sitting here must be a nice way for you to unwind."

"It is. I've spent many an afternoon or evening out here, reading a book or just listening to music and watching the birds. It's…"

"Calming," Brody said.

"Yes. Very." Except with Brody in the room, calm didn't describe the riot of awareness rocketing through her. Her mind went back to that almost kiss the other day. For the hundredth time, she wished they'd finished what they'd started.

Who was Brody McKenna? Between the flirting and the compliments and the help in the bakery, he seemed interested in her, but when it came to moving things to the next level, he backed away instead. Was she misreading him?

"When I was in…" he stopped, started again, "overseas, we stopped in this tiny village for several days. It sat in this little oasis, a valley of sorts, nestled between several mountain ranges." As he spoke, she had the feeling in his mind, he'd gone to that destination, and his voice softened with the memory. "Not many places over there had trees, but this one did. The room where I stayed looked out over a stone wall and a field, all shadowed by the majesty of the mountains. When the sun rose, it painted an exquisite picture. Gold washing over purple, then over green, like unrolling a blanket of yellow. It was simple and beautiful."

"It sounds it."

"The days there were long, and tough." He ran a hand through his hair and sighed. "Some days, that mountain range restored my sanity, brought me back to reality. To what mattered."

"My brother talked about something similar. He said that every day he spent in Afghanistan, he made it a point to find something beautiful wherever he went. And when things got tough, he'd just focus on that one beautiful thing, and it would remind him of home and why he was there."

"Those moments brought him peace?"

"I think they did." She looked at Brody McKenna and saw a man who needed that same kind of peace.

He carried a load of troubles on his shoulders. What troubles, she wasn't sure, but she suspected it stemmed from a recent tragic event. Maybe she could help him find a little solace, or if nothing else, show him she understood. He was trying to do that for her, and the least she could do was the same.

Kate got to her feet, and crossed to a cedar box that sat on the shelf. All this time, the box had sat, closed, waiting for her to be ready. To open it, to share the contents, to tell the story. She realized as she carried the small wooden container back to the loveseat, that for a month, she'd put her emotions on a back burner. She'd done that long enough.

"I want to show you something." Kate settled herself beside Brody, and opened the lid. "I haven't shown this to anyone, except my grandmother." She pulled out a trio of velvet boxes, and laid them on the coffee table. "Andrew's medals, given posthumously. Odd word, isn't that? Posthumously. Like it was funny afterwards or something." She shook her head, then reached into the box, and withdrew another item. "The flag from his funeral." She placed the triangular folded item on the table, giving it one lingering touch then reached inside one more time. "And the four leaf clover necklace he wore. He called it his good luck charm."

Brody remembered.

In that moment, he was back in the first village they'd stayed in, sitting outside, watching the sun go down behind the mountains. Andrew sat beside him, fingering the necklace. The clover had caught the last of the sun's rays, bouncing them off like an aura. Brody had asked Andrew about the emblem, and that conversation had built the beginnings of a friendship between the two men.

The memory sent a rush of emotion through Brody. He glanced at the necklace in Kate's hand. The explosion had chipped off one corner, twisted another, doing the same damage to the jewelry as it had done inside Andrew's body. He could see Andrew all over again, lying on the ground, torn apart by the blast, while his friends lay nearby. Blood mingled with fear, and Brody and the other doctor with him rushing to try and save them all. Knowing at least one would die before the day ended.

Brody's throat grew thick, his eyes burned. "You okay?" Kate asked, placing a hand on his arm. Her comforting him, when he should be the one comforting her.

"Yeah." A lie. He hadn't been okay in a long time, and the necklace brought back all the reasons why. "My father used to have a four leaf clover necktie. He wore it whenever he called on a new client." Brody had shared the same story with Andrew, all those weeks ago and sharing it now with Kate was like being back there on that porch while the sun sent the world a goodnight kiss. "One of us inherited the tie when my father died. Finn, I think. We're Irish, so you know the four-leaf clover superstition is alive and well."

"Andrew just liked them. When we were kids, we spent an entire afternoon, combing the yard, looking for one." She ran her thumb over the four heart shapes that converged to form the trademark leaves. "We never found one, but we tried our best."

"Maybe that's because luck isn't something you find. It's something you...create."

"True." She gave the necklace one last touch then

lowered it to the table, one link at a time. "That's why I don't want to open another location. Because I'm afraid that…"

When she didn't go on, he turned to her, took one of her hands in his and waited until her gaze met his. "Afraid of what?"

"Afraid that I'll be as unlucky as Andrew." The truth sat there, cold, stark. "That I'll take a risk and I'll fail, and I'll…" Her hand ran over the folded surface of the flag, "Let him down. Let myself down."

"You're smart, Kate. Talented as hell. And you have something that people love and enjoy. That's a recipe for success." He closed her palm over the charm. "With or without a good luck charm, you're going to do just fine."

"I hope you're right." She gave him a watery smile. "There are days when it's hard to find that view, and focus on the good."

"I know what you mean. I don't think I've seen that view in a long, long time."

She gave the box a loving touch then raised her gaze to Brody's. "I shared all this with you because I wanted you to know that I understand what it's like to need that one little thing that restores your sanity, gets you back on track. I don't know what's bothering you, but it's clear something is weighing heavy on your shoulders." She picked up the necklace and dropped it into Brody's palm. "I want you to have this. Let it be your view, Brody. It worked for Andrew, and I'm sure it'll work for you."

The gold weighed heavy in his palm. "I…I can't take this, Kate."

"But—"

Brody glanced at the medals, the flag, lying on the

table, and knew he could delay this no longer. Kate deserved to know the truth, even if it hurt. Even if it went against her brother's wishes. Maybe Andrew was wrong. Maybe his sister could handle more than he'd thought.

"Kate, there's something I want to tell you." Against Brody's hip, his cell phone began to ring, the distinctive trilling tone that meant his service was trying to reach him. Routine calls, like appointment changes, were routed to voicemail, but emergencies went straight to Brody's cell. He cursed under his breath. "I have to get this."

He flipped out the phone, and answered it. In seconds, the operator relayed the information—one of his patients had landed in the hospital a few minutes ago with heart attack symptoms. The cardiac team wanted the primary care physician's input before proceeding. "I'll be right there." He closed the phone and put it back in the holster. "I'm sorry. I have to go."

"Duty calls?"

He nodded. "It's an emergency. Listen, I'll catch up with you tomorrow, okay?"

"I can't. My grandparents and I are going up to Maine for the day to visit my mom. How about Monday?"

"I'll be there." Even though he dreaded the conversation he needed to have with her, a part of him couldn't wait to see her again. Today had been fun, and brought an unexpected lightness to his heart. He craved more of that.

Craved more of Kate.

"You'll be there on Monday, with your apron on?" She gave him a teasing wink.

He chuckled. "Of course. I'm starting to see it as the

next best fashion accessory. What all the cool docs will be wearing this winter."

She led him to the door, then paused and put a hand on his arm. Her gentle touch warmed his skin. "Brody?"

"Yeah?"

"Thank you for today. You made me laugh, and you made me forget, and it was...wonderful." A smile curved across her face, this one a sweet, easy smile. "I needed that. A lot."

All Andrew Spencer had wanted was his older sister's happiness. Brody had done his best to ensure that, and to ensure she followed the path she'd been on before she lost her brother. A win in that column, but a loss in the other, where the truth lay. And complicating the equation—

Brody liked Kate Spencer. A lot. He wanted more, wanted to make her his. Wanted to take her in his arms and kiss her until neither of them could see straight. To do that, he had to start them off on the right foot—

And tell her why he had walked into her shop that first day. Was she ready to hear the truth? Or would it set her back even more?

His phone buzzed a second time, reminding him the patient came first. Before what Brody wanted, before what Brody craved. And that meant any relationship with Kate Spencer fell far down the line from the promise Brody had made in that dusty hut.

# CHAPTER EIGHT

THE Morning Glory Diner promised good home cooked meals according to the sign in the window and the delicious scents emanating every time someone opened the door. Kate stepped inside, and opted for a table by the window. The flowers of the namesake ringed the bright diner's walls and decorated everything from the menus to the napkin holders. The counters were a soft pale yellow, the seats a deep navy blue, which offset the border of violet morning glories well.

A smiling blonde came over and greeted Kate. Her nametag read Stace, but somehow Kate would have pegged her for a McKenna fiancé without it. She had the kind of bright, happy personality that seemed to fit with what Kate knew of the McKenna men so far. "Welcome to the Morning Glory," Stace said. "Can I get you some coffee?"

"Sure." Kate put out her hand. "And if you have a sec, I'd love to chat with you. I'm Kate and I'm making your wedding cupcakes this week."

"Kate, how nice to finally meet you in person." The other woman smiled. "Brody told us about you. And so did Riley's grandmother. She said you made amazing chocolates."

"Thank you." Brody had been talking about her. At first, it flattered her, then she realized it made sense. He'd hired her to make Stace's wedding cake, after all, and giving her business a plug would be part of that. Kate had been puzzling over Brody's words from Saturday all weekend. Something troubled him, but what it was, she didn't know. He'd left the necklace behind, right next to a whole lot of unanswered questions.

"Listen, I need to get a couple orders on the tables, but then I should have a few minutes to sit and chat. I'll bring us coffee." Stace cast a glance toward the clock on the wall. "And knowing my husband-to-be, he'll be walking in those doors in about thirty seconds for his omelet fix, so you can meet Riley, too."

"Sounds great." Kate gave Stace a smile.

A few seconds later, the door opened and a man who looked like a younger version of Brody strode inside, straight to Stace. He took her in his arms, gave her a quick dip that had her laughing, then a longer kiss that had her blushing. She gave him a gentle swat, then gestured in Kate's direction.

Riley crossed the room, a wide smile on his face. He slid into the opposite seat and put out a hand. "Riley McKenna. The youngest and cutest McKenna brother—and you can tell Brody I said so."

Kate laughed and shook hands with Riley. She liked him from the start. "Nice to meet you. Kate Spencer, owner of Nora's Sweet Shop."

"So you're the one that has my brother all distracted. The man doesn't know if he's coming or going lately."

Had he said that? Been talking about her? "Brody and I are just working together. He's helping me out while my assistant is out of town."

"Well, for Brody it's more than some baking and measuring. The man can't stop talking about you." Riley leaned across the table. "He's smitten, I'd say. Though if you tell him I said that, I'll deny it."

Kate put up her hands. "Brody and I are not dating—" well, Saturday had been kind of a date, and the tension between them spoke of something more than friendship "—I'm not sure he's interested in me that way." Because despite the day they'd spent together, the flirting and the jokes, he kept taking two steps forward, one step back. The mixed signals confused her, and as much as she'd told Riley and Stace she'd come here to get more details for their wedding cake, she knew the truth. She'd stopped in to pump those who knew Brody best for more information. Something to help her solve the puzzle of the enigmatic Brody McKenna.

"Tell me," Riley said, "is Brody there pretty much every day?"

"Well, yes, but—"

"Is he doing nice things like opening the door for you?"

"Well, yes, but—"

"And is he finding excuses to run into you when he doesn't have to be there?"

"Well, yes, but—"

"Then he's interested. Trust me, Brody doesn't waste his time on things that don't matter to him. If he's around you all the time, he's interested. Not to mention, he manages to bring up your name about... oh, a hundred times in conversation."

Stace slid into the booth beside Riley and handed Kate a cup of coffee. "You talking about Brody?"

"Yup. And how the middle brother is the last to learn

that a good woman is the secret to happiness." Riley pressed a kiss to Stace's cheek. "It's always the smart ones that are the dumbest."

"I agree with that." Stace gave him a gentle nudge, then turned to Kate. "Riley was just as bad as Brody. Kept on pretending he didn't have any interest in me. And meanwhile, he was drooling behind my back."

Riley feigned horror. "I was not. That was Finn with Ellie."

Kate laughed. "Brody mentioned him a few times."

"The first to fall and get married, and he surprised the hell out of all of us by eloping. He's got one kid already, another on the way. By taking the plunge, he blazed the trail for the rest of us." Riley chuckled. "And this weekend, it'll be my turn. I can't wait."

Stace beamed at him. "Neither can I." Riley slipped his arm behind Stace and drew her a little closer, a little tighter.

Kate dug a notepad out of her purse. "While I have you two here, I wanted to ask you some questions about the cupcakes. Brody gave me information, but—"

"He's a guy and they aren't big on details, right?" Stace said. "Whatever Brody told you, though, is probably just fine. I'm the least fussy person you'll ever meet. Just make them edible and pretty and I'll be happy."

"Because all you want to do is marry me, right?" Riley said.

"No. All I want to do is gorge on cupcakes." She laughed. "Okay, and marry you."

Riley swiped a hand across his forehead. "Phew. You had me worried there for a minute. I thought the wedding was all an elaborate plot for dessert."

"Oh, it is," Stace said with a grin. "And you're the dessert I'm getting."

The two of them embodied happiness. Kate envied them a bit. No, a lot. Would she ever meet a man who would love her that much? "I'm not sure my cupcakes can live up to that," she said with a smile.

"I'm sure they'll be all that and more. I heard all about your chocolates from Mary at dinner last week."

"A family dinner that Brody skipped," Riley said. "I heard it was because he was working with you."

"I'm sorry, if I had known he should have been at a family dinner—"

Riley put up a hand to stop her. "It was no big deal, really. Honestly, we're all glad Brody started working with you. It's been good for him."

Stace nodded. Concern filled both their faces. "Be patient with Brody. He's been through a lot."

Did that explain the distance he maintained? The way he pulled back every time they got close? What could possibly be that bad that he felt he couldn't tell her?

"He told me his parents died." Kate shook her head. "I meant yours, Riley. I'm sorry about that."

"Thanks, but that isn't what troubles Brody these days. He's been through something…traumatic. In the recent past." Riley exchanged a glance with Stace.

Something Brody hadn't shared. The big thing he kept dancing around, then dropping? Hurt roared inside Kate. She had sat there with him and poured her heart out, sharing her deepest fears, and he had yet to do the same. Why?

"He said he's working with me because it helps him

get his mind off things," Kate said. "I'm glad that baking can do that for him."

*And that he can avoid the hard topics yet coax them out of me.*

"Brody hates to cook," Riley said with a laugh. "Like seriously runs the other way if someone turns on the oven. He's a takeout only man."

"Then why would he offer to help me?"

Again, Riley and Stace exchanged a glance and again, Kate got the feeling there was something—something big—they weren't telling her. "You need to ask him about that," Riley said. "Just know that if Brody is there doing the thing he hates the most in the world, there is a really, really big reason for him doing so."

"Bigger than your wedding?" Kate asked.

Riley thought a second. "Brody's not there for our wedding. He's there because—" Stace laid a hand on Riley's arm and he cut off the sentence. "Brody's a good man," Riley said instead. "And he's trying his damnedest to do the right thing. So before you judge him, think about that. And give him the benefit of the doubt."

Thursday afternoon, Brody sat in his office, surrounded by charts he needed to finish up and notes he should be reviewing, and ignored it all. He'd come so close to telling Kate the truth on Saturday, but at the last minute, chickened out, using the emergency as an excuse to get out of there. And in the days since, he'd found one excuse after another to avoid the bakery. Instead, he'd gone for long, hard, punishing runs that hadn't solved a damned thing.

The problem? He liked Kate. Liked her a lot. And he knew if he wanted a future with her, then he had to start being honest. Trust that she could handle the information, and not be worse for knowing it.

Andrew's concerns continued to nag in the back of Brody's head, though. Who would know her better than her brother? Maybe Andrew was right to protect her, or maybe he didn't realize his sister's strength.

How well did Brody know her, though, after only a couple weeks? Better than her own flesh and blood?

Mrs. Maguire gave his door a soft knock, and came inside. "Do you need anything else before I leave, Doctor?"

"No, thanks, Mrs. Maguire." His head nurse had been a model of efficiency this week, and kept him on track despite his uncharacteristic lack of attention to his practice. She'd noticed, and mentioned it a few times. He'd attributed his inattentiveness to exhaustion, an excuse that didn't work, given he'd worked half days all week.

She lingered in the doorway, then came inside and put a hand on the back of his visitor's chair but didn't sit. "I've noticed you've been troubled lately, Doc." He put up a hand to argue, but she cut him off. "Can I give you some advice? The same advice Doc Watkins gave me one day?"

Concern etched her features. Working side by side with him for years had given Mrs. Maguire an insight into what made Brody tick. Maybe she'd share something that could take the edge off his emotions, give him a way to find his direction again. "Sure."

She swung around to the front of the chair and eased into it. "Did I ever tell you about my daughter, Sharon?"

"Just that she's married and given you two, no, three grandchildren to spoil." Every day it seemed Mrs.

Maguire put out a new picture of one of the three kids on her desk. Or a new drawing colored with thick crayons, and marked with love for Grandma. The kids lived a couple towns over, and Brody knew Mrs. Maguire devoted every spare minute to seeing them.

A smile curved across Mrs. Maguire's face. "She has indeed. But for a time there, I didn't think she was going to do anything with her life, anything except die."

As far as he could remember, Mrs. Maguire had only shared the good news about her family, never any kind of troubles beyond the typical colds or restaurant meltdowns. "I didn't know that. What happened?"

"This was before your time, and back when it was just me and Doc Watkins. As a single mom, I juggled everything—work, school, soccer matches. Sharon felt neglected, I think. When she got to high school, she made a lot of bad choices. Fell in with the wrong crowd. Pot led to coke, led to crack. In those days, crack ran rampant." She shook her head. "I thought I was going to lose her. I did everything I could to try to keep her safe. Console her, stay home with her, whatever it took to keep her on track. But nothing worked. One day at a time, I watched my baby die."

"Oh, Mrs. Maguire, I'm so sorry." He couldn't imagine the stress on her shoulders during those days, coupled with working full-time and paying the bills.

"And here I was, a nurse. The kind of person who should know better, you know? I kept trying to fix it, like putting a band-aid on a cut, but it wasn't a cut, it was a hemorrhage, and she didn't want the help."

"What did you do?"

"I came in here one day and I cried to Doc Watkins. Told him I had to quit so I could take care of my baby.

I was going to devote myself full time to trying to fix Sharon. And you know what he told me?"

Brody shook his head.

"He said if I quit, it would be the worst thing I could do. Well, he said more than that, and a whole lot more colorfully than I would. You know Doc Watkins. He was nothing if not direct."

Brody chuckled. "I remember."

Mrs. Maguire crossed her hands in her lap and dropped her gaze to her fingers. "Back then, there wasn't a lot of that fanciness about enabling and co-dependency, but that's what it was. I just didn't see it. All I saw was that I was protecting my daughter, help-ing her. Doc gave me the number of a great rehab. Told me to drop her off and drive away. I did, but damn, I didn't want to. She was crying and screaming and call-ing me names, then begging me to come back in the same breath. I had to shut the windows, turn the rear-view mirror, so I wouldn't give in." Tears filled the older woman's eyes at the memory, and she leaned forward, grabbed a tissue from the box on his desk, and dabbed at her face. "I left her there. Hardest damned thing I ever did in my life, and also the best. Three months later, she came out clean. Moved to Brookline, got herself a job in a dress shop, and after a year or so, met the man that became her husband."

"I'm glad that all worked out." He'd admired Mrs. Maguire before, but his esteem for her increased ten-fold. The woman sitting across from him possessed an incredible inner strength. "You must have been so worried."

"I was, but more than that, I was beating myself up for not fixing it. It took me a long time to realize that some things are out of my hands. I couldn't make her come clean. I couldn't make her want it; she had to want it for herself. Just because I have medical training doesn't make me a miracle worker." She crumpled the tissue into her fist, then leaned forward. "Most of all, I had to learn that sometimes, you just have to cut yourself some slack. You and me both."

"I try, Mrs. Maguire. I really do."

"No, you don't. I've seen your face ever since you got back from Afghanistan. Whatever happened over there, you are blaming yourself for and now that weight has become an albatross around your neck." She put up a hand. "Now I don't know the whole story, and I might be just talking out of my hat, but all I can say is that I have been in shoes similar to yours, and if you put your faith in others, and stop beating yourself up for what you can't control, what you couldn't fix, it'll all work out. You are a doctor, and you're used to fixing, bandaging. Not everything can be fixed. Some things just have to be." She got to her feet, and smoothed a hand down her jacket. "I've said my piece, and I'll let you be. I'm not trying to tell you what to do, Dr. McKenna, just trying to offer you a solution. Take it if you want." She gave him a kind smile, then left the room.

Brody got to his feet and went to the window. He looked out at the busy streets of Newton, beginning to fill with cars now that the clock had ticked past five. For the next few hours, it would be bumper to bumper with people trying to get home to their lives, their homes, their families. They would sit around the table and talk about their days, and few, if any, would realize just how lucky they were to be together.

He thought of Mrs. Maguire and her daughter, and

how close his head nurse had come to losing her only child. He thought of albatrosses and choices, and after a long time, he pulled out the card, read it over for the millionth time, then tucked it back into his wallet. It was time he told Kate the real story about her brother.

And let the chips fall where they may after that.

# CHAPTER NINE

KATE had baked and decorated, frosted and sugared. But it hadn't been enough to make her forget what Riley and Stace had said. Or to put Brody McKenna out of her mind.

Because she'd started to like him. He kept his cards close to his chest—heck, hidden inside his chest—but every once in a while, the other side of Brody peeked out. A playful, sweet side. Like when they'd danced together at the rest home. When he'd dug in and started baking, even wearing the pink apron. At the same time, he showed this dimension of caring. Like the kind of man a woman could lean against, depend upon. Even if being around him stirred her in a way she hadn't been stirred before.

Would it be worth it to take the risk and fall in love with him? Or would she be burned by a man who was keeping part of himself hidden? She'd seen her mother do it time and again with her father. Giving, giving, giving, and never receiving his full heart in return. Would Brody be the same? Would she be repeating her mother's mistakes?

Her conversation with Riley and Stace had only stirred the pot. What had Brody been hiding behind those blue eyes? The flame of Brody McKenna drew her again and again. She needed to exercise caution— or she'd get burned.

"Somebody's got a lot on her mind."

Kate jerked her head up and looked at her grandmother. "Huh?"

"You just turned that rose into a radish." She pointed at the red clump of buttercream on top of the cupcake.

"Oh, no." She swiped the ruined decoration off, then set down the piping bag. "I guess I am a little distracted."

"And I know why." Nora hefted a heavy tub of frosting onto the counter and started to peel off the lid.

"Grandma, quit that!" Kate said, sliding in to finish the job before her grandmother hurt herself. "No helping."

"You need the help. I have the experience. Let me give you a hand."

Kate sighed. She knew her grandmother. She wouldn't give up. "Okay. If you promise to take it easy, and sit down while you work, can you frost those cupcakes over there?"

Nora laughed. "You sound like you're the grandmother and I'm the granddaughter."

"Just watching out for my favorite grandma." Kate slid a stool over to the counter, then plopped a platter of red devil cupcakes and a piping bag of cream cheese frosting in front of her grandmother. She laid a hand on Nora's shoulder. "Thanks, Grandma."

Nora took Kate's hand and gave it a squeeze. "Anytime, sweetie. I love this place almost as much as I love you."

"Ditto." She grinned, then dipped her head to focus

on assembling the order she'd been working on. Maybe talking about work would keep her from thinking about Brody. "By the way, I looked at that second location the other day."

"You did? What'd you think of it?"

"It was…perfect. In this quaint little town square in Weymouth, across the street from an old-fashioned movie theater. There's a florist and a café nearby, and a hospital right down the street."

"I don't think it gets much better than that," Nora said. "Did you make an offer?"

"Not yet."

"What are you waiting for?"

Kate shrugged, then threw up her hands. "I don't know. A sign? A big, blinking, this is the right decision to make sign."

Nora laughed. "Life never gives us those. If it did, every choice we make would be easy as pie."

"True."

Nora laid a hand on her granddaughter's shoulder. "You'll know the right answer when the time comes. Meanwhile, you have a big night tonight. Are you ready?"

Kate glanced down at the dress she'd put on, the heels she'd brought to work just for tonight. "As ready as I'll ever be. If I just stick with the desserts, I'll be fine. Either way, I'm packing tissues in my purse."

Her grandmother gave her a quick hug. "Such a smart, practical girl. No wonder I'm so proud of you."

The bell over the door rang, and Kate turned to go out to the shop when she heard Brody's voice call out a hello. Her heart tripped, and a smile curved across her face. Not thinking about Brody had worked for, oh, five seconds.

"Hmm…and you wonder why you're distracted," Nora said. "I think the reason just walked in."

"It has nothing to do with him," Kate whispered. "Nothing at all."

"Mmm, hmm." Nora drew a little frosting heart on the stainless steel counter. Kate swiped the romantic symbol onto her finger and plopped the sweet treat in her mouth before Brody walked in and saw it.

Damn. Every time she saw Brody McKenna, she forgot to breathe. He had on a suit jacket with his shirt and tie today, and he looked so handsome she could have fainted. "Hi," she said, because her brain wouldn't process any other words.

"Hi, yourself." He started to shrug out of the jacket. He had a tall, lean body, defined in all the right places. His muscles rippled under the pressed cotton of his shirt, and she wondered what he'd look like bare-chested. She'd seen him in a T-shirt and shorts and that had been a delicious sight that had lingered in her mind. What would he look like, wet from the shower? Fresh out of bed in the morning? In the dark of night, slipping under the sheets?

Damn. Why did this man affect her so?

"Uh, you might want to keep that on," she said, putting up a hand to stop him. "I have another delivery tonight. I forgot to tell you earlier. If you don't mind helping me, there'll be a free dinner in it for you."

"A free dinner? One that doesn't come out of a microwave or a drive-through? Who can turn down that offer?" He grinned, then entered the kitchen.

Her stomach flipped, her heart tripped, and she knew

why her thoughts lingered on him whenever they were apart. That smile. And those eyes. And everything else about him. In that second, she decided she'd take the risk, open her heart.

"Hello, Mrs. Spencer," he said to Kate's grandmother.

"Why hello, Dr. McKenna. So nice to see you again."

"You, too, ma'am."

"Why, would you look at the time?" Nora said. She took off her apron, and laid it beside the piping bag. "I completely forgot I promised your grandfather I'd go out with him for the early birds dinner special tonight. I better go." She shrugged into her coat. "You two can handle this alone, can't you?"

She laid a slight emphasis on the word "alone" and gave her granddaughter a knowing smile. Behind Brody's back, she drew a heart in the air and pointed at Kate. "Oh, and, Brody," Nora said, "I'd love to have you over for Wednesday night dinner at our house next week."

"I'd be honored, Mrs. Spencer. Thank you."

"Good. I'll see you at six. Kate knows the address." She gave her granddaughter a smile. "Maybe she'll even drive you."

Kate had no doubt her grandmother would drive over and pick up Brody herself if her granddaughter didn't. Matchmaker Nora at work again. Andrew had had some of those tendencies himself, always telling Kate he'd keep an eye out for the perfect man for his amazing sister.

"Do you need me to bring anything?" Brody asked.

"Aren't you sweet? No, nothing at all. Just bring yourself." Nora shot Kate another smile of approval for Brody. He'd racked up several brownie points and had clearly moved to the top of Nora's list. "That'll be enough."

Nora headed out the door. Kate wished the floor would open up and swallow her but it didn't. Or a customer would come in and save her from the awkward silence. None did. Or the sky would fall and create a distraction—

None of that happened. Instead, the room became a warm, tight space of just her. And Brody. Her gaze roamed over him. Desire pulsed in her veins. He wore a half smile, and in an odd way, that turned her on more than a full smile. She wanted to feel his hard chest beneath her palms, but most of all, she wanted to kiss him.

Why had he yet to make a move in that direction? Brody didn't strike her as the shy type. She had read attraction between them, she was sure of it. What was holding him back from pushing this further?

She watched him loading the finished cupcakes into boxes, and read tension in his shoulders, a distance in his words, his smile. She kept on talking, filling the room with endless chatter, if only to keep from asking the obvious question—

What's wrong?

They worked together for several minutes, exchanging small talk about their days. The whole thing seemed so ordinary, smacking of a domestic life with Brody. She could imagine a future like this—her coming home from the shop, sitting across the dinner table from him, and talking about everything, and nothing at all. Like ordinary couples with ordinary lives.

Already, that told her that her heart had connected

with him. A lot. She was falling for him. But the falling felt nice, like tumbling into a warm pool.

As much as she wanted to linger in that pool, she held back, because she sensed a reservation in Brody. Maybe he didn't feel the same way. Maybe he did, as though it was moving too fast. Or maybe she had read him wrong. And she could be making the mistake of a lifetime.

"There, that's the last one," she said, sandwiching the last cupcake in the container. She closed the lid and handed it to Brody. He stacked them together, then gave her a grin.

"Another job done."

"Yep." Joanne would be back Saturday, and then her afternoons of working with Brody would come to an end. Already, she could see that finish line, and it saddened her. She'd gotten used to having him here.

"I'm sorry about my grandmother earlier," Kate said, "but you don't have to go to dinner if you don't want." Her roundabout way of saying if you aren't interested in me, here's your out.

"I'd love to go. Your grandmother didn't bother me at all by asking me over. I think there's something in a grandmother's DNA that makes them bound and determined to matchmake," Brody said. "When I saw mine a few days ago, she said the same thing. That I should bring you to the next family dinner, which in case I get in trouble for not inviting you, is at Mary McKenna's house in Newton, on Sunday at two. She's just a few blocks north of here."

Kate laughed. "Seems like our grandmothers are determined to bring us together."

"Mine heard glowing reports from Riley about how

nice you were. And that got her wheels turning, thinking that you and I…" His voice trailed off.

"Yeah, my grandmother, too." Kate let out a nervous
laugh. She brushed at her hair. Damn. She was acting
like a schoolgirl. Her face heated under Brody's lingering gaze. She turned away to grab a spoon and moved
too fast, unnerved by the tension, by the unanswered
questions. Did he like her? Or not?

As she pivoted, her arm bumped the bowl, and sent
it tumbling onto the floor. When it hit the concrete, the
violet frosting in the bowl splattered upward, and out-
ward, spreading in a burst of color on Brody's shirt and
his suit jacket. "Oh no! I'm sorry."

"No problem. I've had worse on my shirt. Especially
during flu season." He slipped off the jacket, then, just
like in her fantasy, he began to undo the buttons. Her
heart skipped a beat, and nearly stopped when he peeled
apart the panels of his shirt and revealed, a lean, muscled chest.

Oh. My. God. Kate opened her mouth. Closed it
again. "Uh…I can get you a T-shirt. If you don't mind
one that says Nora's Sweet Shop."

"Better to wear the words than the actual sweets."
Brody grinned.

Kate spun away before she reached out and ran a
hand down his chest. Or worse. Like threw him onto
the stainless steel counter and ravaged his body. She
grabbed a T-shirt from the glass case out front and
brought it back with her. "At least this is brown, instead of pink like the aprons."

"It's almost manly. Thanks."

"Anytime." And anytime he wanted to take his shirt

off in her presence, he could. But she didn't say that, either.

He moved closer, standing inches away now, that broad chest so close she could feel the heat against her own skin. "Do you, uh, want to give it to me?"

*Way to go, Kate, hold the man's shirt hostage.*

"Oh. Oh, yes. I'm sorry. I…got distracted." She inhaled, and caught the woodsy scent of his cologne. Dark, mysterious, like wandering a forest in the middle of the night.

"Distracted by what?"

"You." There. The truth hung there, in plain sight. "You distract me, Brody McKenna."

"I don't mean to." He reached up a hand and cupped her jaw. His hand was big, strong, yet gentle against her skin. "I keep telling myself not to do this, not to take things further, but then every time I leave here, all I do is think about you. And when I'm near you, all I can do is think about kissing you."

"Really?" She swallowed. "But…"

"But what?"

"But…you haven't."

A smile curved across his face. Slow, sexy. "No, I haven't. And maybe it's time I remedied that."

"Maybe it is."

"Do you want me to kiss you, Kate?"

"Yes." She exhaled. "Yes, I do."

"Good." He leaned in, winnowing the gap between them until a fraction of space separated them. Her pulse rumbled like thunder and a craving for Brody grew inside her until the world disappeared.

She watched the gold flecks dance in his eyes. Her heart stuttered, stopped, stuttered again.

"Ah, Kate…" he said, her name a harsh whisper, then he closed the space and kissed her.

His lips were hard against hers at first, a strong, wild kiss, like a sudden summer storm. His hands tangled in her hair, and he pulled her to him, tight against his chest. She curved into Brody, heat racing through her body, charging up her spine. Her hands worked against his back, feeling the ripple of the muscles she had fantasized about. The warm expanse of his skin, the hard places of his body. He plundered her mouth, his tongue dancing hot and furious with hers.

She couldn't think. Couldn't breathe. Couldn't move. Desire pounded a hard rhythm in her body, and for a long, long second she forgot where she was. She only knew Brody was kissing her and it was the sexiest, most exquisite experience of her life. She shifted against him, pressing her pelvis to his erection, wanting more, wanting—

Brody broke away. He cursed and spun toward the window. "I'm sorry, Kate. I shouldn't have done that. I wasn't thinking. I…"

She laid a hand on his bare shoulder and waited until he'd pivoted back to face her. "It's okay, Brody. I wanted that as much as you did."

"I know, but… I need to talk to you before we take this any further."

The clock chimed the half hour. She cursed the timing. "Can it wait? We have to get going before we're late. Already, with the traffic and set up time, we're likely to barely make it there before the event starts."

"Yeah, it can wait." He drew the T-shirt over his head, and she bit back a sigh of disappointment. "A little while, but not too long, okay?"

"Sounds serious." She grinned. "You're not giving me a fatal diagnosis, Doctor, are you?"

"No, no." He fiddled with the stack of orders on the counter beside him. "Just something I've been meaning to tell you."

"Okay." She lifted the boxes of cupcakes, then placed them in his arms. Curiosity piqued inside her but she had to concentrate on work for now. Like he said, they'd talk later. "We'd better head out now or we'll be late."

"If you don't mind, we can stop by my office. I keep an extra shirt and tie there, for accidents just like this."

"Sure." He helped her load the cupcakes into the van, repeating what they had done two nights before, with her driving, him sitting in the passenger's seat. They drove the few blocks to his office, and Kate waited in the van while he went inside and traded the T-shirt for a clean shirt and suit jacket. When he returned, she put the van in gear.

Brody glanced over at her. "You look beautiful."

"Thank you." She smoothed a hand over the black jersey fabric of the sweetheart neckline dress she'd chosen. "This is a special event."

"Big one for Nora's Sweet Shop?"

"You could say that." She paused. "Really, it's a big one for me."

"Sounds important."

"It is. It's a way of thanking the people who have been there for me when I needed them." She glanced over at him. "It's a thank you for the troops."

He tensed beside her. Whatever he'd been holding back seemed to be bubbling under the surface. Why?

"Is something bothering you?" she asked.

He glanced out the window, as they headed out of

Newton and into the city, against the flow of outgoing traffic. Horns honked. Lights flashed. But Kate's attention stayed on Brody.

"Yes and no," he said after a while.

"You want to talk about it?"

He didn't say anything for a long time, so long she thought he hadn't heard the question. Finally, he let out a breath. "I've been wrestling with something for some time now and I know I need to talk about it, but…" he shook his head, "doing so is a lot harder than I expected." He paused again, and she waited for him to continue. "The last medical mission trip I took was really difficult. I lost a patient, and it's been haunting me."

"Oh, Brody, I'm sorry."

"I made a promise to the patient, one I'm not so sure I can keep anymore. He didn't want me to say what happened to him. He just wanted me to encourage someone very close to him to focus on the future, not on what happened in the past, and I just don't know if that's the right thing to do." Brody hesitated again and then looked at her. "If it were you, what would you want?"

She thought about her answer. "I don't know. A part of me feels like I've just started moving forward, and knowing more, or going back there would be like the day I found out. I just…don't want to go there again. I'm just getting out of that cement, you know?"

"So you're saying it would be better not to know?"

"For me, for now…that's what I'd want. Maybe down the road, it would be easier."

"Thanks for the advice. I'll keep that in mind." He turned to the window, and watched the world go by, a clear sign the subject was closed.

The sun had started to set, casting a golden lake over the rippling green waters of Boston Harbor, and twinkling halos over every skyscraper.

"The city is amazing, isn't it?" Kate said. "Every winter, I say I want to move and open up a location in Florida or Hawaii, or any place that doesn't get snow. But there's just something about Boston, something... magical, that I love. No matter where I go, my heart will always be here."

"I feel the same way. I've traveled all over the country, seen a lot of the world, and there's still nothing like Boston. I love it here, for all its faults...and traffic."

Kate laughed. "Yeah, the traffic is one thing I can do without. My grandparents don't mind it. They say it gives them extra alone time in the car. They're old romantics that way."

"They sound it." Brody glanced out the window, watching the city go by in a blur of buildings. "I guess everyone hopes to find a true love like that, the kind that can last a lifetime. I know my grandparents were like that. My parents, not so much. They fought all the time. Then they'd make up, and it'd be fiery in a different way. I think they were two opposite souls, who just couldn't let go of each other."

"Sometimes the fireworks are good." Though for her parents, attraction hadn't been enough to sustain their marriage. They'd been too different to make it work, too infatuated to slow down and think before they tied the knot.

Still, fireworks summed up what had been going on inside her ever since she'd met Brody. And every time he smiled at her. Or touched her. And, oh, yes, when he kissed her.

Fireworks. Bottle rockets—no, Roman candles—of desire, launching in her chest. Fireworks alone didn't create a relationship, and she needed to remember that.

Brody had turned his attention on her, and it took all her effort to keep her eyes on the road and not on him. "Is that what you're looking for? The fireworks and happiness, even in a traffic jam?"

She sighed. "I gave up on that a long time ago. My parents were like yours. All fireworks, no substance. I guess watching their marriage disintegrate made me lose faith in ever finding Mr. Right."

"And who is your Mr. Right?"

"Why, are you applying for the job?" She cast him a grin, pretending the question was a joke. But after that kiss, a part of her hoped like hell the answer was yes.

"Can't do that if I don't know the qualifications." He grinned. "I could be all wrong for you."

"Could be." Or he could be all right. She didn't know yet, but a part of her really wanted to find out. "I guess my brother is the one I hold up as the ideal for all the men I meet. Andrew was smart, and funny, and driven, and above all, a hero. The kind of man who was true to those he loved, loyal to everyone he knew, and braver than anyone in the world. You could count on him to be honest, to be the one you depended on, rather than him depending on you."

"He sounds like the perfect guy."

She laughed. "Oh, he was far from perfect, believe me. There was a time when we were little, like nine and seven. He and I were fighting over a toy, and he slugged me, hard. My eye swelled up, my cheek turned purple, and he felt so bad, he carried me to my grandmother, and stood over me for hours, changing out the ice pack and worrying like a new mother. He got in a lot of trouble that day, and for years, would tell me how bad he felt about it. I, of course, being the evil older sister, milked that injury for all I could."

Brody laughed. "I know that trick. Riley and I have given Finn a hard time and taken him on a guilt trip more than once."

"I've met Riley and I can see that about him. He seems like he was…mischievous as a child."

Brody laughed. "He still is."

"What's Finn like?"

"The total opposite of Riley. Finn is an architect, all straight lines and organizational charts, although marrying Ellie and adopting a child has loosened him up a lot. Riley runs an after school program at Wilmont Academy. He was the slowest to grow up, but he's making us all proud now."

"And you, of course, being a doctor who also volunteers his time to help the needy. You must make them all proud, too."

His gaze went to the window again. For a long time, he was silent, just watching the traffic go by, the houses yield to skyscrapers. "Some days I think I do. Other days…not so much."

He didn't elaborate and she didn't press. Once again, Brody had closed a door between them, and Kate reminded herself she didn't need a man like that. At its heart, this wasn't a relationship, it was a business deal. He was helping her and in exchange, he'd get the cupcakes for Riley's wedding. Fireworks or not, if there was no substance, there wasn't anything to build on.

Then why did she care what troubles lay behind those blue eyes? Why did she keep pressing for more?

Because she sensed something good, deep inside of Brody. Something worth fighting for.

"So, who's your ideal Mrs. Right?" she asked, up-ending her own vow to stay neutral. She exited the highway, and came to stop at a red light. A sign for her and Brody? "The perfect doctor's wife with the gloves and pillbox hat?"

"Lord, no, that would drive me nuts." He chuckled. "I'm not that formal. Ever. I like women who are... natural."

"As in no makeup, wearing sandals and T-shirts?" The light turned green, and Kate accelerated again.

"As in they act like themselves all the time. I hate when people act one way but feel the opposite. I don't like secrets or surprises."

"Me, too. If you asked me my relationship deal-breaker, it would be dishonesty. I can't stand being lied to. Have the courage to tell me the truth, or don't waste my time." She flicked on her directional, then pulled into the hotel's parking garage. The van bumped over a speed strip. Kate cast a quick glance at the cargo, but nothing had moved. "If you want people who are true to their word and to those they care about, then you've come to the right place tonight."

Brody didn't say much as they pulled the boxes out of the van, then loaded them onto a cart and headed up the to the third floor in the hotel elevator. Once inside the ballroom, a hotel staffer directed Kate to the banquet table, telling her to set up dessert on the far corner.

She glanced at Brody several times, but the easy banter between them had disappeared. Had she said something wrong? Or was he still thinking about the patient he had lost?

"We only have a few minutes before everyone arrives, so we need to hurry," she said. They worked out an assembly line of sorts, with Brody handing Kate the cupcakes while she laid them on tiered trays she had brought with her.

"Red, white and blue?" he said, noting the arrangement of the desserts. "It almost looks like you've made flags."

"I did." She pointed to the array of cupcakes, set in the familiar pattern of the flag for the USA. Then she drew in a deep breath. Tonight would be difficult, no doubt, but the cause was a worthy one, and Kate vowed to suck it up and not cry. "Okay. Here they come."

The ballroom doors opened and dozens of men and women in uniform strode into the ballroom, chatting in low tones as the band took up the stage and began to play "America the Beautiful." The room filled with a sea of green and camouflage, flanked by bright flags on either end.

"I haven't seen these people in a long time. I'm so nervous and excited."

"I thought you said it was a thank you," Brody said.

"It is." She leaned in and lowered her voice. "For the members of Andrew's unit, along with several other units from Massachusetts who returned to the States in the last few weeks. It was originally supposed to be a retirement party for the top ranking general in the area, but the general put up his own money and paid to have a party for the troops instead. So it mushroomed into this big event. They came to me for the cupcakes because they knew my brother had…" She bit her lip and shook her head. She would not cry tonight. Would not. "Well, that he didn't come home."

The troops settled into chairs that ringed tables decorated with patriotic colors. An honor guard marched in, raised the flag, and the whole room stood at attention to sing "The Star Spangled Banner."

"There are members of Andrew's unit here tonight?" Brody hung back behind the banquet tables with Kate, his stomach riding his throat.

"Yes. I can't wait to introduce you to them."

Introduce him? The thought hit Brody in the chest like an anvil. Kate had said the one thing she couldn't abide was someone who didn't tell the truth. All Brody had done since he met her was lie. Lie about who he was. Lie about why he was in her shop. Lie about his volunteer work. He'd done it because it had been Andrew's last request, but now...

Now he wasn't sure it had been the right decision. How could he expect her to move forward, to look to the future, if Brody was holding a key to her past in his hands?

"These are the true heroes," she whispered to Brody. Tears filled her eyes, while she watched the general take the stage and thank the brave men and women who had given their lives in defense of their country. "The people who risked everything for those back home."

Brody had thought he was doing the right thing by not telling Kate about Andrew's death, but he'd been wrong. The woman beside him was no daisy. She was as strong as an oak tree, and the time had come for him to tell her the truth. He'd be there to help her through it, and she would be okay. He'd make sure of it.

The general finished his speech, then began introducing the vendors who had donated their time and products to the event. "And I'd also like to introduce

Miss Kate Spencer, owner of Nora's Sweet Shop. She lost her brother, Andrew, in Afghanistan last month. A tragic accident, that occurred while Andrew and members of his team were accompanying a medical team helping local villagers. Kate, come on up here." The general waved to her.

She hesitated. "I don't know if I'm ready for this," she whispered. She spun toward Brody. "Go with me? At least until the stage?"

"Of course." He took her hand, and they walked across the room and over to the stage. Kate gave Brody a smile, then climbed the few steps and crossed to the podium. "Thank you, General Martin. I'm afraid you've given me too much credit. I didn't do anything but make cupcakes. It's all of you who made the sacrifices and gave of yourselves. I hope these desserts thank you, at least in some tiny measure, for all you have done. I know my brother was proud to be in the National Guard, but not as proud as I was to call him my brother."

A roar of applause and hearty agreement went up from the crowd. Kate gave them all a smile, then climbed back down the stairs and took Brody's hand again. "Thank you."

"You did great." She'd been poised and brief, and delivered a speech that touched people with a few words. He'd never seen another woman who could do so much, and touch so many, so easily.

Damn, he liked her. A lot.

And because he did, he would tell her who he really was, and what had happened in that dusty hut, and pray it all worked out. In his practice, he'd seen a thousand times that the truth gave patients power. To make their own decisions, to handle a diagnosis. Kate needed that, and Brody was done waiting to give it to her.

"I'm just glad I got through it without crying." She smiled again, but this time her eyes shimmered. "It's still hard to talk about him sometimes."

"I understand. More than you know." He led her through the crowd and toward the banquet tables. Maybe they could slip out for a few minutes and he could talk to her. Or maybe it would be better to wait until they had left, and they could find a quiet place to talk alone.

Along the way, several troops got to their feet to offer condolences, and thank-yous for the cupcakes. Brody's feet sputtered to a stop when a familiar face rose to greet Kate. "Hey, Kate. Nice to see you again."

"Artie! Oh my gosh, it's been so long since I've seen you!" She let go of Brody's hand and gave the tall man a big hug. "How have you been?"

Artie Gavins, one of the other men in Andrew's unit. Brody forgot what his job had been, but he knew his face. He'd bandaged it the same day that Andrew had died. A serious man, who the others had dubbed "Straight Line" because he rarely cracked a smile. Andrew said Artie kept them all on track, but had also respected the other man's common sense approach.

"Fine, just fine," Artie said. Then his gaze traveled past Kate, and landed on Brody. It took him a second, but Brody could see him making the connection in his brain, processing the man in the suit jacket and tie, and connected him with the doctor in a khaki coat and jeans that he'd known last month. "Doc? Wow, I can't believe it's you. Hell, I almost didn't recognize you all dressed up and wearing a suit and tie."

Brody put out his hand and shook with the other man. "Good to see you, too."

And it was. There'd been so many wounded that day, so many to tend to. Seeing one of the men as hearty and hale as ever, gave Brody more reward than any paycheck ever could.

Still, he prayed Artie wouldn't say anything else. Brody didn't want Kate to find out who he was like this. He wanted time to explain it to her, time to get the words right, and here, in a public place, among all these people, wasn't the right place or time. "We, uh, better get back to the dessert table," he said to Kate. "I think we forgot to unload one of the boxes."

"Oh, yes, we need to get that done. Wouldn't want anyone to miss out on dessert." She gave Artie's shoulder a squeeze. "We'll catch up later."

"We will. Nice to see you, Kate, Doc." Artie took his seat again.

Brody hurried through the rest of the crowd with Kate, and back over to the banquet table. He wanted to pull Kate aside, but they were pinned in by the banquet tables and people were already lining up for food. No discreet way to duck out of the room.

"I didn't know you knew Artie," she said. "What a small world. How did you meet him?"

"He was…my patient once." Brody cast a glance down the long white tableclothed space. The hungry crowd was closing the gap between the chicken cordon bleu and dessert.

"Wow, and you remember him? That's pretty impressive, Doc."

"There are certain patients I never forget." Understatement of the year. "Listen, can we get out of here? I really want to talk to you."

"I can't leave. I promised the general I'd stay and eat with the troops. Plus, I'd love to catch up with Andrew's unit. It makes me feel closer to him. Why don't you stay? I promise, none of them bite." She grinned.

"I...I can't. I..." How could he explain it? The gap had closed, and the diners were now ten feet away. In that crowd was Artie, and most like Sully and Richards, the other two who had been on that mission with Andrew, also wounded, also part of the mad rush between Brody and the other doctor to save lives. "I...I need to talk to you, Kate."

She put a hand on his arm "Are you okay? You look...pale."

He glanced at the troops heading toward them, then at the woman who had just talked about the one army man who wouldn't be coming home, and the guilt hit him again in a wave so hard, he had to take a breath before he spoke again. "No, I'm not okay. Not at all."

"What is it?"

Andrew's last words rushed over Brody. *Don't tell her. She'll only grieve more.*

But that bequest warred with everything Brody knew to be true. A patient couldn't mend if they were in the dark about their ailment. Kate's heart was hurting her, and keeping the truth from her even one second longer wasn't going to help her heal. No amount of cupcake baking or location scouting could do what the simple truth could.

He was standing in a room with the bravest people in the world, and standing across from one of the bravest women he had ever met. He was doing her a disservice by keeping this tucked inside one minute longer. "Remember I told you about that patient I lost when I was on the medical mission?"

"Uh-huh." She pivoted a cupcake to the right, straightened another, until the frostings were aligned and the colors made straight lines in the flag design.

"That patient was someone you know."

She jerked her head up. "Someone I know?"

The hungry troops had reached the cupcakes. They exclaimed over the design as they selected one and moved on. "We need to go somewhere private, Kate."

"What, now?"

"Yes. It can't wait any longer. In fact, what I have to tell you shouldn't have waited as long as it has."

"Kate, I've saved a seat at the head table for you," the general said. "Come on and join me for dinner."

She glanced at Brody then back at the general. "I will, sir. Can you give me one second, please?"

The general nodded. "Take all the time you need."

She grabbed Brody's hand and they scooted along the wall, and out of the ballroom. Kate glanced back at the room as the doors shut. "I only have a minute, Brody."

He reached into his pocket and pulled out his wallet. Then he withdrew the card he had carried for so long and handed it to her. A parade of emotions washed over her face. Confusion, shock, hurt.

"How…how did you get this?" she asked.

The moment had come, and dread rumbled in Brody's gut. How he wished he didn't have to tell her this, didn't have to watch the happiness dim in her eyes. "Artie knows me…because I was his doctor."

"You said that."

"I was his doctor in Afghanistan. In fact, I treated several of the troops in that room."

"Wait. You were in Afghanistan? When?"

He let out a long breath. "I was part of a medical team that was going from village to village, helping provide care to people too poor or too far from a doctor, and also tending to those who had been injured because of the war. A National Guard unit had been dispatched to serve as protection for us because it was still a dangerous area." He met her gaze. "It was Andrew's unit, Kate."

"I don't understand. How did you know my brother? Is that how you got my card?"

"Remember that town I told you about? The one with the mountain range? We were there for several days and while we were, Andrew received one of your care packages."

She clutched the card tighter, her face pale. "I sent him those baskets every week, like clockwork. Lord only knows how the military got them to him, but they did."

"He loved those baskets." Brody chuckled a little at the memory of big, strong Andrew, as happy as a kid on Christmas when he received a box from home. He'd handed out cupcakes to all, boasting about his sister as he did. "I know he kidded you about them, but he kept every card, and talked about you all the time. When I met you, I felt like I already knew you."

"He talked about me?"

He nodded. "He was a good guy, your brother. Really good. It was probably a boring detail, just going from town to town with a couple doctors, but he treated it like the most important mission he had ever been on."

A smile wavered on her face. "That was Andrew. His whole life was about taking care of other people."

"He did a good job at it," Brody said.

"That still doesn't explain why *you* have the card I sent him."

Brody let out a long breath. He crossed to the brick wall and laid his palm against the cold, hard stone. The words stuck in his throat, churned with bile in his gut, but still he pressed forward. "I got to know your brother while he was with our group. We talked a lot. We had a lot in common, you know, both being from around here, and both being Red Sox fans and…"

"That's good. I'm glad he made a friend." Her voice broke a little.

"He was my friend," Brody said, turning to Kate. "I need you to know that. I cared about him a lot. And I wanted to save him. So badly, I really did."

"What do you mean?"

In the room behind them, the party rolled on. Someone laughed at a joke, and the band shifted into a pop song. Forks clanked, voices hummed.

Brody bit his lip. Damn. "All he ever talked about was you, and this shop, and getting back here to help his family out. He loved all of you very much, and he wanted nothing more than to see a chain of Nora's Sweet Shops someday. He told me you'd be scared to death to do it alone, but I should encourage you to go after your dreams. He worried about you. Worried that you'd get scared, or be too overwhelmed by his death, to keep going forward." Brody swallowed hard. Forced the words out. "He wanted me to make sure you did that. It was his dying wish."

"You…you were with him when he died?"

Brody nodded. He wanted to look away when he said the next part, but Kate deserved the truth, deserved the unvarnished, painful as hell truth. So he met her gaze, and said it. "I was his doctor."

"His doctor?" She pressed a hand to her forehead. "When were you going to tell me?"

"I tried to. A thousand times. But I didn't..." He sighed. "I didn't want to hurt you."

"You took care of him?"

"He was badly injured, and so were several other guys. That blast...it hurt them all. Some worse than others. The second doctor on the team was over-whelmed, less experienced, and there was a lot to deal with, all at once. It was chaos, Kate, sheer chaos. I did my best, believe me, but his injuries were too severe."

The words hung in the air between them for a long, long time. He watched her process them, her eyes going wide with disbelief, then filling with tears, then nar-rowing with anger. "You...why didn't you save him? What kind of doctor are you?"

"I tried, Kate, I tried. But you've got to understand, we were in the middle of nowhere, and our supplies were low. We'd just come from a village that had a lot of wounded and sick people, and we were on our way to the rendezvous spot for a resupply, when Andrew's truck went over the IED. All of them were hurt, and we had to try to help everyone, all at the same time. We did our best, but Andrew was badly injured. There was nothing I could do for him."

"Did he..." She bit her lip, swiped at the tears on her cheeks. "Did he suffer?"

People asked that question and never wanted the truth. They never wanted to know that their loved one had been in pain, or lingered with a mortal wound. They wanted death to be quick, painless, as simple as closing your eyes. "He wasn't in any pain," Brody said, which was the truth. The one thing they'd had in good supply was painkillers. "And we talked a lot during his last hours."

"Hours? He suffered for *hours?* Why…why didn't you get more help? Call in a helicopter? Do something… else? Why did you…let him die?"

"I didn't let him, Kate. I did everything I could."

"But it wasn't enough, was it?" She shook her head, then glanced down at the card. When she raised her gaze to his, those emerald eyes had gone stone cold. "And so you came here, came to me, on what, a mercy mission? Take care of the grieving older sister?"

"It wasn't like that. I—"

"I don't care anymore, Brody. I don't care what you intended or what you meant. You let my brother die and then you stood in my shop and watched me cry and never said a word." She flung the card at him. It pinged off Brody's chest and tumbled to the carpeting. "Stay away from me. I'm not your pity case anymore."

Then she turned on her heel and headed back into the ballroom. The door shut, and Kate was gone.

# CHAPTER TEN

BRODY stood beside his brother and watched Riley and Stace pledge till death do us part, with ridiculous, happy smiles all over their faces. Frank, Stace's head chef, longtime friend and business partner, watched from his seat, tears streaming down his face. Gran sat beside Frank, dabbing at her pale blue eyes. Stace's sister and nephew sat on the other side of Frank, beaming like proud parents.

The wedding had been simple, the service lasting just a few minutes, with Brody and Finn serving as ushers. Finn had been best man, and gave Riley a hug of congratulations when he handed the youngest McKenna the rings. As soon as the minister pronounced them man and wife, Jiao, Finn and Ellie's adopted daughter who had served as flower girl, scooted out of her mother's arms, and scattered more rose petals on the altar. The guests laughed, and Jiao ducked back behind her mother again. Ellie chuckled, and wrapped a protective arm around the small dark-haired girl.

The minister introduced Mr. and Mrs. McKenna, then Riley and Stace turned toward the small crowd of guests, hand in hand. Applause and cheers went up, and the couple headed down the makeshift aisle in the center of the diner, while guests showered them with rose petals and Jiao brought up the rear, scattering flowers in their wake.

Throughout the wedding, Brody had forced himself to keep his attention on the front of the room. Not to turn back and see if Kate was one of the guests seated in the diner. But now, as Riley and Stace walked away, his gaze scanned the crowd, searching for long brown hair, deep green eyes.

Disappointment sunk like a stone in his gut. She wasn't here.

He'd hoped, even though he had heard the finality in her voice, but still he'd hoped that she would change her mind. His heart kept looking for her, kept hoping to see her when there was a flash of dark brown hair or the sound of laughter.

The band began playing, and several waitstaff hurried in to move the seating around to accommodate a dance floor in the center of the diner. The cupcakes had been delivered early this morning, probably part of Kate's plan to avoid him. Before Brody arrived, she'd stacked them on a towering stack of circular plates, decorated with fresh flowers and strands of iridescent pearls, like a real wedding cake. As always, Kate had surpassed expectations. The guests oohed and aahed, and Riley pointed to Brody. "Don't tell us, tell my brother over there. I believe he made each one himself."

"It wasn't me," Brody said, "it was all the work of—"

The door opened. Kate strode inside. She had her hair up in a loose bun, with tendrils tickling along her jaw. She wore a pale blue dress that floated above her knees in a swishy bell, and floral heels that accented her legs, curved her calves. Brody reminded himself to breathe.

He couldn't dare to hope for forgiveness for lying to her for so long, regardless of how many times he'd apologized. But a part of him was damned glad to see her, and wishing anyway.

"Thank that beautiful woman there." He pointed at Kate. "Kate Spencer, the owner of Nora's Sweet Shop, which makes amazing cupcakes and chocolates."

Several guests swarmed Kate, singing her praises over the floral decorated cupcakes. She thanked them, the admiration causing her to blush. After a while, she broke away from the group, accepting a glass of champagne from a passing waiter. She chatted with Ellie while Brody watched and wished she was talking to him.

Riley strode over to Brody. "I see your baker is here. You going to ask her to dance?"

"She's not my anything." She never had been, really. The relationship he'd built with her had been built on a lie, and everyone knew a castle constructed on sand would never last.

Riley arched a brow. "What happened?"

"I told her about Afghanistan. That I was the doctor with her brother when he died. And that her brother had asked me to watch out for her."

"How'd that go?"

Brody scowled at his little brother. "How do you think?"

"I'm glad you finally talked about it, Brody."

"Yeah, well, I'm not. Now I've lost her, and all because I was trying to do the right thing."

Riley clapped a hand on Brody's shoulder. "Remember

when you and me tricked Finn into seeing Ellie, with that old bait and switch we did with the bagels?"

"Yeah." Brody watched Kate across the room. Stace had moved on to greet other guests and now Kate stood away from the crowd, sipping her champagne, and watching the guests. Avoiding all eye contact with him.

"You need to do the same thing, and find a way to get that pretty girl to talk to you again."

"She doesn't want to see me."

"Did you ask her?"

"Of course not. I just assumed—"

Riley let out a gust. "Geez, Brody, now I'm the expert in relationships in this family? If that's the case, then you'd better check the sky, because I think pigs are flying. You don't assume, brother, you go find out. You have to get in there and take a shot before you can score."

Brody arched a brow. "Did you just tell me to score?"

"Hey, I may be grown up and responsible and married now," he sent a wave over to Stace, "but I'm not perfect." Riley gave Brody a nudge. "Now go over there and take a chance. The woman really likes you. Lord only knows why, but she does." He grinned. "So don't let her get away, or Finn and I will have to take charge."

Riley joined his wife. Brody waved off the waiter's offer of champagne and threaded his way through the tables and chairs until he reached Kate. Up close, she looked a hundred times more beautiful. With her hair up, he could see the delicate curve of her neck, the tiny diamond earrings in her lobes. He caught the scent of vanilla and cinnamon, and a bone deep ache to hold her rushed through his veins.

Brody headed over to her. "Can we talk?"

"I think we've talked all we need to," Kate said, her tone short, cold. "Our business is concluded, and I've found out who you really are. What else is there to discuss?" She raised her eyes to him. Hurt and disappointment pooled in those emerald depths.

"Kate, let me explain."

"Why? What are you going to tell me that's going to change anything?"

"Just hear me out. Please. Five minutes, that's all I ask."

She bit her lip, considering. "Fine. Five minutes."

A start. Right now, Brody would take any start he could get.

"Let's get out of here, okay?" He led her through the diner, into the kitchen, then out the back door and into the alley that ran behind the Morning Glory. He propped the back door open with a rock, then turned to Kate. The sun danced off her hair, shining on those tempting curls, and it was all he could do not to take her in his arms. "I'm sorry for not telling you who I was right off the bat. I was wrong."

She shook her head, tears welling in her eyes. "You should have told me."

"I know. You're right." If he could have done it differently, he would have. All this time, he'd thought he was doing the right thing, but he hadn't been. Looking at Kate now, at the hurt in her face, he wished he could start over. "That last conversation I had with Andrew, when he knew he was dying, he asked only one thing of me."

She raised her gaze to his. "What?"

"That I make sure you were okay. That you were moving forward with your life. He said he was afraid you'd be stuck in your grief. He begged me not to tell you the truth because he was afraid it would make things worse for you."

"Worse? How can knowing the truth make it worse?"

Brody wanted to reach for Kate, but he held back. "He was afraid you would blame yourself all over again. He said you told him that if anything ever happened to him, you'd feel responsible."

She nodded. "I did say that. And he was right. If I hadn't—"

"The last thing he wanted was for you to think you were the reason he was over there." Brody reached for Kate's hand. "Andrew loved his job, and he loved you. He didn't join the military because of you, he joined because he was doing what he does best."

"What's that?"

"Protecting the people he loves. He was doing it then, and he's been doing it ever since he died, through me." Brody let go of Kate's hand and dropped onto the concrete stoop to face a few self truths. "I can relate, because that's what I've done all my life. I've protected my family. Protected myself. I nag my grandmother about getting checkups, harass my brothers about annual physicals. I take care of those around me, because if I do, I can…"

"Prevent another tragedy."

"Yeah. Or at least that was my plan. I thought I went into medicine to change people's lives," he said, "but in reality, I did it to change my own. When my parents died, I remember thinking how powerless I felt. One minute they were here, the next they were gone. I didn't have any say in it. I didn't have any control over it."

"You were eight, Brody. There was nothing you could do."

"Try telling that to an eight-year-old whose world just turned inside out. I became a doctor, I think partly as a way to change that history. You know, save someone else's loved ones and do it often enough, and it would make up for my loss. But it never did. I kept thinking if I could find the right prescription, make the right diagnosis, it would be enough. Change a life, in some small way. And most of all, control the risks, as best I could."

"And thus control the outcome."

He nodded. "But then I went to Afghanistan and realized that sometimes you have to let people take risks. If your brother hadn't been the one in the lead, if he and his team hadn't hit that bomb, it would have hit us. And those villagers would have died. He gave his life for us, because that was his job. He protected us, by risking himself."

She bit her lip. "That was Andrew. He did it all his life."

"You once called him a true hero, and I agree. He was an example for the rest of us to live up to," Brody said. "When that patient of mine at Mass General died, I had to go and tell the family. It was my first notification and the attending thought it would be a good idea for me to learn how. The whole thing was…agonizing. Horrible. The patient's sister was there, and his mother and father, and all I remember seeing was the grief in their eyes. I knew I was causing it, by my words, and I couldn't stop it, because it was the truth. There was no going back and bringing that man back to life. Or bringing him back to his family."

"But you're a doctor. You deal with life and death

every day. Why was this any different?" She took two steps closer and bent her knees until they were eye level. "I *deserved* to know, Brody. You lied to me, over and over again. Why would you do that? To me? Why couldn't you—"

"Because he was my *friend,* damn it!" The last words ripped from Brody's throat, leaving him hoarse. All those weeks he'd spent overseas with Andrew by his side, he'd imagined the two of them meeting up again in Newton, sitting down to watch the game, have a few beers, trading stories about their time in the Middle East. He'd never expected that a bright, sunny morning in the middle of fall would be the day Andrew Spencer, that vibrant, strong young man, would breathe his last breath. "I watched my friend die and it tore me apart. It was like I was losing a brother. I kicked myself for every decision, every moment. I wanted to go back and undo it, to change the course of destiny, and I couldn't. I couldn't do it, Kate, no matter how much I wanted to." He ran a hand through his hair. "I thought it was hard losing that first patient, but at least there, I had all the tools I needed, all the medical staff I could want. The best hospital, the best tests. When he died, I knew I had done everything I could. But when Andrew died—" Brody cursed and turned away.

"What about when Andrew died?"

Brody was back there again. The heat of the Middle East a powerful, shimmering wall. At every turn, the smell of poverty, desperation, lost hope. "We were in this tiny little dirt floor hut in the middle of nowhere. Hours from a hospital. There was me and one other in-experienced doctor, and that was it. No X-ray machines. No operating rooms. No specialists on call. We'd just come from a village that had a lot of sick and wounded people, and our supplies were low. If I'd been in a hospital, I could have hooked him up to a machine. I could have bought him some time. I could have..." He cursed again. The ground blurred before him.

"Changed the ending?"

Brody closed his eyes and drew in a long, deep breath. All these weeks, the what ifs had plagued him. He'd replayed the entire day a hundred times in his mind, but in the end, always came to the same conclusion. The one ending that in his heart he couldn't accept, even though he knew it was the only one. No matter how many hospitals or experts had been on the scene of that explosion, the outcome would have been the same. Sometimes, people just died. And it sucked, plain and simple. "No. He had deep internal injuries from that bomb. The best hospital in the world would have only been able to do one thing." He lifted his gaze to Kate's. "Buy him more time."

"To do what?" Kate asked. "To suffer?"

"To say goodbye."

And there, Brody realized, lay the crux of what had dogged him all these weeks. What had kept him from sleeping. What had laid guilt on his shoulders like a two-ton wall. "I wanted him to have time to talk to you. The cell service where we were was non-existent, and I kept hoping he'd get well enough that we could transport or that a signal would magically appear. I just wanted Andrew to have time to tell his family he loved them. I didn't want to be his messenger, damn it, I wanted him to talk to his family himself. He tried to hold on, he really did, I could hear the helicopters in the distance and I kept hoping, and praying, and trying to keep him alive." Brody's voice broke, and he raised his gaze to her. "But I couldn't fix this, Kate. I...couldn't. I failed and I'm sorry, Kate. I'm so, so sorry."

She buried her face in her hands. Her shoulders shook with her tears, and Brody got to his feet, wrapped an arm around Kate and drew her to him. She tensed, then finally leaned against him. She cried for a long time, Brody doing nothing more than holding her and running a hand down her back and whispering the same thing over and over again. *I'm sorry.*

He could have said it a thousand times and never felt like it was enough. Finally, her tears eased, and so too did the stiffness in her body, the tension in her features. She drew back, the dark green lakes of her eyes still brimming. "Don't you understand, Brody?" she said. "My brother did say goodbye to me and did tell me he loved me. He did it through you."

Perhaps. But had Brody done all he could have to ensure Andrew's final message had been delivered? "The only thing I could do afterwards was fulfill his last wishes. It wasn't enough, but it was all I had, and for a friend like Andrew, I couldn't let him down again. I wasn't a very good messenger. I should have..." he threw up his hands, "done more."

"Sometimes you do all you can and you accept that it's enough. You said something like that to me just the other day. Remember?"

He could hear the band playing inside, music celebrating a new beginning, a new life, while outside in the alley, he and Kate were discussing a loss and trying like hell to move forward with their own lives.

"I'm a doctor," he said. "I'm supposed to heal people. It's in the Hippocratic Oath, for God's sake. Do no harm. And I did harm by treating him in the middle of nowhere, in a place that didn't have everything I needed. I did him harm by not giving him the time to say good-bye." He cursed and shook his head. "I did my best, and I fell short. Maybe I'm not the doctor I thought I was."

"Let me ask you something." She laid a hand on his. "What would have happened to my brother if you hadn't been there? If he'd been alone and that bomb went off?"

"He'd have suffered. It would have been long and slow, and painful." A horrible, undeserved end for a hero like Andrew.

"And you eased that pain, didn't you?" Kate asked.

"Yes. We had plenty of painkillers."

"I meant you eased that pain by talking to him. By making him forget what was happening. He didn't suf-fer because he had you. A friend, when he needed one most." She held Brody's hand tight in her own, her touch a soothing balm for his tortured thoughts. "Thank you for being with him. Thank you for taking care of him. Thank you for making it easier for him."

The words came from Kate's heart. She didn't blame him. She'd absolved him. "He cared about you deeply. I wish I could have brought him home to you."

Tears spilled from her eyes. "I do, too."

His entire goal for the last few weeks had been to help her move forward, to help her go after her dreams, and even if she never spoke to him again after today, he wanted to know she was at least driving down that path and he had done what Andrew asked of him. Then he could take satisfaction in that. He told himself it would be enough. "You have to move forward, Kate. Rent that building. Expand the business. The one thing Andrew wanted more than anything was for you to be happy.

For you to go after your dreams. We stood in that shop in Weymouth and I could see in your eyes that you wanted to take that chance, but in the end, you walked away. You've stood still for weeks, Kate, instead of taking the leap."

"I wasn't the risk taker. That was Andrew. And without him—" She shook her head. "I can't do it. Nora's Sweet Shop is doing just fine where it is. I don't need to expand."

"Because you're afraid of failure."

"I'm done." She turned away. "I didn't come here for you to tell me what I'm doing wrong with my life."

"You're just going to run away? Because the conversation got tough?"

"I'm not doing that, Brody." She pressed a finger into his chest. "You are. Quit telling me how to change my life until you have the courage to change your own." She crossed to the door and jerked it open.

She was about to leave, and he knew, as well as he knew his own name, that he would never see her again if he let her go now. He had done what he always did— protect, worry, dispense advice and medicine—and had been too afraid to do the same for himself.

*Doctor, heal thyself,* she'd joked.

How true that was.

If he didn't change now, he'd lose everything that mattered. Brody was tired of losing what was important to him. Not one more day, not one more minute, would he live afraid of the risks ahead. Afraid of loss. Afraid of being out of control.

"Kate, wait." He let out a gust. She lingered at the door, half here, half gone. "We're two of a kind, aren't we? Both in fields that require us to take a chance every day, and both of us too scared to do that. You would think I wouldn't be, because I've seen risk and loss firsthand, felt it under my hands, heard it in the slowing beep of a heart rate. But I am. I'm scared as hell to lose a patient. And scared as hell to lose you."

"Me? Why?"

"Because you're the first woman I've ever met who has shown me my faults and dared me to face them. You're right about me. About my need to fix everything. I think it's part of why I do the medical missions. It wasn't enough to change lives here. I needed to do it in other towns, other countries. And I thought I was doing just fine." Now the words that he had always kept to himself, the tight leash he had held on his emotions, uncoiled, and the sentences spilled out in a fast waterfall. "Until I went to Afghanistan. There, I was stuck in the middle of nowhere with a dying man and a roomful of wounded. Not enough time, not enough supplies, not enough medicine in the world to save everyone. Medicine couldn't save him, and all I could do was watch him die." Brody ran a hand over his face. "I have been scared, all this time, of not having control over the situation. Of exactly what happened with your brother." He took in Kate's delicate features, her wide green eyes. In the past few weeks, she had changed him in dozens of ways, by encouraging him to step out his normal world. He wanted more of that. More of her. And that meant changing, right this second. "I'm done being afraid of risk, Kate. It's kept me from doing what truly makes me happy."

"Like what?"

"Like expanding the medical missions to be bigger, to take on new challenges. Like doing more to change the lives of the people here in Newton. And most of all," he paused, "like falling in love."

"Falling in love? You have?"

"A long time ago." As he said the words, he realized they were true. "I think I fell in love with you before I even met you."

She shook her head. "That's impossible. How could you do that?"

"Andrew and I talked about you all the time. Whenever we were between towns, or between shifts, we talked. He told me all about the shop and your grandmother, and you." Brody grinned. "He made you sound like Mother Theresa and Santa Claus, all rolled into one."

And finally, Kate laughed and Brody saw a bit of her fire return. "I'm not that nice or that altruistic."

"He thought you were. And the more he talked, the more I saw you through his eyes. I saw you in the care packages you sent. In the notes you wrote. In the memories he shared. And I thought, damn, what would it be like to have someone love me that much?" He took her hands in his and held tight. "It took me over a month to work up the courage to walk into your shop. I would walk down there every day during my lunch break, and after I got done for the day, and every time I would turn around. Partly because I was dreading telling you who I was and why I was there, and partly because I was afraid I'd meet you and you wouldn't be what I imagined."

"I wouldn't live up to the hype?"

He smiled. "Something like that. But then I met you, and you were all Andrew said, and more. You were kind and funny and smart and beautiful. Very beautiful." He closed the gap between them and took both her hands in his. "More than I deserved. More than I ever hoped."

"Brody—"

"You knocked me off my feet so badly that first day, I didn't even realize I picked out a sports basket for my grandmother, who is as far from a sports fan as you can get. All I knew was that I wanted to talk to you, wanted to get to know you. And…" He let out a breath, and faced the last bit of truth. That for all these years, he had held back from love, protecting his own heart, because of one failure. Which had cost him true happiness. No more. "I want more of that, Kate. I want you. In my life now and for always."

She shook her head and broke away from him. "Brody, I can't do this right now. I'm supposed to be at the wedding, and so are you, and—"

He reached for her again, this time cupping her face with his hands. "Take a risk with me, Kate."

Her eyes grew wide, and her cheeks flushed. "I…I can't." She shook her head. "You need to quit believing in the impossible, Brody McKenna, and look at the facts. We're not meant to be together. We started out on a lie, and you can't build anything from that. Nothing except goodbye."

Then she headed back inside. The door slammed shut with a loud bang that echoed in the alley for a long, long time.

# CHAPTER ELEVEN

THE ruined cupcakes sat on the counter, mocking Kate. Distracted and out of sorts, she'd burned two batches this morning. She'd thought coming in on a Sunday would allow her to get caught up, but it had only put her further behind. When Joanne had come in to help, Kate almost burst into tears with relief. "I hate to abandon you on your first day back," she said to Joanne, "but I really need to get some air. I think I'll go for a run."

"Go, go. I'll be fine. Besides, your grandmother is due to stop by for her daily sugar fix. She'll keep me company."

Kate tossed her apron to the side and headed out to the front of the store. Just as she did, Nora entered, making a beeline for the cupcake display. She placed a small box on the counter beside her, then lifted the glass dome. "Good morning, granddaughter."

"Good morning." She pressed a kiss to Nora's cheek. "How are you?"

"Just fine, just fine, or I will be when I get my daily cupcake." Nora's hand hovered over the red devil, then the peanut butter banana, then the chocolate cherry. "Off to see the cute doctor?"

"No. I'm just heading out for a run."

"Well, before you go, maybe you should open this package. I found it on the doorstep when I came in." Nora settled on the chocolate cherry, and replaced the glass dome. She leaned against the counter, peeled off the paper wrapping and took a bite. "Amazing. As always."

"That package is for me?" Kate grabbed a box cutter from under the counter. Maybe she'd ordered something for the shop and forgotten. She slipped the knife under the tape, and as she peeled it off, she realized the box had no stamp, no delivery confirmation tag. And it was Sunday, a day no service delivered. "You just found it out front?"

"Yup." Nora took another bite, and smiled. "Delicious. Sometimes the best and sweetest one is the one you missed, in your rush to make a choice. Don't you think?"

Kate peeled up one flap, then the other. She reached into the cardboard container and pulled out a small black velvet box. A card had been attached to the top, and she opened that first.

*Sometimes all you need is a little luck before you leap.*
*—Brody*

"What do you have there?" Nora asked.

"I don't know." Kate pried open the hinged lid of the box, and let out a gasp when she saw the contents. A four leaf clover, a real one, encased in a glass dome, and attached to a heart shaped charm, dangling from a wide silver ring. A keychain, waiting for keys.

"That man knows you well," Nora said.

"He does. But—"

Nora laid a hand on Kate's shoulder, cutting off her words. "Before you go spouting off all the reasons why you shouldn't love him, let me ask you something. Did I ever tell you the story of who named the shop?"

Kate nodded. "Yeah, but tell it again. It's my favorite."

A soft smile stole across Nora's face as she talked. "When we were first married, your grandfather knew how much I wanted to open a little shop like this, but I was young and had a child on the way and a husband going off to war, and the whole idea just scared the pants off me. The day he left, I woke up and found a spatula on my pillow. Tied up with a bow. He'd carved Nora's Sweet Shop into the handle. Did it by hand, with a pocketknife I gave him for his birthday. He told me the sweetest thing I could ever do for him was to go after my dreams. And I did. I never regretted it, not for a second. I've been so proud to see you and Andrew take up the reins and carry that dream forward." Nora put a hand on Kate's. "Now it's your turn to run with the ball and carry it the rest of the way. To take Nora's to new heights."

"I'm scared, Grandma." Kate ran her hands over the silver ring. "What if I fail?"

"Just by having the courage to go after your dreams, you've already won, my dear." She drew her granddaughter into a long, tight hug. "And no matter what, I'll be here to support you."

Kate fingered the charm, then lifted her gaze to the newspaper article on the wall. Andrew seemed to be smiling his support from across the room. He would want her to do this. To move forward, and as Brody had said, quit standing still. "Thanks, Grandma."

"You're welcome. Now go for that run, and clear your head. I'll stay here and," she lifted the glass dome and snagged a peanut butter banana cupcake this time, "guard the cupcakes."

Kate laughed. She slipped the keychain into her pocket then headed out the door. A few minutes later, she had stopped at her townhouse, changed her clothes, and started toward the reservoir. The Sunday morning sunshine warmed her, and she found herself slipping into the rhythm and peace of running.

Her mind drifted to Brody and she found herself looking for him, hoping to see him running, too. The keychain bounced in her pocket, a reminder of his gift. A little luck to encourage her to take a risk.

A risk like opening a second location?

A risk like...

Opening her heart?

She rounded the bend of the reservoir, startling a flock of pigeons. They burst into flight, with a chatter of wings. The contingent of pigeons circled away, opting for greener pastures, while several settled back onto the ground in Kate's wake. She watched the ones in flight, their squat bodies becoming sleek gray missiles against the sunny fall sky.

Her steps slowed. She glanced to her right, and saw two paths. One that led toward home. One that led another direction. The opposite from the one she'd always taken. Kate drew in a breath and started running again.

The smell of braised beef filled the kitchen of Mary McKenna's Newton house. Finn, Ellie and Jiao stood in the sunroom and talked with Mary, while Brody hung back in the library and pretended to look for a book he had no intention of reading.

His attempt to show Kate he cared, that he supported her, had gone bust. He'd dropped off the package early this morning, tempted to deliver it in person, but not sure what kind of reception he'd get. After the way things had ended yesterday, he wasn't sure she ever wanted to see him again. Still, he couldn't get her out of his mind, no matter how hard he tried.

"Come join us, Brody," Ellie said to her brother-in-law. "Your grandmother's about to open a bottle of that '92 Merlot you like." She rubbed a hand over her stomach. "Though I'm sticking to apple juice for a while."

Brody waved off the offer. "I'm not in a wine mood tonight. I'll be out shortly."

Ellie sighed and leaned against the doorjamb. "You McKenna men are all the same." A soft smile stole across her face. "Stubborn, determined and impossible."

"Hey. How's that supposed to make me feel better?"

"It's not." Ellie pushed off from the door and crossed to Finn. Her pregnancy had just started to show, giving her a tiny bit of a curve to her belly. "Those are the qualities I love the most in Finn. He's like a bulldog, only cuter."

Brody laughed. "I don't know about the cute part."

"I heard what you did." Ellie paused before him. She took the book in his hands away and shoved it back on the bookshelf. "Both in Afghanistan and with Kate. I think you did the right thing."

He shook his head. "I lost her in the end. How is that the right thing?"

"You were doing what all three of you do. Protecting

her. Taking care of her. She'll realize that and come around."

"I hope so."

"She will." Ellie laid a hand on Brody's arm, the loving support of a sister-in-law who had already become an indelible part of the McKenna family tree. "And it'll all work out. A wise man once told me that the smart man lets the woman he loves go, so that when she returns, it'll be because she truly loves him." She poked a finger at his chest. "That smart man was you. That day in the coffee shop, remember?"

"I do." He and Riley had dragged Finn down there and surprised him with Ellie, all in hopes of spurring the two to work it out. Which, clearly, they had. "Thank you, Ellie."

"You're welcome."

"You're a smart woman," Brody said.

She laughed. "Well, be sure to tell Finn that."

"I think he already knows."

Ellie smiled, the same private smile that Brody had seen on Riley, Stace and Finn. The smile of someone deeply in love and happy as hell.

She gave his arm a gentle tug. "Come on, Brody, have a glass of wine with your family and have a little faith that it will all be okay."

He headed out of the library and into the hall with Ellie. "You do know I'm a doctor, right? Faith is a hard commodity to come by in a world of tests and logic."

"I know. But you're also an Irishman and if anyone trusts in luck and faith, it should be you." She gave him a grin, then stepped away and waved toward the front door.

Brody turned. Kate stood in the doorway, wearing a

T-shirt, shorts and running shoes. A fine sheen of sweat glistened on her skin. To Brody, she'd never looked more beautiful or desirable. He caught his breath.

"I'm sorry for just showing up, but…" she bit her lip and gave him a tentative version of a smile, "does that offer for a family dinner still stand?"

Joy burst in his heart and he closed the distance between them in a few short strides. "Yes, every Sunday. Two on the dot," he said, then let out a gust. "Oh, God, Kate, I wasn't sure I'd see you again."

"I got the package." She reached in her pocket and held up the keychain. It tick-tocked back and forth on her finger. "Thank you."

"You're welcome."

She turned it over in her palm, and dropped her gaze to the small green leaves. "When I got it, my first instinct was to do what I've always done. To run from the risk and the fear. And I literally did just that."

"I can tell." He grinned. "But you still look sexy, even after a run."

"I thought running would help me forget," she said, "but all I did was look for you. At every turn, at every stop. I didn't want to run around the reservoir. I wanted to run to you, Brody. And so…"

"You did." If happiness were a meter, Brody's would shoot off the charts. "I'm glad."

"You were right. I was scared. When I was a kid, I was the one who had to be the steady rudder for Andrew. And he worried about me. The two of us, taking care of each other. Our parents fought all the time and it was just…chaos. I didn't want my little brother to worry or get scared, so I became the practical, dependable one. I let him dream big, and I kept my feet firmly on the ground. Then when he died, it shook me badly. So I did what I do best, and kept those feet cemented in place. I thought if I did everything the same, no surprises, no risks, I wouldn't have to experience that kind of loss or pain again. But I was wrong. Because in the end, it cost me you."

"I'm still here, Kate." He brushed a tendril of hair off her forehead. "And I always will be."

"When you told me you'd fallen in love with me, all I could see was this big cliff and you standing beside it, asking me to jump with you. I got scared and I ran, instead of doing what I should have done."

"Which was…?"

She smiled and winnowed the gap between them, lifted her arms to wrap around his neck and raised on her tiptoes. She pressed a kiss to his lips, then drew back. "That."

"Much better than walking away." He tightened his hold on her, then kissed her back. God, he loved this woman. Loved her smile. Loved her smarts. Loved everything about her. "Much, much better."

"I got scared, because I fell in love with you, too. I found a hundred reasons not to be with you, because I couldn't believe that a man like you really existed. One who could light fireworks inside me and at the same time understand my deepest needs." She tangled her fingers in his hair and her eyes shimmered with emotion. "A real hero."

He glanced away. "That's not me."

"It is." She drew his face around until he faced her again. "You saved my brother. And you saved me. You put everyone else ahead of you and you took the risks no one else wanted to take. That's a hero to me."

He still disagreed about the real hero here, but if the woman he loved saw him as one, he wouldn't argue. To Brody, Kate was the heroic one, determined and smart, the one who had saved him from an empty life. He cupped her jaw, and ran a thumb along her chin. "I love you, Kate Spencer."

A smile burst across her face, bright as the sun. "I love you, too, Brody. I think I fell for you the minute you brought that silly basket up to the counter for your grandmother."

He chuckled. "I was too distracted by you to make a smart buying decision."

"Good thing." She grinned. She held up the key ring again. "You know, there's only one thing this ring needs now."

"What?"

"Keys to a second location. As soon as I get home, I'm calling that realtor. There will be a Nora's in every town, or at least a lot of them." She laughed.

"And I'm thinking of taking on a partner for the practice, so I can keep treating people here in Newton, but also step up my mission work."

She smiled. "Both of us, taking risks."

"Together. The best way to do it."

She laid her head against his chest. "I agree, Brody. I agree."

"The best choice I ever made was that basket. And… you." His heart, no his entire world, were complete now with Kate in his arms. He could see their future ahead, one where she brought smiles to people everywhere there was a Nora's Sweet Shop, and he healed the sick and wounded in far-flung places. There would be some compromises ahead, making both her business and his mission trips work, but Brody had no doubt they'd find a way because in the end, he and Kate had the same core values. The same goals. To create a world full of heroes. And he couldn't wait another minute to start on that path. "I meant what I said. I want to spend the rest of my life with you. Will you marry me, Kate?"

She drew in a deep breath, then exhaled it with a smile. "Yes, I will, Brody."

A burst of applause sounded from behind them. Brody turned to find Finn and Ellie, flanked by his grandmother and Jiao, all clapping and beaming their approval. "I only have one thing to say," Finn said, crossing to his middle brother. "It's about damned time."

Brody laughed. "Always direct and to the point, Finn."

Finn drew Kate into a hug, so tight she squeaked. "Welcome to the family, Kate. The McKennas are a rowdy bunch, so be prepared."

"For what?" Kate asked.

"For the happiest time of your life." He clapped Brody on the shoulder, offered the two of them congratulations, then headed for the dining room. "Now let's eat."

\* \* \* \* \*

# *Mills & Boon® Hardback*

## *September 2012*

# ROMANCE

| | |
|---|---|
| **Unlocking her Innocence** | Lynne Graham |
| **Santiago's Command** | Kim Lawrence |
| **His Reputation Precedes Him** | Carole Mortimer |
| **The Price of Retribution** | Sara Craven |
| **Just One Last Night** | Helen Brooks |
| **The Greek's Acquisition** | Chantelle Shaw |
| **The Husband She Never Knew** | Kate Hewitt |
| **When Only Diamonds Will Do** | Lindsay Armstrong |
| **The Couple Behind the Headlines** | Lucy King |
| **The Best Mistake of Her Life** | Aimee Carson |
| **The Valtieri Baby** | Caroline Anderson |
| **Slow Dance with the Sheriff** | Nikki Logan |
| **Bella's Impossible Boss** | Michelle Douglas |
| **The Tycoon's Secret Daughter** | Susan Meier |
| **She's So Over Him** | Joss Wood |
| **Return of the Last McKenna** | Shirley Jump |
| **Once a Playboy…** | Kate Hardy |
| **Challenging the Nurse's Rules** | Janice Lynn |

# MEDICAL

| | |
|---|---|
| **Her Motherhood Wish** | Anne Fraser |
| **A Bond Between Strangers** | Scarlet Wilson |
| **The Sheikh and the Surrogate Mum** | Meredith Webber |
| **Tamed by her Brooding Boss** | Joanna Neil |

0812 GEN STD HB

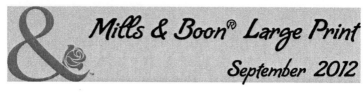

*Mills & Boon® Large Print*

*September 2012*

# ROMANCE

# HISTORICAL

# MEDICAL

## *Mills & Boon® Hardback*

### *October 2012*

# ROMANCE

| | |
|---|---|
| **Banished to the Harem** | Carol Marinelli |
| **Not Just the Greek's Wife** | Lucy Monroe |
| **A Delicious Deception** | Elizabeth Power |
| **Painted the Other Woman** | Julia James |
| **A Game of Vows** | Maisey Yates |
| **A Devil in Disguise** | Caitlin Crews |
| **Revelations of the Night Before** | Lynn Raye Harris |
| **Defying her Desert Duty** | Annie West |
| **The Wedding Must Go On** | Robyn Grady |
| **The Devil and the Deep** | Amy Andrews |
| **Taming the Brooding Cattleman** | Marion Lennox |
| **The Rancher's Unexpected Family** | Myrna Mackenzie |
| **Single Dad's Holiday Wedding** | Patricia Thayer |
| **Nanny for the Millionaire's Twins** | Susan Meier |
| **Truth-Or-Date.com** | Nina Harrington |
| **Wedding Date with Mr Wrong** | Nicola Marsh |
| **The Family Who Made Him Whole** | Jennifer Taylor |
| **The Doctor Meets Her Match** | Annie Claydon |

# MEDICAL

| | |
|---|---|
| **A Socialite's Christmas Wish** | Lucy Clark |
| **Redeeming Dr Riccardi** | Leah Martyn |
| **The Doctor's Lost-and-Found Heart** | Dianne Drake |
| **The Man Who Wouldn't Marry** | Tina Beckett |

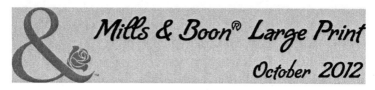

# ROMANCE

| | |
|---|---|
| **A Secret Disgrace** | Penny Jordan |
| **The Dark Side of Desire** | Julia James |
| **The Forbidden Ferrara** | Sarah Morgan |
| **The Truth Behind his Touch** | Cathy Williams |
| **Plain Jane in the Spotlight** | Lucy Gordon |
| **Battle for the Soldier's Heart** | Cara Colter |
| **The Navy SEAL's Bride** | Soraya Lane |
| **My Greek Island Fling** | Nina Harrington |
| **Enemies at the Altar** | Melanie Milburne |
| **In the Italian's Sights** | Helen Brooks |
| **In Defiance of Duty** | Caitlin Crews |

# HISTORICAL

| | |
|---|---|
| **The Duchess Hunt** | Elizabeth Beacon |
| **Marriage of Mercy** | Carla Kelly |
| **Unbuttoning Miss Hardwick** | Deb Marlowe |
| **Chained to the Barbarian** | Carol Townend |
| **My Fair Concubine** | Jeannie Lin |

# MEDICAL

| | |
|---|---|
| **Georgie's Big Greek Wedding?** | Emily Forbes |
| **The Nurse's Not-So-Secret Scandal** | Wendy S. Marcus |
| **Dr Right All Along** | Joanna Neil |
| **Summer With A French Surgeon** | Margaret Barker |
| **Sydney Harbour Hospital: Tom's Redemption** | Fiona Lowe |
| **Doctor on Her Doorstep** | Annie Claydon |

# "It's been three years. Too long to just take up where we left off."

"Not so long that I don't remember where you like to be kissed."

Surprise turned to shock when he lowered his head to touch his lips to the sensitive spot beneath her earlobe, slowly sliding them to the hollow of her throat.

His voice vibrated against her skin. "How you like to be kissed."

"Chase, stop." A delicious shiver snaked its way down her body before he lifted his head to stare into her eyes. "We—"

His mouth dropped to hers and, despite part of her brain protesting that a kiss between them just complicated things, her eyes slid closed. The soft warmth of his lips sent her spiralling back to all the times they'd sneaked kisses between patients, celebrating successful outcomes, or held each other in wordless comfort when a patient was lost. To all the times they'd tramped in the mountains and made love anywhere that seemed inviting.

Apparently her hands had their own memories, slipping up his chest to cup the back of his neck, his soft hair tickling her fingers. *He's right.* The vague thought flitted through her head as his wide palm slid between her shoulderblades, pressing her body closer as he deepened the kiss. It had been very, *very* good between them. Until it hadn't.

**Dear Reader**

When I decided to write a Medical Romance™ set in an exotic place Benin, West Africa, was an easy choice. I could still see the gripping photographs my husband had taken when he worked in a mission hospital there some years ago, and enjoyed hearing his account of the months he was there. It was interesting learning more about Benin and thinking about the kinds of people who dedicate their lives to medical work there and elsewhere.

My story's hero is Dr Chase Bowen, who grew up in mission hospitals and is now dedicated to his patients and to the work he considers his calling. Because he knows from experience that it isn't safe for non-native children in the countries where he works, Chase believes having a family of his own isn't an option. Until Dr Danielle Sheridan returns to his life, bringing with her the son he didn't know he had.

Danielle believed she was doing the best thing for her son, keeping him a secret, since Chase had made it clear he never wanted children. Now that Chase knows, can they make a new relationship work with the challenges of their careers and fears? Chase wants marriage, but Dani isn't convinced. Then a terrifying event challenges them both.

I hope you enjoy reading CHANGED BY HIS SON'S SMILE as much as I enjoyed writing it!

*Robin Gianna*

# CHANGED BY
# HIS SON'S SMILE

BY
ROBIN GIANNA

Published in Great Britain 2014
by Mills & Boon, an imprint of Harlequin (UK) Limited,
Eton House, 18-24 Paradise Road, Richmond, Surrey, TW9 1SR

© 2014 Robin Gianakopoulos

ISBN: 978 0 263 24360 4

Printed
by

After completing a degree in journalism, working in the advertising industry, then becoming a stay-at-home mum, **Robin Gianna** had what she calls her mid-life awakening. She decided she wanted to write the romance novels she'd loved since her teens, and embarked on that quest by joining RWA, studying the craft, and obsessively reading and writing.

Robin loves pushing her characters to grow until they're ready for their happily-ever-afters. When she's not writing, Robin's life is filled with a happily messy kitchen, a needy garden, a tolerant husband, three great kids, a drooling bulldog and one grouchy Siamese cat.

To learn more about her work, visit her website, www.RobinGianna.com.

**CHANGED BY HIS SON'S SMILE
is Robin Gianna's debut title**

## Dedication

To George, my own doctor hero husband.
Thank you for supporting me in my writing dream,
for answering my endless medical questions, and for
putting up with the piles of books and pens and papers
and Post-it® notes that clutter our house. I love you.

## Acknowledgments

For me, it takes a village to write a Medical Romance™!

Many thanks to:

Kevin Hackett, MD and Betsy Hackett, RN, DSN, for
tolerating my frantic phone calls and hugely assisting me.
SO appreciate the awesome scene, Kevin!

My lovely sister-in-law, Trish Connor, MD,
for her great ideas and help.

Critique partner, writer friend, and pediatric emergency
physician Meta Carroll, MD, for double-checking scenes
for accuracy. You're wonderful!

The many writer friends I can't begin to thank enough,
especially Sheri, Natalie, Susan and Margaret. Without
you, my bootstraps might still be laying on the floor.

My agent, Cori Deyoe of 3 Seas Literary Agency,
for her tireless assistance with everything.

# CHAPTER ONE

THE POOR WOMAN might not be able to have more babies, but at least she wasn't dead.

Chase Bowen's patient stared at him with worry etched on her face as she slowly awakened from surgery.

He leaned closer, giving her a reassuring smile. "It's okay now. You're going to be fine," Chase said in Fon, the most common language in The Republic of Benin, West Africa. If she didn't understand, he'd try again in French.

She nodded, and the deep, warm gratitude in her gaze filled his chest with an intense gratitude of his own. Times like these strengthened his appreciation for the life he had. He couldn't imagine doing anything else.

Chase understood why, despite their family tragedy, his parents still spent their lives doctoring the neediest of humankind.

"Her vital signs are all normal, Dr. Bowen," the nurse anesthetist said. "Thank God. I've never seen hemoglobin as rock bottom as hers."

"Yeah. Ten more minutes and it probably would've been too late."

He pressed his fingers to her pulse once more and took a deep breath of satisfaction. Ectopic pregnancy from pelvic inflammatory scarring was all too frequent in this part of the world, with polygamy and the diseases that came with that culture being commonplace. He'd feared this was one of the patients who wouldn't make it.

There'd been too many close calls lately, and Chase tried to think what else they could do about that. Their group had an ongoing grass-roots approach, trying to encourage patients to come in before their conditions were critical. But people weren't used to relying on modern medicine to heal them. Not to mention that patients sometimes had to walk miles just to get there.

"Will there be more babies?" the woman whispered.

He couldn't tell if the fear in her voice was because she wanted more children, or because she didn't want to go through such an ordeal again.

"We had to close off the tube that had the baby in it," he said, gentling his voice. "But you still have another tube, so you can probably conceive another baby, if you want one."

Whether she was fertile or not, Chase didn't know. But the children she did have still had their mother. He squeezed her hand and smiled. "Your little ones who came with you looked pretty worried. Soon you'll be strong enough to go home, and they'll be very happy to have their *maman* again."

A smile touched her lips as her eyelids drifted shut. Chase left her in the capable hands of the nurse anesthetist and stripped off his gown to head outside. Moist heat wrapped around him like a soft, cottony glove as he stepped from the air-conditioned cement-block building that made do as the clinic and O.R. for the local arm of Global Physicians Coalition.

Dusk still kept that particular inch of sub-Saharan West Africa bathed in low light at nine-thirty p.m., and he didn't bother to pull his penlight from his pocket. The generators would be turned off soon, and the growl of his stomach reminded him he hadn't eaten a thing since lunch. Finding dinner in the dark was a crap shoot, so a quick trip to the kitchen had to happen before the lights went out.

He strode around the corner of the building and nearly plowed down Trent Dalton.

"Whoa, you off to save another life?" Trent said, stumbling a few steps. "I heard your patient's sister calling you '*mon héros*.' I'm jealous."

"I'm pretty sure you've been called a hero once or twice, deserved or not," Chase said.

"Not by such a pretty young thing. I recall it coming from an elderly man, which didn't stroke my needy ego quite as much."

Chase snorted. "Well, thank the Lord the pregnant sister was my patient instead of yours. Your ego would explode if it got any bigger."

"I'm confident, not egotistical," Trent said, slapping Chase on the back. "Let's see what there is to eat. I've gotta get some food before I have to scrounge for a coconut by the side of the road."

"With any luck, Spud still has something in there for us."

"No chance of that. He left a while ago to pick up the new doc who just arrived from the States."

Spud wasn't even here? Chase's stomach growled louder as he realized the chances of finding anything halfway decent to eat was looking less likely by the minute.

The place would doubtless fall apart without Spud Jones, the go-to guy who cooked, ordered all the sup-

plies, transported everyone everywhere and pretty much
ran the place.

"How come I didn't know there was a new doc coming?" Chase said as they walked toward the main building.

"Well, if you weren't wrapped up in your own little world, maybe you'd enjoy more of the gossip around
here."

"Do you know who he is?"

"Not a he. A she. A very pretty she, according to
Spud," Trent said. "Thank God. As a constant compan-
ion, you're not only the wrong gender, you're dull as
hell. We're overdue for some new female beauty to spice
things up around here."

"We? You mean you," Chase said with a grin. "There's
a reason Dr. Trent Dalton is known as the Coalition Casanova."

"Hey, all work and no play makes life all work." His
light blue eyes twinkled. "She's coming to finally get
electronic clinic records set up on all the kids. I can't
wait to offer my suggestions and assistance."

Chase laughed. As they neared the building, the sight
of a Land Rover heading their way came into view within
a cloud of dust on the road. Chances were good he'd
worked with the new doctor before. The Global Physicians Coalition was a fairly small group, and most were
great people. Medical workers who saw mission work as
a calling, not just an occupation.

The sound of the Land Rover's engine choked to a stop
just out of sight in front of the building, and Trent turned
to him with a smile of pure mischief. "And here's my lat-
est conquest arriving now. What a lucky lady."

Trent took off towards the front doors and Chase followed more slowly, shaking his head with an exasper-

ated smile. One of these days Trent's way of charming
the pants off women then leaving them flat with a smile
and a wave was going to catch up with him. Not that his
own record with females was much better.

"*Bon soir*, lovely lady. Welcome to paradise."

Trent's voice drifted across the air, along with Spud's
chuckle and a few more words from Trent that Chase
didn't catch.

Feminine laughter froze Chase in mid-step. A bubbly,
joyous sound so distinctive, so familiar, so rapturous that
his breath caught, knowing it couldn't be her. Knowing
he shouldn't want it to be her. Knowing that he'd blown
it all to hell when he'd last seen her anyway.

Without intent or permission, his feet headed towards
the sound and the headlights of the dusty Land Rover.
Shadowy figures stood next to it, and he could see Trent
taking the new arrival's bulky shoulder bag from her.
Spud was obviously introducing the two, with Trent giving her his usual too-familiar embrace.

Chase had to fight the sudden urge to run forward,
yank Trent loose, and tell him to keep his hands off.

He hadn't needed to see the curly blonde halo glowing
in the twilight to know it was her. To see that beautiful,
crazy hair pulled into the messy ponytail that was so right
for the woman who owned it. A visual representation of
impulsive, exuberant, unforgettable Danielle Sheridan.

Chase stared at her across the short expanse of earth,
his heart beating erratically as though he'd suddenly developed atrial fibrillation.

He'd always figured they'd run into one another again
someday on some job somewhere in the world. But he
hadn't figured on it stopping his heart and shortening
his breath. Three years was a long time. Too long to still

be affected this way, and he didn't want to think about what that meant.

She was dressed in her usual garb—khaki shorts that showed off her toned legs and a slim-fitting green T-shirt that didn't attempt to hide her slender curves. In the process of positioning another bag on her shoulder, it seemed she felt his gaze and lifted her head. Their eyes met, and the vibrant, iridescent blue of hers shone through the near darkness, stabbing straight into his gut.

Her big smile faded and her expression froze. A look flickered across her face that didn't seem to be just a reflection of what he was feeling. The feeling that it would've been better if they hadn't been stuck working together again. Bringing back memories of hot passion and cold goodbyes.

No, it was more than that. The same shock he felt was accompanied by very obvious dismay. Horror, even. No happy reunion happening here, he guessed. Obviously, the way they'd parted three years ago had not left her with warm and fuzzy feelings toward him. Or even cool and aloof ones.

"Chase! Come meet your new cohort in crime," Spud said.

He moved closer to the car on legs suddenly gone leaden. Dani's heart-shaped face wore an expression of near panic. She bent down to peer into the backseat of the Land Rover then bobbed back up, their eyes meeting again.

"Danielle, this is Dr. Chase Bowen," Spud said as he heaved her duffle. "Chase, Dr. Danielle Sheridan."

"Dani and I have met," Chase said. And wasn't that an absurd understatement? They'd worked together for over a year in Honduras. The same year they'd made love nearly every day. Within warm waterfalls, on green mountain meadows, in sagging bunk beds.

The year Dani had told him she wanted to make it permanent, to have a family with him. For very good reasons, a family couldn't happen for Chase, and he'd told her so. The next day she'd left the compound.

All those intense and mixed-up memories hung in the air between them, strangely intimate despite the presence of Trent and Spud. Suddenly in motion, she surprised him by moving fast, stepping around the hood of the car in a near jog straight towards him, thrusting her hand into his in a brusque, not-very-Dani-like way.

"Chase. It's been a while. How've you been?"

Her polite tone sounded strained, and he'd barely squeezed her soft hand before she yanked it loose.

"Good. I've been good." Maybe not so good. As he stared into the blue of her eyes, he remembered how much he'd missed her when she'd left. More than missed her sunny smile, her sweet face, her beautiful body.

But he'd known it had been best for both of them. If a family was what she wanted, she should marry a guy rooted in the States. No point in connecting herself to a wandering medic who wouldn't have the least idea how to stay within the confines of a white picket fence.

Apparently, though, she hadn't found husband and father material, because here she was in Africa. The woman who had burrowed under his skin like a guinea worm, and he had a bad feeling that her arrival would start that persistent itch all over again.

"Dani," Spud called from across the car, "I'm going to take your duffle to your quarters, then be back to help you get—"

"Great, thanks," Dani interrupted brightly. "I appreciate it."

She turned back to Chase, and he noted the trapped, almost scared look in her eyes. Was the thought of having to work with him again that horrible?

"I thought the GPC website said you were in Senegal," Dani said. "Are you...staying here?"

"No, just stopped in for a little day tour of the area."

The twist of her lips showed she got his sarcasm loud and clear. What, she hoped he was about to grab a cab and head to the next tourist destination? He couldn't remember Dani ever saying dumb things before. In fact, she was one of the smartest pediatricians he'd had the opportunity to work with over the years. One of the smartest docs, period.

"Well. I..." Her voice faded away and she licked her lips. Sexy, full lips he'd loved to kiss. Tempting lips that had been one of the first things he'd noticed about her when they'd first met.

"So-o-o," Trent said, looking at Dani, then Chase, then back at Dani again with raised brows. "Chase and I were about to have a late dinner and a beer. Are you hungry?"

"No, thanks, I had snacks in the car. You two go on and eat, I'm sure you're starved after a long day of clinic and surgeries." She put on a bright and very fake smile. "I'll get the low-down on the routine around here tomorrow. Right now I'm just going to have Spud show me my room and get settled in. Bye."

She walked back to the other side of the Land Rover and then just stood there, hovering, practically willing them to leave. Well, if she wanted to act all weird about the two of them being thrown together again, that was fine by him.

"Come on," he said to Trent as he moved towards the kitchen. While his appetite had somehow evaporated, a beer sounded damned good.

"Mommy!"

The sound of a muffled little voice floated across the sultry air, and Chase again found himself stopping dead. He slowly turned to see Dani leaning into the back of the Land Rover. To watch, stunned, as she pulled a small child out through the open door and perched him on her hip.

Guess he'd been wrong about her finding husband and father material. And pretty damned fast after she'd left.

"Mommy, are we there yet?" The sleepy, sweet-faced boy of about two and a half wrapped his arms around her neck and pressed his cheek to her shoulder. A boy who didn't have blue eyes and crazy, curly blond hair like the woman holding him.

No, he had dark hair that was straight, waving just a bit at the ends. A little over-long, it brushed across eyebrows that framed brown eyes fringed with thick, dark lashes. A boy who looked exactly like the photos Chase's mother had hauled all around the world and propped up in every one of the places they'd lived. Photos of him and his brother when they were toddlers.

Impossible.

But as he stared at the child then slowly lifted his gaze to Dani's, the obvious truth choked off his breath and smacked him like a sledgehammer to the skull. He didn't have to do the math or see the resemblance. The expression in her eyes and on her face told him everything.

He had a son. A child she hadn't bothered to tell him about. A child she had the nerve, the stupidity to take on a medical mission to a developing country. Something he was adamantly against...and for good reason.

"I guess...we need to talk," Dani said, glancing down at the child in her arms. She looked back at Chase with a mix of guilt, frustration and resignation flitting across her face. "But let's...let's do it tomorrow. I'm beat, and I need to get Andrew settled in, get him something to eat."

"Andrew." The name came slowly from his lips. It couldn't be a coincidence that Andrew was his own middle name. Anger began to burn in his gut. Hot, scorching anger that overwhelmed the shock and disbelief that had momentarily paralyzed him. She'd named the boy after him, but hadn't thought it necessary to even let him know the kid existed?

"No, Dani." It took every ounce of self-control to keep his voice fairly even, to not shout out the fury roaring through his blood and pounding in his head. "I'm thinking a conversation is in order right this second. One more damned minute is too long, even though you thought three years wasn't long enough."

"Chase, I—"

"Okay, here's the plan," Trent said, stepping forward and placing his hand on Chase's shoulder. "I'll take Andrew to the kitchen, if he'll let me. Spud and I'll rustle up some food. You two catch up and meet us in the kitchen in a few."

Trent reached for the boy with one of his famously charming smiles. Andrew smiled back but still clung to Dani's neck like a liana vine.

"It's okay, Drew," Dani said in a soothing voice as she stroked the dark hair from the child's forehead. "Dr. Trent is going to get you something yummy to eat, and Mommy will be right there in just a minute."

"Believe it or not, Drew, I bet we can find some ice cream. And I also bet you like candy. The kids we treat here sure do."

The doubtful little frown that had formed a crease between the child's brows lifted. Apparently he had a sweet tooth, as he untwined his arms from Dani and leaned towards Trent.

"And you know what else? It's going to be like a camp-out in the kitchen, 'coz the lights are going out soon and we'll have lanterns instead. Pretty cool, huh?"

Andrew nodded and grinned, his worries apparently soothed by the sweet adventure Trent promised.

Trent kept talking as he walked away with the child, but Chase no longer listened. He focused entirely on the woman in front of him. The deceiving, lying woman he'd never have dreamed would keep such an important thing a secret from him.

"I want to hear it from your lips. Is Andrew my son?" He knew, *knew* the answer deep in his gut but wanted to hear it just the same.

"Yes." She reached out to rest her palm against his biceps. "Chase, I want you to understand—"

He pushed her hand from his arm. "I understand just fine. I understand that you lied to me. That you thought it would be okay to let him grow up without a father. That you brought *my son* to *Africa*, not caring at all about the risks to him. What is wrong with you that you would do all that?"

The guilt and defensiveness in her posture and expression faded into her own anger, sparking off her in waves.

"You didn't want a family, remember? When I told you I wanted to marry, for us to have a family together, you said a baby was the last thing you would ever want. So, what, I should have said, 'Gosh, that's unfortunate because I'm pregnant'? The last thing *I* would ever want is for my child to know his father would consider him a huge mistake. So I left."

"*Planning* to have a child is a completely different thing from this and you know it." How could she not have realized he'd always honor his responsibilities? He'd done that every damned day of his life and wasn't about to stop now. "What were you going to do when he was old enough to ask about his father? Did it never occur to you that if his dad wasn't around to be a part of his life, he'd feel that anyway? That he'd think his father didn't love him? Didn't want him?"

"I…I don't know." Her shoulders slumped and she looked at the ground. "I just… I know what it's like to have a father consider you a burden, and I didn't want that for him. I thought I could love him enough for both of us."

The sadness, the pain in her posture stole some of his anger, and he forced himself into a calmer state, to take a mental step back. To try to see it all from her perspective.

He *had* been adamant that children wouldn't, couldn't, fit into his life, ever. He'd learned long ago how dangerous it could be for non-native children in the countries where he worked. Where his parents worked. He couldn't take that risk.

So when she'd proposed marriage and a family, he'd practically laughed. Now, knowing the real situation, he didn't want to remember his cold response that had left no room for conversation or compromise.

No wonder she'd left.

She lifted her gaze to his, her eyes moist. "I'm sorry. I should have told you."

"Yes. You should have told me." He heaved in a deep breath then slowly expelled it. "But I guess I can understand why you didn't."

"So." She gave him a shadow of her usual sunny smile. "We're here. You know. He's still young enough that he won't think anything of being told you're his daddy. My contract here is for eight months, so you'll have a nice amount of time to spend with him."

Did she honestly think he was going to spend a few months with the boy and leave it completely up to her how—and where—his son was raised?

"Yes, I will. Because I accept your marriage proposal."

# CHAPTER TWO

"EXCUSE ME?" DANI asked, sure she must have heard wrong.

"Your marriage proposal. I accept."

"My marriage proposal?" Astonished, she searched the deep brown of Chase's eyes for a sign that he was kidding, but the golden flecks in them glinted with determination. "You can't be serious."

"I assure you I've never been more serious."

"We haven't even seen each other for three years!"

"We were good together then. And we have a child who bonds us together now. So I accept your offer of marriage."

The intensely serious expression on his face subdued the nervous laugh that nearly bubbled from her throat. Chase had always been stubborn and tenacious about anything important to him, and that obviously hadn't changed. She tried for a joking tone. "I'm pretty sure a marriage proposal has a statute of limitations. Definitely less than three years. The offer no longer stands."

"Damn it, Dani, I get it that it's been a long time." He raked his hand through his hair. "That maybe it seems like a crazy idea. But you have to admit that all of this is crazy. That we have a child together is...crazy."

"I understand this is a shock, that we have things to

figure out." Three years had passed, but she still clearly remembered how shaken she'd been when she'd realized she was pregnant. Chase obviously felt that way now. Maybe even more, since Andrew was now here in the flesh. "But you must know that marriage is an extreme solution."

"Hey, it was your idea to begin with, remember? You've persuaded me." A slight smile tilted his mouth. "Besides, it's not extreme. A child should have two parents. Don't you care about Andrew's well-being?"

Now, there was an insulting question. Why did he think she'd left in the first place? "Lots of children are raised by unmarried parents. He'll know you're his father. We'll work out an agreement so you can spend plenty of time with him. But you and I don't even know each other any more."

Yet, as she said the words, it felt like a lie. She looked at the familiar planes of his ruggedly handsome face and the years since she'd left Honduras faded away, as though they'd never been apart. As though she should just reach for his hand to stroll to the kitchen, fingers entwined. Put together a meal and eat by candlelight as they so often had, sometimes finishing and sometimes finding themselves teasing and laughing and very distracted from all thoughts of food.

A powerful wave of all those memories swept through her with both pain and longing. Memories of what had felt like endless days of perfection and happiness. Both ridiculous and dangerous, because there was good reason why a relationship between them hadn't been made for the long haul.

Perhaps he sensed the jumbled confusion of her emotions as his features softened as he spoke, his lips no longer flattened into a hard line. "I'm the same man you proposed to three years ago."

"Are you?" Apparently his memory of that proposal was different from hers. "Then you're the same man who didn't want kids, ever. Who said your life as a mission doctor was not just what you did but who you were, and children didn't fit into that life. Well, I have a child so you're obviously not the right husband for me."

His expression hardened again, his jaw jutting mulishly. "Except your child is *my* child, which changes things. I'm willing to compromise. To adjust my schedule to be with the two of you in the States part of the year."

"Well, that's big of you. Except I have commitments to work outside the States, too." For a man with amazing empathy for his patients, he could be incredibly dense and self-absorbed. "We should just sit down, look at our schedules for after the eight months I'm here and see if we can often work near enough to one another that you can see Drew when you have time off."

"I will not have my son living with the kinds of dangers Africa and other places expose him to."

"You grew up living all over the world and you turned out just fine." More than fine. From the moment she'd met him she'd known he was different. Compassionate and giving. Funny and irreverent. Book smart and street smart.

The most fascinating man she'd ever known.

The unyielding intensity in his eyes clouded for a moment before he flicked her a look filled with cool determination. "I repeat—my son needs to grow up safe in the States until he's older. Getting married is the most logical course of action. We figure out how to make our medical careers work with you anchored in the U.S. and me working there part of the year. Then we bring him on missions when he's an older teen."

"Well, now you've touched on my heart's desire. A marriage founded on a logical course of action." She laughed in sheer disbelief and to hide the tiny bruising of hurt she should no longer feel. "You've got it all figured out, and you haven't even spent one minute with him. Or with me. So, I repeat—I'm not marrying you."

Frustration and anger narrowed his gaze before he turned and strode a short distance away to stare at the dark outline of the horizon, fisting his hands at his hips, his broad shoulders stiff. In spite of the tension simmering between them, she found herself riveted by the sight of his tall, strong body silhouetted in the twilight. The body she'd always thought looked like it should belong to a star athlete, not a doctor.

She tried to shake off the vivid memories that bombarded her, including how much she'd loved touching all those hard muscles covered in smooth skin. All the memories of how crazy she'd been about him, period. Three light-hearted years ago the differences they now faced hadn't existed. Serious differences in how Andrew should be raised, and she still had no proof that Chase wouldn't be as resentful in his reluctant role as father as her own parent had been.

Now that Chase would be involved in Andrew's life, she had to make sure her son never felt the barbed sting of being unwanted.

Tearing her gaze from his stiff and motionless form, she turned to find Andrew and get him settled in. Chase must have heard her movement as he suddenly spun and strode purposefully towards her.

The fierce intensity in his dark eyes sent an alarm clanging in her brain. What was coming next she didn't know, but her instincts warned her to get ready for it. He closed the inches between them and grasped her waist in his strong hands, tugging her tightly against his hard body.

A squeak of surprise popped from her lips as the breath squeezed from her lungs.

This she was definitely not ready for.

His thick, dark lashes were half-lowered over his brown eyes, and her heart pounded at the way he looked at her. With determined purpose and simmering passion.

"I remember a little about your heart and your desire." His warm breath feathered across her mouth. "I remember how good it was between us. How good it can be again."

She pressed her hands against his firm chest but didn't manage to put an inch between them. Her heart thumped with both alarm and ridiculous excitement. "It's been three years. Too long to just take up where we left off."

"Not so long that I don't remember where you like to be kissed."

Surprise turned to shock when he lowered his head to touch his lips to the sensitive spot beneath her earlobe, slowly sliding them to the hollow of her throat, his voice vibrating against her skin. "How you like to be kissed."

"Chase, stop." A delicious shiver snaked its way down her body before he lifted his head to stare into her eyes. "We—"

His mouth dropped to hers and, despite the part of her brain protesting that a kiss between them just complicated things, her eyes slid closed. The soft warmth of his lips sent her spiraling back to all the times they'd sneaked kisses between patients, celebrating successful outcomes, or held each other in wordless comfort when a patient had been lost. To all the times they'd tramped in the mountains and made love anywhere that had seemed inviting.

Apparently, her hands had their own memories, slipping up his chest to cup the back of his neck, his soft hair tickling her fingers. *He's right.* The vague thought flitted through her head as his wide palm slid between her shoulder blades, pressing her body closer as he deepened the kiss. It had been very, very good between them. Until it hadn't been.

Through her sensual fog the thought helped her remember what a strategic man Chase could be. That this wasn't unchecked, remembered passion but a calculated effort to weaken her resolve, to have her give in to his marriage demand.

She broke the kiss. "This isn't a good idea."

"Yes, it is." His warm mouth caressed her jaw. "I've missed you. I think you've missed me, too."

"Why would I miss being dragged out of bed to do calisthenics at six a.m.?" The words came out annoyingly breathy.

"But you missed being dragged into bed for another kind of exercise."

His mouth again covered hers, sweet and insistent and drugging. One hand slipped down her hip and cupped her bottom, pulling her close against his hardened body.

He'd always teased her about how she couldn't resist his touch, his kiss. A pathetically hungry little sound filled her throat as she sank in deeper, doing a very good job proving he'd been right.

*But that was before,* her sanity whispered.

Yanking her mouth determinedly from his, she dragged in a deep, quivering breath. "This won't work. I know your devious strategies too well."

His lips curved and his dark eyes sparked with liquid

gold. "I think you're wrong. I think it's working." He lifted one hand to press his fingers to her throat. "Your pulse is tachycardic and your breath is all choppy. Both clear indications of sexual desire."

"Thanks for the physiology lesson." She shoved hard at his chest to put a few inches between them and felt his own heart pounding beneath her hands. At least she wasn't the only one feeling the heat. "But memories of good sex do not make a relationship. And definitely not a marriage."

"So we make new memories." His big hands cupped her face as his mouth joined hers again, and for a brief moment she just couldn't resist. Softening, yielding to the seductive, soft heat of his kiss, to the feel of his thumbs feathering across her cheekbones, until her brain yelled his words of three years ago. That, despite what he said now, marriage and a family were the last things he ever wanted.

She couldn't let him see the pathetic weakness for him that obviously still lurked inside her. She had to stay strong for Andrew.

The thought gave her the will to pull away completely and shake the thick haze from her brain, ignoring the hot tingle of her lips. "This is not a good idea," she said again, more firmly this time. "Our...relationship...needs to be based on logic, just like you said. None of this to muddy things up."

"You used to like things muddied up."

The teasing half-smile and glint in his eyes made her want to kiss him and wallop him all at the same time. "I need to rescue Trent. You can meet Andrew, but I don't want to tell him about...you...tonight. Let him spend a little time with you first."

"So long as you understand this conversation isn't over."

Conversation? Was that what they'd been having? "I'd

forgotten what a prince complex you have, bossing everyone around."

She headed in the direction Trent and Andrew had disappeared, relieved to be back on stable ground without the confusion of his touch, his kiss. Then realized she hadn't a clue where they'd gone. "Where is the kitchen anyway?"

Chase strode forward with the loose, athletic stride she'd always enjoyed. As though he was in no hurry to get where he was going but still covered the ground with remarkable speed.

"This way."

His warm palm pressed her lower back again as he pulled a penlight from his pocket, shining it on the ground in front of her. "Watch your step. Rocks sometimes appear as though they rolled there themselves."

As they walked in the starlight, the whole thing felt surreal. The heat of his hand on her back, the timbre of his voice, the same small, worn penlight illuminating the dusty path. As though the years hadn't passed and they were back in Honduras again, feeling close and connected. She stared fixedly at the uneven path, determined to resist the gravitational pull that was Chase Bowen.

Chase shoved open a door and slipped his arm around her waist, tucking her close to his side as he led her down a short hallway. Quickly, she shook off his touch.

"Stop," she hissed. "Drew needs to get to know you without your hands all over me."

"Sorry. It's so nice to touch you again, I keep forgetting." He raised his palms to the sky, the picture of innocent surrender, and she again had the urge to punch the man who obviously knew all too well how easily he could mess with her equilibrium.

Several camp lights dully lit the room, showing Drew

sitting at a high metal table, his legs dangling from a tall stool. The low light didn't hide the melted ice cream covering the child's face from the tip of his nose down, dripping from his chin.

"Hi, Mommy!" He flashed her a wide grin and raised the soggy cone as if in a toast, chocolate oozing between his fingers. "Dis ice cream is good!"

"I can see that." She nearly laughed at the guilty look on Trent's face as Drew began to lap all around the cone, sending rivulets down his arm to his elbow.

"I'll clean him up." Trent waved his hand towards Drew, looking a little helpless. "Didn't see the point of it until he was done."

"Don't worry, making messes is what Drew does best," she said, giving Trent a reassuring smile. "Right, honey?"

"Wight!" Drew shoved his mouth into the cone, and the softened ice cream globbed onto the table. He promptly dropped his face to slurp it straight from the flat metal surface then swirled his tongue, making circles in the melty chocolate.

"Okay, no licking the table." Chase probably thought she'd never taught the boy manners. Hastily, she walked over to lift his wet, sticky chin with her palm. "Finish your cone, then we'll find out where we're sleeping. And you'd better do it quick, 'coz it's about to become all cream without the ice part."

"You know, Drew," Chase said in a jocular tone that sounded a little forced, "when you stick your tongue out like that, you look like a lizard. We have big ones around here. Maybe tomorrow we'll look for one."

Drew's eyes lit and he paused his licking to look up at Chase. "Lizards?"

"Yep. Maybe we'll catch one to keep for a day or two.

Find bugs to feed it." Chase moved from the sink with two wet cloths in his hands. His thick shoulder pressed against Dani's as he efficiently wiped the chocolaty table with one cloth then handed it to Trent, whose expression was a comical combination of amusement and disgust.

Chase lifted the other cloth to Drew's mouth, his gaze suddenly riveted on the little boy's face. *Their* baby's face. Still cupping Drew's chin in her hand, Dani stared at Chase. Every emotion crossed his face that she'd long imagined might be there if he knew about his son. Within the shadowy light she imagined that through all those mixed emotions it wasn't horror that shone through but joy. Or was that just wishful thinking?

Her breath caught, remembering how many times in the past two and a half years she'd thought about what this moment might be like. After the miracle of Drew as a newborn and when he'd cried through the night. When he'd first smiled. Crawled. Run.

Her throat closed and she fought back silly tears that stung the backs of her eyes as Chase lifted his gaze to hers, wonder filling his.

The sound of Trent clearing his throat broke the strange spell that seemed to have frozen the moment in time.

"I'm going to head to my room, you three. See you in the a.m.," Trent said, smiling at Drew.

Heat filled Dani's face. "I appreciate you getting him the ice cream. I don't think there's much doubt he enjoyed it."

"Yeah, thanks, Trent." Chase and he exchanged a look and a nod before Trent took off, and Dani could see the two of them were good friends. Something that often happened when working in the GPC community, but not always. Occasionally personalities just didn't mesh and a strictly professional relationship became the best outcome.

Then there were those rare times that an intimate relationship took over your whole world.

"I think this one's done, Lizard-Boy," Chase said, taking what remained of the soggy cone and tossing it in the trash. He took over the clean-up with an efficiency that implied he'd had dozens of children in his life, wiping Drew's hands then pulling Dani's hand from her son's chin, about to take care of his gooey face, too.

The frown on Drew's face as he stared at the stranger washing his face while his mother stood motionless snapped her out of her stupor.

She tugged the cloth from Chase's hand and took over. "I'm not sure if you ate the cone, or the cone ate you," she said lightly. She rinsed it again, along with her own sticky hand, before dabbing at the last spots on Drew's face.

"Dat's enough, Mommy." Drew yanked his head away as she tried for one last swipe of his chin.

Spud poked his head into the kitchen. "Everything's ready, if you are, Dani. Tomorrow Ruth is coming to meet both of you and take care of Drew while we give you the low-down around here."

"Great. Thanks." She lifted Drew onto her hip and turned to Chase, inhaling a fortifying breath. "We'll see you tomorrow."

"Yes." His gaze lingered on Drew. When he finally looked at Dani, his eyes were hooded and his expression serious. "Tomorrow will be a big day."

Dani awoke to a cool draft, and she realized Drew was in the process of yanking off her bed sheet.

"Hey, you, that's not nice. I'm sleeping."

No way could it be morning already. She pulled the covers back to her chin but Drew tugged harder.

"Get up. I hungry."

She peeled open one eye. From the crack visible between the curtains, it looked like the sun had barely risen above the horizon. "It's too early to be hungry."

"Uh-uh. My tummy monsters are growling."

Even through her sleep-dulled senses Dani had to smile. Drew loved the idea of feeding the "monsters" that growled in his stomach. "What color monster's in there today?"

"Blue. And green. Wif big teeth."

He tugged again. Dani sighed and gave up on the idea of more sleep. Doubtless both their body clocks were off, and no wonder. Sleeping on a plane was something she never managed to do well, but Drew had conked out both on the plane and in the car, and she'd been amazed he'd slept at all once he'd got into bed.

"All right. Let's see what there is to eat."

She threw on some clothes but left Drew in his Spiderman pajamas. It took a minute to remember which door led to the kitchen, and she hesitated in the hallway. Getting it wrong and ending up in someone's bedroom was an embarrassment she didn't need. Cautiously, she cracked open the door, relieved to see a refrigerator instead of a sexy, sleeping Chase Bowen.

"Let's see what your monster wants," she said, pushing the door wide as she nudged Drew inside. To her surprise, Trent was sitting at the table, sipping coffee and reading.

"When I took this job, no one told me the hours here were dawn to dusk," Dani joked as she plopped Drew onto the same stool he'd sat on the night before.

"Spud's a slave driver, I tell you," Trent said with an exaggerated sigh. "Actually, I just finished up an emergency surgery. Clinic hours don't usually start until nine. Coffee?"

He started to get up, but she waved her hand when she spied the percolator on the counter. "Thanks, I'll grab it myself." Last night, the darkness had obscured most of the kitchen, but this morning showed it to be big and functional, if a bit utilitarian.

"So, do you and Chase share a room?" As soon as the words left her mouth she wondered why in the world she'd asked. She stared into her cup as she poured, heat filling her face at the look of impassive assessment Trent gave her in response.

"No. The medical workers used to stay with families nearby, but they built the sleeping quarters you're in a couple years ago, with small rooms for everyone."

"Oh. Can you tell me where there's oatmeal or something for Drew?"

"Top cupboard on the left. Spud fixes breakfast around eight. Chase runs every morning." He leaned his back against the table and sipped his coffee. "But you probably know that."

She did know. The man was a physical fitness nut. "How long have you worked with Chase?"

"We've worked together in the Philippines and Ghana. Been here a year. Both our commissions are up, but we're hanging around until there are other surgeons here and we get new assignments."

Did that mean Chase might not be here long? A sharp pang of dismay stabbed at her, which was both ridiculous and disturbing. Shouldn't she feel relief instead? It would be so much better for Drew if Chase moved on before the two got too close.

"Mommy, I need food," Drew said, fidgeting on his stool.

Lord, she had to be sure this whole mess didn't distract her from the work she'd come to Africa to do. If she couldn't even get Drew's breakfast going, she was in serious trouble.

In a sign that their new, temporary home was practically made for her and Drew, two of his favorite foods sat in the cupboard. Dani microwaved the apple-flavored oatmeal and opened a box of raisins.

Trent got up and pulled some construction paper and crayons from a drawer to place them in front of Drew, poking a finger at his pajama top. "While your mom gets your breakfast, how about drawing me a picture of Spiderman climbing a wall?"

Wow, the man sure knew kids, and she wondered what Trent's story was. Just as she was about to ask, he beat her to the questions.

"So, obviously you and Chase go back a while. Where did you meet?"

"Honduras." Back then, her expectations for mission work had been so starry-eyed and naive. And the last thing she'd expected was to meet a hunky, dynamic doctor who'd knocked her socks off. Among other things.

Apparently, Trent expected more than a one-word answer, looking at her speculatively. It was pretty clear he wondered if her arrival was bad for Chase. Her stomach twisted. Who knew if this situation they were in was good or bad for any of them?

"I'd just finished my pediatric residency and wanted to do something important for a while," she said, tucking raisins into the steamy oatmeal to make a smiley face. "Go where kids don't get the kind of medical care we have at home."

She didn't add that she'd stayed months after her contract was up because she hadn't been ready to say goodbye. Knew she'd never be ready. Until she was forced to be.

She slid Drew's artwork aside to make room for his breakfast. He picked the raisins out one at a time and shoved them in his mouth. "He can't see now! I ate his eyes!"

A smile touched Trent's face as he watched Drew dig into his breakfast, but when he turned to Dani, his expression cooled.

"So, why didn't you tell Chase? Frankly, I think that's pretty lame."

She gulped her coffee to swallow the burning ache in her chest that was anger and remorse combined. Who was he to judge her without knowing Chase's attitude? Without knowing she'd had to protect her baby? Without knowing how hard it had been to leave the man she'd fallen crazy in love with?

"Listen, I—"

The kitchen door swung open and the man in question walked in, which immediately sent her pulse hammering at the thought of what lay ahead of them. Telling Drew, and what his reaction would be when he learned Chase was his daddy. What demands Chase might or might not make in being a part of his son's life. How it all could be balanced without Drew getting hurt.

Chase filled the doorway, sweat glistening on his tanned arms and face, spikes of dark hair sticking to his neck. A faded gray T-shirt damply clung to his broad chest, his running shorts exposing his strong calves and thighs. His brows rose as he paused in mid-stride, wiping his forehead with the sleeve of his shirt.

"What is this, a sunrise party? Not used to seeing anyone in here this early."

She tore her gaze from his sexy body to focus on

wiping Drew's chin. "Andrew needed food more than he needed sleep. Guess we're not on West Africa time yet."

Chase grabbed a bottle of cold water from the fridge and took a big swig as he leaned his hip against the counter, his attention fixed on Drew. Dani found herself staring as he swallowed. As his tongue licked droplets of water from his lips.

Quickly, she glanced away and swallowed hard herself. Why couldn't she just concentrate on the serious issues that lay between them, instead of wanting to grab him and sip that water from his lips herself?

Toughening up was clearly essential, and she braved another look at him, sternly reminding herself they'd been apart way longer than they'd been together. His demeanor seemed relaxed, but she could sense the undercurrent of tension in the set of his shoulders, the tightness in his jaw. Obviously, he felt as anxious about their upcoming revelation to Drew as she did.

Trent stood. "Think I'll get in a catnap before the clinic opens."

"Don't worry about getting to the clinic at nine. I can't take how cranky you get when you're tired," Chase said.

"Better than being cranky all the time, like you," Trent said, slapping Chase on the back. "See you all later."

The kitchen seemed to become suffocatingly small as Chase stepped so close to Dani that his shoulder brushed hers. His expression told her clearly that it was showtime, and her pulse rocketed.

Why did she feel so petrified? At least a thousand times since he'd been born, she'd thought about how or if or when she'd tell Drew about his daddy. He was still practically a baby after all. Like she'd said last night, he probably wouldn't think anything of it.

But as she looked at her little boy, the words stuck in

her throat. She turned to Chase, and he seemed to sense all the crazy emotions whirling through her. The intensity on his face relaxed, his deep brown eyes softened, and he slipped his arm around her shoulders.

"I promise you it will be okay," he said, dropping a kiss on her forehead. "No. Way better than okay. So stop worrying."

She nodded. No point in telling him she'd been worrying since before Drew had been born, and couldn't just turn it off now. But deep inside she somehow knew that, even though he hadn't wanted a child, Chase would never say and do the hurtful things her own father had.

Chase released her shoulders and pulled two stools on either side of Drew's before propping himself on one and gesturing to Dani to sit on the other. She sank onto the stool and hoped her smile covered up how her stomach churned and her heart pounded.

She wiped the last of his breakfast from Drew's hands and face and slid his bowl aside. "Drew, you know Mommy brought you to Africa so I could work with children here. But I brought you here for another reason, too."

Okay, so that was a total lie, and the twist of Chase's lips showed her he was still ticked about not knowing about Drew. But she was going with it anyway, darn it.

"And that reason is…because…" She gulped and struggled with the next words. "Dr. Chase here is, um…"

She was making a complete mess of this. Drew looked at her quizzically and she cleared her throat, trying to unstick the words that seemed lodged in there.

Chase made an impatient sound and leaned forward. "What your mom is trying to say is that I'm really happy to finally meet you and be with you because—"

The door to the kitchen swung wide and Spud strode in with hurricane force. "A truck plowed down two kids walking to school. One's pretty beat up. I have them in pre-op now."

Chase straightened and briefly looked conflicted before becoming all business. He stood, downed the last of his water and looked at Drew, then focused on Dani, his expression hardened with frustration. "We'll talk later."

Spud turned to her. "Ruth is on her way to take care of Andrew," he said. "I'll show you the facility and the clinic schedule after he's settled in."

"I want to help with the injured children as soon as she gets here," Dani said. She wasn't about to let the drama with Chase interfere with her reason for being here in the first place, and caring for sick and injured children was a big part of that reason.

Spud inclined his head and left. Chase paused a moment next to Drew and seemed to hesitate before crouching down next to him.

Dani's heart pinched as she saw the usually decisive expression on Chase's face replaced by a peculiar mix of uncertainty, determination and worry.

"Later today, how about you and your mom and I go look for those lizards?"

"'K." Drew beamed at Chase before grabbing his crayons to scribble on his Spiderman artwork.

Chase strode to the door, stopping to give Dani a look that brooked no argument. "Plan on a little trek this afternoon."

# CHAPTER THREE

WITH DREW HAPPILY playing under the watchful eye of a gentle local woman, Ruth, Dani hurried to the prep room Spud directed her to.

The room, only about fifteen feet by twenty or so, echoed with the whimpers of a child. The harsh, fluorescent light seemed to bounce off the white cinder-block walls, magnifying the horror of one child's injuries.

Chase was leaning over the boy as he lay on a gurney, speaking soothingly in some language she'd never heard as he focused on the child's leg. She'd almost forgotten how Chase simply radiated strength, calm, and utter competence when caring for his patients. The boy nodded and hiccupped as he took deep breaths, an expression of trust on his face despite the fear and pain etched there.

Dani looked at the boy's leg and nearly showed her reaction to his injury, but caught herself just in time. Jaggedly broken, the child's femur protruded through the flesh of his thigh. Gravel and twigs and who-knew-what were embedded in the swollen wound. His lower leg was badly scraped and lacerated and full of road debris too, and his forehead had a gash that obviously required suturing.

The other child, at first glance anyway, seemed to have suffered less severe injuries.

She looked to be about eight years old. Her wounds would need suturing, too, and before that a thorough cleaning. A woman, presumably her mother, sat with her, tenderly wiping her scrapes and cuts with damp cotton pads.

"What do you need me to do first?" Dani asked. She'd probably be stitching up the girl but, as bad as the boy's injuries looked, Chase might need her help first.

"Get a peripheral IV going in the boy. His name's Apollo. Give him morphine so I can irrigate and set the leg. Then you can wash out his sister's cuts, scrub with soap and stitch her up. I have her mom putting a lidocaine-epinephrine cocktail on her to numb the skin."

Dani noted how worried the mother looked, and had to applaud her for her calm and efficient ministrations. A cloth that looked like it might have been the boy's shirt lay soaked with blood on the floor next to her, which, at a guess, she'd used to try to stop the bleeding. The mother's clothes were covered in blood too, and Dani's throat tightened in sympathy. The poor woman had sure been through one terrible morning.

"Where are the IVs kept? And the irrigation and suture kits?" If only she'd had just an hour to get acquainted with the layout of the place. Right now, she felt like the newbie she was, and hated her inadequacy when both patients needed help fast.

"IVs are in the top right cupboard. The key to the drug drawer is in my scrub pocket."

She stepped over to Chase, and he straightened to give her access to his chest pocket. As she slipped her hand inside, feeling his hard pectoral through the fabric, their eyes met. The moment took her rushing back to Honduras, to all the times just like these, as though they had been yesterday instead of three years ago. To all the memories of working together as a team. To all the times he'd proved what an accomplished surgeon he was.

Heart fluttering a little, she slipped the key from his pocket, trying to focus on the present situation and not his hunkiness quotient. She turned and gathered the morphine and IV materials and came back to the whimpering boy, wanting to ease his pain quickly.

"Tell him he'll feel a little pinch then I'm going to put a straw in his hand that'll make his leg hurt less," she said, concentrating on getting the IV going fast.

"Damn," Chase said.

She looked up and saw him shaking his head. "What?"

"I'd forgotten how good you are at that. One stick and, *bam*, the IV's in. I don't think he even felt it."

His voice and expression were filled with admiration, which made her feel absurdly pleased. "Thanks."

He leaned closer. "He's lucky you're here."

"And he's lucky to have you to put his leg back together."

He smiled and she smiled back, her breath catching at how ridiculously handsome the man looked when his eyes were all fudgy brown and warm and his lips teasingly curved.

"The little girl's going to get the world's most meticulous stitcher-upper, too," Chase said, still smiling as he tweezed out lingering pieces of gravel from Apollo's wound. "I remember a button you sewed so tightly on my shirt I couldn't get it through the little hole any more."

"Well, I only did it for you because, considering you're a surgeon, you're really bad at sewing on buttons."

His eyes crinkled at the corners as they met hers again, and her heart skipped a beat, darn it all. With the IV in place, the boy's eyes drooped as the morphine took effect. Chase placed an X-ray plate under the boy's calf, then rolled a machine across the room, positioning its C-arm over his shin, obviously suspecting, as she did, that it also might be broken.

"Is the X-ray tech coming soon?"

"No X-ray tech. Honduras was loaded with staff compared to this place. I'll get this film developing before I work on the compound fracture."

Wow. Hard to believe they had to take and develop the X-rays. "I'll get started with the girl. Where's irrigation?"

He nodded toward the wide, low sink. "Faucet. The secret to pollution is dilution. It's the best we have."

Her eyes widened. "Seriously? I stick her wounds under the faucet?"

"Attach the hose. We've found it provides more force than the turkey basters we use on less polluted wounds. It's how I'm going to get him cleaned up now that he's had pain meds. You're not in Kansas any more, Toto. Be right back." With a wink, he left with the X-ray cartridge in his hand.

Dani grabbed a pair of sterile gloves from a box attached to the wall and rolled a stool from under the counter to sit next to the gurney. She smiled at the wide-eyed girl and her mother.

If only she spoke their language, or even a little French. The girl looked scared but wasn't shedding a single tear. Hopefully, when the local nurse arrived, she could interpret for Dani. Or Chase would. One of the many amazing things about the darned man was all the languages he could speak fluently or partially. He had a true gift for it, while Dani hated the fact that it had never come easily to her.

"I'm going to wash—*laver*—her cuts to get all the gravel and nasty stuff out of there." Lord, was that the only French word she could come up with?

The mother seemed to understand, though, nodding gravely. Dani rolled the gurney to the low sink and couldn't believe she had to stick the child's various extremities practically inside it, scrubbing with good old antiseptic soap to clean out the debris. Thank goodness the numbing solution seemed to be working pretty well, as the scrubbing didn't seem to hurt her patient too badly.

"You're being very brave," she told the little girl, who gave her a shy smile in return, though she probably didn't understand the words.

The mother helped with the washing, and Dani thought about how her own perspective had changed since she'd had Drew. When she had been in med school, and then when she'd become a doctor, she'd thought she'd got it. But now she truly understood how terrifying it must be to have your child seriously injured or ill.

When Chase returned, Dani had finished prepping the girl and helped him get the boy's wounds washed out. Not an easy task, because tiny bits of gravel seemed determined to stay embedded in his flesh. Thank heavens the morphine made the situation tolerable for the child.

"You want me to stitch this big lac on his head, or do you want to do it after I work on his leg?" Chase asked, then grinned. "Or maybe we should call in the plastic surgeon."

"Funny. I'm as good as any plastic surgeon anyway. Tell his mom he'll be as handsome as ever when I'm done."

Chase chatted with the mother as they laid the boy back on the gurney, and the woman managed a smile, her lips trembling and tears filling her eyes for a moment.

"I haven't seen anything like this since Honduras," Dani said quietly to Chase as they got the patient comfortable and increased his morphine drip in preparation for setting the leg. "Been in a suburban practice where the bad stuff goes to the ER. The roughest stuff I dealt with was ear infections."

"So you're sorry you came?"

"No." She shook her head and gave him a crooked smile. "Even though you're here, I'd almost forgotten how much we're needed in places like this."

"Except you shouldn't have brought Drew. Which we'll be talking about." His expression hardened.

Oh, right. Those deep, dark issues they had to deal with separate from what they were doing now.

Yes, Chase was a great surgeon and good man, but she had to remember why she'd left in the first place. Because he didn't want a child. And she wasn't about to let him bully her into doing things his way and only his way, without regard for how it would affect Drew.

Glad to be able to put some physical distance between them to go with the emotional distance that had suddenly appeared, she stepped away to stitch the girl's cuts.

"I'm taking him into the OR to set the bone and put a transverse pin in the distal femur," Chase said, wheeling the gurney to the swinging door that led to the operating room. "If Trent comes down, tell him I'm just going to splint it and put drains in for now, until the swelling goes down. When the nurse anesthetist gets here, tell her to grab the X-rays and come in."

He stopped to place his hand on the mother's shoulder, speaking to her in the soothing, warm tones that always reassured patients and family and had been known to weaken Dani's knees. From now on, though, when it came to Chase, she had to be sure her knees, and every other part of her, stayed strong.

"Once you heal, it's going to take a while to get your leg strong again. But I promise we'll help you with exercises for that, and you'll be playing soccer again in no time." Chase smiled at the boy, now in a hospital bed with a trapeze apparatus connected to his leg with a counterweight, which had to feel really miserable in the hot, un-air-conditioned hospital ward.

Lucky, really, that it wasn't a whole lot worse, with bad internal injuries. Barring some hard-to-control infection, he'd eventually be running again. Damned drunk driver apparently hadn't even seen the poor kids. Chase's lips tightened.

As Chase suspected, in addition to the compound fracture, the boy's tibia had been broken too, and he'd put a cast on it before finally getting him set up in bed. It would be damned uncomfortable for the kid, but would keep the bones immobile so he could begin to heal.

"Nice work, Dr. Sheridan," he said to Dani as he looked closely at the boy's forehead, which she'd nearly finished stitching. Dani looked up at him from her sitting position next to the bed, a light glow of perspiration on her beautiful face. Her blue, blue eyes smiled at him in a way that made him want to pick up where they'd left off the night before. If they'd been alone, he would have. Convincing her to marry him was a pleasure he looked forward to. Except he needed to stop thinking about all the ways he planned to accomplish that before everyone in the room knew where his thoughts had travelled.

He could tell Dani already did. "I've always appreciated the superior techniques you implement for everything you do," he said, giving her a wicked grin.

Her smile faded and her fair skin turned deeply pink, and she quickly turned to finish working on the boy's forehead. He nearly laughed, pleased at how easily he could still rattle her.

The nasty gash was now a thin red line within the tiny

stitches Dani was currently tying off. If anything, she'd gotten even better at it than when they'd been in Honduras. Even back then he'd been amazed at her talent for leaving only the smallest scar.

"Tell him he looks very handsome and rugged, like a pirate," she said, smiling at the boy. "His friends will be jealous."

Chase translated and the kid managed a small smile, but his mother laughed, the sound full of relief. She'd been fanning the child practically non-stop with a home-made fan, trying to keep him comfortable in the stifling heat of the room and to ward off pesky flies that always found their way into the hospital ward, regardless of everyone's efforts to keep them out.

They'd set Apollo's sister up in the bed next to him, though she didn't really need to stay in for observation. Their mother, though, would be bringing food in for her son and sleeping next to him on the floor to help care for him, so it made sense to keep the little girl here too, as the bed was available.

"We'll be putting a new cast on his whole leg some time after the swelling goes down, but for now we'll be keeping him comfortable with some pain medicine," he said to the mother. "I'll be back later to check on him."

He tipped his neck from side to side to release the kinks that always tightened there after a long procedure. With everything they could do for the kids finished for now, he felt suddenly anxious to find Drew and tell him the truth. He gathered up Dani's suture kit. "Ready to go, Doctor?"

"Not really," she mumbled under her breath as she stripped off her gloves.

She looked up at him as she stood, her face full of the same uncertainty and anxiety that had been there earlier. Why was she so worried about telling their son that he was the boy's father? If she didn't look so sweet and vulnerable, he'd be insulted.

Sure, he'd said he didn't want kids, but that had been before he'd known it was already moot.

She'd see how good it would be. He'd reassure her, romance her, be a good dad to Drew, and she'd realize that everything would be okay. His mood lifted, became downright buoyant, and he tugged at one of the crazy blonde curls that had escaped from her ponytail.

Last night when he'd kissed her, she hadn't been able to hide that she still wanted him the way he wanted her. She'd come round. Marry him. He'd find a good job for her in the States where he could work sometimes, too, and Drew would be safe.

Yeah, it was a good plan. He knew he could make it happen.

He tugged another curl.

"You know, you're like a second-grader sometimes," she said, pulling her head away with a frown. "Next, you'll be putting a frog down my shirt."

"No. A lizard." He folded her soft hand into his. "Let's find Drew."

# CHAPTER FOUR

"THIS LOOKS LIKE a good lizard spot." Chase maneuvered the Land Rover off the dusty road and around some scrub towards a grouping of rocks.

"I can't believe you're really planning on catching one," Dani said, shaking her head. "I know you have quick reflexes, but I think even you are a little slower than a lizard. And if you do catch one, it'll probably bite you."

"Watch and learn." He grinned at Dani but the smile she gave in return was very half-hearted, and shadows touched the blue of her eyes. He stuffed down his impatience to tell Drew and get it over with so she'd relax and see what a great dad he was going to be. So she'd get over her illogical attitude and say yes to marrying him.

Chase stopped the vehicle by the rocks, which would hopefully prove to be a good hiding place for the reptiles. Not that the primary reason for coming out this afternoon was really about lizards. But he wanted Drew to like him and remembered how much fun he'd had searching for lizards and various other creatures with his own dad and brother.

"Spud packed an old blanket we can use as a sort of tablecloth on the rock," Chase said. He turned to the child sitting in the car seat in the back. Every time he looked at the boy the wonder and worry over having a child slammed him in the chest all over again. "How about a snack, Drew? Then we'll go hunting."

"I'll get the picnic bag Spud put together for us," Dani said.

He watched Dani slide from the front seat, enjoying the view of her perfect, sexy behind in her khaki shorts. Her lean, toned legs. She opened the back door and unlatched their son from his car seat.

His son. Such a crazy word to think. To have rolling from his lips when he'd been alone and tried out how it would feel to say it. *My son.* But none of it was as strange as how normal it felt to look at the child and know Drew was his. To feel the strong tug of emotion that pulled at his heart for the sweet-faced boy he barely knew.

If Drew wouldn't have balked at it, Chase would've taken his son from the seat himself and carried him to stand tall on the biggest rock where they planned to enjoy a picnic before going lizard hunting. Now that he knew about Drew, it felt oddly natural to be a father, and that itself seemed more than surprising.

During his run this morning, he'd found himself thinking of all the things he wanted to do with Drew. All the things he'd loved as a kid. All the things his own father had shared with him, taught him. Except so many of those things stemmed from having lived in other places and cultures around the world. He'd have to figure out which of those things they'd be able to do together in the States, where Drew belonged.

While he'd never been particularly comfortable in the U.S., he was more than willing to work there part of the year to spend time with his child and his wife. Seeing them every day while he was there would make it worthwhile. And with global communications being what they were these days, it would be easy to stay in touch, even close, when he worked missions.

He knew in his bones it would work out fine for everyone. His family.

Chase grabbed the blanket from the back of the car, along with a wooden box he'd brought for any lizards they'd manage to catch.

The savannah stretched for as far as they could see to the hilly horizon, with scruffy trees here and there amid lush grasses and brown scrub. He headed to a nice, flat rock perfect for a picnic and began to lay the blanket across it.

"Let me help." A few soft, blonde curls that had escaped Dani's ponytail fell across her cheek as she leaned over the rock. He wanted to drop the corner he was holding and feel them wrapped around his finger. Tickle the shell of her ear as he tucked them there. Bring her mouth to his.

*She doesn't like it when you push.* He grabbed one end of the fabric and together they smoothed it across the rock. Or attempted to smooth it, with Drew scrabbling across the rock on all fours looking a bit like a crab and bunching up the blanket until Dani grabbed him up and swung him in circles.

"We can't eat with you messing up the blanket, silly."

"I a lizard!" Drew protested as Dani set him on his feet and kissed the top of his head.

"I know. And I have yummy bugs to feed you if you sit on the rock like a good reptile."

"Okay. I like bugs." Drew quickly climbed onto the rock and sat, comically sticking out his tongue and giggling.

Chase and Dani both chuckled. The kid was so damned cute. He and Dani reached for the food bag at the same time, and her eyes met and locked with his. For a moment they just stared at one another, and Chase nearly reached for her, wanting to kiss away the worry behind her smile and whatever other emotions he saw flickering in their blue depths. The beautiful blue he'd seen so many times in his dreams after she'd left Honduras.

He gave up resisting and lifted his hand to cup her cheek, placing a quick, gentle kiss on her soft lips. "Why so gloomy? The Dani I remember was full of sass and saw everything as an adventure. Not a worrywart," he said. "You've been adventuring with Drew alone. All I want is to jump in and join you."

She gave him a twisted smile and shook her head. "Maybe today. But what about tomorrow? What about next year, when you're who-knows-where and have forgotten all about us?"

What a damned insulting thing to say. As though he'd ever forget all about them. "If you'll just—"

"I want my bugs!" Drew began lizard-walking again, sticking out his tongue and tangling the blanket.

"Okay, lizard-boy. Let's see what's in here." Chase huffed out a frustrated breath at both her attitude and his apparent inability to just shut up about the subject for one minute.

Except he knew why he'd opened his mouth. He'd wanted to wipe that worry from her face. Wanted to see the sunny, vibrant Dani again. But pushing her was the wrong approach, and he knew it. Showing her his commitment to making a marriage and family work was the way to convince her, not with words. Not by getting irritated with her doubts, which he supposed he couldn't blame her for having.

He pulled out the grilled chicken on sticks that Spud always made and looked to see what else was in the bag.

"Here are the best-tasting bugs in Benin," Chase said, pulling a box of raisins from the sack. Drew sat back on his haunches and opened his mouth. They began a comical game, with Chase tossing the raisins into Drew's mouth and the child slurping up any that fell onto the blanket.

"Okay, you two. Even lizards need more substantial food than bugs," Dani said.

She put the rest of the picnic on metal plates. "What's this stuff?" she asked, lifting the foil from a plastic bowl to expose soft, lumpy, brown and beige discs.

"Those are *akara*," Chase said. "Fried fritters made from black-eyed peas. They're kind of ugly but they're good."

Dani handed one to Drew as she assembled a few other things on the child's plate. Holding it in both hands, he took a big bite then promptly spit it out right onto the blanket, leaving his tongue hanging from his mouth with a comical look of anguish on his face. "Cookie yucky!"

Chase didn't want Drew to think they were laughing at his distress, and tried to keep his face from showing how hilarious the poor kid's expression was. "Sorry, buddy. That's not a cookie. Guess we should have made that clearer."

"Poor Drew. Have a drink to wash it down." Dani handed him a water bottle and wiped up the food. Apparently she wasn't too worried about Drew being offended, as a laugh bubbled from her lips, and the sound of her amusement stole Chase's breath. He looked at the curve of her sexy lips and the sparkle in her beautiful eyes, beyond relieved that she was finally more relaxed and happy.

He'd always loved her laugh, her smile, her sense of humor. Kissing that laughing mouth was almost as high on his agenda as telling Drew that he was his father, but he reminded himself he had to go slowly.

But not too slowly. Who knew when his next assignment would come through? The thought of having to leave before Dani believed in their relationship again scared the hell out of him.

After they'd eaten, Chase grasped Dani's hand to let her know the time had come to tell Drew, together. Instantly, a grim expression replaced the soft happiness on her face of just a moment ago, and he shoved down the disappointment he felt at the transformation. What had he ever done to make her look at him like that?

"Andrew." The child stopped banging a stick against the rock and looked up at him expectantly. Chase figured he should take the lead in this, as he had a feeling Dani would be as tongue-tied as she'd been earlier if he left it all up to her. "This morning your mom was telling you she brought you to Africa for two reasons. Besides helping kids here, she wanted you to meet me. And I really wanted to meet you."

He looked at her and the worry—damn it, he'd even call it torment—in her eyes made him pause. Did she need to be the one to say it?

"Yes, Drew." Her voice sounded strained and her grip on his hand tightened. "I'm so happy because, believe it or not, you finally get to meet your daddy. Dr. Chase is your daddy. Isn't that great?"

To Chase's shock, her lips quivered and fat tears filled her eyes and spilled over. She quickly swiped them away, but not before they hit him hard in the gut.

Dani wasn't an over-emotional woman, crying over any little thing. That she was moved to tears now showed him what he hadn't even thought about. How hard all this had been on her, no doubt from the beginning. Being pregnant with Drew, alone. Giving birth to him, alone. Raising him, alone.

Painful guilt swamped him. No, he hadn't known about Drew. But he should have been more intuitive when she'd proposed to him, damn it. And it had been his words that had driven her to secrecy.

He wrapped his arm around her shoulders and pulled her close, kissing her salty cheek and giving her a smile he hoped would show her that her solitary hardship was over. That, even when she was in the States while he worked elsewhere, she would never be truly alone.

He looked at Drew, whose head was tipped to one side, his big brown eyes studying Chase. "Your mom told me you're the best boy in the whole world, and I'm incredibly lucky to be your dad. I'm really happy to get to spend time with you now."

Drew looked at his mother then jumped off the rock to start banging the stick on it again. "I thought maybe Mr. Matt was gonna be my daddy."

*Mr. Matt?* Chase stiffened and his arm dropped from Dani's shoulder. Was Dani involved with someone? His brain froze. Why hadn't he even thought to wonder? Or ask?

A short, uncomfortable laugh left Dani's lips. "Mr. Matt is just a friend. Dr. Chase is your daddy, and I think he'd like it if you called him that."

"Yes, I'd like that, Drew." He only half heard himself speak. What the hell was he going to do if Dani was in love with someone else? A strange sensation gripped his heart that was panic and anger combined. They had a son together, and she belonged to him. It would be over Chase's dead body if another man tried to claim her. Tried to make decisions that affected Drew. That affected where his son lived and who he lived with.

"'K." Drew smiled then shrieked. "A lizard! Look!"

The boy ran, chasing a tiny lizard through and around the rocks, and Chase turned to Dani, trying to speak past the tightness gripping his throat and squeezing his chest.

"What the hell? Do you have a boyfriend?"

"What do you mean, 'What the hell?'" Dani said, frowning. "You act like you and I were still together. In case you've forgotten, we'd both moved on with our lives until yesterday."

The primitive possessiveness that roared through his blood shocked him in its intensity. "You can tell this Mr. Matt to get lost. That you're getting married."

She looked at him like she thought he was crazy. Which was fine, because he suddenly felt a little crazy. She made him crazy.

"I'm pretty sure I already told you I'm not marrying you. Can't you just stop with the full court press and get to know Drew? Like I said, we'll work out a solution where you can spend time with him each year."

"Are you—?" Chase realized he was practically shouting and lowered his voice. "Are you in love with this guy?"

"My feelings for Matt are irrelevant. What is relevant is figuring out how to make sure Drew knows he's important to you. That he's not just some in-the-way, annoying afterthought in your life."

He grasped her shoulders in his hands and pulled her close. "You know, I'm getting damned tired of you implying I'm going to be a deadbeat, rotten, selfish father. I've known Drew barely one day, but if you don't think I'd throw myself in front of a truck for him, you don't know me at all."

She drew a deep breath, and stared at him searchingly as she slowly released it. "Okay. I'm sorry. Let's...

let's just enjoy the day with Drew. We'll figure out the rest later."

Jealousy and frustration wouldn't let him agree. He glanced over at Drew to see him occupied, enthusiastically poking his stick into a crack in a rock. "Is this Matt guy the reason you won't agree to marry me?"

"No. I won't marry you for all the reasons I've already said. I believe two people should get married because they want to live together and be together and love one another. Not so you can call the shots or because it's a logical course of action."

There was damned well nothing logical about the way he was feeling. Nothing very mature or sophisticated either. He wanted to throw her over his shoulder and make her his right then and there. Then he wanted to find this Matt guy and punch him in the face. But since he couldn't do either of those things, he settled for the one thing he could do.

He pulled her tightly against him and kissed her. Without finesse. Without thoughts of reminding her what they'd had three years ago. He kissed her with the anger and fear and uncertainty that pummeled his heart. He kissed her with the release of a deep and pent-up hunger for her he hadn't even realized was there until she'd come back into his life.

Her palms pushed against his chest and she pulled her mouth from his. She stared at him, both confusion and desire swimming in her eyes. The memories of past kisses, of yesterday and of three years ago, crackled between them. Her breath mingled with his. Her clean, sweet scent enveloped him. And there was no way he could keep from taking her mouth with his again.

This time her palms swept up his chest, her cool fingers slid across his nape. A low moan sounded deep in her throat, and he tasted the same wild desire on her tongue that surged through every nerve in his body. He cupped the back of her head, tangling his fingers in her thick hair, wanting to release her ponytail and feel those crazy curls slide across his skin.

The anger, the jealousy that had shoved him headlong into the kiss faded. Replaced by the warm and heady craving that had always burned between them. The taste of her, filled with a soul-deep passion and the promise of intimate pleasures only she could give.

He let his hand wander, cupping her bottom and pressing her against him. Her heat sent his thigh nudging between her legs and he felt her respond by rubbing against him, a sweet murmur of pleasure vibrating from her lips to his.

"Mommy! I catched the lizard! I catched it!"

They pulled apart, and he was sure he wore the same shocked and slightly horrified expression she did. Both their chests were heaving with rapid breaths, and she lifted shaking fingers to her lips as she turned towards Drew.

Damn. Chase scrubbed his hand across his face. He'd like to think he would have remembered Drew was there. That he wouldn't have put his hand up her shirt or down her pants or any of the many things he'd been about to do. But he had to grimly admit that he'd been so far gone, he just might have done any and all of it anyway.

He'd have to be more careful. Remember there were three of them now, not just him and Dani. Of course, she'd goaded him into it with the whole thing about her refusal to marry him. Her damned boyfriend.

But with that thought came a smile of grim satisfaction. If Dani thought she was in love with this Matt guy, the spontaneous combustion they'd just shared had surely proved her wrong. The way it had always been between them, from the very first weeks they'd met.

"Chase!"

Dani's slightly panicky voice had him quickly heading to her and Drew.

"Chase, are you sure these things don't bite? I think you should drop it, Drew. Now."

"No. It mine." The boy's chin jutted mulishly. "Daddy said we could catch some."

*Daddy.* To hear Drew call him that in such a natural way, like they hadn't met just yesterday, was inconceivable yet wonderful, and the tight band constricting his chest eased slightly.

The boy's stubby little fingers grasped the tail of a lizard no bigger than a mouse as it writhed to get loose. He had to chuckle at the triumph on Drew's face and the distaste on Dani's.

"A master lizard-catcher. Like father, like son." Yeah, the boy was a true Bowen. If only his brother was here to share the moment.

The thought brought his enjoyment down a notch, at the same time reinforcing exactly why he was adamant that Drew grow up in the U.S. He reached for the wooden box he'd found at the compound. "Here, Drew, I brought this to put it in. We can only keep it for a day then we'll let it go so it stays healthy. Okay?"

"Okay." Drew dropped it into the box, a huge grin on his face. "I a good lizard-hunter, aren't I?"

"The best." Chase's heart filled with something powerful and unfamiliar as he looked at the boy's adorable little face, lit with the kind of joy unique to children.

Drew's smile was blinding. The boy might look like him, but that beautiful smile was all Dani.

He lifted his gaze to Dani's and their eyes locked in a wordless connection. So many emotions flickered in her eyes. Wariness, apprehension, anxiety. Warring with the remnants of their intoxicating kiss. His gaze dropped to her full lips, still moist, and it was all he could do not to grab her and start what they hadn't been able to finish.

He forced himself to step back and give her the breathing room, the time she'd asked for. Waiting wasn't one of the things he was best at, but he'd try. With maybe just a little nudge to shorten the wait.

"So, is there any chance you and Dad can make it down here?" Finally, his mother had returned his call. Chase had begun to wonder if something was wrong, or if they'd left Senegal and hadn't told him, with sketchy cell service somewhere remote.

"We'd love to see you, honey. It so happens we have a few days off," his mother's voice said in his ear. "But it's usually me trying to get us together, not you. Anything going on?"

"Actually, yes." He paced in his room, still undecided whether he should tell them about Drew over the phone or just let them meet him.

"Well? Are you going to tell me or keep me in suspense?"

He wasn't sure exactly what to say but decided he should just let them know so they'd be prepared. "I want you to meet your grandson. Andrew. He's two and a half and cute as can be."

There was a long silence, and Chase could just picture his mother's stunned expression. Probably similar to his when he'd first seen the boy who looked exactly like him and his brother.

"Are you there?" he asked.

"Yes. It's just that I thought you said I have a grandson. A grandson?"

Her voice rose in pitch, and Chase was pretty sure it was with excitement. Of course she'd be excited. Both his parents loved children and knew he'd always said he'd never have kids. Most likely, this was a dream-come-true for her.

"Yes. I just found out… It's kind of a long story. But Drew's mother is here with me, and we're getting married soon." True, she hadn't yet agreed to that. But if he had to move mountains, she would. And having his parents come was another step towards convincing her. They'd love Dani and Drew, and she'd love them, too. It would give her a chance to see how good they'd be as a family.

"Oh, Chase, I can't believe it!" His mother laughed, and obviously pulled her mouth from the phone as she spoke to his dad. "Phil! Phil, we have a grandson! Get on the internet and book a flight to Benin right now."

Chase grinned. He'd had a feeling his mom would drop everything to meet Drew.

"Let me know when you're going to get here, and I'll try to pick you up from the airport. Or Spud will, if I can't get away."

"Okay. Oh, goodness, I can't wait to get there. I'm off to pack. Bye."

She hung up without even waiting for a response, and the disturbing feelings he'd had ever since he'd heard about this Matt character eased a little. Not only would his mom and dad embrace his son and hopefully soon-to-be wife, he'd recruit them to emphasize to Dani how important it was to keep Drew in the U.S. until he was older. Maybe she'd listen to two experienced mission doctors who happened to be Drew's grandparents in a way she wasn't currently listening to him.

The little nudge named Evelyn Bowen was on her way.

## CHAPTER FIVE

WITH CHASE MYSTERIOUSLY gone somewhere, Dani sat in the empty clinic room and tried to focus on the sketchy and incomplete care and immunization records. She was working to get them organized and into the laptop computer she'd brought from the States—fairly unsuccessfully, since she kept wondering where Chase had gone. Kept thinking about the charm he'd been intent on oozing nonstop since yesterday when they'd told Drew that Chase was his daddy.

Kept reliving the feel of his stolen kisses against her cheek or the side of her neck whenever they were together, his fingertips sliding across the skin of her arms. How had she not known her arms were an erogenous zone?

They probably weren't, unless it was Chase touching her. She couldn't help but respond to his teasing caress, the curve of his lips, the sensual promise in the chocolaty depths of his eyes.

She huffed out a frustrated breath. Why, oh, why did she have such a hard time steeling herself against the man's sexual energy and tempting persuasion?

She'd been relieved at how easily Drew had accepted that Chase was his daddy. But, of course, she'd known he was so young he wouldn't have many questions about it. She'd hoped they could tell Drew then ease into a new relationship as two parents living separate lives, with the best interests of their child the only personal connection between them.

But what happened instead? She'd fallen into his embrace, into his kiss, with barely one second of resistance. Her cheeks burned with embarrassment. Especially because his kiss certainly hadn't been full of tenderness. It had been full of anger and possessiveness, no doubt because Drew had mentioned Matt and a competitive man like Chase wouldn't just shrug at something like that.

No, she had a feeling that had just added more fuel to the hot fire already burning within Chase about the two of them getting married.

Matt was the first man she'd dated since Chase, since leaving Honduras to go back to the States to work and start a new life there with Drew. Having a man in her life hadn't been on her to-do list. But Matt had seemed so easygoing, so harmless, really, that she'd finally given in to going out with him a few times the month before she'd left for Benin. He'd been happy to include Drew in several excursions and had been pleasant to spend time with.

Kissing him had been pleasant, too. Pleasant, but not knee-weakening. Not breathtaking. Not so mesmerizing that she'd forget everything except how his mouth tasted and her heart pounded and how much she wanted to get naked and intimate the way she had when Chase had kissed her. So all-consuming that she'd lost all thought about anything but the way he'd made her feel.

And that was bad. In so many ways. More than bad that she hadn't spared one thought about Drew seeing them devouring one another and rubbing their bodies together. Her face burned all over again at the thought,

ROBIN GIANNA 63

even though Drew was too young to think much of it, even if he'd noticed.

It was bad because she had to keep her focus. She had to resist the intense, overpowering attraction she'd felt for Chase since practically the first moment she'd met him and which clearly hadn't gone away with time and distance.

As she'd told him before, great sex wasn't a reason to get married. Neither was a feeling of obligation on Chase's part. Or a need to control their lives. If she ever did marry, she wanted it to be because her husband loved her more than anything. Wanted to be with her more than anything. Believed she was every bit as important to him as his work.

And that obviously just wasn't true with Chase.

Love had nothing to do with him wanting marriage, and she shoved away the deep stab of pain that knowledge caused. His reasoning that she and Drew should stay in the States while he lived his life the way he always had, or close to it, just wasn't enough. Not for her and not for Drew.

Working with underprivileged people around the world was important to her, especially after she'd seen all the need in Honduras. She had her career plan all worked out, where she'd be employed in the U.S. for two years, spend nine months abroad, then head back to the States for two more years. And giving Drew exposure to other cultures couldn't be anything but good for him.

Not to mention that, if Chase was still going to live all over the world, it made no sense to get married and pretend they were a family the years they lived in the U.S. Didn't he see that Drew would always know he wasn't as important to his dad as his job? But if they weren't married, Drew would accept that his parents were no longer together, and would understand why his dad lived somewhere else.

She believed Chase when he said he wanted to be part of Drew's life. It would probably work out okay if he saw Drew several times a year for a few weeks each time. After all, they lived in a global world now. With phone calls and video chats online, being close to one another shouldn't be too hard.

What a tangled mess. But she was here to do a job, not think endlessly about the problems. She stared at the scribbled index cards, and wondered why some of the previous doctors and nurses had even bothered to record the unreadable notes.

"Dani, are you in here?"

"Yes." She absolutely wouldn't ask Chase where he'd gone. For all she knew, he'd been seeing a woman. And it was none of her business.

Chase strode into the room, looking so good in jeans and a pale yellow polo shirt that showed off his tanned skin and dark hair and eyes that she caught herself staring. She pulled her gaze back to the cards, typing what she could into the computer.

"Making progress?" he asked, leaning over her to look at her work, resting his palm between her shoulder blades.

"Not much. I can't even read most of them. We're just going to have to start with new records of children as we see them." She stared fixedly at her work. "I'd like to talk with you about ways we can get parents to bring their kids in for checks."

"It's not easy. A lot of folks don't have transportation, so they only come when there's a serious problem. Some believe Vodun will keep their children from getting sick."

"Vodun?"

"Voodoo. The word translates as 'spirit.'" His hand slid up her back to cup the back of her neck, his breath whispering across her cheek. "We'll talk about all that when we go into the field soon to do immunizations in various villages."

His mouth dropped to caress the skin beneath her ear-lobe, which sent a delicious shiver across her throat until she jerked her head away.

"You know, back home that would be considered sexual harassment. Don't make me contact the GPC to lodge a complaint."

"You think a tiny kiss is sexual harassment?" His low laugh vibrated against her skin. "I can think of lots more ways to harass you sexually. If you ask nicely."

"You're ridiculous." She shook her head, feeling slightly dizzy. She should be annoyed, but instead had to desperately will herself to be tough and strong against the seductive temptation of his lips. "In case you haven't noticed, I'm trying to work here. Leave me alone. Seriously."

To her surprise and relief, he straightened and his warm hand left her nape. "Take a break from that for a minute. Ruth and Drew need you to come outside."

"Why?" She swiveled to look at him. He had an odd expression on his face, slightly amused and clearly anticipatory. Obviously nothing was wrong and her curiosity was piqued, in spite of herself.

"You'll see. Come on."

He grasped her hand and she rose from the chair, tugging her hand from his as she followed him out the clinic doors.

As they approached the small enclosure that served as a playground for patients' children and siblings, she could see Drew scooting around on a plastic ride-on toy train that hadn't been there earlier, a wide grin on his face. And two people standing next to him with equally ecstatic expressions.

Who...?

"Toot-toot! Toot-toot!" Drew exclaimed, scuffing his shoes in the dirt as he rode.

Chase put his arm across Dani's shoulders before they stepped inside the gate of the wooden fence. "Mom and Dad, I'd like you to meet Dr. Danielle Sheridan. Dani, my parents, Drs. Philip and Evelyn Bowen."

His parents. Drew's grandparents. Stunned, Dani smiled and reached to shake Chase's father's hand. "It's nice to meet you." Nice and shocking. They just popped in for a quick trip to Benin to meet Drew?

About to shake Evelyn's hand, the woman gave her a warm embrace instead. "It's so delightful to meet you, dear. And our Andrew is so adorable. Precious! I can't believe how he looks just like Chase did at that age. You have no idea how happy you've made us."

*Our Andrew.* The words put a funny little flutter of joy in Dani's chest. She had to smile at the lovely woman's greeting and obvious sincerity. How wonderful that Andrew had grandparents who would clearly want to be a part of his life. Her own mother lived pretty far from where Dani had gotten a job and, as a nurse, worked a lot of hours. Not the kind of grandmother who would be baking cookies and babysitting.

Then again, neither were the Drs. Bowen, working in mission hospitals around the world. Nonetheless, it was nice.

"I'm...surprised you're here," Dani said, giving Chase a look he couldn't misinterpret. He responded with a grin that showed no guilty feelings at all about his subterfuge. "Where do you live?"

"We're working in Senegal right now. Benin's a pretty quick airplane ride from there, really." The woman clasped her hands together, her eyes sparkling. "When Chase told us about Drew and you, we were over the moon. We brought the little train and a few other gifts. I hope that's okay?"

"Of course." Dani smiled. "But I can't tell if he likes it or not, can you?"

They all chuckled, as it was more than obvious he loved it. Scooting around, toot-tooting endlessly and grinning.

"They'd barely taken it from the box before he jumped on it," Chase said as he watched Drew, his gaze soft with a hint of pride. "He's going to be riding a bike in no time."

"We're happy he likes it," Phil said. "I'm especially pleased because if he didn't, I have a feeling Evelyn and I would be heading straight to another store to look for something else, even if we had to fly to Cotonou. I kept having to remind her we were bringing everything on a plane, she had so much stuff."

"It's a grandparents' prerogative to buy their grandchildren presents," Evelyn said, an indulgent smile on her face as she watched Drew. "Especially the very first one."

*First* one? She couldn't know Chase's attitude about having children if she thought there would ever be more.

That thought led Dani in a nasty and very uncomfortable direction it hadn't gone before, making her stiffen. What if Chase did marry someday? What kind of woman would be stepmother to Drew? Just thinking about it made her stomach twist. She reminded herself he'd be working in remote places around the world, so Drew wouldn't be around a stepmother much anyway, but didn't succeed in ridding herself of a slightly sick feeling in her gut.

Evelyn turned her attention to Dani. "I hear there's to be a wedding soon. Have you decided on a date?"

*What?* One look at Chase proved he really had told his parents they were getting married. How arrogant could the man be? He had an infuriatingly smug smile on his face, and an expression that said he couldn't wait to see how she'd react to his mother's question.

"A wedding? I hadn't heard about one. Is it someone I know?" She kept her voice light, her expression bland, but knew Chase could see the challenge in her gaze. So he thought this was one big chess game? He'd forgotten she'd learned to play from him.

His parents looked at one another then at Chase, obviously confused. "Chase said—"

"I said we were getting married. I didn't say Dani had agreed yet," Chase said smoothly, with a look that said, *Answer that.* "But wouldn't it be great to make it happen some time when you could be here to share it with us? Please help me convince her how nice it would be to celebrate our marriage as a family."

Damn the man. He'd certainly played his turn well, with both his parents staring at her with bemused expressions.

"Chase and I just recently met up again," she said, trying to figure out exactly what to say. It was a battle to keep from narrowing her eyes and scowling at Chase for putting her in such an awkward position. Though she was pretty sure that, even if they didn't know the details of her relationship with Chase, his parents knew how babies were made. "I don't feel we know each other well enough again to consider something as important as marriage."

Both his parents looked back at Chase, and Dani felt a slightly hysterical desire to laugh, thinking they looked like they were watching a tennis match.

"All I want is for the three of us to be a family, and I'm sure you'd agree that's the best thing for Drew. But Dani's being difficult." Chase rocked back on his heels, his hands in his jeans pockets. "It's hard to believe, because any woman would be lucky to put my ring on her finger, right, Mom?"

That smile continued to play about his lips. He'd always been good at that delicate combination of joking humor while making a very serious point.

Dani looked at Evelyn, figuring that, as his mother, she doubtless agreed he was an awesome catch for any woman.

"Dr. Bowen, I..." Dani began, not even sure what she was going to say.

"Please, call me Evelyn." She reached to squeeze Dani's arm. "Pay no attention to Chase's heavy-handed attempts at manipulation. I'm surprised, really, at his clumsiness. From the time he was little, he could get whatever he wanted without anyone even knowing he was leading them there."

Astonished at his mother's words, Dani was also more than amused at the surprised and outraged expression on Chase's face.

"What the hell?" He folded his arms across his chest. "You don't think Dani should marry me? What about Drew? What about us being a family?"

"Don't drag your father and me into this." His mother held up her hand. "Obviously, there's some reason you didn't even know about Drew until now. While we'd love to welcome Dani as our daughter-in-law, you two will have to figure all this out on your own. As long as I get to play doting grandmother to our darling baby, I'm happy."

Phil chuckled. "And I have a feeling that 'doting' will be an understatement."

Evelyn grasped Phil's hand and they walked over to stand on either side of Drew, forming a bridge with their arms. "Drive through the tunnel, engineer Andrew. But watch out, there might be a landslide and it could collapse on you," Phil said.

Drew shrieked in delight as he drove around their legs and through the "tunnel," ending up trapped as their arms surrounded him.

As she watched them, Dani's heart filled with how lovely Chase's parents were and how lucky Drew was that they wanted to be a part of his life, even though their time together would doubtless be infrequent.

"I can't believe this," Chase said.

She looked at his disgusted scowl and knew he wasn't talking about his parents' game with Drew. "Is this finally the proof you need that you should get over the unpleasant controlling streak you have? Even your mother thinks so."

"She didn't say I'm controlling. And I'm not."

He stepped close and she was glad his parents were here. Surely Chase wouldn't touch her and kiss her and make her feel all weak and out of control while they were around.

"But convincing?" His mouth came close to her ear, and he smelled so good, like fresh soap and aftershave and him, that it was all she could do not to turn her head for a kiss anyway. "Convincing you will be a pleasure."

He backed off a few inches, and the promise in his dark eyes told her resistance would be tough going. But she could do it. She *would* do it. To protect Drew and to protect her own heart.

"Lunch, everybody!" Spud bellowed from the door.

Drew jumped off the plastic train, knocking it over onto its side, and ran to Dani. He flung one arm around

Dani's leg and wrapped the other around Chase's. "I hungry! Daddy, will you feed me more bugs?"

"You bet. I've got some big, fat ones picked out just for you." Chase lifted his gaze to Dani. His eyes turned from soft and smiling to hard and cool in an instant. "Drew, at least, knows we're already connected, no matter what you want to believe." He reached down to lift Drew into his arms, kissing his round cheek before settling the child against his shoulder like he'd been doing it fo rever.

The image of father and son, of their brown eyes and thick dark hair so like the other, along with the tender expressions on his parents' faces, gave Dani another pang of guilt. But she reminded herself she hadn't really robbed all of them of two and a half years of togetherness. Chase and his parents would have been living who knew where in the world without her and Drew anyway.

"Whatever Spud made, it'll be good," Chase said, his head tipped against Drew's for a moment before he looked at his parents. "Then we'll make a plan for the rest of your visit with your grandson."

# CHAPTER SIX

"To think you've always hassled me about my smooth moves when you're the true master," Trent said as he and Chase pulled off their gloves and gowns after surgery and headed toward the hospital corridor.

"What smooth moves?"

"Getting your parents to come and gush over Drew and put the pressure on Dani. Brilliant." Trent grinned. "Except, of course, that my moves work and yours are a pathetic failure."

"Glad you think it's funny," Chase said, still stunned at his parents' reaction to Dani not wanting to marry him. He'd been so sure his mother would have seemed, at the very least, disappointed. And with Dani's eyes looking so soft and tender as she'd watched them with Drew, he had been positive a little pressure from them would have been a big help toward his goal.

"I still can't believe they didn't back me up. Even threw me under the bus completely when they said it was between the two of us and didn't care whether we got married or not."

"I never thought I'd hear you say you wished you had more interference from outside forces in your life." Trent chuckled. "Seems to me you always complain when anybody at GPC sticks their nose in your business."

"Interference wasn't what I had in mind. Coercion was what I had in mind. Helping Dani see what's obviously the best solution here." No, the interference he was worried about might come in the form of a jerk named Matt he didn't even know. Except the guy was halfway across the world, while he had Dani with him, and there was some old saying about possession being nine-tenths of the law. He planned to take full advantage of it.

"You have no clue about women," Trent said, shaking his head. "The harder you push, the faster she'll run. Show her what a great dad you'll be to Drew and give her time."

"There might not be much time. Who knows how soon you and I'll be relocated?"

"True. But you've got to relax a little instead of bugging her to death. Let her remember why you two were together in the first place. Lord knows, I can't figure out why, but a lot of women do like you."

"I'm just trying to remind her what we had before." Seemed to have worked, for a moment at least, both times he'd kissed her. Just thinking of the feel of her mouth on his, her sweet body pressed close, made his body start to react all over again.

"Then lay off and play hard to get. I guarantee she'll start thinking of your old times in Honduras and come back for more. Women are perverse like that."

"I'm beginning to see why your relationships with women last a nanosecond." Part of Chase wanted to laugh, but Trent's words did make him pause. Could giving Dani a day or two to take the lead be the answer to speeding things up? Just the thought of heading to his next job without his ring on her finger filled him with cold anxiety. Especially with "Mr. Matt" waiting in the wings, four thousand miles away or not.

"Trust me. She won't be able to figure out why you're suddenly not touching her and annoying her all the time. It'll drive her crazy and she'll want to jump your bones. Then she'll say yes, and you can get married." He slapped Chase's shoulder and grinned. "We'll get three weeks off before we start our new jobs. Plenty of time for a honeymoon. I bet your parents would love to have Drew stay with them up in Senegal while you and Dani go somewhere alone. You'd better start deciding where."

The thought of a week or two alone with Dani shortened Chase's breath and sent his thoughts down the erotic path they persisted in going. Not good, because he and Trent had just entered the hospital to do rounds on patients.

A halo of curly blonde hair immediately caught his attention. Dani moved her stethoscope here and there on a child's chest, and while he couldn't really see her expression, he knew it would be intent and focused.

As though she could feel him looking at her, heart-stopping blue eyes lifted to him, and for a moment they stared at one another across the room. She seemed so far away and yet not, as though they were touching one another, breathing one another's breaths, sharing one another's thoughts, despite the expanse between them.

Trent leaned closer and in an undertone said, "Yeah, she's crazy about you. Take my advice, and I'll call the preacher." With an unholy grin he headed towards one of his patients.

Chase inhaled a deep, mind-clearing breath. Why not give Trent's method a try? What he'd been doing the past few days hadn't seemed to convince her, that was for damned sure.

He joined Dani as she checked on her patient to find out what she thought of the child's condition. She smiled at the boy before turning to Chase. "His lungs seem to be clear today. I think it's fine for him to go home tomorrow. Will you tell him?"

The boy grinned at the good news and pumped his arms in the air victoriously. Dani joined him, smiling brightly, mirroring his fists pumps with her own as she exclaimed, "Yahoo!"

The boy laughed, and Chase marveled at her cheerful exuberance. From the very first moment he'd met her he'd noticed that whenever she walked into a room, worries cleared, people smiled, and the rise in energy seemed palpable. His own energy included.

He turned to Dani. "I'm about to check on Apollo. Want to join me?"

Her beautiful eyes smiled at him. "Yes. I was waiting for you."

He liked the sound of that. More than liked it, and wished it was true in more ways than for work. Like in her room at night. In her life, for ever.

It was all he could do not to clasp her face between his palms and give her a soft kiss. He turned away and walked toward Apollo's bed.

The boy's mother had gone somewhere for the moment, with the blankets she used as she slept on the floor carefully folded and stacked. Apollo looked uncomfortable with the apparatus holding his leg in traction to keep the bones aligned, and his expression reflected his misery. He touched the child's forehead with the backs of his fingers, and it felt thankfully cool. No fever was a good sign.

"Does your leg hurt?" he asked. They'd kept him on painkillers, but sometimes it just wasn't enough. "Is the traction rubbing against you anywhere?"

The child shook his head then turned his attention to

Dani as she stopped at the other side of the bed. And who could blame him for wanting to look at her? He himself could look at her all day and night, and never tire of her sweet face and vivacious smile.

"The nurses tell me he's eating and drinking okay, so that's good," Dani said to Chase. She examined the stitches in Apollo's forehead closely, then put her stethoscope in her ears and pressed the bell of it to his chest.

Chase studied the pin he'd placed in the bone as it protruded from the boy's skin. Thank God it wasn't bleeding and didn't show signs of infection. The boy was lucky. "Your leg looks good. Pretty soon we'll change the cast to cover your whole leg, okay?"

Apollo nodded, still looking miserable, poor kid. Chase wished he could hurry the process, but controlling the pain was the best he could do for now.

*"Vous avez...un coeur...très fort,"* Dani said haltingly to Apollo.

Chase had to grin at her accent, which was pretty bad, but he gave her credit for trying. "She's right," he said in Fon, in case the boy wasn't adept at French. "You do have a very strong heart. And your leg will be strong again, too. I promise."

"You'll be getting better every day, and that should make you smile." Dani placed her fingers gently on the corners of Apollo's mouth and tipped them up, and he gave her a small, real smile in response. "Maybe we need to find a way to help you remember that smiling and laughing will make you heal even faster."

She picked up the homemade fly swatter fan, composed of a dowel rod with cardboard taped to it. She pulled a marker from her pocket and drew a smiley face on it before turning it to fan Apollo.

"Don't worry, be happy," she began to sing in her

sweet voice. And then, in typical Dani style, she began cutely bobbing from side to side, smiling her dazzling smile.

"Don't worry, be happy." She waved the smiley-face fan and twirled around. Between singing, she coaxed, "Come on, sing with me! Don't worry, be happy."

The child attempted a feeble version of the song then laughed for the first time that day, looking starstruck.

Probably the same expression he wore when he was around her, Chase thought. He watched her slim figure dance around, looked at the sparkling blue of her eyes, and thought about the moment he'd first met her. How she'd stopped him in his tracks for a second look. And a third. Gorgeous and adorable didn't begin to cover the impact she made on everyone the second she walked in a room with that blinding smile.

At that moment Apollo's mother arrived, and beamed at Dani and her dancing and singing. Chase reassured her on the boy's progress, and Apollo turned to his mother, looking much more cheerful than when they'd first examined him. The child spoke to her in Fon, and she smiled and nodded, looking warmly at Dani and thanking her.

"What did he say?" Dani asked.

"He says he likes the pretty doctor. But that's no surprise." He wanted to say how much he liked the pretty doctor too, but remembered he was supposed to be playing hard to get. Though that seemed kind of stupid, like he was in middle school. But he was going to give it a try, damn it.

Dani turned a bit pink. "Tell him I like him too. And that I'm glad he's starting to feel better."

After Chase did as she asked, she handed the fan to Apollo, patted his shoulder and moved to their next patient. Chase followed and focused on being all business.

Just a colleague, not her former lover. Not the man who wanted to marry her and become her current lover as soon as possible. When they finished rounds, they headed back to the housing compound.

"Is it okay with you if I spend some time with Drew and my parents before we hand him back to you tonight?"

She looked surprised. "I… Sure. You don't want me there, too?"

He shrugged nonchalantly, proud of his acting skills. Yes, he wanted her there but, no, he wouldn't show it. "I just figured you'd like some time to yourself for a change. We'll play with him for a while then bring him in for dinner. Sound okay?"

"Sure," she said again, a slight frown on her face.

Cautious optimism bloomed at the confusion on her face as she clearly wondered why he wasn't touching and teasing her as he had been before. Damn it, maybe he *had* let his worry and frustration push him to come on too strongly.

Maybe Trent's idea was a good one after all.

## CHAPTER SEVEN

"GOT EVERYTHING?" CHASE asked.

"I think so." Mentally, she reviewed her supply list as she looked inside her backpack. Vaccines, syringes, antibiotics, blood-sugar monitor. "Did you say there's a blood-pressure cuff already there?"

"Yeah. We keep a lockbox in the building with various things in it. Otoscope, flashlight, and a small pharmacy for drugs that don't need to be refrigerated." He threw the strap of his battered doctor's bag over his shoulder, lifted up a small box that held more of the supplies Dani carried in her backpack and headed out the door of the clinic.

She followed, refusing to notice his flexing triceps and wide, strong shoulders beneath the white polo shirt he wore. The sky was an iron gray but even without the scorching sun the air rested hot and heavy against her skin.

"You don't think it will be too much for your parents to watch Drew all day? Maybe Ruth should come give them a break."

"Are you kidding?" Chase rolled a dusty motorcycle from beneath an overhang. "They were practically rubbing their hands together with glee at the prospect of having him to themselves."

"All right, then, I won't worry. Though you already

know that when he's on the go, he's like a rubber-band-powered balsa-wood plane. He keeps going until he conks out."

"Yeah. He's a lot of fun."

The indulgent smile on his face was filled with pride. Why had he been so adamant he didn't want children? It was so obvious he already adored their little boy.

"I'm sorry about having to ride the motorcycle," Chase said. He slipped the box into a bigger container attached to the bike. "I usually go alone, and didn't think to talk to Spud about the car. Didn't know he needed to get supplies today."

"In case you don't remember, we rode all over Honduras on a bike like this." As soon as she'd said it, she wished she hadn't. Memories of Honduras weren't something she wanted to think about. Memories of her body pressed against his as they'd ridden to an off-site clinic like they were today, or when they'd had a day off to spend together and find a great hiking spot. A great love-making spot.

Dani shook her head to dispel the thoughts. It should be easy to forget how close they'd been back then. For some reason Chase had stopped the constant touching and teasing and tiny stolen kisses he'd been assailing her with. Surely he didn't really think she'd report him for sexual harassment?

Chase swung his leg over the bike's seat and curled his fingers around the handlebar grips, turning to look at her. "This village is only about a half-hour ride. But I warn you," he said, his teeth showing white in his smile, "the road can be rough at times. So hang on tight."

"Got it." Sitting on the back of the bike, she slipped her arms around him, her fingers curling into his taut middle.

"Ready?"

"Ready." Actually, she wasn't ready at all. Not ready for the feel of her breasts pressed against his hard body. The sensual feel of her groin pressed against his backside. The clean, masculine scent of his neck filling her nostrils.

He opened the throttle and the motorcycle took off down the dirt road. Soon there was nothing visible but groves of trees here and there and lining the bumpy road, the occasional car or truck passing them, and scooters and motorcycles often carrying as many as four and even five people. Bumps in the hard earth jammed her body against Chase and she threaded her fingers together against his sternum to keep from bouncing right off.

"You okay?" Chase shouted over the engine, glancing over his shoulder at her.

"Yes." Except for that urge she kept feeling to slip her hands beneath his shirt to feel the smooth skin she knew was right there, like she'd used to. The urge to touch more private parts as she had in Honduras when they'd been riding together, making Chase laugh and accuse her of trying to make him crash the bike. Then quickly finding the best place to enjoy finishing what she'd started.

Her own body part that she currently had pressed hard against Chase's rear began to tingle at the memories and she wished she could loosen her grip on Chase's middle to smack herself.

She had to stop thinking about their past and focus on the future. On her job. She was here to work and now to establish the framework they'd agree on regarding Drew. A second broken heart over Chase she didn't need, and the future he envisioned for them would mean exactly that.

Finally, the wide and desolate savannah showed signs of habitation. Small rectangular structures made of mud-baked walls, some with thatched roofs and others covered with corrugated steel, were scattered here and there. Happy, smiling children, many naked or wearing only colorful bottoms and beaded jewelry, played in the dirt or worked with their mothers, hanging laundry or grinding some kind of food in large vessels. A group of men and boys, their hands covered in wet, orange mud, were building a new house. As she and Chase rode by, the men waved and shouted, grinning with pride at their work.

Chase stopped the bike next to a small, worn, cinderblock building with an open doorway and windows. When he turned off the engine, the sudden silence was a relief, with the sound of the breeze in the trees and children laughing the only things to be heard.

Dani slipped off the bike and Chase followed. "Did GPC have this place built for a clinic?" she asked.

"No. I'm told some other group built it to be a school but had to abandon the project. We use it on the first of each month so folks who aren't from this village will know when we're coming, too."

An odd stack of stones and other things atop what looked like a mud sculpture caught her eye. Nestled beneath a nearby tree, there were chains and beaded necklaces looped around the entire thing. "What's that?" she asked, pointing.

"A fetish. It's like a talisman. Voodoo to keep away bad spirits."

"Really?" She walked closer to examine it. "Does all this stuff have a special meaning?"

"I don't know about that one in particular, but it's animism. Belief that everyday objects have souls that will help and protect you."

"Do their beliefs make it hard to get people to come to the clinic, if they think the voodoo will keep them healthy and safe?"

"Sometimes. Like anywhere, it depends on the person." Chase pulled the supply box from the motorcycle and stepped towards the door. "About two hundred people live in this village, and we get quite a few from elsewhere. I think they appreciate knowing we'll be here, and rely on modern medicine more than they used to because of it. Which makes it worthwhile to come."

Dani followed him into the little building, the darkness taking a minute to get used to after the comparatively bright daylight. The single room was certainly sparsely furnished, with only a rickety-looking examination cot, a small table, and a few old chairs inside.

"So they don't use voodoo to treat illnesses?"

"They do. Sakpata is the Vodun god for illness and healing, and many call on him and offer sacrifices when someone is sick. Priests also use healing herbs." He organized the supplies on the little table. "Vodun is an official religion in Benin, and a lot of people who are Christian or Muslim still use voodoo elements in their lives, especially when somebody's sick."

"So are you going to have someone make a little doll of me and stick it with pins to make me marry you?" She meant it as a joke, but then had to ask herself why she'd brought up the subject of marriage when he hadn't mentioned it all day.

"Don't I wish there was some way to make you agree to marry me." His lips twisted into a rueful smile. "Unfortunately, the dolls and pins thing is mostly Hollywood. While there is some black magic, it's not a significant part of voodoo. It's really about belief in ancestry and calling on the spirits to help with their lives. Peace and prosperity."

"Well, shoot, that's too bad. I was just thinking about the list of people I might want dolls made of."

"Sorry. Except not really, because I'm probably on your list." Chase stepped over to the locked box and pulled out a stethoscope, blood-pressure cuff, and some drugs to bring back to the table. "You'd be amazed by some of the fetishes, though. Hippo's feet and pig genitalia and even dog and monkey heads." He grinned. "In bigger towns there are voodoo festivals worth seeing. Drew would probably like all the colorful clothes and dancing."

"I bet he would. Maybe we could find a day to go to one." She smiled then looked out the door. Nobody seemed to be heading their way. "So now what? Do you go round people up and bring them in?"

"Round them up?" He smacked his palm against his forehead. "Darn, I forgot my lasso."

"You know what I mean." She placed her hand on his thick shoulder and gave him a little shove. "Let them know we're here."

Her vision had become used to the low light, and she could see the curve of his lips and the little crinkles in the corners of his eyes before he gave a low laugh.

"I'm sure they saw us." He reached out to tuck loose strands of her hair behind her ears, of which there were many after their ride. As he curled one strand around his finger, his smile faded, replaced by something in his gaze that sent her heart thumping. "No way they could miss the beautiful blonde as she rode into town."

His finger travelled down her jaw and she found herself standing motionless, staring into his eyes, holding her breath. His hand dropped to his side and he turned away to briskly finish organizing the supplies.

"As people arrive, you can take care of the children and I'll look at the adults. I'll translate when you need me to. I have the records for the kids we've immunized here since I've been in Benin."

The shift in his demeanor was startling. What had happened to the Chase of yesterday who doubtless would have taken advantage of them being alone and kissed her breathless? Or, at the very least, continued with the flirting he was so good at?

She'd been sure she didn't want that from him. But when he'd turned away, suddenly all business, the traitorous part of her that had been thinking about sex during their entire motorcycle ride wanted to grab him and kiss him instead. Wanted to feel that silky skin covering hard muscle she'd been itching to touch the whole time her arms had been wrapped around him.

She mentally thrashed herself and pulled her own supplies from the backpack. Apparently her libido, which had come to life since seeing him again, wasn't up on the fact that her sensible brain wanted to keep their relationship platonic.

As if by voodoo, the first patients suddenly appeared at the doorway and the next hours were filled with basic examinations and immunizations, distribution of drugs for various problems, medicine to rid children of intestinal worms—which were apparently common here, as they had been in Honduras—and topical or oral antibiotics for the occasional infected wound.

Communicating with the children and their parents was surprisingly easy, with hand gestures working pretty well and Chase translating over his shoulder for the rest.

After being concerned at first that they'd have few patients, Dani couldn't believe the line of children, standing three and four deep, waiting for their shots. After being so frustrated at the sorry state of the immunization records they had, she was more than pleased at how much she'd be able to add to the database after today.

What a great feeling to know that coming here could

make such a difference in the health of these kids. More than once during the day she smiled at Chase and his return smile was filled with a sense of connection, the same understanding of exactly what each was feeling that they'd shared long ago.

By late in the afternoon the line had dwindled to just a few stragglers. The work left Dani feeling both tired and energized at their accomplishments.

"How long do you usually stay?" she asked Chase as she cleaned her hands with antiseptic and looked at the few people remaining outside. "Do you hang around until there's nobody waiting?"

"It depends. Obviously, at some point you just need to shut it down, especially when it gets dark early. Believe me, you don't want to be riding home on a motorcycle after the sun sets. It's not common to be robbed, but it does happen." He grinned at her. "And the last time I rode on all those rough potholes without being able to see, I was more convinced I might not live another day than the time I walked across a frayed rope bridge over the Amazon in a windstorm."

Now, there was a image. Dani laughed. "Then let's be sure to wrap it up before then. We don't want to orphan Drew."

The thought squashed her amusement. In her will she'd listed her own mother as guardian to Drew if anything ever happened to her. But her mother was alone, and tremendously busy. Now that Chase was involved in Drew's life, should they make other arrangements?

"You know, we should talk about that, unlikely as it is, as we figure out our future arrangements with regard to Drew," she said. "If something happened to me, I figured my mother should take him. But maybe your parents would be a better choice."

Chase's expression turned fierce. "No. That's not a good option. Nothing's going to happen to us."

"But we—"

Distraught shouting interrupted her thought as a man pushed his way through the few people standing in line and burst through the doorway.

# CHAPTER EIGHT

Chase stepped over to him, speaking in an authoritative yet calming voice that seemed to help the man get himself under control. Dani wished she knew what was going on, but it was clearly something that would need their attention. The man spoke fast with frantic gestures, and the frown and concern on Chase's face grew more pronounced.

Chase spoke to Dani as he shoved some items in his medical bag and flung the strap over his shoulder. "I need to go with him. He lives about half a mile away, so I'm going to take the bike to get there fast. I'll tell the last in line we'll come back next week so you can put stuff away and lock up the drugs as quickly as possible. Someone can show you where I am. You'll have to walk, but I think I might need you there."

"What's wrong?"

"His wife's in labor and something's not right. She's bleeding and in abnormal, extereme pain—the midwife doesn't know what to do. Assuming we have a live infant, your expertise may help."

He spoke quickly to a man in line, who nodded. "This man will show you where she is."

"Okay." She'd barely uttered the words before Chase

left with the worried husband, and the sound of the motorcycle engine came to her just moments later.

Dani quickly stashed the medical supplies and pharmaceuticals in the lock box then followed the man Chase had asked to guide her through the village.

A rusty bike leaned against the wall of the clinic building and to her surprise he gestured for her to get on it. While it would be great to get there faster than it would take to walk, it wouldn't help to ride it if she had no idea where she was going.

The man cleared up that question when he straddled the bike himself while still gesturing for her to get on the battered seat. Precariously perching herself on it, she placed her hands on the man's shoulders and he pedaled off.

At first their wobbling movement was so slow she ground her teeth in frustration. They'd never get there at this rate, and an increasingly disturbing feeling fluttered in her stomach that the situation just might be dire.

Thankfully, the guy seemed to get the hang of pedaling standing up with her weight behind him, as they picked up speed on the bumpy dirt path, passing a hodgepodge of straw huts and mud houses.

The sound of a woman's moans and cries made the skin over her skull tighten and the bike stopped outside a hut that seemed larger than several others nearby.

She jumped off the bike. "Chase?"

"In here."

She followed his grim voice and stopped just inside the doorway, stunned at the scene. The writhing and moaning woman in labor lay on a pad on the floor that had at one time been some yellowish color but was now stained red with the blood that was literally everywhere. All over the poor woman's lower body. The dirt floor. The mid-wife, crouched beside her and holding her hand. Chase.

"What's wrong?" Her heart tripped in her chest. "What can I do?"

"Placental abruption. You can see the pain she's in, and her abdomen is rock-hard." He finished swabbing the woman's belly with antiseptic wipes and drew some drug into a needle. "Got to do an emergency C-section. I'm about to give her a local anesthetic, which is the best I can do here. Then we've got to get that baby out."

She crouched next to him. "Tell me what to do."

"Get my knife out of my bag. The ball suction to clear the baby's mouth and nose. The ambu-bag. Then get ready, because when I pull the baby out I'm handing it to you and praying like hell."

She grabbed the bag and went through its contents to find what he needed. She snapped on a pair of gloves and grabbed some antiseptic wipes to clean the knife.

Chase injected the woman's stomach in multiple lo-cations until there was nothing left in the syringe, then tossed it aside to take the knife from Dani.

"Are you going to do a low, transverse incision?" She had a feeling the usual C-section standard wouldn't apply here in this hut, with the poor woman likely bleeding to death.

"No. We'll be damned lucky if a vertical gets the baby out in time."

With a steady hand Chase made a single, smooth slice through the skin beginning at the woman's umbilicus down to her pelvis, exposing the hard, enlarged uterus within the cavity. Chase looked briefly at Dani, his jaw tense. "Ready?"

She nodded and prepared herself for fast action. Adrenaline surged through her veins as she knew the infant had probably lost its oxygen connection to its mother and would need immediate help to breathe on its own. If it was still alive.

Chase began the second incision through the uterus itself, exposing the infant. He reached into the womb and carefully lifted the baby out, using his fingers to wipe the baby boy's tiny face and body gently to remove the tangle of clotted-off blood vessels that had torn and lead to the abruption.

"Here." He passed the motionless baby to Dani and began scooping out the loosened placenta from the mother's uterus. "I've got to get her bleeding stopped or we'll lose her."

The infant was dark purple, his lips nearly black from lack of oxygen. Dani quickly used the bulb suction to clear the amniotic fluid, mucus, and black meconium from his mouth, nose, and throat, but he still didn't breathe.

Heart pounding, she attached the smallest mask to the ambu-bag then placed the mask over the baby's nose and mouth. She slowly and evenly squeezed the bulb, praying the air would inflate the baby's lungs.

After what seemed an eternity a shudder finally shook his tiny body. He coughed and drew in several gasping breaths before weakly crying out. His little arms and legs started jerking around and as his cries grew stronger, Dani sagged with relief.

She grabbed one of the stacked cloths the midwife must have put by the mother and quickly wiped the baby down. Getting him dryer and warmer was critical to keeping him from going into shock.

Satisfied that he was now warm enough, she grasped the umbilical cord and milked it gently, trying to get every drop of the cord blood into the baby's body. She then cut the cord and clamped it off.

Looking into the baby's little face, she saw he was no longer crying, his eyes wide as he saw the world for the first time, and it filled her heart with elation. "We did it! We did it!" she said, turning to Chase.

"Good. Give him to the midwife and get me another clamp."

His tone and expression were tight, controlled as he worked to sew the woman's uterus, and Dani's jubilation faded as she switched her focus from the infant to his mother.

The woman was speaking between moans, looking at her baby, but blood still flowed from her body. Such a frightening quantity that Dani knew they had very little time.

She quickly stood to pass the baby to the midwife then grabbed a clamp from his bag. She kneeled next to him again, heart racing. Why was the woman still bleeding? It looked like he'd already tied off the big uterine veins and stitched the uterus itself.

"What's wrong, Chase?"

He shook his head. "Uterus can't seem to naturally clamp down and stop the flow. Check her pulse."

Dani pressed her fingers to the woman's wrist and stared at her watch. "One-forty," she said, dismayed. Clearly, the woman's pulse was rocketing to compensate for her blood volume loss.

He worked several more minutes in silence. "Damn it!" Fiercely intense, he turned to look at Dani. "Get me the garbage bag that's in the motorcycle box and the sponges and gauze in there. Hurry."

She ran to grab what he asked for, wondering what he could possibly have planned but not about to ask with the situation so dire. As she hurried back into the hut she heard him barking orders and the few other women in the room ran off.

Blood literally dripping from his hands and arms, he grimly took the garbage bag from Dani. He slipped his hands inside the bag and began to ease it into the woman's belly cavity.

"What in the world are you doing?" In her astonishment the question just burst from her lips.

"Packing the belly. Like a big internal bandage. It's her only chance. I'll stuff it with the sponges and strips of cloth the women are getting. Tamp it down and apply pressure to stop the bleeding. Pray like hell."

He grabbed the sponges and gauze and stuffed them inside the garbage bag. Then he yanked off his own bloody shirt and rapidly tore it into small strips before stuffing them, too, into the bag. The women returned with cloth strips and he shoved them inside before pressing on it all with his hands.

He kept the pressure on the woman's belly for long minutes before lifting his gaze to Dani. With blood spattered across his face and naked torso, his eyes looked harshly intense. "Check her vitals again."

She quickly took the woman's pulse, and her heart tripped. "One-fifteen. It's working!"

She doubted they'd get it down to a normal reading of seventy, but at least it was heading in the right direction.

"Call Spud. Tell him to get a car here stat to take her to our hospital. We can't transfuse there, but if we pump her with fluids, it should be enough."

She stepped outside the hut to call Spud, and when she returned she saw that Chase was stitching the woman's belly closed with the filled garbage bag still inside.

"So, you leave it in there until she clots well enough?

Then take it out?" Dani had never seen such a thing. Never even heard of it. Amazement and awe swept through her at Chase's incredible knowledge and skill.

"Belly-packing is battlefield medicine." He continued his steady, even stitches to completely close the incision except for the very top of the garbage bag, which was still exposed. The plastic extended outside the woman's body as he stitched around it. "Eventually, we'll be able to pull the sponges and cloth out piece by piece, then the empty bag, and hopefully not have to open her up again."

The woman started speaking again in barely a whisper. In spite of what she'd been through, she extended her arms towards the midwife. Holding her new, tiny son close to her breast, she kissed his head and managed a weak smile.

Dani's throat filled and tears stung her eyes. Chase had done this. He'd somehow, miraculously, saved this woman's life. Her baby hadn't lost his mother.

Chase spoke to the women who'd fetched the strips of cloth, and they brought several pads and put them beneath the patient's legs. Obviously, Chase was concerned about her going into shock before they got her to the hospital.

The women brought some water and, silently, Chase stripped off his gloves and washed the blood off his chest and arms as best he could, with Dani following suit. Spud arrived with a nurse from the hospital, and they carried the woman and her baby to the car and drove off.

Other than quick instructions to Spud and the nurse, Chase had barely spoken for fifteen minutes. Standing next to the motorcycle after they'd packed everything up, Dani touched his arm.

"That was amazing. I've never seen anything like it. You should be very proud of what you did today."

He didn't respond, just looked at her. She couldn't decipher the emotion on his face exactly but it definitely wasn't triumph, which was what she thought he'd be feeling. It seemed more like despair.

He reached for her, grasping her shoulders, and slowly pulled her against his bare chest, which was still sprinkled with dried blood. His lips touched her forehead, lingered, until he stepped back to mount the bike.

Chase was quiet the entire ride back to the GPC compound. Not that there could be much conversation over the loud engine, but on the way to the village he'd managed to throw the occasional comment or observation over his shoulder. Probably the low light made it even more important that he concentrate on avoiding precarious ruts and potholes.

This time her arms were wrapped around a naked torso, and she had to control the constant urge to press her palms to his skin, slide them across the soft hair on his chest, down to the hard corrugated muscle of his stomach. Distracting him while driving in the near dark was definitely not a good idea.

After they'd unpacked the items they hadn't used and returned them to the clinic, Chase seemed remote, preoccupied. "I'm going to go clean up. See you and Drew at dinner."

"Okay." She didn't know what to think of his demeanor. Distance. The lack of touching and flirting earlier that day. And for the past forty-five minutes he'd spoken to her as though they were strangers.

Annoyed with herself at the hurt she felt because of the sudden change in him, she decided to check on Drew before she, too, washed off all the road dirt and changed her bloody clothes. She knew the Bowens had Drew, but had no idea exactly where they were. She turned to find out and felt a hand close over her forearm.

"Do you have pictures of Drew when he was first born? When he was a baby?"

"Of course. Though I don't know how many I have with me. Some on my laptop and a few on my phone."

"I'd like to see them."

Why did he appear so oddly somber? How could he not be elated that fate had sent them to the village that day? "You know, you did just save two lives today. I'm surprised you aren't exhilarated." She certainly had been, until his seriousness had tempered it.

"We saved their lives together." He placed his hand on her cheek. "And three years ago we made a life together."

His eyes were now darkly intense, and she tried to decipher the jumble of emotions there, all mixed up with his somber demeanor and the grim lines around his mouth. He almost looked... Could the word be vulnerable? She searched his face and realized, stunned, that was exactly the word. Never would she have guessed the *über*-talented, ultra-confident Chase Bowen could ever look or feel vulnerable in any way. No matter what the circumstances, he always seemed...invincible.

"Yes, we did," Dani said softly. "And I can see you're as proud of him as I am. I'll find what photos I can and show them to you after dinner."

He nodded and turned to walk to his room, leaving her staring at his back and asking herself if she really knew him as well as she thought she did.

She went to find Drew, and had to wonder. In her infatuation with Chase, with his obvious strengths that had dazzled her so, had she never taken time to look inside at the rest of the man? At all facets of him and his life and what had shaped him to become the person he was today?

Chase was her son's father. They might not be spending much time together in the future, but the emotion on Chase's face tonight proved she needed to understand better what made the man tick.

# CHAPTER NINE

CHASE LAY ON his bed, his hair still wet from his shower, and stared at the cracked ceiling. He hoped everyone went ahead and started dinner—he and Dani had arrived back much later than they'd expected as it was. But he needed a few more minutes to deal with the overwhelming feelings that had unexpectedly swamped him after the birth of the baby that afternoon.

Damn it, he'd never wanted this. Never wanted to be susceptible to the same kind of pain he'd felt when his brother had died. Never wanted to feel vulnerable to his whole universe being crushed in an instant.

But when he'd brought that baby into the world, the moment had taken away his breath.

In his career he'd delivered more babies than he could possibly guess at. Had always appreciated the miracle of birth, the joy of the mother, the pride of the father. Had enjoyed gently passing a healthy infant to suckle at its mother's breast, and sympathized with the loss when a baby hadn't made it.

Never had it felt personal. Until today. The first baby he'd delivered since he'd found out he had a child of his own. Seeing the baby's tiny body, hearing his first cries, watching him looking with wide eyes at the world for the very first time had clutched at his heart like nothing before.

And the mother. She'd suffered so much with the baby's birth and yet, barely escaping death and in tremendous pain, she'd smiled through it all when she'd first seen her son.

He'd missed that with Drew. Missed being there to help Dani. And he hated that he'd never even thought to ask her if it had been an easy birth or a hard one. Even with all the modern technology in the U.S., not all babies were born without complications.

He scrubbed his hands over his face. He never wanted to feel the cold terror for Dani and Drew that had gripped him as he'd worked with mother and infant today. The sudden fear that if something happened to either of them, his entire world would be ripped to pieces. How did people cope with that? Did they just refuse to see the dangers? The risks?

Inhaling a shaky breath, he swung his legs off the bed and sat up. The past couldn't be changed. Andrew had been conceived and born healthy and he was the most beautiful child Chase had ever seen. And Dani was a very special woman. An incredible woman.

He'd do whatever he had to do to keep both of them safe.

As he stepped through the doorway of the kitchen, it looked like everyone had finished eating but Dani. The scene was much livelier than usual, the room filled with Spud, Trent, Dani, his parents, and Drew, who obviously enjoyed being the center of everyone's attention. Laughter at his antics bounced off the walls of the room, but Dani's big smile faded as he walked in, her blue gaze seeming contemplative.

He hoped like hell she hadn't sensed how disturbed he'd felt. He also hoped he had all those feelings under control.

"Daddy!" Drew grinned and raised his arms toward Chase, his fingers gooey with mashed yams.

Chase's chest felt peculiarly heavy and light at the same time. He couldn't believe how quickly Drew had accepted him as his dad. How he wanted to be held by him. To be played with by him. He had to swallow hard to shove down the emotions that had swamped him earlier.

"Hey, lizard-boy. What have you been up to today?" He grabbed a wet towel, partly to give himself something to do, and wiped Drew's hands before sitting next to him.

"Your mother and I showed him the technique for shinnying up a palm tree today," Phil said. "He's a natural. Even better than you when you were that age."

"Yes," Evelyn agreed with a proud smile. "He made it up at least three feet. With us spotting, of course. Pretty soon he'll be getting all the way up to grab a coconut or two."

"Little did I know this was a Bowen family tradition," Dani said with a smile. "When Chase first showed off how he could climb a coconut tree, I thought it was just a macho thing he did to impress women."

"It worked, didn't it?" Chase asked. He conjured up a smile and took a swallow of beer, hoping it would help him relax and feel more normal. Last thing he wanted was to have anyone guess at his feelings. Or, worse, ask.

"A few of the places we lived actually had palm-tree climbing contests. Chase and his brother even won occasionally," his mother said.

Chase stiffened and glanced at Dani. He'd never mentioned Brady to her. Or to Trent or Spud, for that matter. What were the chances they wouldn't ask questions?

"Chase has a brother?" Dani looked questioningly from his mother to him, her eyebrows raised.

Obviously, no chance. Chase gritted his teeth. The last

thing he wanted to talk about was Brady. Not ever and especially not today.

"Had." Evelyn's eyes shadowed. "He—"

"Dani said she'd find some pictures of Andrew when he was a baby," Chase interrupted. He wasn't hungry anyway, and stood to gather empty plates, with Spud following suit. "I know you two proud grandparents want to see them as much as I do."

Dani looked at him for a long moment before speaking. "Yes. I had more downloaded than I realized."

She stood to retrieve her computer from a kitchen shelf, and Chase drew a deep breath of relief. Not that she wouldn't ask again, but at least he'd be prepared to give the most basic account possible, without his parents around to embellish it, before changing the subject.

Everyone crowded around as Dani gave a slide show on her laptop. Drew had been so damned cute as a baby, with a shock of dark hair sticking up around his head, his brown eyes wide, his cheeks round and pink. Sitting on the floor amid a pile of blocks, a big grin showing just a few teeth, drool dripping from the corners of his mouth like a bulldog. She even had a video of him crawling up to the hearth in her little house, pulling himself to his feet then yanking to the floor the houseplant perched there, scattering dirt everywhere.

It was a hell of a thing that he'd missed it all.

Amid the laughing and *aww*s echoing in the kitchen, and Drew's delight at his photos, Chase found himself looking at Dani between nearly every picture. The love and tenderness in her eyes as she looked at the captured moments in time. Not so very different from the expression on her enchanting face when they'd shared so many intimate moments in Honduras.

Her smiling gaze met his more than once, warm and

close, and he almost blurted out the words right there in front of everyone. Almost asked why she was being so stubborn about marrying him when they had this beautiful child between them. The closeness they'd shared before and could share again. Why? Did she still honestly not believe him, or trust him, when he promised they could make it work? Was it her feelings for that Matt guy?

"That's it, I'm afraid." Dani shut her laptop with a smile at Drew. "I need to remember to take more pictures while we're here in Benin. You seem to grow bigger every day."

"The good news there is that Drew has grandparents with a very nice camera who now have a new favorite subject," Phil said. "We've taken so many of him it's a good thing I brought an extra memory card. Too bad we have to leave in a couple days."

"Perhaps you and Dani can bring Drew to Senegal," Evelyn said to Chase. "How much longer are you here in Benin?"

"Not sure." He wasn't about to go into that potential problem right now. He didn't know if Dani knew he'd be leaving soon, and the last thing he wanted to give her was another reason to think they shouldn't make things permanent between them.

Drew yawned, and Chase grabbed the excuse to get out of there. "Looks like a certain tree-climbing monkey needs to go to bed," he said, lifting him into his arms. Drew snaked his arms around Chase's neck and he held the child's little body close. Would he ever stop feeling the amazement, the joy that nearly hurt at having this little guy in his life?

"I a lizard, not a monkey," Drew said with another yawn.

His eyelids drooped and Chase headed for the door

then stopped to look at Dani. He realized he didn't know Drew's bedtime routine, and that had to change. "You coming?"

She nodded, saying her goodnights to everyone before following him down the hall to her room.

"I'll get him ready. You don't have to stay," Dani said as she pulled Drew's Spiderman pajamas from a drawer.

"I want to know what's involved in getting him ready for bed," Chase said. He gently sat a half-asleep Drew on the edge of the bed and took the pajamas from Dani. Afraid the child would conk out before he'd even had a chance to change him, Chase quickly pulled Drew's little striped shirt over his head and finished getting him into his PJs.

"We usually read a book after using the bathroom, but I don't think he's going to stay awake for that tonight," Dani said as she put Drew's discarded clothes away.

Together, they took him down the hall to take care of bathroom necessities before tucking him into bed.

"'Night, Daddy," he said, lifting his sweet face for a kiss.

"'Night, Drew. Sleep tight."

Drew did the same with Dani, and as Chase watched her soft lips brush their child's cheek, saw her slender fingers tuck her unruly hair behind her ears, saw her tempting round behind as she bent over, he knew he couldn't play the hard-to-get game any longer. Not just because it hadn't seemed to work, he thought wryly.

He had to touch her. Had to kiss those soft lips. Had to satisfy the desire, the longing he'd barely been able to contain since she'd first arrived. Since he'd first seen her silhouetted in the sub-Saharan twilight.

He needed her tonight, and could only hope she'd give in to the feelings he knew they'd both shared, remembered, since finding one another again. Let him show her what she meant to him. Let him show her how good their future could be.

She straightened and stepped closer to Chase in the small room. "He's already sound asleep," she said with a smile. "Your parents wore him out. Or he wore them out. They've obviously had a wonderful day. Thank you."

"For…?"

"For bringing them here. For Drew getting to know them. He hardly has any family and yours is…special."

Her luminous eyes looked up at him, held him, and he closed the gap between them. He pulled her close, hoping she wouldn't resist, object. "Not as special as you. No one is as special as you."

Then he kissed her. Slowly. Softly. Not wanting to push, to rush, to insist. He wanted her to want the same thing he wanted. For them to join together and make love in a way that made everything else fade away. All the worries, the fears he'd felt earlier buried beneath the kind of passion only she had ever inspired in him.

She tasted faintly of coffee and vitality and Dani, and she kissed him back with the same slow tenderness he gave her. So different from the spontaneous combustion of their previous kisses. The kisses he fed her, that she gave in return, were full of a quietly blossoming heat. Slowly weakening him as they strengthened his need.

Her hands tentatively swept over his chest and shoulders to cup the back of his head, her tongue in a languid dance with his. He pulled her tightly against him, loving the feel of her soft curves molded perfectly to his body. Made for him.

She broke the kiss. "You are the most confusing man."

"Not true." He brushed her lips with his because he

couldn't stand even a moment's distance. "There's nothing confusing about what I want right now."

He kissed her again, and her sigh of pleasure nearly had him forgetting about gently coaxing. Nearly had him lifting her to the bed and yanking off their clothes to tangle their bodies together, to feel every inch of her skin next to his.

She pulled her mouth away with a little gasping breath. "A couple of days ago you wouldn't stop touching and kissing me then all day today you acted like we barely knew one another."

"So it did work." He pressed his mouth below her ear. Tasted her soft throat. Breathed in her sweet, distinctive scent.

"What worked?"

"I was playing hard to get. Trent told me to. Said you'd want to jump my bones."

She gave a breathy laugh. "I swear, boys never grow up, do they?"

"So, do you?" He slipped his hands up her ribs, let one wander higher. "Want to jump my bones?"

Her lips curved, but she shook her head. "I don't think that's a good idea. We have…issues to resolve without making things harder."

"Except something's already harder."

She chuckled, her eyes twinkling, and he knew he could look into the amazing blue of them for ever. He kissed her again, hoping to make her forget about any and all issues and just feel.

Surely she could sense, through his kiss, what she meant to him. That she wouldn't stop and pull away and end the beauty of the moment before it began. That she could feel what she did to him through the pounding of his heart and the shortness of his breath.

Dani pulled her mouth from his and untwined her hands from behind his neck. She stepped out of his hold, and Chase tried to control the frustration that had him wanting to grab her and refuse to let her go. "Dani—"

"Shh." She pressed her fingers to his lips then slid their warmth down his arm to grasp his hand. "Your room is close by, right? Let's go there. We'll hear Drew if he wakes up."

Relief practically weakened his knees. Or, more likely, he thought with a smile, they'd already been weakened by her. "Come on."

Dragging her behind him, Chase could hear her practically running as he strode the short distance down the hall to his room, but slowing down wasn't an option. He'd barely shut and locked the door behind them before he grabbed her again.

This time the kisses didn't start out sweet and slow. He found himself in a rush, his mouth taking hers with a fierceness and possessiveness he couldn't seem to control. His hands slid over her bottom, up her sides to her belly and breasts, further until he cradled her head. He released her ponytail, and the tangle of her hair curling around his hands took him back to the first time he'd kissed her, when those ringlets had captured his fingers and refused to let go.

"I've always loved your crazy curls," he said. "Love the way it feels, tickling my skin."

"Well, if you really love it..." Her soft fingers slipped up his ribs and he shivered as she pulled his shirt over his head. She leaned forward and nuzzled his neck, her wild hair caressing his shoulders, and he couldn't control a groan.

"I love your hair, too," she said. Her hands traveled back up his chest before she buried her fingers in his hair, pulling his mouth down to hers for a deep kiss. "It's like thick silk. Drew's lucky he has your hair and not mine."

Her lips were curved and her eyes were full of the same desire that surged through his every cell. "I can't agree," he said. "But arguing with you isn't on our agenda right now. Getting both of us naked is."

He tugged off her shirt then reached for the button on her shorts before desperation seemed to grab both of them at the same time and every garment was quickly shed until both stood naked in front of each other.

His breath caught in his throat. Three years since he'd seen her beautiful body. Three years without enjoying her small, perfect breasts. The curve of her waist, her slim hips and legs, the blonde curls covering the bliss between them. Three years without touching and tasting every inch of her soft, ivory skin, and suddenly he couldn't wait one more second to join with her.

He reached for her at the same time she reached for him, and they practically fell onto his bed with a bounce.

Her breasts grazed his chest and he dipped his head to take one pink nipple into his mouth. With his eyes closed, tasting first one taut tip then the other, he could imagine they'd been together just yesterday, without the three years of distance between them. He could hope, as his lips traveled over her flat abdomen, that she had missed him as much as he'd missed her. He could believe, as his fingers explored the moist juncture of her thighs, as he breathed in the scent of her, as he listened to her moans of pleasure, that she was already his, for ever.

"Chase." As she gasped his name, her hands tugged at his head, his arms, his torso.

He rose to lie above her and she opened her arms and body to him, a beckoning smile on her beautiful lips.

"You said your goal was to make me want to jump

your bones." Her voice vibrated against his chest. "You've succeeded. So do it."

She held him close, wriggling beneath him, trying to position herself in a way that left him no option for staying strong and enjoying her body for a whole lot longer.

He managed a short laugh. "And you call me bossy." He wanted to kiss that smiling mouth of hers, but wanted to watch her, too. He slipped inside her heat, and was glad he could see her eyes, her lips. See her desire, her pleasure. Knowing he gave it to her.

He wanted, more than anything, to give her pleasure. He wanted to make this moment last, to show her he would give her everything. To assuage whatever worries she had about them staying together for ever.

As they moved, he tried to take it slowly. To draw out the distinctive rhythm the two of them had always shared. But the little sounds she kept making, the way she kissed him, the way she wrapped her legs around him and drew him in drove him out of his mind.

He couldn't last much longer. He reached between them to touch her most sensitive place as they moved together, and was rewarded as she closed her eyes and uttered his name. Saw the release on her beautiful face as he let himself fall with her.

The quiet room was filled with the sound of their breathing as they lay there, skin to skin. He buried his face in the sweetly scented spirals of her hair, stroking his hand slowly up her side to cup her soft breast.

He smiled. After what they'd just shared, even stubborn Dani couldn't deny they belonged together.

Neither seemed to want to move, and they lay there for long minutes, skin to warm skin. Until her hands shoved at his shoulders and he managed to lift himself off her and roll to one side. With his fingers splayed across her stomach, he finally caught his breath.

"If I didn't know better, I'd think I didn't have any bones left for you to jump," he said, kissing her arm.

"I have to check on Drew."

She struggled to get up and Chase swung his legs off the bed to give her room. Then, shocked, he saw the expression on her face.

It wasn't full of blissful afterglow, the way he knew his had been. It was sad and worried. Distant.

What the hell had happened?

"Dani." He reached for her hand, but she shook him off, grabbed up her clothes and quickly put them on.

"I'm sorry." Her voice was tight, controlled, so unlike the Dani he used to know as she struggled with the button on her shorts. "This was…a mistake. We shouldn't have complicated an already complicated problem."

Chase tamped down a surge of anger at her words. "You're the one making it a complicated problem. To me, there's no problem at all."

"Our…making love…doesn't change anything. Doesn't solve the problem of you wanting us to be married and act like we're a normal family while you live halfway across the world."

"Damn it, Dani." He grasped her arm and halted her progress in getting on her shoes. "We *can* be a normal family. How many people travel on business while their spouse keeps things going at home? It's the same thing."

She pulled her arm loose and slipped on her sandals. "It's not the same thing. Do I have to keep saying it over and over? Seeing you just a few months a year, Drew would wonder why your work is more important than he is."

"I'd make sure he knows he's the most important thing

in my life. That you both are." He wanted to shake her. How could she still put up this damned wall between them after what they'd just shared?

She shoved her glorious curls from her face and finally looked him in the eye. He saw the same despair and anxiety that had been there from the minute she'd arrived in Benin, and didn't know what the hell to do about it. Hadn't he given her every reason to trust him? Why could she not see what was so very clear?

He tried to reach for her, but she stepped to the door, shaking her head. "I need to check on Drew," she said again. "And I need to think. About you and me and my own mission work and Drew. I'll...see you tomorrow."

As the door clicked behind her, he nearly dropped down onto the bed in frustrated defeat.

After what they'd shared, he'd been sure he'd won her tonight. And didn't know what the hell his next move should be.

# CHAPTER TEN

CHASE WALKED INTO the kitchen after his run and workout to make coffee for Dani. An extra five miles had cleared his head and brought renewed optimism. Surely, after last night, she'd dreamed of him the way he'd dreamed of her. Relived every achingly sweet moment in her arms and body.

He'd hated feeling so shaken and disturbed last night before dinner. Not a feeling he was used to, and definitely a feeling he didn't like. But making love with Dani had calmed him, soothed him, deep within his soul, and he wanted that again. And again.

Hopefully, she was over whatever had prompted her doubts and regrets and quick exit last night. And if she wasn't over it, he had a plan to get her over it.

His plan was to take a cup of coffee to her room, awaken her with a kiss then, assuming Drew was still asleep, kiss her and touch her and convince her that a morning shower together was the perfect way to start the day. Just thinking about kissing her soft lips and soaping her every delicate curve had him breathing faster.

Maybe he should just forget about waiting for the coffee to brew and head in there that minute. Except the woman was addicted to her morning coffee, and the gesture would probably soften her up and help him get what he wanted. Her, naked, wet, and slippery against his equally naked, wet, and slippery body.

Reminded yet again of what they had together. Why they belonged together.

Despite the uncertainty of his plan, he had to chuckle, thinking about how irritated she used to get when he dragged her out of bed early in the morning to do push-ups and sit-ups with him. A cup of coffee under her nose, though, always seemed to bring down her annoyance and bring up that sunny smile that had him starting the day with a smile of his own.

Drumming his fingers against the countertop as he listened to the coffee perk, he spotted yesterday's mail in a small pile. After being gone all day then preoccupied afterwards, he hadn't looked at it. A good distraction from his currently surging libido.

He shuffled through the envelopes then stopped cold when he spotted one addressed to him with the GPC logo and return address. The back of his neck tightened and he had a bad, bad feeling he knew what it was.

He ripped open the envelope and unfolded the letter. It didn't take more than a quick skim of its contents to see he'd been right.

Damn it! Half crumpling the letter, he pressed both palms to the countertop.

Panama. His new assignment. One more week here, three weeks off, then Central America.

What the hell should he do now?

No way was he heading to Panama before Dani became his wife. Even if he stayed here for the three weeks' vacation, she'd have plenty of work to do with the two new surgeons arriving to replace him and Trent. Unless she was willing to share her room and single bed, which she apparently wasn't ready to do, he'd have to find another place to stay. Acquire his own car or scooter to get around.

He straightened. Those were easy things to accomplish. The hard part was convincing Dani that marriage between them was best all round. The way they'd burned up the sheets last night should have shown her they still had what they'd shared in Honduras and had her saying yes right then.

Damn it to hell. Could GPC have possibly sent him farther away? It couldn't have been the Congo, or someplace close where he could fairly easily hop a plane to see her and Drew?

No, it had to be literally halfway across the world from Dani.

Without a guarantee that he could charm and cajole her into marriage before he had to leave, he couldn't afford to just hope absence would make the heart grow fonder, or however that stupid old saying went. More likely it would be out of sight, out of mind, and she'd end up back with Matt in less than eight months, leaving *him* in the cold and with no influence at all about what mission trips she might head to in the future with their son in tow.

An icy hollow formed in his chest at the thought of never again holding her or kissing her. Maybe even having to see her with some other man when he visited Drew.

No. Not happening.

Various solutions spun through his mind until he struck one that seemed viable. He'd been with GPC a long time. Year-round, unlike a lot of docs. And his parents had worked for them at least thirty years. Surely all that gave him some clout.

In a few hours, when the GPC offices opened, he'd make a phone call. Tell his old buddy Mike Hardy that

Dani and her son needed a change of assignment from Benin, and to find someone to replace her. That she needed to join him in Panama for the duration of her contract commitment.

He sucked in a calming breath and nodded. Yeah. It could work. Somehow he'd get the folks at the GPC to keep mum on why she was being reassigned with him. Come up with a good reason she'd believe.

The kitchen door swung open and he jumped as he turned to see who it was.

Trent. A breath of relief whooshed from his lungs.

"What are you up to?" Trent asked, eyebrows raised. "You look like you just robbed the GPC piggy bank. Shake out your pockets so I can see if there's more than a buck fifty in there."

Thank God it wasn't Dani, because if Trent was getting guilty vibes from him, she'd be sure to suspect he was up to something. She'd always had a sixth sense when it came to what he was thinking and feeling.

"Just wondering how I can snitch that fancy watch you bought in Switzerland before you head to your next assignment." Chase threw out a grin he hoped was convincing. The last thing he wanted was another lecture from Trent on how to deal with Dani. On playing hard to get or letting things unfold as they would or whatever the hell he came up with next. "So, where are they sending you?"

"Eastern India. West Bengal, to be exact." Trent grabbed a cup and poured the coffee Chase hadn't noticed had finished brewing. "How about you?"

"Panama." Just the word made his stomach churn.

Trent sipped his coffee and gave him a measuring look. "So, now what?"

Chase didn't pretend to not know what he meant. "Not

sure. I'm thinking I'll call Mike at GPC and have Dani reassigned with me."

Trent nearly spit out his coffee as he choked. "Reassigned with you?" He burst out laughing. "Oh, man, I want to be in the room when she finds out you're moving her halfway across the world without even asking."

"None of this is funny." Chase gritted his teeth. "I can't go all the way to Panama without things tied up between us. Or anywhere else, for that matter. And since it's not looking like that's going to happen in a few weeks, the logical solution is for her to come with me."

"You are so delusional." Trent shook his head. "Do you really think Dani would want to marry a guy who's so controlling that he first demands marriage and then, when she says no, manipulates the whole world so things will turn out the way he wants them to?"

"This has nothing to do with being controlling." Why the hell did everyone keep accusing him of that? "This has to do with making the best decision and getting married because of Drew."

"*Your* best decision. Which isn't necessarily *her* best decision."

"What, you think I'd be a lousy husband? Thanks a hell of a lot." Surprise and anger burned in his chest. "You know, I'm damned tired of my friends and family turning on me this way. I try to do right by my own son and all I get is a raft of crap over it." He grabbed a glass of orange juice and downed it in one gulp. "I'm calling the GPC. And once Dani and I are married and happy, there's no way she'll be mad about moving with me."

Trent looked at him steadily before he gave a small shrug. "You know her better than I do. And I honestly wish you the best of luck because, of course, I know you'd be good to her and Drew. But I think you're making a mistake if you don't talk to her first."

The sound of squeaking hinges preceded Dani as she came into the kitchen. Absently, Chase recognized the anticipation in her eyes—it was her I-smell-coffee look. Her pleased expression morphed into a frown as she looked first at Chase then at Trent then back at Chase, a question in her blue eyes.

"You two fighting about something?"

"No." Chase stalked over to Dani, placed his hand behind her head and gave her a hard kiss. To show Trent and her and himself that she belonged to him—would belong to him for ever—no matter what the obstacles. No matter how stubborn she was.

Her shocked eyes widened and she opened her mouth to speak but Chase had had enough talking for one morning. He dropped his hand. "I'm going to check on Drew before I take a shower." He knew his voice was tight, barely controlled, but it was better than yelling at both of them, which was what he wanted to do. "See you in the clinic."

"See, that wasn't so bad, was it?" Dani rubbed the arm of the little girl she'd just immunized and smiled, holding out a sheet of the stickers she'd brought from the States for the girl to choose from. The child's dark eyes lit up at a sparkly fairy, and she carefully stuck it to the big index card Dani gave her.

With any luck, the children's families would pay attention and bring both the child and the card back when her next shots were due. Of course, they didn't have calendars so they would doubtless have trouble remembering exactly when they should return. And, sadly, most couldn't even read. But the double system, with Dani having the information entered into the laptop, too, just might help keep track of their care better than before. If and when they showed up again.

Spud and the local nurses had gone into different communities to let people know they'd be doing immunizations all week, and it seemed to have worked pretty well. Trent had the day off, but she and Chase managed the substantial turnout.

Dani was surprised and thrilled with the slow but steady stream of children that arrived, some on bicycles, some on scooters, some on foot. One entire family showed up in a rickety horse-drawn cart, and Chase had teased her again about not being in Kansas any more, as it was apparently a common occurrence.

Dani smiled at the next child in line and, for at least the fiftieth time that day, found herself momentarily distracted by Chase standing ten feet across the room. Her gaze catching on his profile as he listened with his stethoscope. Staring at the strong muscles in his arms, his big gentle hands as they moved over a patient's body. The creases in the corners of his eyes as he caught her looking and gave her a knowing smile that showed he, too, was remembering last night.

This was exactly why she'd practically run from the room. Chase was a dangerous drug she wasn't sure she should keep taking. Bringing a euphoria that made her want to forget about anything but the scent of his skin, the delicious feel of his heavy body atop hers, the mind-blowing pleasure only he had ever given her.

She just might have been able to resist his magnetic pull. Stayed strong despite the way her pulse tripped and her breathing suspended every time he touched or teased her. But watching his amazing work yesterday had filled her with awe. Not that she'd forgotten what he did every day. What miracles he could accomplish when a situation demanded it.

But seeing how disturbed he'd obviously felt after the difficult birth of the baby and nearly losing the mother, combined with the admiration that had filled her heart, had touched the healer in her.

It seemed obvious he must have been thinking about Drew and how blessed they both were that their son had been born without complications. Asking to see pictures of Drew as a baby and toddler must mean he'd been painfully thinking about having missed those years.

She hadn't made a conscious decision to give in to her desire to be with him. But when she'd seen the haunted look in his eyes, she'd wanted to make it all better. To bring back the normally tough and confident Dr. Chase Bowen who never showed the vulnerability that had so surprised her.

Even now there was tenseness about his mouth and eyes. Edginess that had been there when he'd given her that hard kiss in the kitchen right in front of Trent. Like he had been staking his claim.

She dragged her attention back to the child she was about to immunize. The bad news was that their lovemaking had done more than momentarily take the strain from Chase's face. It had touched the wound deep in her heart she'd thought had healed and scarred over. The wound she absolutely did not want ripped open again.

But apparently her self-protective mechanism wasn't working quite right, because she couldn't stop thinking about what they'd shared last night. Couldn't stop thinking about how wonderful and special and overwhelming it had been, and how she wanted it again.

Which was very, very dangerous.

You'd think she'd never made love to him before.

Hadn't spent an entire year exploring every inch of Chase's body in every possible location.

Disgusted with herself for thinking about every inch of his body for the hundredth time that day, Dani finished the little girl's immunizations. She looked around the room and saw Chase locking some drugs in the drawer.

He must have felt her gaze on him because his brown eyes met hers. "Need some help?" Chase asked.

She turned back to her work table, smiling at a little boy now ready for his shots. "A back rub would be nice. I feel like my spine is frozen in a permanently bent position."

And wasn't that kind of invitation a totally stupid thing to say? She gulped and focused on making the boy feel at ease as she poked him with a needle. Suddenly, right next to her, Chase placed his hands on her shoulders, gently kneading, lowering his head next to hers. "I'm very good at the kind of doctoring where we find a new position for your back. I can make it feel all better."

The sensual promise in his voice took her right back to last night, suspending her breath and making her heart flutter. The boy she'd just immunized left with his stickered card clutched to his chest and she glanced up at Chase. At the curve of his lips. At his eyes, smoldering and dark. And somehow shadowed, too, with something else she couldn't figure out. Worry? She'd thought that was her domain.

"How's that feel? Better?"

"Yes. Good. Thanks, that's enough." She stood and stepped to a cupboard, gulping in oxygen not infused with Chase's scent.

Why, oh, why did her body and mind so want to get physical with him again, instead of listening to logic? But it was more than obvious it would take very little persuasion on his part to start what they'd had last night all over again.

*And why not?* that traitorous part of her brain whispered. Just like last night, she was finding it harder and harder to come up with a good reason why she couldn't just enjoy the unbelievable way he made her feel. To give herself up to it until he left.

Until he left. How she'd feel then, she had no clue. Tough as it had been leaving him three years ago, she'd survived it. Even managed to stop thinking about him constantly. Stopped wondering where he was and what he was doing and who he was doing it with.

But this time would be different, and that knowledge brought heaviness to her chest and a painful stab to her soul.

This time, because they had Drew to share, she'd be in contact with him. Know all that she hadn't known before, including if he had a serious relationship with someone else. That most definitely would not be a good feeling, but she'd have to toughen up and deal with it. The question was, would making love with him or not making love with him while they were here together make it any less painful in the future?

Was it worth the risk to her heart to fall headlong into the heady, emotional crevasse that was Chase Bowen? A crevasse she'd foolishly thought three years ago that he'd fallen into along with her?

Through the doorway the sun glowed low in the sky and the tall man walking in seemed to bring a sweep of muggy heat along with him. He wore a cylinder-shaped striped hat and a bright and colorful tunic completely at odds with the grim exhaustion etched on his face. A boy of about fourteen followed him. Nearly expressionless except for his deeply somber eyes, he had a length of equally bright fabric wrapped around his shoulders and arms like a cape.

Chase stepped over to them and spoke to the man, who turned to the boy with a single nod. Like an unveiling, the child slipped the fabric from his arms.

Dani's breath stopped and she stared in disbelief. She'd thought Apollo had had a terrible injury? This was something straight out of a horror movie.

# CHAPTER ELEVEN

TWO LONG BARE bones stuck out below the child's elbow from what was left of his arm. The normal soft tissue abruptly ended, with the skin black and mummified.

Dani could hardly believe what she was seeing. Her chest constricted at what unimaginable pain the boy had to have suffered over what must have been weeks, or even longer. Clearly his hand had completely rotted off and left behind what they were staring at.

Dani lifted her gaze to Chase's. His expression was carefully neutral as he asked questions of the father and the boy. But his dark eyes held grave despair.

"Okay." Chase's chest rose and fell in a deep breath as he turned those eyes to Dani. "I don't have to tell you we have to remove what's left of his arm. I'll take it off above the elbow. You'll have to act as my assistant. If you don't want to, we can have them spend the night and I'll have Trent or the nurse help me tomorrow."

"Of course I'll assist." Did he think she couldn't handle the tough stuff? She'd feel insulted if the situation wasn't so awful.

"Let's get him set up in the OR. I'll scrub then get him anesthetized."

With a few quick words to the father he laid his hand gently on the boy's back and guided him through the doors to the OR. Dani tried to give a reassuring smile to the man, reaching out to touch his forearm, trying to let him know it would be okay, but the man's expression didn't change.

The ache in her chest intensified, imagining what not only the boy but his parents, too, had been through with this. Why, oh, why hadn't they come in sooner? It was a miracle that infection hadn't killed the child.

As she entered the room, she was struck by the stoic expression on the boy's face. Just lying there, quiet and still, looking at her and Chase with serious, deep brown eyes. Not upset. Not even grim. Just accepting of this horrible thing that had happened to him, which would affect him for the rest of his life. She swallowed down tears and busied herself getting the surgical equipment together.

Chase put the boy under sedation with some antiquated-looking equipment. "I've never seen a machine like this," Dani said, both because she wondered about it and to distract her from what was about to happen. "Does it ever fail?"

"It looks like hell, I know. But it's reliable and safe, believe it or not. A hospital in Cotonou donated it."

Dani watched Chase prep the skin above the boy's elbow, waiting for him to tell her the story about the child. When he said nothing, she had to ask. "Did they tell you what happened? Why they waited so long to come in?"

"This kind of thing happens way too often." Chase picked up the knife. "He fell from a tree. They live over sixty kilometers away, with no easy way to get here."

Dani thought about Drew learning to shinny up the palm tree, at the climbing competitions Evelyn and Phil had told her about, and her heart stopped. "If kids fall from trees all the time, why do parents allow it? Why did *you* do it?"

"They're not climbing for fun. They're gathering leaves for their livestock. During the drought that can follow the rainy season, there isn't enough food to feed the animals. After a long time working in the trees, they get careless or just lose their footing."

Chase seemed fiercely focused on making a circumferential, fish-mouth incision above the child's elbow to leave plenty of skin and flesh to fold beneath what would end up being the stump of his arm. Dani noted the tightness of his lips, his jaws clamped together, and knew that, no matter how many times he'd seen these kinds of horrific things, he never got used to it. Never just took it in his stride but felt deep empathy for all the people born without the privileges so many others took for granted.

She suddenly saw what she hadn't completely understood before. Why he'd said this wasn't just what he did but who he was.

He had been born into this life. Accomplished more in a year to help people on this earth than most did in a lifetime. And she again felt overwhelmed with the admiration and respect she'd felt yesterday. Had felt in Honduras when she'd seen the lives he'd changed.

From the moment she'd met him, she knew he was like no one she'd met before. And with painful clarity, she understood even more what a nearly insurmountable situation yawned between them. His work was his life, and while he wanted to be a good father, he'd never be able to be that unless they lived together. He didn't want Drew anywhere but the U.S., but she, too, wanted to make at least a small contribution to people like this young boy. So where did that leave them?

There was no good answer. Marriage? Leaving her alone and Drew wondering why his dad didn't want to live with them? No marriage? Leaving them even more distant from one another? Dear Lord, she just didn't know.

Chase clamped off the artery and vein then reached for the bone saw. As he sawed through the humerus she clenched her teeth at the horrific sound and thought of her own son. Wanted to know more about why the family had waited until the situation was this bad.

"Why didn't they come in sooner?"

"I told you. They live far away. Just spent two days walking here. Obviously, it was a compound fracture, and the local healer tried splinting it and called on the spirit Sakpata to help him heal. They probably thought it would be okay. But I'm sure it was full of debris just like Apollo's and got infected."

He set aside the bone that would never again be a part of the child. With heavy sadness weighing in her chest, she pressed sponges against the opening to soak up blood and fluids. "But they must have seen that it wasn't getting better. I can't even imagine what it must have looked like."

"Don't judge them. Don't impose your Western views on the life they have to live here." His voice was fierce as he clamped off the artery and vein and began to sew the fish-mouth incision back together over the stump. "They didn't know what to think. Thought maybe it was healing, part of Sakpata's plan when his hand turned from pink to purple to black."

He leaned more closely over the gaping, raw flesh, carefully stitching the tissue. "But, as you can tell, there was superficial dry gangrene of the exposed tissue. He must have a good immune system, which sealed the gangrene off in the junction between the wound and the rest of his arm. Kept him alive. By the time his hand was mummified and hanging on by just the neurofiber bundle, they knew it was too late."

"My God," she whispered, and tears stung her eyes again. It was hard to even process what the child had gone through.

Chase glanced at her, and his grim expression softened slightly. "Please don't cry. It doesn't accomplish a damned thing. These people are tough and used to challenges we can't even imagine. To absolute hell being handed to them on a platter."

A tear spilled over and Dani lifted her shoulder to swipe it away. "I'm not as hardened as you are to all this."

"I hope I'm not hardened." He laughed without any humor in the sound at all. "I'm just determined. Determined to get more doctors and nurses in places like this. Determined to get more funding. And as much as you might not understand his parents letting this happen, I give the father huge credit for bringing him in now. I've seen people who lived with something this bad for years that was never addressed by modern medicine."

She looked at him, at the intensity in his eyes as he worked. "If more doctors are needed here, why are you so determined that I take Drew to live in the States? Why wouldn't you just want us to stay here? For me to work alongside you?" Wasn't that the obvious solution? He claimed to want her to marry him. At least that way they'd be together as a family.

"Didn't you just hear me say it can be hell in a place like this? Drew doesn't belong here. Not until he's an adult."

"It's not the same thing for him as it is for the people who live here. Obviously, he wouldn't be exposed to the same problems."

"To some of them he would." His anger seemed to

ratchet higher, practically radiating from him as he pinned her with a ferocious gaze. "He cannot and will not live in developing countries. Period. Now, are you going to just stand there or are you going to help?"

Sheesh. "Yes, Dr. Bowen." She couldn't remember him ever being this domineering and cranky before. Must be the stress of this poor boy's injury compounded by the stress of their personal situation.

She grabbed thin suture material and handed it to Chase to finish tying off the artery and vein, then continued to sponge out the blood as he worked. There was clearly no talking to the man once his mind was made up, and now wasn't the right time anyway. Though, so far, there hadn't seemed to be any right time to come up with a solution they could agree on.

"While I finish the ligation of the artery and the stitching, you can pull together the sterile cotton dressing and elastic wrap."

When it was over, all that was left of the child's arm was a stump neatly rounded in a compression dressing. Dani wondered if he'd be relieved at no longer looking at his own bones, or if the final loss of his arm would grieve him, too.

Her heart squeezed. As Chase had said, the boy had been handed hell and, unlike in the U.S., would probably never have a prosthesis that would give him a usable limb. Her own mom had always told her to remember that life wasn't fair, and wasn't that the truth? Next time she felt like complaining about something, she'd step back and picture this boy's arm and his tragically stoic expression.

They settled the boy into a bed, and Chase told the father they could stay for three days until it was time to change the dressing.

"Usually, we'd just send him home tomorrow and have

them come back to have the dressing changed in a few days, as we're pretty full up in the hospital," Chase said as they headed out the doors to find Drew. "But I bet they wouldn't come back, because they live so far away. We can't risk infection."

Dani nodded, and they continued walking, not saying anything. His expression was still grim and she wasn't sure if it was because of the boy or their conversation about Drew or both. She felt emotionally spent from the whole experience and, really, what more was there to say?

"I forgot to tell you," Chase said, shoving his hands in his pockets as they walked side by side. "Mom has a bee in her bonnet about going to some hotel in Parakou that a friend of theirs owns before they leave. It's about thirty kilometers from here. Wants to have lunch there. I guess there's a nice pool too, and as we have tomorrow off, she wants us to take Drew swimming. Is that okay with you?"

"Drew doesn't know how to swim. He's only two." Climbing trees and swimming with the child barely out of diapers? What was with this family?

"Two and a half," he said, his expression lightening in a slight smile. "I'll teach him. The sooner he learns, the better."

"I assume you won't just throw him in the deep end and tell him to flap his arms and kick?"

"Don't worry. I'll show him the basic moves before I send him off the diving board."

"Chase!" She stared at him then frowned as he chuckled. He'd always delighted in teasing her, and too often she fell for it.

He put his arm around her shoulders. "I promise not to scare him. We'll just have fun. He won't learn how to be really safe in the water for a while, but it's a first step."

Apparently his anger with her had cooled, as he touched his warm lips to her temple, lingering there for a moment, sending a tingle across her cheek and down her neck. "If it works out, we could probably take him to the hotel weekly, even though Mom and Dad will be gone."

She looked into his deep brown eyes and wanted to ask the question hanging between them. What was going to happen when he was gone, too?

"Sure. Sounds fun. I'd like to see more of the countryside. And another city."

"Good." He stopped walking, and since his arm was around her she stopped, too. He used his free hand to cup her cheek and gave her a soft kiss she should have stepped away from. Should have prevented from quickly morphing into something hotter, needier.

His tongue slipped inside her mouth and the taste of him was so delicious, so overwhelming she couldn't resist. One tiny taste. One more minute. One more time.

On their own, her arms wrapped around his waist and held tight as he moved his hands down her body, firm and sure and insistent. One large palm cupped her behind as his other hand slipped beneath her shirt, caressing her skin, making her gasp as he pulled her close against his hardened body.

His lips separated a whisper from hers, his breath quick against her moist skin. "Dani." His mouth covered hers again, slanted to deepen it, intensify the taste and feel of his kiss, and the heat between them became so scorching she was sure she just might combust right there outside the building.

He tore his mouth from hers, his eyes passion-glazed and nearly black as he stared at her. "How about that back rub? Like now, and naked?"

Now and naked sounded very, very good, but the

moment without his lips on hers gave her enough time to gather a tiny semblance of sanity. A second to protect her heart. "I just…don't know if that's a good idea. I admit last night was wonderful. But I'm afraid it just makes things more…confusing."

She pulled out of his arms completely, regretting no longer having his arms around her, his fingers touching her skin, his mouth igniting hers. But her brain told her she should stay strong. Wouldn't having sex, being together again intimately, just lead to heartache?

For a moment he didn't speak, and she wasn't sure what emotions flickered across his face. Frustration? Contemplation? Agreement? She was surprised he didn't reach for her again, and quickly turned to continue into the building before something else happened that might put her yet again under his spell. Again weaken her resolve.

"Dani—"

"Let's not talk about any of this right now." She kept going, counting the steps to the door. Maybe it was cowardly, but she needed a minute to regroup. Some time to get her breath back and her heart back into a normal rhythm. Some time to figure out the confusing messages her brain and body kept sending through every nerve. "After your parents leave, we'll sit down together and discuss options. When we make some decisions, I promise to be reasonable."

He grasped her arm and stopped her progress, turning her to him. His gaze no longer passionate or angry, he looked beyond serious. "Reasonable is marrying the man who cares about you and our son. Reasonable is planning our future together. I don't get what's not obvious about that."

"Because I don't want to be married to someone who

doesn't live with me. I don't want Drew to wonder why his father's work is more important to him than he is." *I don't want to be hurt again.* "Why don't you understand that?"

"Dani." He cupped her face in his hands, and the tender and sincere expression on his face gripped her heart. "I promise I'll be with you as much as I can. I've already talked with the GPC and asked about eight-month assignments. I admit it'll be hard for me to adjust to working in the States some, but I'm willing to do it. For Drew and for you. What more can I say and do to convince you it will work out?"

Maybe the words *I love you*? She wanted to say it aloud—nearly did—but bit the inside of her cheek just in time. She'd refused to even think about that being part of the equation. Until last night. Until they'd practically set the bed on fire and her along with it. Their time together brought back every single memory of the intense physical and emotional intimacy they'd shared in Honduras.

True, he had told her he loved her back in Honduras. Once or twice had uttered those three little, wonderful-to-hear words.

Then he'd turned her down flat when she'd asked him to marry her, saying he just wasn't the marrying kind. Knowing that he only wanted to marry her now because of Drew still pained her more than she wanted to admit.

Was she able to be in the kind of marriage he was offering? Would it be okay for Drew? Could she convince Chase how important it was to her to spend at least some time doing mission work? After a few years, would Chase feel a need to work full time outside the U.S. again, leaving them alone almost all year?

She didn't know. And all the uncertainty weighed

heavily in her chest. All the questions spun in circles in her mind.

"Like I said last night, I need time to think." She tried hard to ignore the delicious feel of his thumb gently sliding across her cheekbone, his breath touching her skin. "I've asked you before, and I'm asking again. Please stop pushing for an answer. Let's let…things unfold….as they will. Without you confusing me with your hot kisses."

"Since you think my kisses are hot," he said, a smile finally touching his lips, "and you asked nicely, I'll be good. For how long I can't say, but I'll try."

He touched his mouth to hers, light and quick, and the, oh, so brief touch still made her feel weak. His five o'clock shadow gently abraded her cheek as he whispered in her ear, "If you change your mind tonight, though, you know where my bed is."

# CHAPTER TWELVE

"Eat up your breakfast so we can get going," Dani told Drew as he fidgeted on the kitchen stool, just poking at his oatmeal. "I've already got your swimsuit and everything packed. We're waiting for you."

"I ready to go."

"Not until you eat." Her cellphone rang and she pulled it from her pocket, wondering who could be calling.

"Dr. Sheridan here." She touched Drew's hand, mimed him eating, then jabbed her finger at his bowl.

"Hello, Dr. Sheridan, this is Colleen Mason from GPC. How are you?"

"Fine. How can I help you?" She picked up Drew's spoon and poked oatmeal in his mouth, to his frowning annoyance.

"I'm Director Mike Hardy's assistant. I wanted to let you know that your request for a transfer to Panama has been granted, and we have arranged for a replacement for you in Benin. You'll start four weeks from today. Would you like for me to make all your travel arrangements?"

"I'm sorry, there must be some mistake. I didn't ask for a transfer to Panama."

"This is Dr. Danielle Sheridan? Currently in Benin?"

"Yes." What a weird error. "But I'm scheduled to stay here for eight months, and I only arrived a week ago."

"Well, I'm confused now. I'll have to check with Mike, but it was my understanding that you're scheduled to re-locate with Dr. Bowen at the same time he goes to work in Panama."

Her breath backed up in her lungs and she nearly dropped her phone. "Dr. Chase Bowen? Is he moving to Panama?"

"Yes. The same date I have you scheduled to go."

Shock and anger welled up in her chest and threatened to choke her. It didn't take a genius to realize this was no mistake. That this was the work of a certain master manipulator determined to have everything his way and make decisions for her, and to heck with talking to her about it beforehand.

She could barely catch her breath to speak. "Well, I'm afraid this is a mistake. I have no intention of mov-ing to Panama. Let me speak with Dr. Bowen and I'll call you back."

"All right. And I'll speak with Mike, too, to see what the mix-up is. Thanks."

Normally, Dani was pretty easygoing and couldn't remember ever feeling quite like this. Her whole body shook and her head tingled with fury. "Eat your food, Drew. I'll be right back."

She stalked towards the door but before she could push it open to go find the controlling man and let him have it, the jerk in question walked in.

"The car's packed up. Are you—?"

She flattened both hands against his chest and gave him a shove. "Who do you think you are?"

His eyes widened and his brows rose practically to his hairline. "What?"

Her jaw clenched, she glanced back at Drew to see him finally eating, and grabbed Chase's arm. She pulled him into the hall and had to rein in her desire to pummel him with her fists just to release the wild anger welling within her.

"You're moving to Panama." She dragged in a breath so she could speak past the pounding of her heart. "You didn't even tell me. And you didn't even ask what I thought about moving there and working there with you. You just decided Drew and I should go and that's that?"

The surprise on his face settled into grim seriousness. "Okay. I get it that you're upset. Let me explain."

"There's no explanation necessary. It's pretty obvious what you think."

Her anger morphed into a different emotion, and she found herself swallowing a huge lump in her throat and the tears that threatened to accompany it.

Now she knew. Knew how she'd feel when he moved away. And it was so much worse, so much more painful than she'd expected. As she stared at his face, she knew without a doubt she'd miss him horribly. Even more than when she'd left Honduras, though she would never have dreamed that was possible.

And Drew. Drew would miss the daddy he'd so easily embraced and now loved to be with. What she'd feared and dreaded all along.

But moving with him? What would that solve?

Nothing. It would just delay the inevitable. She and Drew would move back to the States when her contract was up, but Chase wouldn't. It was as simple and wretched as that.

"I'm not moving to Panama with you. I'm not moving anywhere with you."

He grasped her arms and narrowed his eyes, his voice tight. "Listen. Panama is safer for Drew than Africa. And it would give us almost eight more months together, for you to think about us. For you to see we belong together. I'm not leaving here without this resolved between us."

"Then don't leave." She tipped her chin and stared at him. The man she knew never backed down from a challenge. "Stay here. Tell the GPC you're taking a leave of absence."

"I can't do that." Now he too was angry, his brows deeply furrowed over fierce brown eyes. "I have a contract with them. I have work to do."

"Well, so do I." She tried to shake free of his grip, but he held her tight. "This is why—"

"Is our baby ready to go?"

Evelyn's cheerful voice came down the hall with her and Phil, but both of them stopped short near the kitchen door.

"I'm sorry." Chase's parents looked at them with obvious uneasiness. "Are we…still on for today? Would you like us to take Drew by ourselves?"

"No. We're coming." Chase released Dani's arms and his chest rose and fell as his expression cooled into stone. "Where's Drew?"

"Eating. I'm sure he's done."

Without another word she stepped into the kitchen to gather up her son and his gear. Drew deserved a nice day with his grandparents, who were leaving tomorrow, and his daddy, who was leaving very soon. Before they went back to life as it had been. Back to just the two of them.

So much for worrying about Drew maybe being intimidated by the swimming pool. Dani sat with Evelyn at an ornate wrought iron table and watched her son splash with delight in the warm, crystal-clear water.

Drew's silliness and his grandparents' laughter at everything he did and said had made the drive to the hotel bearable. Had given Dani time to cool off, toughen up, and accept that Chase was leaving. To swallow that pain. To even forgive his audacity at trying to get them moved with him, because he thought, in his twisted sort of way, that it would have given them more time together. How could she really be angry about that?

No, her anger had proved to be as fleeting as their relationship had been. And she was left with only bleak resignation weighing heavily on the depths of her soul.

Chase stood in the shallow end of the pool, holding their son's little body with both hands around his ribs while Phil tossed him a plastic ball, and she had to admit the child looked practically ready to do breaststroke.

Breaststroke. An unfortunate name for a swimming position that made her think, with an ache in her heart, about their time together last night. Since he was leaving, she figured she deserved to stare at Chase's half-naked body. To imprint it one last time upon her memory.

She'd had her turn in the pool with Drew before they'd taken a break for lunch. Twists of both pain and pleasure had knotted her stomach as Chase had watched her swim with Drew. With his eyelids low, his gaze had been filled with the same emotions swirling through her now. A heightened sensual awareness tempered by frustration and dejection.

After having chlorine repeatedly stinging her eyes, she'd been more than happy to hand Drew over to Chase, quickly moving across the tiled floor because having her damp body brushing against his skin was torture. Thankfully, the hotel gift shop had a white terrycloth swimsuit cover-up she could buy, as she wasn't about to sit there in a bikini in front of Chase. Or while sitting next to his mother.

At first she'd tried hard not to eye Chase in the pool

the way he'd eyed her, but failed miserably. The wetness
of his bronzed skin seemed to emphasize every inch of
his muscled strength. As he dunked Drew partway into
the water then back up, to the child's laughing delight,
his biceps bulged and his six-pack rippled, and the dark,
wet hair in the center of his chest ran in a damp arrow to
disappear beneath his black swim trunks. Why couldn't
the man be growing a paunch and losing his hair?

"Our Andrew is a fish, just like his father," Evelyn
said.

Dani yanked her attention back to Chase's mother,
thankful Evelyn was watching the action in the pool instead of noticing the way she was staring at the woman's
son. Evelyn wore what seemed like a permanent expression of happy pride, and Dani felt gratified and blessed
that Chase's parents already adored their grandchild.

"Is Chase a fish?" She tried to remember if she'd ever
seen him actually swim, but could only come up with
the times the two of them had splashed in waterfalls
with shallow pools. Not that she'd be surprised, since he
seemed to be good at everything physical. Which started
her thoughts down that painful path again, and that had
to stop. Chase wouldn't be around to show her his various physical skills, and she again pulled her attention
back to Evelyn.

"Oh, yes. Many of the places we lived had lakes. When
he was older, he started doing triathlons and trained in
the ocean when we lived somewhere near a coast." She
smiled, obviously enjoying the memories. "When we
worked at big hospitals, he was on a few swim teams and
won a number of trophies. He and Brady would swim
laps for ever, it seemed, though, of course, Chase lasted
longest as he was older."

Brady. Obviously, Chase's brother. "I hope you don't

mind if I ask you about Brady," she said quietly. "Chase has never talked about him."

"No, he wouldn't." She sighed, her eyes shadowed as she stared at the pool. "It was a terrible thing for all of us when Brady died."

Dani sat without speaking, hoping she'd continue. Eventually, though, she had to ask her to elaborate. "What happened?" she asked gently.

"We were living in the Congo. Working at a small hospital there. Chase was sixteen, Brady fourteen." Evelyn turned her now serious gaze to Dani. "We knew it must be malaria, though, of course, we'd taken the usual precautions. Took one chloroquine once a week. Had mosquito netting over the beds and used repellent."

Her expression grew grimmer as she turned her gaze to the pool again. "But Brady presented with high fever. Was lethargic. We immediately gave him more chloroquine and kept an eye on him, giving him fluids." She closed her eyes for a moment. "But he got sicker. We tried quinine with the chloroquine but after another couple days, he couldn't eat or drink. We put a tube down his nose to rehydrate him, but knew we had to get him home to a U.S. hospital."

"Did Chase go with you?" Dani could only imagine how scared a sixteen-year-old boy would be when his beloved brother was so sick. Or maybe, as a teenager, he hadn't fully understood how serious it was.

Evelyn shook her head. "No. And that was a mistake. He was in the middle of mid-term exams, had his friends there, and we were blindly sure that, once in the States, Brady would get better." She turned her brown gaze on Dani, and tears filled her eyes. "But he didn't. Turned out he had a strain of malaria resistant to chloroquine. The malaria went into his brain and it was over."

"I'm so sorry." Dani's throat closed, and she rested her hand on the older woman's arm, knowing the touch was little comfort. What else was there to say? An unimaginable loss for any parent.

Evelyn nodded and wiped away her tears. "It was a terrible time for all of us. But in some ways it was worst for Chase. He never got to say goodbye to Brady. Wasn't there at the end, holding his hand, like we were. It wasn't his fault, but I know he felt guilty and selfish that he'd stayed in Africa to take a test and hang with his friends instead of being there for his brother."

Finally, Dani saw everything very clearly, as though she'd been looking through binoculars and had suddenly found how to focus them.

She saw why Chase was so insistent that Drew not live in Africa. Or any developing country. He'd experienced first hand the worst that could happen.

Obviously, it was also why he hadn't wanted children, ever. Doctoring the neediest of humankind, as he'd so often said, was what he did. Who he was. And he couldn't do that, and be that, with a family he wanted to keep safe.

His rejection of her marriage proposal hadn't been all about him, as she'd long assumed. About having a woman in every port, so to speak, which she'd bitterly wondered after she'd left. It was about his deep caring for others, and she should have known that all along.

"Thank you for telling me, Evelyn," Dani said. "I would guess you're in agreement with Chase that I shouldn't have Drew here in Africa."

Evelyn gave her a sad smile. "There are risks no matter where you live. I'm not sure what the right answers are. I do know Chase didn't particularly like living in the States."

But he wanted her and Drew there. "Do you know why not?"

"We sent him to a boarding school for a year after Brady died, and he hated it. He was too used to living in unusual places around the world with all different kinds of people and couldn't tolerate what he saw as the superficial things important to American kids of his own age." A genuine smile lit her face, banishing the shadows. "I told him he's a reverse snob. That it's okay to want to have nice things and live in a nice house. It's all a matter of balance."

Wasn't that true about life in general? Balance. It was what she needed to find with Chase in their decisions about Drew. Marriage or no marriage.

"Don't look so stressed, dear." It was Evelyn's turn to press a reassuring hand to Dani's forearm. "I know my son can be a bit on the domineering side when he makes up his mind, but things will work out the way they're meant to. I don't know why you kept Andrew a secret from Chase, but after meeting you I would guess you had your reasons. Now that we have Andrew in our lives, you already know we're here to stay."

"Yes." Dani looked at the steadiness in Evelyn's eyes, the warmth, and knew Chase had been blessed with special parents as he'd grown up. Part of what had shaped him to be the special man he was today. "I do know."

# CHAPTER THIRTEEN

BY THE TIME they returned from Parakou, the moon was rising and darkness was closing in. Spud had a simple, late meal waiting for them, ready to be warmed.

Swimming was clearly an exhausting activity, as Drew's eyes kept closing at dinner, his face nearly dropping into his plate of spaghetti. With his grandparents chuckling, Dani decided there was no hope in trying to get more food in the child that night. She followed Chase as he carried Drew, barely able to awaken him enough to get bedtime necessities done before he was in a deep sleep.

Dani pulled Drew's covers over his shoulders and kissed his cheek, his little rosebud lips already parted in deep slumber. "'Night, baby boy."

She pulled the mosquito netting around the bed before turning to Chase in the darkened room. He stood there with his hands in his pockets, staring at her with such intense concentration it was almost unnerving.

"I guess we should get back to dinner," she said. "Help clean up."

He stood silently for another long moment before he finally spoke. "Thank you for today. I know my parents had a great time with you and Drew. And I did, too."

"I couldn't believe how much he loved the water. You

were right—at this rate he's going to be swimming be-fore his next birthday."

He placed his wide palm against his chest and raised his eyebrows. "Did I hear you say I was right about some-thing? I need to sit down."

"I'm pretty sure I give you credit when you actually *are* right. Which does happen occasionally," she said, trying to lighten the mood, which had weighed heavily on both of them all afternoon.

He didn't even smile, his serious eyes seeming to study her. Maybe he could see what she was thinking. Feeling. Finally understanding.

"I'm…sorry about the Panama thing. It was wrong of me to not talk to you. I just…" He shoved his hand into his hair. "I felt desperate. I don't want to leave without you agreeing we should get married. Without us *being* married."

After learning what she had today about his brother, she understood much more than she had just hours ear-lier. And the pain of his rejection when she had proposed to him didn't hurt quite as much as it had before.

As she looked into his eyes, she allowed herself to see what she hadn't looked for back then. Hadn't bothered to observe. The vulnerability deep within their chocolaty depths when all she'd noticed had been his utter confi-dence. His utter determination.

What must it have been like for him to be living his carefree teenage life, focused on school and his friends, only to lose his brother so suddenly and shockingly? The fact that she'd known Chase for over a year and he'd never mentioned it showed her he still carried the pain of it deep inside.

"I'm not ready to make a commitment to marriage, Chase. But I understand things better now." She clasped his hand. "We have a little time before you go to Panama. When you leave…"

He pressed his finger to her lips. "Shh. I don't want to talk. I don't even want you to say you'll marry me right now. We've done too much talking in circles, arguing, trying to figure out what to do and how to do it. All I want is to kiss you and be with you." He cupped her face in his hands and gave her the softest of kisses, and like before, it was too much and not nearly enough.

Too much to be able to walk away, feeling nothing. Not nearly enough to satisfy the craving her body couldn't help but feel for him. The craving she was no longer trying to resist.

She wanted those same soft kisses everywhere on her body.

Need bloomed within her as she wrapped her arms around his body and pulled him close, her breasts tingling at the heavy beat of his heart against them. "The only talking I was going to do was to say, 'Make love to me.'"

His lips curved and his eyes gleamed in the low light. "Now, that kind of talking I'm good with."

He kissed her, soft, teasing, coaxing. But coaxing wasn't necessary. The moment his mouth covered hers, gently drawing her tongue inside to dance slowly with his, she was lost. He tipped his head to one side, exploring her mouth so thoroughly she could barely breathe. His fingers pressed into her hips and pulled her against his hard body. Her heart thumped hard against her ribs and just as she sank deeply into his kiss, fumbling at the button of his shorts, wanting him so much her knees wobbled, his hands dropped to her shoulders and he set her away from him.

She stared at him, confused. His eyes smoldered, dark and dangerous, and the curve of his lips promised all things carnal and wonderful. So why wasn't he touching her? "What—?"

"I found a place for us that's a little more fun than a bed." His voice was low and sexy. "More like what we enjoyed in Honduras. For days, I've been thinking about you and me, there, naked under the stars. Let's get in the car and go."

She couldn't wait to make love with him, and he wanted to go on a road trip? "We made love in a bed plenty of times in Honduras. I'm for that. Your room. Like now."

He laughed, a deep, smoky rumble. "I like it when you're all bossy." He pulled her close again for a hard, intense kiss that was over all too soon before he set her away from him and pulled his phone from his pocket.

She folded her arms across her thumping heart, staring at his phone in disbelief. "You going to call 911 for help? Good idea, because I just might have to hurt you if you don't immediately demonstrate some of your amazing sexual skills."

That low laugh of his, louder this time, seemed to reverberate in her own chest. He pressed his palm to her mouth. "We agreed on no talking, remember?" With that annoying smile still on his face, he lowered his head to nibble her neck, her lobe, his moist tongue touching the shell of her ear. "Unless the subject is sex. So let me tell you what I want to do to you."

His breath slipped across her skin and the rumble of his voice was filled with desire. "First, I want…"

"Less talk, more action." She slipped her hands inside his T-shirt, up the smooth skin of his ribs to lightly abrade his nipples with her short fingernails as she ran her mouth across his jaw. Beneath her hands, his heart pounded and his muscles bunched.

"To strip off all your clothes and see every inch of your skin," he continued in that deep voice so full of sexual promise she about threw him down on her bed to get on with it. "All day you teased me, wearing that little bitty swimsuit of yours. I want to—"

"Get naked and horizontal right this second?" She slipped her hand down into his shorts, seeking the biggest object of her desire.

He quickly pulled her hand out of his pants and heaved a breath. "You always were an impatient cheat." He texted into his phone as she massaged the hard ridge beneath his zipper. He grabbed her wrist again with a breathless laugh. "Damn it, stop."

"You kiss me until I can't remember my name then say stop?" Nearly dizzy with wanting him, she forced herself to step to the bed and sat, but the distance barely slowed the aching heat pooling low in her body. "Fine."

If he planned on continuing his hard-to-get game, he was in for a surprise. On alert, she watched him, ready to make her move. Which would be that as soon as he came close enough, she'd pounce and yank him down next to her.

Yeah. She felt her own lips curve, anticipating what fun it was going to be, wrestling around on the bed and stripping off their clothes. Somehow she doubted he'd keep up the delay tactics and resist.

Except he was still looking at his phone, and her amusement faded into downright irritation. All the teasing all week, even their lovemaking of a few nights ago, had left him cool and in control while she was practically melting for him?

Then the surprise move was his. Two steps to the bed, and he effortlessly scooped her up into his arms. With quick strides he carried her out into the hall.

Okay, maybe he had a good plan after all. She pressed closer, wrapping her arms around his neck and nibbling at his lips. Beneath her hands, his back muscles flexed and tightened. "I hate to remind you," she said, giving his lips a teasing lick that left his own tongue chasing after hers, "but we can't just leave Drew."

"What, you thought I was texting my broker?" He practically kicked open the door and carried her out into the warm, sultry night. "Mom says she'll watch Drew."

Her blood began to pump faster and her body hummed in anticipation. He'd thought to call for babysitting, which must mean he had something very delicious in mind. She ran her mouth across his skin, loving the taste of him, the curve of his jaw, the slight abrasion of his skin.

"If you don't stop, we're not going to make it any farther than the backseat of this car." His eyes glinted down at her, eyelids half-closed, and it wasn't too dark to see that the smile was gone from his face, replaced by a hunger that was exactly what she wanted to see. The same hunger rising within her and leaving her breathless.

He yanked open the door of the Land Rover and practically dumped her inside, before shutting the door and jogging to the driver's side.

The engine grumbled to life and Chase hit the gas, apparently in a hurry. And that was fine with Dani.

Wondering why such an old car had bucket seats instead of a nice, long bench, she attempted to cuddle up close to him, touching her lips to his chin, his cheek, his ear. It wasn't too difficult to ignore the hard plastic between the seats, but the gear shift was darned annoying.

She wrapped one hand behind his head and flattened her other palm against his body, giving him slow caresses that made him suck in his breath. Teasing touches beneath his shirt to feel the smooth skin over hard muscle there. Combing through the soft hair in the center of his chest then down. Pressing against the zipper of his pants, which was currently strained to its limit.

He grasped her hand and held it motionless and tight in his. "You trying to make me wreck the car?"

"No. Just trying to hurry things up." She pressed closer against his shoulder, ignoring the stupid gear shift digging into her thigh. She sucked gently on his throat, every sense tuned to his scent and his taste and the feel of his skin.

"I do have to actually change gears, Dani." His voice was a low growl. "Please move over for just one minute. We're almost there."

Oh, right. The gear shift wasn't just an in-the-way annoyance. "Sorry." She straddled his lap and the bounce of the car on the rutted road pushed his hard erection right where she wanted it. The sensation was so erotic, she moaned. She tunneled her fingers into the thick, soft hair she loved to touch and very nearly gave him a full mouth-to-mouth kiss, but figured that wasn't compatible with him actually being able to see and drive.

"God, Dani." He gave a breathless laugh. "If you wiggle against me one more time, I'm gonna run off the road into a tree. Do you have some kind of death wish?"

"No." She knew the man could practically drive in his sleep. "Just remembering how much fun we had in Honduras. How crazy you made me back then. How crazy you make me now."

"You're crazy, all right. But I like it."

The car suddenly veered to the right and bounced even more for another thirty feet or so before coming to a jarring stop.

Immediately, his arms wrapped around her, and the kisses between them became frenzied, their bodies rubbing together until Dani thought she might come undone with all her clothes still on.

Chase yanked his mouth from hers, and their panting breaths mingled in the air between them. His eyes glittered in the darkness. "I didn't drive all the way out here to make love to you against the damned steering-wheel. Come with me."

"I just about did."

His quiet laugh filled the car before he shoved open the door. Still holding her in his arms with her legs wrapped around his hips, he somehow managed to grab thick blankets from the backseat and stride with her toward a small cluster of trees.

She quit nibbling his face and neck to see where they were going. Probably would be a good idea to help with the blankets instead of just hanging onto him like a baboon.

She slid her legs off his hips and wasn't sure she could actually stand up. "Give me one."

Together, they laid the blankets over whatever spongy, soft, and dark plant life was thriving beneath the trees. "What is this stuff?"

"I don't know. Don't care either, except that the minute I saw it, I thought of lying here with you, watching the stars."

"I didn't know you'd gone anywhere since I've been here."

"I haven't."

His eyes, shining in the darkness, were filled with both desire and tenderness, and his meaning finally sank in. "You mean, you thought of me even before I showed up in Benin?" she whispered.

"Thought of you. Wondered about you. Dreamed of you."

His quiet voice slipped inside her heart until it felt so full, it was hard to breathe. He reached for her, held her close, and for a moment the heady sexual desire that had consumed them earlier gave way to a quiet, aching connection. To what they'd had before.

To what they still had now.

He loosened her hair from its band. Pulled off her shirt between kisses. Caressed her collarbone, her shoulders, her back as he slipped off her bra. Pleasured her breasts with his mouth as he pushed off the rest of her clothes.

Then it was her turn. But she couldn't go slowly, as he had. His kisses, his touch had ignited the smoldering fire he'd lit within her earlier, and she made quick work of his clothes until they were both naked, with the cool night air skating across their skin.

She pushed him down onto the blanket and looked into his handsome face. At his shining eyes and sensual lips curved in a smile.

"You make me think of a wood nymph up there, naked and beautiful with your curly hair shining in the dark." His big hands slid up her thighs and his thumbs slipped into the juncture between them, stroking her slick skin until she gasped with pleasure.

"If I recall my mythology, Greek gods liked to play with wood nymphs. Are you a Greek god?" She said it teasingly, breathlessly, but it was, oh, so true that he looked like one, with his gorgeous, muscular physique, his dark hair, his eyes flecked with gold, and the kissable shape of his beautiful lips.

"If I need to be to play with you, the answer is yes," he said on a heavy breath, smiling. "Playing with you is my number-one fantasy."

"Good. Because I'm liking being a wood nymph. Playing with my Greek god." She slowly moved against his talented fingers, the tension coiling and rising deep inside. She ran her hands slowly over his chest, his shoulders, his arms, loving the feel of his skin, the breeze touching her body, the moonlight dancing across his face, his skin, his hair.

"I'm liking it, too." That smile still played about his lips. "It was worth nearly ending up in a ditch as we drove here."

She had to kiss those sensual, smiling lips and leaned over to cover his mouth with hers, slipping her tongue gently inside to touch his. He tasted so good, so wonderful, his skin so warm against hers, his chest hair tickling her sensitive breasts, she wanted to just stay there, draped over him, kissing him in the moonlight. Making up for all the lonely nights she'd missed his moist lips, his warm body, the shivery touch of his hands.

But the slow circles he was making with his thumbs turned her insides to a liquid fever and the fact that he was naked and right there wouldn't let her draw out the moment any longer. She rose up to sheath him with her wet heat, and the throaty groan he gave in response made her move faster, more urgently. His hands grasped her hips as he moved with her, their gazes locked.

"Dani." His voice a harsh whisper, he suddenly bent at the waist and took her into his arms, reversing their position so she lay beneath him. Their pace quickened, the night air filling with the sounds of their pleasure. His hands were everywhere, gently squeezing, caressing, holding her close, their mouths and bodies joined in a dance that took her back to every achingly beautiful day they'd shared deeply hidden in the mountains of Honduras.

"Dani," he said again against her mouth. She heard herself crying out against his lips, and he joined her with a groan that came deep from within his chest and reverberated within her own.

They lay there for a long time, their breathing slowly returning to normal. The feel of his face buried in her neck, the weight of his body pressing hers into the spongy mattress, his hand cupping her breast, was perfection.

Cool air slipped between them as he shifted, lying just off her, skin still pressed to skin. His finger slipped across her ribs to trace lazy circles on her stomach.

"I want you to know I'm planning to stay in Benin for my vacation time until I leave for Panama." He paused. "If that's okay with you."

"That would be good." Drew would get to spend even more time with Chase if he wasn't working. And she'd have a little while to make sense of all her confusion about the future.

He propped himself on one elbow, his face close to hers. He splayed his big hand over her navel as he looked down into her eyes. "About my wanting you to marry me—"

She pressed her fingers to his lips. "I thought we weren't going to talk about that. I just want to lie here with you and look at the stars. After the next couple weeks, we'll…figure out what's best for everyone."

"I'm not asking for an answer right now. I can wait. But there's something I need to say." His dark eyes had lost their sensual glow and were now deeply serious. "I'm sorry I was so…unpleasant when I said, back in Honduras, that I never wanted to get married and have kids. If I'd known about Drew, you know my answer would have been different."

A sharp pinch twisted her heart as she stared at his somber face. Was that supposed to make her feel happy? What did he want her to say in response? She already knew that was the only reason he wanted to marry her now.

She turned her face to look at the stars, their twinkling points blurring as unwelcome tears stung her eyes. The last thing she wanted was for Chase to see her all teary over him. To feel guilty that, even though he'd said he loved her back in Honduras, he hadn't loved her quite enough.

"It's all right. I understand."

"I haven't finished." He gently grasped her chin between his thumb and forefinger and brought her gaze back to his. "The reason I acted like such a jerk was because it crushed me to realize it was about to be over between us. I knew I couldn't live a regular, suburban life in the States. I couldn't be the husband you wanted and give you the family you wanted. And that hurt like hell."

She pressed her palms to his chest, feeling his heart beat strong and steady. "I figured you were the kind of guy who just wanted to be free. That I wasn't enough to make you think otherwise."

"Not enough?" He cupped her head between his hands and kissed her hard, as though she'd made him angry. When he broke the kiss, he looked down at her with disbelief etched on his face. "Too much. More than I deserved. A woman who was everything—a caring doctor who made everyone around her smile, a woman with an adventurous spirit, a woman any man would be damned lucky to have in his life. And on top of all that, so beautiful you made my chest ache every time I looked at you."

His eyes seemed to look deep into her heart. "I love you, Dani. You're everything I've ever wanted in a woman. And now you've given me Drew. He's a miracle I didn't think I could have in my life, but a miracle I can't imagine being without now."

Her throat closed and she wrapped her arms around his neck to give him a kiss she hoped showed him how much his words had moved her. How much they'd given her hope that a good life for the three of them really might be possible.

Their lips separated, and the emotion shimmering between the two of them caught her breath and expanded in her heart. The clear night, the fragrant air, the softness beneath their blanket, all wrapped them in a quiet intimacy neither wanted to have end just yet.

Chase settled back to lie flat next to her, shoulder to shoulder, fingers curled together as they stared at the stars.

## CHAPTER FOURTEEN

DANI FINALLY BROKE the long, relaxed silence. "I'm always amazed at how the Big Dipper looks just the same here as in the States and Honduras," she said, trying to lead up to the conversation they needed to have about Brady.

He chuckled. "Yeah, amazing, Miss Astronomy. Remind me to not have you teaching Drew about physical science."

She playfully swatted him. "You know what I mean. That the world, really, is such a small orb in all of the universe, with billions of people floating together through space."

"Yeah."

She turned her head to look at him. "Your mom told me about Brady."

Silence again stretched between them, this time no longer calm and relaxed. The sound of his heavy sigh mingled with the chirp of crickets until he finally spoke. "Because we moved so much, Brady and I were best friends. We did everything together, even when we made friends with local kids and kids of other doctors and med professionals."

"I never had a brother or sister, and always wished I did." She squeezed his hand. "I can't imagine how hard it was for you to lose him."

"Yeah. One minute he was with us, the next he was gone."

He turned his head toward her, the softness that had been in his eyes earlier now gone. Replaced by the hard and determined stare she'd become accustomed to when he objected to Andrew being in Africa.

"Now you understand why Drew can't live here. Why, short term, Panama would be safer. Why it's best for the two of you to live in the States until he wouldn't be as susceptible to a serious illness."

"So you'd be okay with our living there and you living here, or in Central America, or in India?" Trying to wrap her brain around how that would work was hard. But his mission work was such a big part of his life, it would be wrong to ask him to give it up completely. Even if he did, he'd ultimately resent it, and very likely Drew would sense that resentment.

Could she give up her desire to do mission work, too? Was it fair of him to even ask? Or perhaps she could convince Chase to compromise, every few years working together in somewhat safer locations like Panama.

"I'd be in the U.S. several months a year." His fingers tightened on hers and his breath brushed her cheek. "It's not a perfect solution, but I know we can make it work."

Could they? Just hours ago she'd been sure the answer was a resounding "No." But maybe, just maybe, an imperfect solution could still be the best solution.

"Now you know about Brady. It's your turn," he said, rolling onto his side, head propped on his hand, his fingers sliding across her stomach again. "You said something about knowing what it's like to have a parent think you're a burden. Why?"

"My parents were college sweethearts. Dad was the only child of a well-to-do family. Apparently there were expectations that he'd concentrate on school, get an MBA and eventually take over the family business."

He touched his lips to her shoulder. "And?"

"Mom got pregnant. And that didn't fit into anyone's plans. They didn't get married, but his family's lawyers set up child support. Which wasn't much because, at that time he was just a student and the court didn't factor in his family's money."

"And he never had much to do with you?"

"No." She shook her head, surprised that, even now, she felt a sliver of hurt over it. "He complained to her all the time about any extra expenses she asked for help with. Sometimes plain refused. When Mom tried to get him to talk to me on the phone, he was curt and got off as fast as possible."

"Did he pay the child support?"

"Oh, he dutifully sent the checks, and his parents even paid for part of my med-school tuition. Which they didn't have to do, and I was grateful for it." His hand moved to cup her ribs and she turned her head to look at him. "But every time I invited them to some school event, they came up with an excuse. Said they were too busy. He married somebody in his social sphere, but never had kids. He and his wife travelled all over the world. Still do, I suppose."

Enough with the self-pity, which was absurd after all these years. She lightened her tone. "Hard to believe I never even got the souvenir shirt that said 'My dad went to Paris but all I got was this lousy T.'"

"So you felt unwanted and unloved by him and that felt like crap. I get why you've been so worried Drew would feel the same way." He cupped her face in his hand, his dark eyes earnest. "You do know I'll always be here for both of you, don't you? Always."

She did know. The man was the most honorable and caring person she'd ever met. "Yes. And if we decide—"

"Uh-uh." He rolled onto her, pinned her beneath him, pulled her hands above her head and silenced her with a kiss. "I know I've been pushing you hard for an answer, but now I'm pulling back. Giving you three weeks before we talk about it at all. Then we'll come back here and have this conversation again."

"Just the conversation?"

His teeth were white in the darkness as he grinned, pressing his body into hers as they sank deeper into the spongy earth. "Well, you know what they say about all talk and no action..." With the sun barely peeking through the curtains, Dani couldn't believe how wide awake she felt. As she stretched, she had to smile at the little aches and twinges from the previous evening's physical activities.

She rolled over and closed her eyes to try to get another hour of sleep. After ten minutes or so it was very apparent that wasn't happening. She stood and pulled on sweats and a T-shirt and peeked at Drew. His sweet lips were parted as he slept soundly and she kissed his head before creeping out the door to make some coffee.

As she expected, the kitchen was quiet and empty, but to her surprise the delicious scent of coffee filled the room. Early-bird Chase must have made it before his run and workout.

Perhaps he was finished and already in the shower. The thought of finding out and joining him there was more than tempting and she walked down the hall to peek into the shower room.

Darn. Dark and quiet. She smirked at the disappointment she felt. Since when had she become a sex maniac?

She knew the answer. Since being with Chase again.

It was hard to believe an entire week had gone by since his parents had left. A week of fulfilling work and lovely family time. Not to mention all those close and intimate moments with Chase after Drew was asleep.

In mere days the man had managed to make her fall headlong in love with him again. Or maybe the truth was she'd stayed in love with him all this time. In love with his strengths and his commitment to others and those deep brown eyes she sank into every time she looked at him.

And, of course, she loved his knee-weakening kisses. The thought sent her mind back to the shower and the fact that he must still be out running and would need one when he returned. Her heart did a little pit-pat, and it was clear she needed a distraction from her libido. A vibrant sunrise peeked through the window, and she wandered outside to enjoy it.

Streaked gray clouds stood out against a magenta sky, the bright orange ball of the sun casting, as it rose above the horizon, a beautiful pink glow across the savannah. She took a sip of her coffee, letting the taste linger on her tongue, then nearly choked as a movement by a nearby tree startled her.

Chase. Doing rapid push-ups like he was in an army boot camp. Doubtless he'd already been for his run and was engrossed in the rest of his fitness regimen. Thank heavens he hadn't dragged her out of bed to join him. Next would come squats and lunges and some kind of upper-body work, and he was the worst drill sergeant ever, with no sympathy for anyone's tired muscles. Not to mention that Chase had given her muscles a very good workout last night.

His biceps bulged and deltoids rippled and just as Dani was admiring all those manly muscles, he jumped up and ran to a tree, leaping to grasp the lowest branch to start on pull-ups.

She'd almost forgotten how beautiful his body was. Even during their lovemaking, when she'd seen him naked, run her hands over his solid strength, she'd been so focused on other things she hadn't taken the time to admire him, which had been pretty much her favorite hobby in Honduras.

But now, with the vivid sun silhouetting his wide, muscular shoulders, his powerful chest, his strong thighs, she let her eyes savor him. It was all she could do not to walk over and slip her hands beneath his T-shirt, currently hiking up with each movement to expose his belly button and the line of dark hair on his taut stomach. To feel his smooth skin all slippery from sweat.

Thinking about that made her feel very warm, like she was the one doing all those pull-ups. Better get back inside before she couldn't resist dragging him into the shower or back to bed, which wasn't a good idea with Drew waking up soon. Or before Chase spotted her and made her hit the ground for push-ups and sit-ups of her own.

Now, there was an alarming thought. She backed towards the door, turning to escape.

"Running away scared?"

She looked over her shoulder as he dropped to the ground and walked towards her in that easy, athletic stride of his.

"No. I'm not afraid of your workouts. You can put me to the test any time." Which he'd done last night. And the night before. Unable to resist his seductive and convincing kisses, she'd completely failed every test. Or aced them, she thought with an inward smile.

"Yeah?" He stopped in front of her and pulled her into

his arms. Warm brown eyes smiled into hers before his lips slipped across hers, feather soft.

With his arm draped across her shoulders, they walked together to the kitchen, and Chase poured more coffee into her cup.

"Thanks for making coffee. You sure know the way to a girl's heart."

"I know a few other ways, too."

"You do?" The way he looked at her, the smile on his beautiful lips, had her leaning in for a kiss, stroking her hand down his damp shirt and over the bulging front of his shorts.

"Is that all you think about?" he teased, his voice a low growl. He picked up a covered plate from the counter and slid the foil off. "I was referring to Ruth's coffee cake."

"Well, that is another way to my heart." The cake did smell delicious, but not quite as delicious as Chase.

"I'm thinking this earns me double points," he said.

"It does." She pinched a piece and stuck it in her mouth. "Definitely. So what do you want to use your points for?"

He pulled her close for a kiss, lips clinging before he pulled back, the corners of his eyes crinkled, his lips teasingly curved. She could get used to waking up to this. To the taste of warm coffee and Chase on her tongue.

She poked another piece of cake into her mouth and Chase licked a crumb from her lips. "I'm thinking my points should get me—"

The kitchen door swung open and Trent walked in then slapped his hand over his eyes. "Could you two please keep your romantic moments out of the public areas of the compound? I'm afraid to go anywhere now for fear of having my innocence corrupted."

"Your innocence was corrupted long, long ago, Casanova," Chase said. He moved to the counter and poured a cup of coffee, handing it to Trent. "When are you leaving for your vacation?"

"In about an hour. I'm meeting a friend in Brussels, and we're going to do a little European tour for a few weeks."

"Would this friend be of the female persuasion?" Chase asked.

"Of course." Trent swigged some coffee and rocked back on his heels. "What would be the point of spending a few weeks with a man? Working with you for the past year has been torture enough."

Dani laughed. She'd heard about Trent's reputation, and wondered how much of it was really true. "I hope you have a great time. And that you enjoy your stint in India."

"Thanks." He turned to Chase and reached to shake his hand. "God knows why, but in all seriousness I'll miss you. I hope we work together next time around."

"Me, too."

They smiled at one another with an obviously close bond forged between two doctors who spent their lives doing what so few others did. As difficult as it would be to pull up roots and start somewhere new every year, part of Dani envied their amazing commitment.

"Good thing you're spending your vacation here as I hear the only doc coming to replace both of us is going to be a week or so late," Trent said.

"Yeah. Think they'll give me double pay for working through my vacation?"

"You'll be lucky if they don't pay you in goats and yams."

Both men grinned, and Trent set his coffee on the table to give Dani a warm hug. "You take care of Drew and keep me posted on how he's doing. And best of luck with this one." He jabbed his thumb towards Chase. "Because you're definitely going to need a lot of luck."

"Thanks. I know." She looked over at Chase's smile, her heart lifting with a sweet ache, and knew she already had a whole lot of luck in her pocket.

Trent left, and Chase pulled her close for another quick kiss. "Tomorrow we'll be busy, with just the two of us here. What do you think about taking Drew back to the hotel today to swim and have lunch? I've got a taste for the burgers they serve there."

"Sounds perfect."

His hands drifted down to cup her rear. "I need a shower. Feel like joining me?"

"If Drew's still asleep, we can—"

He grabbed her hand and practically pulled her out of her shoes as he hurried her down the hall. "I'm ready to redeem my double points. Like right now."

Dani took the last swig of her iced tea and chuckled as she watched Chase and Drew play in the hotel pool. They'd been at it for hours, with only short breaks, and she knew their son would sleep very well tonight.

"And then Superman swoops into the ocean to save Metropolis!"

Chase held Drew's small body between his hands as he dove him headfirst into the water and back up to the surface.

"Again!" Drew swiped his hair and the pool water from his eyes, his grin nearly stretching from one ear to the other. She hadn't realized until she'd seen him all wet how much the child needed a haircut, and made a note to do that tomorrow after work.

She had to laugh at the way Drew held his arms stiffly at his sides like the true Superman, and at Chase's silly comic-book commentary. How amazing that the child who had never liked water being poured over his head to rinse out shampoo now adored being completely underwater. He even liked to jump straight in from the side of the pool, as long as his daddy was there to catch him.

Chase was so good with him that she felt ashamed that she'd ever believed he'd be a distant dad. Yes, there would be physical distance while Chase worked overseas, but Drew would always know how much his daddy loved him, of that she no longer had any doubt.

A few other women sipping drinks by the pool barely concealed the way they eyed Chase, and who could blame them? With his handsome face and bronzed skin over all that muscle, he truly looked like the Greek god she'd teased him about being when they'd made love outside in the moonlight. And he could be...was...all hers.

She stood and walked to the side of the pool. "It's four o'clock, you two. We need to be leaving pretty soon."

"I not done saving Metroplis," Drew said. "Mommy, watch me dive!"

"All right, Superman. Here we go again." Chase grinned at Dani and readjusted his hands on a wriggling Drew before he dunked him beneath the water again.

The grin on Chase's face suddenly died, replaced by a deep frown. He started wading toward the shallowest water, holding Drew up against his chest.

"I not done swimming, Daddy."

"I know. I just want to check something."

The odd expression on Chase's face set off an alarm in Dani's brain. Something was worrying him, and he wasn't a man prone to worry.

Dani's feet landed on the top step of the pool just as Chase stood Drew there. "What's wrong?" she asked.

Frowning, he began to palpate Drew's abdomen, but

the child leaped, trying to jump back into the pool. Chase moved his hands to grip Drew's arms and brought his face close to their son's. "Hold still, Superman. I want to see if you've got kryptonite in your belly."

Drew's eyes lit up at the idea. "Okay."

Dani's heart began to thud and her breath grew short. Why, exactly, she didn't know, but something about the way Chase looked made her feel very, very uneasy. She stepped farther down into the pool next to him and leaned close to Chase, staring as he pressed his fingers gently but firmly into Drew's abdomen and flank.

"What's the matter, Chase?"

He turned to look at her, and his shaken expression, the starkness in his eyes closed her throat. His chest lifted as he sucked in a deep breath before turning back to Drew. "Superman, the kryptonite is going to make you unable to move. Why don't you go up and sit in the chair to finish your smoothie. That'll melt the kryptonite and you'll be strong again."

"Okay. I need to get strong!" Drew grinned and hurried up the steps to grab his drink and sit in the chair.

Dani grabbed Chase's arm. "You're scaring me. What's wrong?"

He closed his eyes for a moment and scrubbed his hand across his face. When he looked down at her, his gaze was tortured. "There's a large mass inside his belly. With its location and his age, my best guess would be nephroblastoma. Wilm's tumor."

"Oh, my God. No," she whispered. Her heart stopped completely. "No. He couldn't possibly have cancer."

# CHAPTER FIFTEEN

CHASE PLACED THE X-ray cartridge beneath Drew's lower back and swiveled the C-arm of the machine over his mid-section, trying to stay calm and professional. The moment he'd touched that hard mass inside Drew's little body he'd felt like someone had kicked in his chest and stopped his heart, and only the fact that he'd taken and developed X-rays hundreds of times enabled him to function at all.

"Okay, Superman? We're going to take some pictures of that kryptonite in there."

"Okay, Daddy."

His son's huge grin made Chase's throat close. He didn't know how the hell he could manage to keep acting like this was all a big game, but somehow he had to stay strong. Had to make sure he didn't scare Drew by showing the gut-wrenching terror that made it hard to breathe.

"After we take the pictures, Mommy's going to fix you your favorite dinner," Dani said. Chase glanced at her as she held Drew's hand and knew she couldn't possibly be holding up any better than he was. The strain and fear on her face made her look suddenly older, and she stared at him in mute anguish.

The car ride back from the hotel had been quiet. Despite Drew falling asleep in his car seat, Chase and Dani hadn't said much. What the hell was there to say? They didn't know anything yet. Didn't know if it was Wilm's tumor or something else. Something non-malignant. Or something even worse than Wilm's.

The shock of it had left both of them stunned and speechless. He hoped to God the X-ray would give them some idea what they were dealing with, but he had a bad feeling they wouldn't know much more than they did now.

"That's it, Superman." Chase pulled out the cartridge and swung the C-arm away. He lifted Drew's small body into his arms and held him tightly against him, closing his eyes for a moment and trying to slow his breathing. Calm his tripping heart.

He headed into the kitchen with the child. "Let's get you something to eat. Your mom will fix your dinner while I get the pictures developed. It'll be important for you to eat good food to build all your muscles."

Drew snaked his arms around Chase's neck. "I will, Daddy. I getting big muscles like you."

Chase sat his son on a kitchen stool and ruffled his hair, somehow managing to force a smile. He turned to Dani, who was busying herself putting together Drew's meal.

"I'll ask Spud to sit with him while he's eating," he said to Dani. "Give me time to get the X-rays developed then come down to the clinic."

She nodded without speaking, without even looking at him, and he headed off and spoke briefly with Spud. Desperately anxious to see what the X-rays showed, he dreaded what they might indicate.

He shoved the films up into the old light box hanging on the wall and peered at them. What he saw made him sway slightly on his feet, unable to catch his breath. It took a Herculean effort to stay upright instead of slumping down into a chair, and he was leaning his hand against the wall to support himself when Dani walked in.

"What do they look like?" she asked, her voice barely above a whisper.

"See the shadow?" He grasped her arm, tugged her closer to look at the films. "There's a suggestion of a large mass in his left flank. Whatever it is, it's big. I'm guessing at least a pound. From what I can see, though, it doesn't look like it's metastasized into the lungs."

"Oh, God." She stared at the films, and tears filled her eyes and spilled over. "Can you take it out?"

"If this was a kid who lived here, whose life was here, I'd do what I had to do." If Dani hadn't been so naive, so damned carefree, they wouldn't be in this situation. "But who knows what the hell it is for sure? We don't have CAT scans and MRIs and ultrasound. We can't even do a biopsy unless we take him to Cotonou."

"I think we should take him to Cotonou right away."

"Are you crazy?" He stared at her and wondered if she was denying the reality staring them both in the face. "We have to make a plan, this second, to get him to the States for a complete diagnosis. Then surgery by someone who knows exactly what they're doing. And chemo, which he'll probably need."

"Maybe it's not malignant. Maybe it's just a benign tumor."

"Maybe. Are you willing to take that chance? Apparently you like taking chances, as you brought him here in the first place. But I'm not willing to take that chance, because you know as well as I do what these X-rays in-dicate. That it's a pipe dream to hope it's not Wilm's or some other cancer."

The dread and anger he'd been shoving down for hours welled up in his chest and burst out in words he knew he shouldn't say. Words he couldn't stop. "If you hadn't brought him here, like I said all along you shouldn't have, he could already be in a hospital in the States. But, no, he's here in Africa. And it's going to take days to make that happen."

He jabbed his finger at the image of the mass inside their baby's body. "And if it *is* Wilm's, you also know how fast it grows. How it can metastasize practically overnight."

Tortured-looking watery blue eyes stared at him. "Are you blaming me for this? I love him more than anything in the world." A sob caught in her throat and she pressed the back of her hand to her mouth.

"That love should have told you to do everything in your power to keep him safe. But instead you brought a two-year-old to a developing country."

"You *are* blaming me," she said, anguish and disbe-lief choking her voice. "He obviously had this before we even left the States. Neither you or I could have protected him from something like this."

"No." He grabbed the films from the light box and shoved them in a folder. "But if you'd kept him where he belongs, Drew would be getting the necessary tests done right this minute. Getting treatment that could very well mean the difference between a good outcome and a bad one." He slammed his hand against the cement wall, un-able to control the fury that kept welling up in his chest, twisting with the icy fear lodged there. "Between life and death."

Dani burst into tears and buried her face in her hands.

Damn it, he shouldn't have yelled at her. But she also needed to hear it. Had to know he was right. Had to know she could never put Drew in a dangerous situation like this again.

He sucked in several breaths before trying to speak again. "What's the best children's hospital near where you live in the States?"

"I rented out my house, so we can't stay there. We can choose any hospital anywhere and just stay at a hotel."

"You're the one who knows the best pediatric cancer hospitals in the U.S. Decide on one, make some calls, and I'll get the plane tickets and other arrangements taken care of."

"And I guess I need to call GPC. Try to get someone here to take my place."

"Somebody needs to be available in the clinic until the new doc gets here and knows what he's doing." The thought of not being able to go with them immediately tore at Chase's heart, but they couldn't just leave the clinic empty. Who knew what desperate patient might walk through the door? "I'll take your place here until I can leave."

"You aren't coming with us?"

The shock in her eyes added to the heavy weight in his chest, but there was no way around it. "You know the new doc isn't coming for another week or so. I can't leave the place with absolutely no one here. But I'll come as soon as I can."

Myriad emotions flitted through her eyes as she searched his face. He wasn't sure what all he saw etched there, but sad and weary disillusionment seemed to shadow her eyes. She nodded and turned away.

"I'll make some calls. Hopefully Drew and I will be out of here by tomorrow."

At the Philadelphia children's hospital, Dani sat alone in the harshly lit waiting room as her son underwent surgery to remove the huge tumor growing inside his small body. She'd kissed Drew as he'd sat in the rolling crib they used to take him to the OR, his little face smiling as though he was on a great adventure, and it had taken all her strength to smile back, to wave as if he was heading off to a play date.

The moment he'd disappeared from sight the tears had begun. Flowing from deep within her soul in what felt like an endless reservoir of dread. She thought of the poor mother bleeding to death whose life Chase had saved, and felt a little like that. That she just might slowly die if she lost her baby boy. Intellectually, she knew life would go on. But it would be forever altered.

She flipped through the battered magazines, but gave up on being able to read anything. So strange to be sitting out in this room with other parents and the siblings of patients instead of on the other side of the wall, involved in a patient's care. Absently, she watched little ones play with the toys in the room, loud and giggling, munching on snacks from little plastic bags and reading stories with their parents, completely unaware of what their families were going through.

Of course, some of the surgeries going on that moment were fairly routine, with little risk. But others? Heart surgeries and brain surgeries.

Cancer treatments.

She leaned her head against the wall and closed her

eyes. Never, in her worst nightmares, would she ever have thought Drew would have to go through something like this. She tried hard to remember that Wilm's tumor, if that was what he had, was highly treatable. That over eighty-five percent of children survived it. Thrived, healthy and happy, the rest of their lives. And she prayed hard, over and over, that Drew would be one of them.

She shoved herself from the chair to grab a cup of coffee from the smiling, elderly volunteer pushing a cart with beverages and snacks. She moved slowly to the rain-spattered window, staring outside at the gray sky, and wondered if the sun was shining in Benin.

She'd forgiven Chase for being so angry with her. For somehow blaming her. He loved Drew nearly as much as she did, and she knew his outburst, his agitation had stemmed from the same shock and terror she'd felt. People did and said things under stress they normally wouldn't.

She'd even forgiven him for not coming back to the States with them. Or maybe forgiven was the wrong word. Accepted, painfully, what she'd known all along but had buried beneath her love for him. Beneath her desire to believe they could have a future together, however complicated.

His work was his life. Who he was. Without it, he wouldn't have an identity that he understood, and that identity took precedence over everything.

But, as bewildered as she felt, one thing became very clear. As she'd taken Drew to his first doctor's appointments, to the first of so many tests, when she'd held his hand as he'd cried during the MRI, and as he'd been poked and pinched as his blood had been drawn, she'd known the life Chase proposed for them wasn't enough.

For a short time, in his arms, through his kisses, she'd

become convinced it was, and just thinking about those moments filled her with a deep longing. But through all the lonely hours since she'd brought Drew back to the States, she'd come to see that she deserved more.

She deserved a husband who would be with her every day. Through good times and bad times. In sickness and in health, as the marriage vows said. And that simply wasn't possible with him living across the world most of every year.

She rested her forehead against the cold pane of glass. She loved Chase. Loved him so much it hurt. But many of the things she loved about him were the same things that drove him to do the work he did.

He couldn't change who he was, and she couldn't even really want him to, because he was like no one else she'd ever known. A man with so much to offer humankind but not enough to offer her.

"I know this cast feels even worse than the last one, but at least you don't have to deal with that apparatus any more, right?"

Chase leaned over Apollo and checked the new cast he'd put on the boy, which extended over his whole leg now that the boy's wound had healed enough to be covered. "Does it hurt?"

The boy shook his head and smiled. "The 'be happy' song makes it better."

Don't worry, be happy. Chase swallowed hard. That wasn't even close to possible.

Apollo's mother reached under the blankets she had stacked next to the bed and brought out a small fetish she'd most likely made herself, handing it to Chase. "I heard the pretty doctor's son was sick and needed to go

back to America," she said. "I wish to give this to her
and her son, asking for Sakpata's healing."

Her son. His son.

"Thank you. I'll let her know." Chase took the beaded
and painted mud statue from the woman and tried to
smile. If only such a thing could really help. But Drew's
health—his survival—would come down to modern medicine and a little luck.

Each time he'd treated small children in the clinic,
their faces had blurred to look like Drew's. His big brown
eyes and his beautiful smile. And through every crisis,
every surgery he hadn't been able to take his mind off
him for even a second. Wondering how he was doing.
What he was going through. If he'd be okay.

Wondering how Dani was holding up through it all.

Chase moved on to the next patient, thinking about
his last phone call with Dani. She'd given him the details
of Drew's tests, what they showed, what they planned
to do. Her voice had sounded calm, her recitation to the
point. She sounded okay, but he suspected it was an act.
His frustration level at not being able to be there with
them threatened to make it nearly impossible for him to
focus on his work.

When the hell was the new doctor going to get here?

His cellphone rang and he pulled it from his pocket.
His mother. Calling for at least the tenth time.

"I'm wondering if there's any news."

Her voice reflected the same tightly controlled fore-
boding he felt that had every nerve on alert. "No, Mom.
She said she'd call after the tumor was removed. After
they do a biopsy to confirm the diagnosis."

"I still think you need to go be with them, Chase. I
think you should book your flight."

"I can't do that yet." Surely she knew he felt as frustrated and anxious as she did? But she also knew that if he left there wouldn't be one damned person here to take care of an emergency. And the nurses would have to take care of the hospital patients alone, with a few in serious condition.

"You do know it's okay to put yourself first once in a while, don't you? You need to be there to support Dani through all this."

"It isn't logical for me to go there where there are umpteen doctors of all specialties ready to take care of Drew, and not a single doctor here to take care of these people. You know that."

"That's not really true, Chase. That hospital has their techs who are well trained for things like hernia surgery, and they'd do the best they could if there wasn't a doctor there." His mother's voice grew more irritated, which he rarely heard from her. "You have your whole life to take care of needy people in the world; you have only this moment to take care of Dani and your son."

He stared at the hospital ward, at all the sick and injured patients, and didn't know what the hell to think. How could he abandon them? Yes, the techs could handle most problems if necessary, but it felt...wrong to leave them without a truly qualified surgeon. And yet the place he wanted to be was with Dani and Drew.

He hung up and pulled out his stethoscope to check the next patient.

"The prognosis is very good, Dr. Sheridan." The surgeon, still wearing his blue cap and surgical gown, sat in the chair next to hers in the waiting room. "I suspect it was, indeed, a Wilm's tumor, but of course we'll have to wait for the biopsy results to confirm that. It was a stage-one tumor, completely isolated in one kidney. With the removal of the tumor, kidney, and ureter, I think only a short course of chemotherapy will be necessary. He's going to be fine."

Dani nearly slid off the chair at his words, tears clogging her throat. Her first thought was to wonder if Drew was awake and wanting her. Her next thought was that she wished Chase was there to embrace in shared relief.

"Can I see him now?"

"He's in Recovery. Still asleep, but you can go on in there so he'll see you when he first wakes up." The doctor smiled and patted her shoulder. "We'll keep him in the hospital a couple of days. Then we'll discuss the next step."

The nurse led her to Recovery and she sat next to Drew, holding his hand, knowing he'd be in pain and maybe confused when he awoke. She'd brought a pillow and blanket to spread on the narrow, but thankfully padded, window seat in his room so she would be right there for him if he needed her.

His eyelids fluttered and he looked up at her. "Mommy?"

"I'm right here, sweetheart." As she squeezed his hand, her own heart squeezed until she thought it might burst wide open. While she knew there was still a slim chance something could go wrong, it sounded like they'd been very, very lucky.

She slowly combed her fingers through his beautiful, thick hair, her heart clutching at the thought that it might all fall out during chemo. She couldn't even imagine it, but would figure out a way to make it seem okay, maybe even fun. After all, he was still so little he might like the adventure of using his noggin as a canvas for non-toxic markers, and managed a smile at the silly thought.

"Is Daddy here?" he asked, his voice sleepy and slurred.

"Not yet." And wasn't that what she'd probably be telling him his whole life? That his daddy would be home whenever he could be there? Maybe soon? Or, more likely, not soon at all.

Tears yet again closed her throat, slipped from her eyes to sting her cheeks, as she told herself it would be all right. It had to be all right. Drew would recover and grow up to be a smart, strong and handsome man like his father. Chase would be there for him when he could be, talk to him a lot, probably send him photos via computer of all the places he was living and all the things he was doing.

And she would be right here for Drew. Every day.

Chase concentrated on his push-ups, trying to block everything else from his mind. Fifty-five. Fifty-six. Fifty-seven.

He never worked out twice in one day. The darkness that surrounded him was usually pre-dawn, not dusk. But he had to do something to deal with the anxious restlessness consuming him.

Dani had said she'd call once she knew anything. Hours and hours ago she'd promised that, but he hadn't heard a word. Kept checking his phone to be sure it was on, that its ringer was turned up, that he hadn't somehow missed her call.

He headed towards his favorite tree, which had lost a few limbs to storms but somehow survived. It stood scarred but still strong, and he leaped to grab the lowest branch. When the phone rang shrilly, he dropped to the ground and nearly fell on his face. Fumbling to snag it out of his pocket, he quickly hit the button.

"Hello? Dani, is that you?"

"Yes. It's me. I wanted to tell you he came out of surgery okay and he's doing fine. It was stage one, so they're sure they got everything. And they expect the biopsy to confirm it was Wilm's, so the prognosis for a full recovery is really good."

His legs felt so weak they seemed to crumple beneath him as he sat on the ground. "Thank God." He swiped his hand across his face and moist eyes, not caring that dust covered his palm. "Are you doing okay?"

"I'm fine." Her voice was calm, cool. "I'll call you to-morrow to let you know how he's feeling."

"Wait." Was that it? She'd barely spoken with him and was going to hang up? "Can I talk to him?"

"He's finally back asleep. He was in a lot of pain and cranky, but they upped his pain meds and he's comfort-able now. Oh, wait, he's crying a little again. I've got to go. I'll call you later."

The phone went dead in his ear and he stared at it. He should feel elated. *Did* feel relieved beyond belief that the tumor had been caught early and Drew would most likely recover completely.

But with that relief came overwhelming disquiet. As he sat there in the dirt, he looked up at the night sky.

He wished Dani was looking at it with him. Not from Philadelphia but from here.

No. He stared hard at the stars, shining steadily and brightly. It seemed he could almost see the slow turning of the earth, the stars growing more brilliant and defined as they rotated infinitesimally in the sky, and knew.

He should be looking at it in Philadelphia with her.

He scrambled up and dialed the airline. He hoped to God the new doc would show up tomorrow as he was supposed to. And prayed that the techs wouldn't have problems covering any emergency, if necessary. But right now, there was only one place in the world he belonged. He belonged with Dani and Drew.

"Come on, you have to eat more than that." Dani poked raisins into Drew's oatmeal to make another smiley face, hoping he'd eat a few of the oats along with the raisins he kept picking out. "Dig out his whole eyeball with your spoon, and gobble it up like the monster you are."

"I not a monster. I a lizard, eating my bugs."

He picked out the raisins again, and Dani sighed. She needed to stop fussing over him, worrying about every bite of food. It was obvious he was feeling better every day, and she couldn't wait until this afternoon when he would get to go home.

"I brought some Benin bugs back for you, lizard-boy," a deep voice said.

Dani swung around and stared, her stomach feeling as if it was jumping up to lodge in her throat. There Chase stood, tall and strong, his brown eyes tired but intense, his entire form radiating energy. She wanted to run to him and throw her arms around him and beg him to never leave again.

"Daddy!" Drew shrieked and tried to scramble out of the bed, but Dani quickly put a restraining hand on his chest.

"You can't just leap out of bed with all this stuff attached to you," she said. "Lie still."

Chase came farther into the room and draped his arm around Dani, pulling her close as he sat on the side of the bed. His eyes met hers, and a familiar ache filled her chest. He leaned forward to give her a soft kiss, and he tasted so good she forced herself to remember all the lonely days and nights and her conviction that she deserved more than he could offer.

Chase turned his attention to Drew, leaned down to kiss his cheek. He stroked one finger across the child's forehead to get his hair out of his eyes then cupped the side of Drew's head with his wide palm. But he kept Dani tugged close against him. "You've been through an awful lot, getting that kryptonite out of your belly, Superman. How are you feeling?"

"Okay. My tummy hurts but Mommy says it'll be better soon."

"I'm sorry it hurts. You're very brave, and I'm proud of you."

"Time to change his dressing," a nurse said with a smile as she walked in.

Chase stood, and Dani stood with him, because she didn't have a choice with his arm tight around her body. They took a few steps away from the bed to give the nurse room.

"I'd like to see the wound." Chase studied it carefully after the nurse had removed the dressing, then nodded in satisfaction. He smiled at Drew. "Looks good, buddy. Your mom and I'll be in the hall while the nurse gets you fixed up. We'll be right back."

Chase moved into the hallway, taking Dani with him, and in some ways she felt like she was right back where they'd been the first time they'd seen one another again in the sub-Saharan twilight. But this time she knew she would remember how much she'd missed him this week. She knew she could stay strong.

He drew her farther down the hall to a darkened nook holding a single chair. He slipped between the chair and wall and pulled her to him, looking down at her eyes, his own deeply serious.

"When did the new doctor arrive?" she asked.

"Thankfully, he showed up at the airport as I was about to leave."

"At the airport?" Had Chase left before the new doctor was in place? She opened her mouth to ask but he pressed his fingers to her lips.

"Before you speak, I have some things I need to say." His hands moved to cup her face, his thumb slipping across her cheekbone. "I was looking at the night sky and saw the Big Dipper. And I thought about you saying that we're all spinning around together on this tiny speck in the universe called Earth. I realized I didn't want to be looking at the stars, knowing you're looking at them too, and not be with you, looking at them together."

Her eyes stung and her fingers curled into his shirt, but she didn't know what she was supposed to say. Didn't know exactly what he was saying.

He brushed her lips softly with his, and she wanted to kiss him longer, wanted to feel his mouth soothe away all the worries, all the loneliness.

"I always said being a mission doctor wasn't just what I did, but who I was." His breath touched her moist lips as he spoke. "I was wrong."

He tucked a strand of hair behind her ear, and she wanted to wrap her arms around him and hold him close. "How were you wrong?"

"It's not who I am. It's just what I do. Who I am is the man who loves you and wants to be with you and share my life with you. Who I am is Drew's father, and I want to share my life with him, too." He pulled her close and buried his face in her hair. "I love you for just you, and

I love him for just him. I love you, and all I want is to share my life with both of you."

He looked at her again, and she knew he meant every word. That it wasn't just a brief reaction to the terrifying crisis of Drew's illness but words from deep within his heart.

"I love you, too," she whispered. "So much. But it scares you to have Drew live in the places you work."

"Which is why I'm staying here. Working here. With you. In whichever one of the fifty United States you choose. My mother pointed out that I—we—have the rest of our lives after Andrew grows bigger to work missions around the world. If you want to. Until then I'm sure I can find work here where I know I can make some kind of difference."

He drew her to the chair and gently sat her in it. His eyes focused on hers, he held both her hands and slowly dropped to one knee. "I know I was pushy and demanding before, and I'm sorry for that. But I can't wait any longer for you to ask me again to marry you."

"Chase, I—"

"No, it's my turn now." His hands tightened on hers. "Will you marry me, Dani? I'll do anything you ask of me if you'll let me be a part of your life. And Drew's. On your terms, not mine. I'm asking you because I can't be complete without you. I'm begging you because I don't want to live without you. Please, will you marry me?"

"Oh, Chase. Yes. I will." She felt her mouth tremble in a wobbly smile. "I've missed you so much."

His chest lifted in a deep breath and he closed his eyes for a moment before looking at her with so much love her heart felt almost too full to hold it all.

"Thank you." He stood and pulled her into his arms,

holding her close. "I missed you for three damned years and I'm not missing you again for even one more day."

He lowered his head and kissed her, and it was so warm and sweet it was like drinking in happiness.

She wrapped her arms around his neck and pressed her cheek to his. "We should probably go back to Drew's room. I get to take him home today. Except that, for the moment, home is a hotel."

"*We* get to take him back home today. And then we'll get started on figuring out where home's going to be."

With the promise of everything she'd ever wanted within his warm gaze, he took her hand and they walked down the hall to be with their son.

Together.

# EPILOGUE

LAUGHTER ECHOED OFF the walls of their new home in Chicago as Drew put on a puppet show for his three doting grandparents. On his hand was a pink pig puppet that was dancing so frenetically he kept knocking down the wobbly, cardboard cutout they'd glued red fabric "curtains" to.

It had been so hard to decide where in the U.S. they should live, but Dani and Chase had finally decided on the Windy City. As Chicago was close to Dani's mother and offered a widely diverse population, they both found work here that they enjoyed, and it was a great place to raise Drew, too.

Along with another little one. Dani placed her hand on her belly to feel the hard kicks the baby kept jabbing into her stomach as she tried to watch Drew's show. Their unborn baby girl seemed to be dancing around as much as Drew's pig was, and Dani grinned at her husband. He grinned back, his lizard puppet making little kisses at her, complete with sound effects.

He turned the puppet toward Drew. "You have any bugs, little pink piggy? I love bugs! I'm gonna lick them up!"

Dani, her mother, and Chase's parents all laughed at the ridiculous falsetto voice he was using, as well as

Drew's comical reaction to the lizard puppet licking and biting him all over.

Evelyn squeezed Dani's arm. "I'm so thrilled we decided to move here for a few years. Think how much we would have missed our Andrew. And our granddaughter too, whenever she decides to meet us."

"Hopefully, very soon," Dani said with a smile, getting up to walk stiffly—waddle was probably a more accurate word—to pour herself decaffeinated coffee and place four candles on Andrew's birthday cake.

"I would have gotten that for you, honey," her mother Sandra, said, rising to busy herself gathering plates from the kitchen. Amazingly, Chase's parents were now employed at the same hospital where Dani's mother worked as a nurse. Unbelievable that a family that had once been scattered all over the world now lived and worked within miles of one another.

With Drew's grandparents in town to care for him when they were gone, Dani and Chase were able to work in El Salvador or Honduras for a week twice a year together. Her mission work and her regular pediatric practice left Dani feeling deeply satisfied, knowing she was making a difference both in the U.S. and abroad. Chase stayed on at the mission another week on his own, which he said was the longest he could be away from his wife. Drew. It was the best of both worlds, as he liked to say, smiling and fulfilled when he returned home to his family.

Drew's pig puppet completely abandoned the cardboard "stage" and began chewing on Phil's leg. With a chuckle Chase stood and walked to stand behind Dani, wrapping his arms around her, his hands splayed across her big belly.

"That lizard's crazy in love with you, you know," he said next to her ear.

"Don't tell him, but I'm crazy in love with him, too." She turned her face to his with a smile. He gave her a soft kiss, but his eyes were filled with mischief. And something else.

"He told me to ask you if he could lick you all over later. What do you say?"

She laughed and turned in his arms, her belly keeping them farther apart than she would have liked. "Tell him yes. I've always had a weakness for lizards."

He lowered his mouth to hers for a long, slow kiss and his lips were a far, far cry from any lizard's. Soft, warm, and, oh, so delicious, they tasted of all he'd given her.

Which was everything.

* * * * *

## *Mills & Boon® Hardback*

### *January 2014*

# ROMANCE

| | |
|---|---|
| The Dimitrakos Proposition | Lynne Graham |
| His Temporary Mistress | Cathy Williams |
| A Man Without Mercy | Miranda Lee |
| The Flaw in His Diamond | Susan Stephens |
| Forged in the Desert Heat | Maisey Yates |
| The Tycoon's Delicious Distraction | Maggie Cox |
| A Deal with Benefits | Susanna Carr |
| The Most Expensive Lie of All | Michelle Conder |
| The Dance Off | Ally Blake |
| Confessions of a Bad Bridesmaid | Jennifer Rae |
| The Greek's Tiny Miracle | Rebecca Winters |
| The Man Behind the Mask | Barbara Wallace |
| English Girl in New York | Scarlet Wilson |
| The Final Falcon Says I Do | Lucy Gordon |
| Mr (Not Quite) Perfect | Jessica Hart |
| After the Party | Jackie Braun |
| Her Hard to Resist Husband | Tina Beckett |
| Mr Right All Along | Jennifer Taylor |

# MEDICAL

| | |
|---|---|
| The Rebel Doc Who Stole Her Heart | Susan Carlisle |
| From Duty to Daddy | Sue MacKay |
| Changed by His Son's Smile | Robin Gianna |
| Her Miracle Twins | Margaret Barker |

# Mills & Boon® Large Print
## January 2014

## ROMANCE

| | |
|---|---|
| Challenging Dante | Lynne Graham |
| Captivated by Her Innocence | Kim Lawrence |
| Lost to the Desert Warrior | Sarah Morgan |
| His Unexpected Legacy | Chantelle Shaw |
| Never Say No to a Caffarelli | Melanie Milburne |
| His Ring Is Not Enough | Maisey Yates |
| A Reputation to Uphold | Victoria Parker |
| Bound by a Baby | Kate Hardy |
| In the Line of Duty | Ami Weaver |
| Patchwork Family in the Outback | Soraya Lane |
| The Rebound Guy | Fiona Harper |

## HISTORICAL

| | |
|---|---|
| Mistress at Midnight | Sophia James |
| The Runaway Countess | Amanda McCabe |
| In the Commodore's Hands | Mary Nichols |
| Promised to the Crusader | Anne Herries |
| Beauty and the Baron | Deborah Hale |

## MEDICAL

| | |
|---|---|
| Dr Dark and Far-Too Delicious | Carol Marinelli |
| Secrets of a Career Girl | Carol Marinelli |
| The Gift of a Child | Sue MacKay |
| How to Resist a Heartbreaker | Louisa George |
| A Date with the Ice Princess | Kate Hardy |
| The Rebel Who Loved Her | Jennifer Taylor |

1213 GEN STD LP

## *Mills & Boon® Hardback*
### *February 2014*

# ROMANCE

| | |
|---|---|
| A Bargain with the Enemy | Carole Mortimer |
| A Secret Until Now | Kim Lawrence |
| Shamed in the Sands | Sharon Kendrick |
| Seduction Never Lies | Sara Craven |
| When Falcone's World Stops Turning | Abby Green |
| Securing the Greek's Legacy | Julia James |
| An Exquisite Challenge | Jennifer Hayward |
| A Debt Paid in Passion | Dani Collins |
| The Last Guy She Should Call | Joss Wood |
| No Time Like Mardi Gras | Kimberly Lang |
| Daring to Trust the Boss | Susan Meier |
| Rescued by the Millionaire | Cara Colter |
| Heiress on the Run | Sophie Pembroke |
| The Summer They Never Forgot | Kandy Shepherd |
| Trouble On Her Doorstep | Nina Harrington |
| Romance For Cynics | Nicola Marsh |
| Melting the Ice Queen's Heart | Amy Ruttan |
| Resisting Her Ex's Touch | Amber McKenzie |

# MEDICAL

| | |
|---|---|
| Tempted by Dr Morales | Carol Marinelli |
| The Accidental Romeo | Carol Marinelli |
| The Honourable Army Doc | Emily Forbes |
| A Doctor to Remember | Joanna Neil |

0114GEN STD HB

*Mills & Boon*® *Large Print*

*February 2014*

# ROMANCE

| | |
|---|---|
| The Greek's Marriage Bargain | Sharon Kendrick |
| An Enticing Debt to Pay | Annie West |
| The Playboy of Puerto Banús | Carol Marinelli |
| Marriage Made of Secrets | Maya Blake |
| Never Underestimate a Caffarelli | Melanie Milburne |
| The Divorce Party | Jennifer Hayward |
| A Hint of Scandal | Tara Pammi |
| Single Dad's Christmas Miracle | Susan Meier |
| Snowbound with the Soldier | Jennifer Faye |
| The Redemption of Rico D'Angelo | Michelle Douglas |
| Blame It on the Champagne | Nina Harrington |

# HISTORICAL

| | |
|---|---|
| A Date with Dishonour | Mary Brendan |
| The Master of Stonegrave Hall | Helen Dickson |
| Engagement of Convenience | Georgie Lee |
| Defiant in the Viking's Bed | Joanna Fulford |
| The Adventurer's Bride | June Francis |

# MEDICAL

| | |
|---|---|
| Miracle on Kaimotu Island | Marion Lennox |
| Always the Hero | Alison Roberts |
| The Maverick Doctor and Miss Prim | Scarlet Wilson |
| About That Night... | Scarlet Wilson |
| Daring to Date Dr Celebrity | Emily Forbes |
| Resisting the New Doc In Town | Lucy Clark |